PRAISE FOR TRACY BUCHANAN:

'I was left absolutely traumatised in a totally brilliant way . . . Beautiful, heartbreaking, uplifting . . . Really worth a read.'

—*HELLO!*

'A pacy read . . . A great book to take to the beach!'

—*Daily Mail*

'I was entranced from the very first page and couldn't put it down until I had all the answers. Tracy weaves a seamless tale while offering brilliant descriptions and raw emotions.'

—Angela Marsons, author of *Child's Play*

'A must read for fans of psychological suspense. Tightly plotted and intense, this novel will have you looking over your shoulder and peeking under your bed. Filled with twists and turns, it will keep you flying through the pages to the shocking end.'

—Heather Gudenkauf, author of *Before She Was Found*

Praise for Tracy's last book, *The Lost Sister*:

'Tracy Buchanan writes moving, gripping, heartbreakingly real family drama.'

—Susan Lewis, author of *One Minute Later*

'Refreshing and intriguing . . . I loved it!'

—Tracy Rees, Richard and Judy bestselling author of *The Hourglass*

'Twisty, emotional and far too hard to put down.'

—Katie Marsh, author of *My Everything*

'I really loved this book . . . Her best yet.'

—*Candys BookCase*

'There are so many twists and turns . . . a heart-rending and thought-provoking book!!!'

—*Book In One Hand Coffee In Another*

WALL OF SILENCE

ALSO BY TRACY BUCHANAN:

The Atlas of Us

My Sister's Secret

No Turning Back

Her Last Breath

The Lost Sister

The Family Secret

WALL OF SILENCE

Tracy Buchanan

LAKE UNION
PUBLISHING

This is a work of fiction. Names, characters, organizations, places, events, and incidents are either products of the author's imagination or are used fictitiously. Any resemblance to actual persons, living or dead, or actual events is purely coincidental.

Published by Lake Union Publishing, Seattle

www.apub.com

ISBN-13: 9781542017091
ISBN-10: 1542017092

Cover design by Ghost Design

Printed in the United States of America

To Nan and Auntie Wendy

'In life we loved you dearly.
In death we love you still.
In our hearts you hold a place
No one else will ever fill.'

Unknown

Chapter One

Thursday 18th April, 2019
4.05 p.m.

I thought Dad's blood would smell of him, that soft citrus scent I've known all my life. But all I can smell on my hands are bitter pennies.

I look down at his face. He's so white, so quiet.

Is this really happening?

'Quick, get up!' A hand grabs at my shoulder, trying to pull me up. 'Mum'll be here soon.'

I think of Mum's reassuring smell. Peach perfume. Sometimes sweat. Chocolate on her breath. I want to squash my face into her neck and tell her everything that's happened, every little detail. Then I want her to tell me it'll all be okay, that she understands, that she will always understand, for ever and ever.

But I can't tell her the truth. I have to be strong. We *have to be strong.*

'Drop the knife,' a voice hisses.

I look down at the large knife that's in my hands. God, I didn't even realise I was still holding it. Only this morning, Mum was using this knife to slice a grapefruit in half. I see the remains of the grapefruit on the side, probably already rotting.

I do as I'm told and the knife clatters to the ground, specks of Dad's blood spotting the kitchen walls as it lands.

The same walls Dad spent all of his birthday weekend painting.

The bitter stench of his blood invades my nostrils again and I'm folding right over, a silent scream coming out.

'What have I done?' I say over and over as I stare at my dad.

A finger is put to my mouth. 'Shhh. Count to five.'

Outside, a bird sings. It sounds all shrill and panicked. Must be a goldfinch. Mum pointed one out to me once. It was in Joel's tree, high up, its little red face staring down at me. Mum said Grandma Quail used to tell her people's souls live on in animals and I remember hoping it was Joel watching us.

Now I hope it isn't. I wouldn't want him to see what I just did.

The clock ticks and the three of us stand around Dad, his blood congealing beneath the soles of our feet as we wait for the sound of Mum's key in the lock . . .

Chapter Two

Thursday 18th April, 2019
4.07 p.m.

Welcome to Forest Grove, Utopia of the Woods
Home to Strong Branches and Deep Roots

Melissa cycled past the village's welcome sign and into the forest, the wheels of her mountain bike juddering over the sludge of leaves and knot of fallen branches. She liked the forest after a downpour, the squish of the damp leaves beneath her wheels, the smell of the mulch and drenched wood drifting up to her. The sun was now scorching those leaves, though, revenge for the shock of rain earlier, and it was warm again.

Prime barbecue weather, Melissa thought to herself as she smiled up at the sun.

She intended to begin the long Easter weekend by kicking back in the garden with a glass of home-made cider in one hand, a barbecued (and heavily buttered) corn on the cob in the other. Screw the diet! In fact, maybe they could invite Daphne and Maddy over, even get Patrick's parents to join them all? Make a night of it.

After, she and Patrick could stay out in the dark and talk all evening like they used to. Patrick needed some chill time. He was running to be a parish councillor and with the local elections coming up in May, combined with his job as a director of a marketing company, he seemed more stressed than usual.

Yep, a few ciders in the evening sun would do the trick!

In fact, they might even have something to celebrate if things had gone well for their elder twin, Lilly (elder by five minutes, as she loved to tell people, not wanting anyone to forget she came out *before* her twin brother, Lewis). Today was the day she'd be finding out if she'd got the lead role in Forest Grove's annual 'Musical in the Woods' production, this year *The Sound of Music.*

It meant a lot to Lilly, nights spent whispering lines to herself over and over, mornings spent scrutinising her expression in the mirror to ensure she was projecting just enough Maria von Trapp without sacrificing the modern take she was giving the role. They were all hoping against hope that all those drama lessons Patrick bought for Lilly after she lost out on the lead the year before hadn't gone to waste. Whatever happened, though, Melissa would be proud of her daughter for working so hard at something she was passionate about.

Melissa pumped her legs to make the wheels turn faster, desperate to get home to her family and that cider. As she enjoyed the breeze on her bare shoulders, a real sense of contentment fell over her. Finally she could say that *yes*, she was at peace here in the forest, the warmth of her family and friends pressing in close to her like the branches of an old oak tree.

She looked over her shoulder briefly, thinking of the ancient oak that sat in the heart of the forest.

The bad times were behind her.

Her street began to come into view then as the forest thinned out. New Pine Road was the closest street to the forest, forming one half of a circle around the woods, the village's original street, Old Pine Road, forming the other half. There was a mixture of four- and five-bed houses on the road, each of them dominated by the same large triangle of a window that looked out over the pine trees from the back. Though Melissa and Patrick were in one of the smaller four-bed houses, they had been lucky enough to get a plot at the end of the road, meaning they were at the curve of the woods, giving them forest views from both the back *and* the side of their house. Nothing beat curling up with Patrick on winter nights, the log fire burning as they looked out at the dark pine columns with a glass of Baileys in their hands. Or summer evenings gathered around their fire pit with the kids as they talked and laughed into the night, the trees swaying in the moonlight before them.

That view was a daily reminder of how very far they had come. How far *Melissa* had come. Yes, their mortgage was astronomical, but all that scrimping and saving, all that hard work, meant she was able to continue living in the town that had been her sanctuary from childhood . . . and now it would be a sanctuary for their three children too.

She pedalled out from among the trees, enjoying the familiar judder of her bike tyres over the gravelled street, a feeling that meant she was nearly home. She passed one of the largest houses, catching sight of its owner, Andrea Cooper, attending to her immaculate lawn. Andrea was the founder of the 'Friends of Forest Grove High' and admin for the town's Facebook group. Melissa's friend Daphne called her 'Scandrea', referring to the fact that she loved a good scandal.

At that moment, Andrea was kneeling down on a floral knee rest, snipping away at her rose bush with the precision of a heart surgeon. She was wearing the Forest Grove 'uniform' of Hunter wellies and Joules raincoat, her platinum hair in a perfect bob. Melissa still remembered her tottering around on stilettos with permed hair and her cleavage spilling out when they were teenagers.

It was only when she met her husband, local police officer Adrian, that she replaced the stilettos with those Hunter wellies.

As Melissa cycled past, Andrea looked up, regarding her with cold eyes. Melissa shot her a smile just to annoy her, then pedalled faster until she got to the end of the street. Melissa jumped off her bike and wheeled it to the front door, surprised not to hear the usual clamour of music, laughter and clattering pots and pans from behind the door. Maybe they were all in the garden?

She pulled her helmet off, her shoulder-length blonde hair sweaty and standing on end, then went to open the front door.

'Hello, you,' a voice called out.

Melissa turned to see her friend Daphne jogging by with her two Jack Russells, Fleetwood and Mac, in pursuit. She was in her usual running gear, her short red hair scraped back beneath a sapphire-blue headband.

'I can't believe you're going for a run,' Melissa said. 'It's *so* hot.'

'You know I'm addicted, sweetie.' Daphne came to a stop in front of Melissa, catching her breath. 'Speaking of which, how's the latest batch of cider?'

'Divine. In fact, I was thinking about popping the barbecue on and having a few glasses. Do you and Maddy fancy joining us all?' she asked.

'Oh, I'd love to, but I have a ton of clothes to go through.' Daphne ran a boutique in the village's small shopping courtyard on the outskirts of the forest, called Déjà Vu. It was essentially a charity shop, but Daphne had cleverly taken advantage of Forest Grove residents' obsession with recycling to brand it as a 'high-end vintage store for the eco-friendly'.

You'd think Daphne was eco-minded herself, but she was the complete opposite. She didn't even recycle her rubbish! But then that was Daphne's way, always going against the grain, something other residents – especially the likes of Andrea Cooper – struggled with. Even though Melissa didn't agree with Daphne's *laissez faire* attitude to the environment, she found Daphne's company refreshing. Sometimes it made a nice change to spend time with someone who wasn't obsessed with the state of the village's ecologically engineered sewage plant or the latest school-run gossip. Daphne kept herself apart from all that, except for the occasional sardonic quip in the village's Facebook group, her comments a source of entertainment for Melissa and Patrick whenever they logged in.

'How was work for you today?' Daphne asked, wiping the sweat from her brow.

'Good, actually. Though I'll miss Jacob Simms; it was his last session today. He's been with me a year.'

Daphne's green eyes flared with anger. 'That poor kid. Honestly, it gets me in a rage when I think of the way the community treated him.'

'He *did* set fire to some of the forest.'

'He was drunk! We've all done stupid things after a few too many Babychams.' Daphne crossed her slim arms across her chest and glared at Andrea Cooper, who was still in her garden. 'People here always talk about dealing with problems themselves and yet they're quite happy to go running to the police over something trivial when it suits them.'

Melissa sighed. Maybe Daphne was right. One stupid mistake and fourteen-year-old Jacob's life had been completely changed the year before. If it weren't for the outrage of the village, maybe he would have been let off with some community service for setting a campfire in the forest that hot summer day. In the end, he had to spend several weeks in a children's home in Ashbridge, called St Fiacre's . . . not to mention now having a criminal record for life. Worst of all, he had been subjected to a severe beating on his last day at the home. 'A little goodbye present' was how the culprit had described it as he pummelled Jacob's legs, meaning his dreams of being a professional football player were completely shattered. At least Melissa's intense physiotherapy over the past few months might mean he'd have a chance of returning to play football one day, even if it wasn't quite of the same quality as before.

'Well, I have high hopes for him now,' Melissa said. 'He's come on in leaps and bounds.'

'Same can't be said about the community, though,' Daphne said. 'Him and his dad were completely blanked in the Neck of the Woods earlier,' she added, referring to the pub next to her shop. 'That's the thing with Forest Grove. One wrong move and it's like you're dead to the residents here.'

'Oh, Daphne, that's not true,' Melissa said softy. 'Look what happened with my mum.'

Daphne put her hand on her hip. 'She didn't make a wrong move, though, did she?'

'She was considered an outsider. People here could have turned a blind eye.'

Daphne went to open her mouth to say something but then sighed, shaking her head. 'God, I'm really on one today, aren't I? I blame that daughter of mine, like walking on eggshells being around her today.'

'That's teenagers for you.'

Melissa had always liked Daphne's daughter, Maddy. She'd been dating Lewis for a year until they surprised everyone by splitting up a few weeks back. Maddy had been good for Lewis, especially at this important point in his school life. He tended to flit from one ambition to the next in his typical erratic fashion, whereas Maddy had known from an early age that she wanted to be a journalist, even setting up a student newspaper for Forest Grove High when she was thirteen. Sure, Lewis was only just fifteen, but they'd be gearing up for their exams in the next school year. Lilly had already decided she wanted to go to a specialist drama college in the next town, and their younger sister, Grace (though it sometimes felt to Melissa like Grace was the *oldest* of her three children, the way she talked), had also decided she wanted to be a journalist, thanks to Maddy's influence.

'Right, better head inside and get the barbie started,' Melissa said. 'Catch you later.'

Daphne checked her Fitbit then gave Melissa a wave before jogging off, her dogs trotting after her.

Melissa placed her hand on the door handle and paused, taking the chance to enjoy a moment of calm before the inevitable noise and rush of family life. She watched the tall pine trees swaying above her. As a child, she would contemplate the trees from the darkness of her bedroom in the small cottage in the woods where she lived with her parents, imagining those trees were alive and watching over her . . . *protecting* her.

Her eyes travelled to the side of her house, taking in 'Joel's tree', as they called it. It was actually two trees grown into each other, crooked and bent but beautiful too with the pretty 'tree charms' hanging from it, colourful glass orbs that had been added over the years in homage to her first son. Melissa's eyes alighted on the latest addition, an orb the size of her fist, sparkling with turquoise green and bright blue swirls. The twins had found it at the craft fair the other day. Melissa smiled as she remembered how excited they'd been to show her.

'It's green,' Lewis had said as he hung it up on the tree.

'Joel's favourite colour,' Lilly had added with a sad smile.

Melissa's eyes filled with tears. Yes, things were a *lot* better than they once were. Joel would be proud of her, of all of them.

She took a deep happy breath then twisted the door handle and pushed the door open. She stepped inside, kicking off her work trainers and taking her light denim jacket from around her waist and hanging it up, noticing the nail on the coat peg was coming loose again. She made a mental note to get Patrick to tighten it up later before the dog had another pile of coats collapse on him. Speaking of which, their golden Labrador, Sandy, came bouncing down the hallway, jumping up at Melissa in his usual forceful and enthusiastic way.

'Hello, baby, hello,' she murmured as she buried her nose in one of the dog's silky ears. 'Down now, down, before you ruin my top,' she said, taking Sandy's paws off her chest and placing them on the floor. 'Too late,' she added with a sigh as she noticed a red mark above the Bodyworks Centre logo on the collar of her white top. She licked her finger and tried to rub it out. 'Don't tell me another jar of chilli got smashed,' she called out as she padded down the hallway, past pale green walls adorned with family photos, and walked into the kitchen. 'You'd better have cleaned up the glass, remember when—'

She paused. Her three children were standing pale-faced in the kitchen, blinking down at something hidden by the wooden island in the middle of the room.

'What's going on?' Melissa asked, her blue eyes scouring the room, taking in more spots of red on the wooden countertops and glossy white cupboard doors. 'Have you been trying to cook dinner on your own again? I texted Dad to suggest we have a barbecue. Where *is* he?'

They didn't say anything, just continued looking down at something.

The hair on Melissa's arms and nape lifted.

Something was wrong.

She walked around the kitchen island then froze, letting out a gasp.

Her husband was lying on the kitchen floor, one cheek squashed against the hard grey tiles, his right arm bent at an awkward angle beneath him.

Chapter Three

Thursday 18th April, 2019
4.15 p.m.

Melissa's first thought as she looked at Patrick was that he was sleeping. It was how she was used to seeing him at night, turning in the darkness to catch him with his eyes closed in the moonlight, cheek pressed against his pillow as he softly snored.

But he wasn't snoring. He wasn't moving at all. And his skin, usually tanned and healthy, was now horribly pale . . . almost blue!

All her senses came alive at once.

'What the hell happened?' she screamed at the kids. 'Did he slip? Have you called an ambulance? Please tell me you've called an ambulance!'

'No,' Lewis said in a trembling voice as he put a protective arm around his little sister, Grace. 'We – we only just found him like this after taking Sandy for a walk.'

Melissa's gaze drew back to the spatters of red around the kitchen, fingerprints of it smeared against the kitchen units, pools of it by Patrick's head. His head, which, as Melissa realised when she crouched down to tend to her husband, was bleeding freely from a wound on the exposed side, his dark brown hair matted against it.

Not chilli sauce, blood.

'Patrick, Patrick, wake up, Patrick!' she said, shaking him.

But he didn't move, just remained motionless, eyes closed. She pressed her hand against his chest, relieved to feel it rising and falling against the skin of her palm.

The kids remained motionless, though, still gawping down at the prone figure of their dad. Sandy padded over to Patrick and lay down next to him, his paws in his owner's blood.

'Are any of you hurt?' Melissa asked her children.

Grace shook her head, wordless, her large oval eyes impossibly wide. Lewis was rocking back and forth slightly and Lilly's gaze was focused on her bare feet, staring at the blood on her carefully painted toenails.

'Come on, phone!' Melissa said, clapping her hands like she did in the mornings to catapult them into getting ready. Lewis blinked then stumbled towards it.

'Patrick, Patrick!' Melissa shouted at her husband as she stretched over to yank a tea towel hanging from the oven handle. She pressed it against the wound on his head, shocked to see how quickly the fabric turned crimson.

Lilly let out a sob.

My poor darlings, she thought to herself.

She grasped her elder daughter's hand. 'Can you take Grace into the living room, Lils? She's too young for all this.' Grace could actually handle things better than Lilly. Even at ten, she had a stoicism about her that her older sister lacked. So it was more about getting Lilly away from the horror of this scene. Though she exuded this aura of being strong and confident, Melissa knew how quickly Lilly could crumble. 'Lewis, give me the phone, sweetheart.'

Lilly grabbed her younger sister's arm and tried to steer her away but Grace refused to move, staring at her father. Lewis stepped around Patrick, flinching when his bare toes made contact with blood, and handed the phone to Melissa with a trembling hand.

'It'll be okay, Lewis,' she said to him, looking her son in the eye and trying to convince him of something she hadn't even convinced herself of yet. 'Dad'll be okay, you hear me?'

He nodded, his face pale with shock as he raked his shaking fingers through the dark hair he'd inherited from his father.

Melissa dialled 999, bloody fingers fumbling over the buttons.

'So you found him like this?' she asked the kids as she waited for someone to answer. 'Just lying on the floor?' They all nodded, wordless. 'What time did you get back from walking Sandy?' She peered at the clock. 'How long did the walk take? Was anyone here when you left?'

Lilly went to open her mouth but Lewis put a hand carefully on her arm.

'The walk took about half an hour,' he said. 'No one was here when we left. We came back about ten minutes ago.'

Ten minutes?

Melissa had been outside talking to Daphne ten minutes ago. That was plenty of time to have called for an ambulance. Why hadn't they called for one?

Those were questions for later, though. Now, she needed to focus on Patrick.

Melissa looked towards the counter to see more blood there, and some strands of dark hair too. Yes, that must be it, Patrick slipped. Slipped and hit his head on the side. She'd always been so worried about the end of that wooden counter, so damn sharp. She'd told Patrick time and again to smooth it out. 'If one of us were to slip . . .' she would say, voice trailing off, unable to say the words.

Well, now the thing that was unsayable was lying right in front of her.

Sandy stood up and padded away from Patrick across the kitchen, leaving bloody paw prints all over the floor.

'Jesus. Sandy!' she shouted. 'Lilly, can you grab him and—' She paused, noticing something lying by Patrick's slippered foot.

A knife.

It was one of their large kitchen knives, the blade slick with blood. She'd only been slicing grapefruits with it that morning!

Her eyes darted from the knife to a pool of blood by Patrick's hip. She leaned over him, letting out a gasp as she saw the bloody slit in the side of his stomach.

'Is – is that a *stab* wound?' She looked at the kids in shock. 'Did you notice?'

'We didn't notice,' Lilly said in a whimper, wrapping her arms around herself.

'Emergency services,' a female voice snapped into Melissa's ear, interrupting her panicked thoughts. 'Which service do you require?'

'My husband's been stabbed!' Melissa said, the words seeming so surreal and horrific as she uttered them.

'Name and address, please,' the operator asked.

'Melissa Byatt. Number one, New Pine Road in Forest Grove. Please come quickly.'

'We'll have an ambulance and the police with you soon, Melissa. Can you check your husband's breathing for me?'

Melissa put her free hand on Patrick's firm chest again, so familiar to her and still warm, thank God. 'I can see he is. His chest is moving up and down but – but he's so pale.'

'Where is the stab wound on your husband's body?'

'Stomach, the right side.'

'You'll need to stem the bleeding,' the operator said.

'Get another towel, there's some in the dryer,' Melissa instructed Lewis. 'My son's getting a towel,' she explained to the operator.

'Good. Ask him to press it against the wound, hard.'

'Press the towel against Dad's wound, okay, darling?' she asked Lewis as he pulled out a mustard-coloured towel. He sank down to the floor, his father's blood pooling around the knees of his jeans as he pressed the towel against Patrick's side.

'How did this happen, Melissa?' the operator asked.

'I have no idea, I came home from work to find him like this. My kids had only been back five minutes; he was like this when they found him.'

'And they didn't call an ambulance?'

'No. They must have been in shock,' Melissa said.

Lilly pulled Grace close to her, leaning down to whisper something in her ear as a lock of her long caramel hair trailed over her little sister's arm.

'How old are they, Melissa?' the operator asked.

'The twins are fifteen, my youngest is ten.'

'Can you pop the phone on speakerphone and ask the children what happened?'

Melissa did as she asked, placing the phone on her leg. 'Guys,' she said, fixing them all with her gaze, 'you need to tell us exactly what happened.'

'We found Dad like this,' Lewis said, brown eyes darting towards the knife and away again. 'Literally just before you walked in, Mum. We didn't know he'd been stabbed, right?' He looked at his sisters, who quickly nodded.

Melissa frowned. She looked over at the knife then at each of her children in turn. She had carried them within her, their fibres mixed with hers, their heartbeats matching hers. She knew them inside out.

And that was why, in that moment, she knew they were lying.

'Okay, the ambulance is just two minutes away now,' the operator said. 'Just stay on the line, okay? Don't touch anything. The police will want to seal the scene.'

Scene . . . as in crime scene.

Melissa felt nausea build inside. She looked at the kids, who all looked panicked.

In the distance, sirens suddenly punctured the air.

Grace jumped at the sound, face terrified.

'Oh, Gracey,' Melissa said. She beckoned her younger daughter towards her. Grace ran over, wrapping her arms around Melissa's waist as she looked down at her father's prone body with wide eyes. Lilly walked over and knelt down by her twin brother, the hem of her dress dipping in blood. She placed her hand over Lewis's to help him stem their father's blood and they exchanged a solemn look.

'We're all here, darling,' Melissa said to Patrick as she leaned in close to whisper in his ear. 'Your family are here.'

Family.

She looked at each of the children. What had happened here? Why were they acting so strangely?

There was an urgent knock on the door then. Melissa gently took Lilly's hand, helping her lay it over the towel covering Patrick's head wound, then she ran down the hallway, opening the front door to two paramedics. They ran into the kitchen with her and started work on Patrick as the children stepped away, going to Melissa.

She held them all close to her as she watched, struggling to comprehend that this was her husband lying before her on their kitchen floor.

Then she froze.

Where was the knife?

Chapter Four

Welcome to the Forest Grove Facebook Chit Chat Group
Home to Strong Branches and Deep Roots
NOT home to spam, self-promotion, cyber bullying or obscenities.
Closed group. 617 members

Thursday 18th April, 2019
4.32 p.m.

Belinda Bell
Does anybody know what's happening on New Pine Road? Rather a lot of sirens and police cars heading that way.

Rebecca Feine
I was just walking the dog down there! I thought I heard sirens but assumed it was coming from Ashbridge.

Peter Mileham
Hope it's nothing serious, know lots of people who live on that road :-(Tommy Mileham, have you seen this, Dad?

Ellie Mileham
I was at the park with the kids, Peter. One ambulance, two police cars. Definitely heading to New Pine Road area. Really worried. Hope everyone's okay.

Tommy Mileham
Yep, lots of sirens, the hounds are going mental.

Belinda Bell
I've headed upstairs so I can see it all from my window. I'm afraid to say the police are outside the Byatts' house.

Graham Cane
You should work for the Daily Express, Belinda Bell.

Belinda Bell
Oh, give over, you.

Andrea Cooper <Admin>
Oh gosh! I only just saw Melissa cycling past. There are an awful lot of police there. Patrick Byatt, is everything okay?!

Rebecca Feine
Not the Byatts! Lovely Melissa saved a baby hedgehog we found in our garden last summer, the care and attention she put into keeping the little thing alive was quite something.

Kitty Fletcher
Oh no! Such a lovely family, hope it's nothing serious, especially after all they went through with little Joel.

Rebecca Feine

Not to mention Melissa's mother all those years ago. Tragedy never seems far from the poor girl.

Jackie Shillingford

Please don't let it be the wonderful Byatts! Rosemary Byatt, have you seen this? Hope they're all okay.

Belinda Bell

Rosemary won't be looking on Facebook, Jackie. I've just seen her and Bill rushing out of their house.

Pauline Sharpe

Oh dear. I used to go to school with Melissa. As Rebecca said, she seems to have nothing but bad luck, just like her lovely mum.

Graham Cane

'Lovely'?! Not sure that's how I'd describe Ruby 'Quazy' Quail . . . !!!

Jackie Shillingford

What a ridiculous thing to say, Graham Cane!

Kitty Fletcher

Yes, not to mention prejudiced against those who struggle with mental illness.

Graham Cane

Oh, here we go, the Snowflake Brigade and their leader, Kitty Fletcher, have arrived.

Rebecca Feine
Andrea Cooper, can we delete these comments about Melissa and her mum, please!

Pauline Sharpe
OMG, my husband just came back from having a look. Patrick was on the floor in the kitchen being tended to by paramedics. He said it looked really bad. How awful!

Tommy Mileham
I can confirm Patrick has been injured. I just spoke to Bill.

Kitty Fletcher
Oh no! Not Patrick! Could it be related to the elections coming up?

Rebecca Feine
They're just local parish elections, Kitty. It can't be related to that! And it's not like Patrick is controversial, is he?

Graham Cane
Always knew trouble would come find the Quails again . . .

Andrew Blake
Speaking of trouble, anyone know where our trusty forest ranger Ryan Day was when this all happened?

Rebecca Feine
Andrea Cooper, where are you?! These posts need to be deleted.

Chapter Five

Thursday 18th April, 2019
4.43 p.m.

We messed up. We didn't think about the knife and the DNA all over it – my *DNA. We had to hide it, quick. I'm pretty sure Mum noticed. She's sitting on the sofa now, jogging her leg up and down as she looks at each of us. She catches my eye. I know she's thinking about the knife, trying to find an explanation other than the possibility that one of us hid it. But Big Foot didn't walk in from the woods and hide it, did he?*

She looks towards the kitchen and I follow her gaze. Two paramedics are carefully lifting Dad on to a stretcher. They told Mum he was stable, he'd be okay, and my head is all mashed up because I can't decide if that's a good thing or a bad thing and I seriously want to barf right here and now, even blurt out to Mum it was me, it was me, it was me!

But the other two are eyeballing me and I need to hold it together. Mum can't know. We talked about it. We all agreed: we found him like that. We don't know who did it.

But the knife – the flipping knife!

And the fact that Dad's alive . . . just. So it's all going to unravel anyway when he wakes up. If *he wakes up. But we've started this now and we have to continue.*

I look at Mum again. Has she got there yet? Has she figured out one of us hurt Dad?

No. No way, she just wouldn't even allow herself to think it.

'So just to confirm, you found Patrick – your dad – injured on the floor?' Adrian Cooper asks. He's a police officer but he's also Dad's friend. His face is all white and sweaty, like never in his life did he imagine he'd be asking questions like this in the very living room where he sits watching football and drinking beer with Dad. I like him. He's a bit of a sap, I suppose, that's what Grandad says. It's true his wife, Andrea, acts more like a police officer than he does, especially the way she lords it over her son, Carter . . . I mean, really, he doesn't have a mobile phone and he's fifteen?! But I like Adrian, he's kind and funny too sometimes, especially when he's drunk.

'Yes,' we all say in answer to his question. He scribbles it down in his notepad, his fingers all trembly.

'Your mum arrived five minutes after you got back from your walk?' he asks. We all nod. 'You say the walk took half an hour . . . and you came back to find your dad like this?' he asks. We nod again, nodding monkeys like the ones we saw for sale when Mum and Dad took us to Koh Samui last year. I get a flash of Dad leaping about in the waves, the smell of frying insects, the taste of Mum's cocktail she let me have a sip of one night.

Things were so different then. Or maybe I told myself they were. Maybe they were all wrong then too.

A man walks in. He isn't wearing a police uniform like Adrian is, but he has 'police' written all over him. He's in a dark suit with dandruff on the shoulders. He's been checking out the scene, all serious like. I can tell from the way he looks around the house and out at the forest that he's not from around here. He leans against the doorway, taking in each of our faces. I try to keep mine straight but my heart feels like it might thump so hard it'll travel up my chest and out of my nostrils.

'I'm Detective Crawford,' he says, voice all soft. 'I'm sorry this is happening to you guys. I have kids your age.' I know what he's trying to do. He's trying to make some kind of connection with us, but lots of people have kids our age. Nobody's had to live with what we have lately, though, have they? 'Was there any sign of a weapon?' he asks. 'A knife? I see one is missing from the knife holder,' he adds, peering towards the knife block by the cooker.

We all hold our breath. Mum too. She looks so confused and there are clusters of pink on her chest like she gets when she's nervous.

Then this steely look appears in her eyes, the same look she had when she and Dad came to view this house six years ago, like 'We really can't afford this house but we're going to bloody buy it even if we don't know how.'

'No sign of it,' she says firmly. 'Kids, did you see anything?'

I want to just jump up and hug her. She has our backs even if she doesn't know why.

'No,' I say.

'No,' the other two say.

My heart soars.

Mum did good. She knew what we needed her to do without us even saying it. Mum knows us more than anyone, though, doesn't she? Like that time I broke my arm while riding my bike, but I was trying to make out it was okay because I didn't want to ruin the family dinner Mum and Dad had spent ages planning for the anniversary of Joel's death. Nobody else clocked on, not even Grandad, who's a bit like Mum too, the way he notices when we're down. But Mum knew, she just knew, and the way she just ploughed into action, taking me to hospital like the family dinner meant nothing to her when I knew it meant everything.

'Can you think of anyone who might want to harm your father, your husband?' the detective asks, looking at us, looking at Mum.

'No one,' Mum says. 'As you probably know, he's running to be a parish councillor and we have elections coming up, but I can't imagine it has anything to do with that.'

I hear familiar voices outside and I feel sick again.

That'll be Nan and Grandad. I peer out, see them talking to Andrea Cooper, who's trying to peer into the kitchen at Dad.

I nearly lose it at the thought of their sad wrinkled faces when they see Dad – their son – on the floor. But I have to hold it together, just like I did when I broke my arm.

It's something you get used to, hiding the bad stuff.

Chapter Six

Thursday 18th April, 2019
5 p.m.

Melissa sat in the ambulance with Patrick, the spatter of blue lights on the road and the high whine of the sirens filling her senses. She clutched on to his hand, telling him he'd be fine, that he was *strong*.

An incessant bleeping suddenly sounded.

'Move,' the paramedic said, gently pushing her out of the way. He jumped into action, pumping at Patrick's chest.

'What's wrong with him?' Melissa cried. 'Is he dying?'

'He's lost a lot of blood,' the paramedic explained between breaths.

They went over a speed bump and Melissa gripped on to the side to keep steady. Patrick's face was a deathly blue.

Oh God, was she about to become a widow?

How could she cope, her husband and her son dying in the space of eleven years?

But then Patrick started breathing again.

'Is he going to be okay?' Melissa asked.

'Sooner we get him to hospital, the better,' the paramedic replied.

When they got to the hospital, Patrick was rushed into the emergency room and it all became a blur of doctors shouting orders and nurses grabbing equipment.

Melissa was aware of Patrick's parents, Bill and Rosemary, turning up at some point, watching in horror as their son was worked on, Rosemary scrunching up tissues to her nose, her short grey hair awry. Bill tried his best to maintain his strong, calm demeanour but failed, stifling a sob as a nurse lifted Patrick's shirt to reveal the stab wound, another nurse carefully examining the bloody gash on his head.

'Oh God,' Rosemary said, putting her hand to her mouth. 'My boy, my perfect boy.'

A nurse came over and ushered them out. Another steered them towards a family room, telling them they'd be updated as soon as there was any news.

News. What kind of news? The bad kind?

'What the hell happened?' Bill asked as the nurse left the room and closed the door.

'The kids found him like that,' Melissa said. 'It's – it's madness.'

'Who would do that to him?' Rosemary asked Melissa.

'I don't know,' Melissa replied.

Rosemary's eyes snagged on Melissa's T-shirt and the blood on there. She pursed her lips and turned away.

They all fell silent, eyes on the small window in the room's door. Melissa found her thoughts flitting between the two halves of her torn mind. First, the brutal fear she felt at the idea of Patrick dying. Then confusion over what on earth had happened. Melissa imagined the kids all sitting on her duck-egg-blue sofa, where she'd left them, as Jackie Shillingford, a family friend, looked after them. They'd been quiet, shocked . . . and hiding something deep inside them.

But what?

They'd all looked so relieved when Melissa told the detective she hadn't seen the knife. She wasn't even sure *why* she'd said it. She'd had to make a decision in a split second and it was all down to gut instinct. She was hoping one of the kids would just say something, *anything*, to make the disappearance of the knife appear completely normal. But they said nothing, Lewis staring at his fists in an anguished way, Lilly sobbing quietly into her hands, her immaculately applied mascara dribbling down her cheeks. Then Grace, blinking in shock. Melissa had wanted to grab them, shake them, ask them what the hell happened to the knife? But she was scared. What would that say about the kids, if they *had* hidden the knife? So instead, she'd lied, and that meant she was part of it now.

Part of what, though? Part of bloody *what*?

The fact was, only the kids could have hidden the knife. That meant they had a *reason* to hide it, a reason with possibilities that made her sick to her stomach. Either they were covering for someone who had done this to their dad . . . or worst of all, one of *them* had done it.

She shook her head. No, how could she even *think* that? It simply wasn't possible. Only that morning, they'd been laughing and joking. Patrick had taken a couple of days off work to be with the kids during Easter half term, giving his parents a break from their usual childcare duties when the kids were off school. They'd discussed whether the twins were old enough to be alone with Grace but had eventually come to the conclusion it wasn't quite time yet, so they were dividing their time between their grandparents, and Patrick and Melissa whenever they could take days off.

They had been planning a lazy day, according to Patrick. When she'd left them, Patrick was joking about Lilly's carefully sculpted 'messy bun' while Lewis slurped up his cereal, still in his PJs. Grace, as usual, had her face stuck in a book, oblivious to it all. What could have happened in just a few hours to tilt their world on its axis so completely it led to Patrick being critically injured by one of them?

No, it had all been perfectly *normal.*

So that left the possibility that the kids were covering for someone. But who? It was all so tame in Forest Grove. The worst that had happened recently was a break-in and, before that, the fire incident with Jacob Simms, but that was over a year ago!

For the kids to be covering for someone, it had to be someone they knew. She should have just told the bloody police about the knife because surely it was better to tell the truth? Surely that was the best way to find the person who did this to Patrick?

Oh, her darling Patrick! She started sobbing.

Bill pulled her into a hug. They rarely hugged nowadays. There used to be hugs like this when Melissa had first come into the Byatts' lives in her teenage years. Hugs that were all-encompassing, reassuring, secure in the storm of tragedy. Patrick once described his parents as like the warmth of a hollow tree protecting you from the rain.

'He'll be fine,' Bill said. 'He's strong, he's a *Byatt.* He'll get through this.'

'But what if he doesn't?' Melissa mumbled into Bill's shirt. 'What will I do without him?'

Melissa had been with Patrick since she was fifteen. That was over twenty-five years of her life. She didn't really know a life without him.

'He will, you hear me?' Bill said.

Melissa nodded, closing her eyes for a moment. There was a distant familiarity to being in this waiting room for her, so many hours spent in this very same hospital with her first son, Joel, waiting for tests, watching as he was prodded and poked. When you're the parent of a child with a degenerative disease, hospitals become your second home.

'Doctor's coming,' Bill said. He stood in the middle of the room and faced the door, looking like he was ready for battle. He was a tall, robust man with a bald head and bushy eyebrows. He too was always so strong in the face of any challenge but Melissa could see the cracks in his tough exterior already, his usually immaculately buttoned-up shirt higgledy-piggledy, a smear of blood on his face from when he'd grabbed his son's hand as he was loaded into the ambulance.

The door opened and a doctor appeared. She was younger than Melissa, maybe late twenties, with perfectly straight red hair and a slim frame. Melissa could feel Bill bristle beside her and she imagined what he was thinking. *That* girl *has been working on my son?* But Melissa was reassured by the doctor's age. All that learning she'd done would be fresh in her mind, like it had been for Melissa just after she qualified to be a physiotherapist four years ago.

The doctor put her hand out. 'I'm Dr Hudson. Shall we sit?'

Melissa started shaking. *Shall we sit* was usually followed by bad news – she'd learnt that with Joel.

Rosemary and Bill both sat down but Melissa remained standing. 'I'd prefer to stand, if that's okay?'

The doctor nodded. 'Of course. Though I hope you don't mind if I sit, it's been a long day.' The doctor sat on the sofa, her blue eyes serious. 'Patrick is currently in a stable condition.'

They all let out a sigh of relief.

'It was touch and go for a while,' the doctor admitted. 'The knife *just* missed a major artery. A few millimetres to the right, and he would have bled to death.'

Rosemary put her hand to her mouth as Melissa's head span.

'But he's all patched up, right?' Bill said, trying to keep his voice steady. 'No more bleeding?'

The doctor nodded. 'Absolutely.' She paused. 'It's actually Patrick's head injury that's worrying us the most. The scan we just did shows Patrick has sustained a traumatic brain injury.'

Bill closed his eyes as Rosemary stifled a sob. Melissa put her hand to her heart, gulping in deep breaths.

'Okay,' Bill said, adopting his no-nonsense voice. 'What does that mean for our boy?'

'There are many possible scenarios,' the doctor said. 'If he—'

'What I mean is, will he be brain-damaged?' Bill cut in.

Melissa could hear the fear in Bill's voice. Patrick was a man who could complete the most complex sudoku puzzle in under an hour. A man who every pub quiz team wanted as a member. A man who flew through school, then university, landing a first-class degree in business studies. A man who was now on the verge of becoming the village's parish councillor. For Bill and Rosemary, Patrick was a living, breathing example of the exemplary Byatt genes at work. The thought of their son being brain-damaged would be too unbearable for them to contemplate.

I'd deal with it, though, Melissa thought to herself.

As long as Patrick lived, she would deal with anything. Hadn't she done the same for Joel?

The doctor sighed. 'What's worrying us right now is that there's a great deal of intracranial pressure on your son's brain, so we feel the best course of action is to place Patrick in an induced coma.'

Melissa frowned. 'Coma?'

The doctor looked at her and nodded. 'An induced coma will allow us to protect the brain and give it time to heal. We'll be able to monitor the swelling, and once that swelling reduces, gradually bring Patrick back out of the coma. He *could* fully recover from this.' Rosemary closed her eyes, nodding to herself. 'But there are also many unknowns. We can discuss those down the line.'

'And his life?' Melissa asked, leaning forward. 'Is his *life* out of danger?'

'Patrick is stable at the moment,' the doctor replied, 'but he's still in a critical condition. An induced coma will greatly improve his chances of survival.'

'Survival?' Rosemary said, the slight tremble in her voice betraying her shock. 'What are we talking here, percentage-wise?'

'A high percentage of survival,' the doctor said carefully. 'But as I said, the trauma to the brain is substantial.'

'So my boy could survive but be a vegetable all his life?' Bill asked bluntly, fists curling. 'Is that what you're saying?'

Melissa took in a sharp breath.

'What a thing to say, Bill!' Rosemary chided him.

Bill sighed, gliding his hand over his head, his shoulders slumping. 'Sorry, love. I just need to know all the details, you know me.'

'Just like our Patrick,' Rosemary said.

Bill smiled sadly, his dark brown eyes, so like Patrick's, filling with tears.

Rosemary grasped her husband's hand as they looked into each other's eyes. 'He'll get through this,' Rosemary said. 'We'll make sure of it.'

They were so good together. Melissa had seen it the moment she'd caught glimpses of them through the woods when they first arrived in Forest Grove twenty-six years ago, this golden couple with their golden children. No fist-dented walls for them, nor bloody tissues in the bathroom bin, she remembered thinking to herself. On the day of her and Patrick's wedding, right in the forest when they were both just twenty, their first son, Joel, growing in her tummy, Melissa had made a promise to herself: she would do *all* she could to have a marriage like Rosemary and Bill's.

In sickness and in health, she thought.

She felt a whirl of panic start to build inside her as she thought of losing Patrick. She clenched her fists, digging her nails into her skin to drive it away. She needed to keep her head.

She turned to the doctor, gathering all her strength. 'How long will Patrick be in a coma?' she asked.

'It could be anything from a few days to a few weeks,' the doctor replied.

'Weeks,' Melissa whispered, contemplating all that time without Patrick. Then she thought of the kids and the secret they harboured. The battle she felt between the relief that she'd have time to find out what happened before their father woke and the fear that Patrick would *never* wake made her head swim with confusion.

'Have you any more questions?' the doctor asked.

Bill leaned forward, looking her in the eye. 'What are your thoughts on the stab wound? Anything to suggest the type of attack this was?'

It was the army sergeant in him coming out. He'd served as a soldier in the British Army for twenty years until he was injured in a bomb during the Troubles in Northern Ireland in the eighties. He then took up a new passion: dog breeding and showing, a hobby that led him to meeting Rosemary and now made them enough money to own the biggest house in Forest Grove.

'Photos have been taken and will be given to the police forensic team,' the doctor said, face very serious. 'Any questions related to the crime should be directed to them, Mr Byatt.'

Bill sank back against the sofa, peering out of the small window towards the spread of trees in the distance that marked out Forest Grove from the surrounding area. He clenched and unclenched his fists and Melissa could see the storm of rage swirling behind his eyes. That would be his focus now, finding out who did this to his son, and it made Melissa shiver – because what if the kids were involved in some way?

'You can come and see Patrick now,' the doctor said, standing.

They all exchanged glances then followed her outside and down the corridor towards the Critical Care ward. The doctor used her security card to let them in and led them past a busy-looking nurses' station. They strode by a shared ward with four beds in it, relatives surrounding some of the patients, who were hooked up to various life-saving machines, some conscious, others not. There was a young girl on one of the beds, just eighteen or so, and Melissa imagined Lilly or Grace lying there. The woman sitting by her bed looked up, catching Melissa's eye, and Melissa could see the despair in her eyes.

She hurried on until they got to the end ward. This was much like the first one, curtains drawn around two of the beds. The exposed beds across from them were home to an elderly woman and a large man in his fifties who seemed happy enough, reading a magazine.

'Patrick's here,' the doctor said quietly, going to the back of the ward and drawing away the blue curtain to reveal Patrick lying in a bed.

Melissa barely recognised her husband.

There was a tall machine next to him with a variety of tubes attached to his body, his heart and breathing constantly monitored. They'd shaved half his head to do the scan and the tube coming from his mouth made his face look lopsided.

Her fingers touched her parted lips in shock and she felt her legs weaken. Bill put his hand on her back and the three of them walked up to Patrick. Melissa took his hand and stifled a sob. It was horrible to see a man so full of life, a man who rarely sat down, now so still and so *tethered*. He was always moving, whether it be on his bike, pedalling madly through the forest, or in the house, fixing something, playing with the kids, dancing, cooking. Even when they had their cinema nights, the five of them on the large corner sofa glued to the TV, Patrick would be getting up every few minutes to do something or another, wanting to perfect some DIY he'd done earlier in the day.

'Sit down, for God's *sake*, man,' Lewis often joked, and Patrick would sigh, flopping down next to his son as Melissa laughed.

Melissa took the seat next to Patrick, and Bill and Rosemary sat opposite her.

'I'll leave you now,' the doctor said in a low voice. 'Stay as long as you like.'

When she walked away, Rosemary burst into tears, grasping her son's hand and leaning her cheek against it.

'Who would do this to you? Who?'

Melissa took a deep breath to stop her own tears coming.

Who *had* done this to Patrick?

Melissa sat with Patrick a few hours later, the skies now dark, the view of Forest Grove from the window of the ward shrouded in night. She felt her heart yearn for the village, for her home, for nights curled up under thick blankets with her family around her, no blood, no secrets, just the sway of pines outside.

She'd been in the room for five hours now, just sitting and holding Patrick's hand, trying to wrap her head around what had happened as her phone lit up again and again with unread messages from well-wishers. Bill was getting a coffee in the café downstairs after giving Rosemary a lift home. Rosemary had her own health problems, having suffered a severe urine infection a few months before that saw her in hospital for a week, so they'd convinced her to go back home and look after the kids, Melissa promising to return in the early hours so Rosemary could come back after she had had some rest.

Melissa smoothed her fingers over her husband's bandaged head now, curling a dark strand of hair around her finger. He'd hate the fact that half his hair had been shaved off but he'd cover that by making a joke of it, say he ought to come to the hospital more often for a shave. She laughed to herself, but then the laugh turned into a sob. She leaned her forehead on his blanketed thigh, tears wetting the wool, feeling the bump of a tube underneath. It was the first thing she'd noticed as she'd glimpsed him through the trees all those years ago: his thatch of wavy hair. He was breathtakingly handsome, even then. She'd never really been into Disney films as a child, but she imagined he was how a Disney prince would look, with that thick dark hair, those broad shoulders and that dimpled chin.

'Looks like a right ponce,' her childhood friend Ryan had said as he and Melissa watched the new family arrive.

For Ryan, Patrick was the embodiment of everything that was wrong about the new 'eco-village' that had been built on the doorstep of the forest they called home. When the letter had arrived informing their parents of the new building works due to take place, the two fourteen-year-old friends had hatched plans to make life difficult for the new residents, even sneaking into the building site at night and smashing new windows in glee.

But as Melissa sat watching Patrick and his sister, Libby, that day, dressed all smart for their great-aunt's funeral, all that resentment had been replaced by pure fascination. These kids weren't like her and Ryan, all grubby-faced and skinny and filled to the brim with sadness and anger. They were rosy-cheeked with health and happiness, smart and smiling. As she'd thought that, Patrick had looked up and spotted the two feral kids staring at him from the trees. He'd raised his hand in greeting and Melissa had gone to raise hers in response. But then Ryan had grabbed her arm and pulled her away.

There was a sound from nearby. Melissa looked up to see Daphne standing at the door to the room, a coffee and a muffin in her hand. She was staring at Patrick in shock, her green eyes brimming with tears. She'd changed out of her gym clothes and was wearing a beautiful cerise silk vest over patterned harem trousers.

'I couldn't just sit at home,' she said. 'I kept thinking about you all alone here.' She walked over to Melissa, giving her a quick hug, her musky perfume wafting over her. 'I know you probably can't eat,' she said as she handed Melissa the coffee and the muffin, 'but I couldn't come empty-handed.'

'Thanks, you're an angel.' Melissa took a sip of the coffee, pleased to have an alternative to the weak coffee she'd been getting from the machine downstairs.

Daphne squeezed Melissa's shoulder then walked around to the chair on the other side of Patrick's bed, sitting down with a sad sigh. Under the light above, Melissa could see Daphne's attractive face was drawn and pale.

'Any idea who did this to him?' Daphne asked.

Melissa shook her head.

'Ryan couldn't believe it when I told him.'

Melissa wondered what her old friend would be making of it all. Ryan had never shaken off his disregard for Patrick. They were civil with each other; they had to be with Melissa and Daphne, his ex, getting on so well, and then when Lewis and his daughter with Daphne, Maddy, started dating. But that was it: no hint of any kind of bromance brewing there. Still, Ryan wouldn't wish this on Patrick.

'How are the kids?' Daphne asked.

'Shocked.' Melissa thought of them back at home. She was itching to get back now and shake the truth out of them. They *knew* something, something more than they were letting on!

Daphne's eyes strayed to the dressing around Patrick's head. 'Unbelievable, something like this happening in Forest Grove. I rip the piss out of it but it's the safest place I know.'

'I know, I can't wrap my head around it either.' Melissa's voice caught in her throat.

'Oh, hon,' Daphne said, leaning over Patrick to take Melissa's hand. 'I'm so sorry you're going through this.'

Melissa felt tears flood her eyes. She pressed her fists into them, desperate not to cry, on the off-chance Patrick could hear her. But she couldn't help it; the sobs began to roll out.

Daphne jumped up and walked around the bed to her, pulling her into a hug. 'Let it all out. Don't worry about my expensive top either.'

Daphne really was *such* a good friend. Melissa still remembered the first time she had met her, while walking in the woods with Patrick on a freezing-cold day over fifteen years ago. Melissa had just discovered she was pregnant with the twins and was still trying to figure out how the hell she'd cope caring for newborn twins and Joel too.

Melissa had spotted her old friend Ryan first. She hadn't seen him much since moving away from the forest with her mother all those years ago, only occasionally during walks in the woods or around town as he attended to people's trees. When she did see him, he was always alone . . . bar his dog, of course. But this time, a glamorous-looking redhead accompanied him, draped in a beautiful sapphire dress. It was so strange to see them together, glamour and grit combined. Melissa could spot the sexual chemistry a mile off, the way Ryan's cheeks flushed as Daphne put her hand to his chest, laughing at something he'd said.

Ryan's making someone laugh? she remembered thinking.

She also remembered feeling oddly jealous. She'd just presumed Ryan would live in the forest alone for ever, still her feral Beast Boy. It was a ridiculous notion, really. Ryan had grown to be impossibly handsome, with his rugged looks and mesmerising blue eyes. The women in town would make up problems with their trees just to call him out and watch him at work with his father.

When Ryan introduced Daphne to Melissa and Patrick that day, Patrick had surprised Melissa by inviting them to a late-summer BBQ they were having that evening. It had been so strange and exotic to see Ryan turn up that night, Daphne looking even more stunning in a short trendy dress with hummingbirds all over it. Melissa had felt dumpy in comparison, bloated and tired. As the night wore on, Daphne sought Melissa out and Melissa realised she was more than just a pretty face, possessing a wicked sense of humour and sharing her love of cider. They instantly hit it off and when Daphne offered her event-planning skills to help Patrick with his schemes to renovate the visitor centre, Melissa would sometimes pop into the centre and catch a coffee with Daphne while there. She was disappointed when Daphne told her she'd be returning to London a couple of months later.

A few months after that, Daphne was back in Forest Grove and pregnant with Ryan's child. Melissa only heard about it through the village grapevine and was disappointed that Daphne didn't get in touch. They were both pregnant, after all. Instead, Daphne stayed huddled up in the forest with Ryan. But when the twins were born, followed by Maddy three months later, the two women inevitably ended up bumping into each other at various playgroups. Daphne didn't seem like her old vivacious self at first, but eventually she came out of her shell again, the two women becoming firm friends. Melissa was sad when Daphne and Ryan eventually split up when Maddy was five, but she wasn't surprised. They were so different, after all, and once the passion wore off, they really didn't have a great deal in common. But it was an amicable split and they did a brilliant job co-parenting Maddy.

'I just can't believe this is happening,' Melissa said to her friend now. 'I thought, after everything with Joel, I could finally say things were working out.'

Patrick moaned slightly.

Melissa pulled away from Daphne and leaned forward. 'Patrick?' His eyes flickered but then he stilled again. 'Oh, darling,' she whispered, stroking his hand.

'I should head off now, I just wanted to check you were okay,' Daphne said, quickly picking her bag up, her own eyes glassy with tears.

'This must be hard for you too, for the whole village,' Melissa said as she watched Daphne. Patrick was so popular, especially with all the work he'd done for the community, raising funds to get the visitor centre renovated, and so much more on top.

'Not as hard as it is for you,' Daphne said. 'But yeah, it's a shock to the system. The Facebook group's alight with it.'

Melissa sighed. She had never thought she'd be the subject of a post on the Forest Grove Facebook group, let alone one as horrific as this. 'Bet there's lots of speculation?' she asked carefully. Maybe someone had seen something, heard something, a clue for Melissa.

'Lots of people heard the sirens, saw the police cars. Everyone's shocked, of course, passing on their good wishes.'

Melissa pulled her phone from her pocket.

'Probably best you don't look at it,' Daphne insisted.

'Oh, I can handle it.' Melissa found the Facebook app and opened it. She took in her Facebook profile picture. It was of her and Patrick with the kids in the forest, bluebells spread out behind them. Bill had taken it just last week during a post-Sunday-roast walk.

They'd been so *happy.*

She looked down at Patrick, taking in his shaven head, the beeping monitors, his middle swathed in dressings.

How could it have come to this?

She sighed and turned her attention back to her phone, finding the post Daphne was referring to. 'Oh, *quelle surprise*, Graham Cane and Belinda Bell are being their usual selves.'

'Ignore them, they're wankers,' Daphne said with a sigh.

'What the hell has my mum got to do with all this? And what does Andrew bloody Blake mean about Ryan?'

Her eyes honed in on Rebecca Feine's comment.

Tragedy never seems far from the poor girl.

Melissa thought of that ancient oak again. A broken branch. A silver ballet shoe on the ground.

She closed her eyes. Why couldn't the darkness just *stop*?

Chapter Seven

Friday 19th April, 2019
6.13 a.m.

I pretend I'm asleep when Mum checks in on us. I wish I could sleep. I haven't all night. I keep feeling the blade slicing into Dad. How hot his blood felt on my fingers. Sticky too. And that gasp of surprise he gave before he fell down.

I press my face into my pillow to stop myself from crying out and Mum's shadow stretches across the room. She begins to walk over and I make my breath slow and deep like I do sometimes when she tries to wake me up for school. She leans down and kisses my cheek.

Can she taste the salt of my tears?

I don't open my eyes no matter how much I want to, because if I do, I think I'll tell her everything and it was agreed earlier that we definitely couldn't.

I think she's going to leave but she stays where she is, watching me, and I can almost hear her brain trying to puzzle it all out. She knows something's up, and we'll be getting the third degree when we wake.

She eventually leaves the room and I let out a quick succession of breaths. Outside, she begins talking to Nan in little whispers. The landing goes silent and I hear them walking down the stairs.

I wonder whether to wake the other two just so I don't feel so alone in Nan and Grandad's massive attic room. I used to get scared here when I was little, swore I could see eyes watching me in the eaves. I'd hide under the covers, get all hot and sweaty and wish Mum and Dad didn't have a social life so we never had to come here some Saturday evenings while they went out. I wonder if Mum used to feel the same when she lived in this attic, first with Grandma Quail then on her own. Nan and Grandad have even kept Mum's drawings of trees on the walls.

There's one drawing I always look for whenever I'm here, of a huge oak tree with two sets of eyes staring out from a hollow inside. The eyes look scared and there's a shadow stretching across the ground in front of the tree.

I know what tree it is. Now I know what happened there as well. I wish I didn't, though.

God, I'm so *tired. I'll be a right state when I get up. What if I slip up and say something I shouldn't?*

I twist and I turn but it's no use, I just can't sleep. So I get up and lie on the floor, ear and cheek to the ground to get as close as I can to Mum's room below. I think I can hear her breathing and I start to cry, my tears soaking the carpet.

I hope she never finds out what happened. I hope she never has to know it was me who did it.

Chapter Eight

Forest Grove Facebook Chit Chat Group

Friday 19th April, 2019
8.56 a.m.

Kitty Fletcher
Just wanted to post my love and sympathies for the whole Byatt family and hope and pray Patrick Byatt makes a speedy recovery. Can't even imagine what they must be going through.

Eamon Piper
What are you talking about? I only saw Patrick at the cafe yesterday.

Belinda Bell
There was a post about it yesterday but looks like it's been deleted this morning. There was an incident at the Byatts' house yesterday afternoon. Andrea Cooper, why did you delete the post? Isn't this group called 'News and Chit Chat'?

Andrea Cooper
Please refer to the rules, Belinda.

Rebecca Feine
Probably because of Graham Cane's moronic comments, Belinda.

Peter Mileham
Back to the topic at hand! Sadly, with Rosemary and Bill's permission, I can confirm my good friend Patrick was injured (stabbed) yesterday in an attack in his own home. They suspect it was a break-in. His kids found him.

Pauline Sharpe
Stabbed? My God. What the hell is happening to Forest Grove lately? Wasn't there a break-in on Birch Road last month? It must have something to do with the factory that opened in Ashbridge and all those immigrant workers. All my prayers and condolences to the Byatts.

Eamon Piper
Have to confess, that thought did occur to me too, Pauline.

Debbie Lampard
My brother knows people who work at the factory through his health and safety work. They're good decent hard-working people, not criminals.

Belinda Bell
Was it a burglary gone wrong, then? Two scruffy-looking police officers knocked at the house earlier asking if I had seen anything but they were rather cagey about what happened when I asked them.

Tommy Mileham
<Angry face> Right, let's get a search party together to find the scum that did this! My hounds will hunt them out.

Graham Cane
You going to bring that gun that's in your profile picture, Tommy?

Tommy Mileham
Don't tempt me . . .

Rebecca Feine
Guns? Don't be ridiculous. Boys and their toys.

Kitty Fletcher
Girls like guns too, Rebecca.

Rebecca Feine

Ellie Mileham
This is terrifying. Can we have a comment from PC Adrian Cooper? Isn't he in this group? If there was an intruder, I'd like to know, please. I live on the next road and I have my kids to think about.

Belinda Bell
Lots of police in the forest at the moment. I can see from my top window, they're all heading to the west of the woods . . .

Andrew Blake
Hmmmmm, who do we know that lives in that part of the forest . . . ;-)

Rebecca Feine
Andrew Blake, what's that supposed to mean?

Graham Cane

Oh, come on, we all know who Andrew means . . . and if I'm right, this thread will be deleted by admin as quick as you can spell out R-Y-A-N!

Rebecca Feine

If you're talking about Ryan Day, you're barking up the wrong tree, literally. Everyone needs to stop speculating on here. Andrea Cooper, can you moderate this, please?

Graham Cane

'Wood' you please stop being such a snowflake, Rebecca Feine? (See what I did there?)

Andrew Blake

Graham Cane, ha ha!

Kitty Fletcher

I can't believe you're making jokes about this, Graham Cane and Andrew Blake.

Graham Cane

Black humour. Best way to 'tree't a tragedy. ☺

Kitty Fletcher

As a certified therapist, I can tell you it most certainly isn't. It's just another way of bottling it up.

Graham Cane

Was wondering when you'd bring up your qualifications, Kitty!

Belinda Bell

Ryan was visiting New Pine Road checking on number 7's tree yesterday afternoon. I saw his van.

Andrea Cooper

Right, everyone, as much as I'm all for freedom of speech, can I remind you all this is an ongoing investigation so comments CLOSED!

Chapter Nine

Friday 19th April, 2019
10.13 a.m.

Melissa woke to the smell of frying bacon and pancakes, her head throbbing as though she'd spent the whole evening before drinking cider. In the few hours of sleep she'd managed to snatch, her dreams had been filled with the forest, of her frantically running through the trees and trying to find her children. She thought of the old oak in the distance, a cracked branch on the ground, a silver ballet shoe below. It was a nightmare she had often. But it was worse than ever. Something was wrong, very wrong, she just couldn't figure out what . . . Then the memory of Patrick lying on the floor and the weight of their children's silence ploughed into her brain.

'Oh, Patrick,' she whispered, tears flooding her eyes.

She quickly grabbed her phone, scrolling past scores of texts of support and Facebook alerts to find the one text she really wanted to read – the promised update from Rosemary, who had gone straight back to the hospital when Melissa had returned in the early hours.

No change. Hope you had a good rest. X

She looked at the clock. She'd already rested too much! The sudden urgency to speak to the kids propelled her out of bed despite her throbbing head, the clarity of morning making her desperately regret keeping the disappearance of the knife from the police.

What had she been *thinking*?

She brushed her teeth and pulled on yesterday's clothes, rubbing some deodorant under her arms before jogging downstairs. It felt strange to be sleeping here again after all these years. It had once been her sanctuary but now she always felt a little uncomfortable here. The kids and Patrick loved it, though. It was the first house to be built in Forest Grove over twenty-six years before, a sprawling lodge, half brick, half wood, with five large bedrooms. The land around it was *huge*, with pastures and meadows plus their own patch of private forest. The kids loved it and would have sleepovers there whenever Melissa and Patrick had their monthly date night. They even had a key to the house, always welcome, whatever the time. The kitchen always smelt of something delicious, from the amazing muffins Bill loved to make to Rosemary's first-rate curries. The large corduroy sofa in the living room was ancient but the most comfortable sofa going, and books filled every shelf scattered around the house.

Even though the house was less than thirty years old, it felt ancient to the kids, who were used to their modern home. Forest Grove had just consisted of the one road of five large properties when it was built, but over the years four more roads had been added, forming circles around the forest, Old and New Pine Road the closest to the woods.

The girls were sitting on kitchen stools now, drinking orange juice as Lewis helped Bill cook some bacon. At first, it seemed a bit inappropriate to Melissa, the way Bill was frying up a breakfast after what had happened the night before. But then she realised he was probably just trying to present a sense of normality for his grandchildren.

The kids were still in their nightwear, faces pale and wan. They always managed to look more vulnerable in their night clothes, even Lewis in his #NOTTIRED T-shirt, which Lilly had got him for his birthday last summer, a reference to how restless her insomniac brother was at night. Sprawled out behind them was the forest, a lone hawk watching from the trees. The morning sun filtered in through the kitchen window, yellow and speckled, like it often was in the forest.

They all looked up when their mother walked in, a flicker of worry in their eyes. They were clearly expecting a grilling from her, and they were bloody right! She peered over at Bill. Should she bring it all up now, in front of her father-in-law: the way the kids had been, the disappearing knife, the lies and the secrets Melissa saw weighing heavily on her children's shoulders? God knew Bill and Rosemary were experts at sharing heavy burdens. But this was different. She wasn't a child any more. She was a mother and her first duty was to her kids. She needed to know everything first, *then* she'd make a decision about who else to tell. Plus, she needed to remember Patrick was Rosemary and Bill's child and he was *their* priority . . . maybe over their own grandchildren. So she needed Bill gone before she could grill the kids.

She looked at the clock. When *would* she be alone with the kids, though?

Sandy trotted over to her, nudging his wet nose into her skin as he tried to get her attention. Bill and Rosemary's two chocolate Labradors sat obediently on their expensive beds in the gated utility room, their coats gleaming. What a contrast they were to Sandy, who still had mud on his golden coat from his walk the day before and was now trying to grab a piece of bacon from Bill's pan as he shoved him away.

Bill and Rosemary bred show Labradors. The famous Byatt Labrador line of show dogs had been on a winning streak for the past thirty years, even picking up a Crufts 'Best in Show' win. The litters their dogs produced were in high demand, with families willing to spend over a thousand pounds for a Byatt Labrador puppy.

Sandy, however, was a happy mistake that had occurred five years ago after one of the Byatt bitches, Bertha, had an entanglement with a golden Labrador during a walk in the woods. Unfortunately, Melissa had been the one walking her. Funnily enough, her in-laws had never allowed Melissa to walk their precious dogs again. Melissa could see on their faces each time they saw Sandy how much they resented the one blip in an otherwise perfect lineage. Bill had even suggested Bertha have an abortion when he found out she'd been impregnated by a 'standard' pet dog. Luckily, the twins had their grandfather wrapped around their little fingers so were able to convince him to keep the puppies, taking one of the four that were born for themselves.

Melissa went to each of the twins now, kissing them on their foreheads and pulling them into a hug, whispering that she loved them as she did so. She then gave Grace a big cuddle. They each relaxed into her, relief exuding from them that she wasn't going to jump in with the interrogation about the missing knife . . . yet.

'How was Patrick when you left him?' Melissa asked Bill.

'Same,' Bill said with a sigh.

'We'll go see him once we're ready, won't we, kids?' Melissa said, examining each of their faces for any clue of what they'd witnessed the day before.

They all seemed to squirm in their seats, avoiding her gaze. Melissa's stomach dropped. Why would they not want to see their injured father?

Bill frowned as he regarded them too, then he took a deep breath, gesturing to the spare stool next to Grace. 'First get a Byatt breakfast in you.'

It was a tradition, the famous 'Byatt breakfast'. Every month, after Patrick and Melissa's regular 'date night', Bill, Patrick and Lewis would prepare a fry-up. The three generations of Byatt men were as tight as you could get, playing football together in the local park each Sunday, always joking around. They were all so similar too, with their tall strong frames and feline brown eyes. Lewis really looked up to his grandad, in awe of the years he'd spent as a soldier, often grilling him about what had happened as he prepared breakfast. Grace would join in, wanting to know all the gory facts as Lilly grimaced in disgust.

There was no animated talk now, though. They were all wordless and exhausted as a breakfast probably none of them would be able to finish was made.

Melissa noticed then that Lilly was wearing an oversized T-shirt from the production of *Wicked* they'd gone to see the summer before.

'Oh God,' Melissa said. 'Your role in *The Sound of Music*. Did you get it?'

Lilly paused a moment then nodded. 'I did!'

'That's just wonderful news!' Bill said. 'I knew you'd do it! Our talented, beautiful Lilly, true Byatt genes at work there,' he said, gesticulating at her with his spatula, grease flying everywhere. 'Your dad will be proud.'

Melissa did her best to ignore the slight from Bill; she was used to it, after all. She leaned across and encircled her daughter's hand. 'Dad *will* be proud.'

Lilly's hand tensed and she pulled it away. Melissa frowned. What was going *on* with these kids?

When breakfast was ready, they all ate silently. Bill, who usually devoured everything on his plate, picked at his food.

'I really think you should get some sleep, Bill,' Melissa said, desperate to question the children. 'Go and have a couple more hours of rest. I'll tidy up and wake you if there's any news.'

Bill didn't answer at first and Melissa began to worry he'd insist on staying awake. 'Maybe I should grab a couple of hours,' Bill finally conceded, placing his fork down and sighing. He stood and kissed each of his grandchildren on their heads before waving at Melissa and walking upstairs. When Melissa heard his bedroom door click shut, she turned to the kids.

'I know the knife was moved.'

She waited to gauge their reactions. They just dropped their gazes to the table, not saying a word.

'It was there, on the kitchen floor,' she continued, 'then it was gone.' She leaned forward, heart thumping. 'Did one of you move it?'

They continued to keep their eyes on the table.

She looked at them in surprise. 'Kids, this is *serious. Really* serious.'

'We *know*, Mum,' Lewis said, peering at her from under his dark fringe.

'So tell me what the hell happened,' Melissa snapped, unable to comprehend why they were being so tight-lipped about it all.

'We told you,' Lewis said. 'We found Dad like that.'

'I'm not asking about that, I'm asking about the knife!' Melissa said.

Lewis blinked at her then shrugged. 'Don't know.'

But he did. She could tell he did!

She jumped up. 'Don't know? Don't *know*? Your dad is lying in hospital clinging to life, and you hid the bloody knife used to stab him. I know you did, because how else did it disappear?'

The three children looked at each other but still didn't say anything.

'Jesus Christ,' Melissa said. 'What's going on? Why are you not telling me? I'm your mother, you have to tell me!'

'Calm down, Mum,' Lilly hissed.

'I will *not* calm down. Tell me right this minute. Right now.'

Still that heavy, impenetrable wall of silence.

'Fine,' she said, her voice trembling with anger as she reached for her phone. 'I wanted to give you a chance to tell me but looks like I'm just going to have to tell the police about the missing knife.'

'We did hide it!' Grace shouted.

'Grace!' Lewis said, glaring at his little sister.

'No, Lewis!' Melissa shouted at her son. 'Let her speak.' She placed her phone down and put her hand on her younger daughter's arm. 'Tell Mum what happened, darling,' she asked, softening her voice.

Grace opened her mouth then she shook her head, shoulders dropping. 'I can't.'

Melissa's mouth dropped open. She turned her attention to her older daughter. 'Lilly, do you have anything to say?'

Lilly shifted in her chair, uncomfortable, but didn't say anything.

'This is ridiculous!' Melissa said, throwing her hands in the air in frustration. Grace flinched at the loudness of her mother's voice and Melissa sighed. Maybe she was being too hard on them, but it *was* ridiculous. How could they keep something so serious from her? 'Look,' she said, trying to calm herself down, 'you three are my priority. You know that, right? All I want is the best for you, as Dad would too. And I'm telling you right now, the *best* thing for you to do is tell me what's going on. I won't be angry at you. I won't go straight to the police if you don't want me to. As long as you tell me the truth, I will *listen*.'

She waited for one of them to say something, but still nothing.

'Are you covering for the person who did it?' Melissa asked, a trace of panic in her voice. 'Is it someone we *know*?'

'We're protecting each other,' Grace said in a whisper.

Melissa froze.

'What do you mean, protecting each other?' she asked. 'From what?'

They gave each other panicked glances.

The voice telling Melissa one of the kids had done it screamed in her mind. She gripped the edge of the counter so tight her knuckles turned white. She felt her breakfast work its way up again.

She got up off her stool and started pacing the kitchen. Then she came back to the counter, placing her palms flat down on it and staring at her kids. 'Was it an accident? A stupid, freakish accident? Because honestly, I'll understand, I just need to know.'

They all remained silent. It was a deliberate silence. A *planned* silence. She could see it in their eyes: they'd made a pact with one another not to say a word.

'This is serious, guys. Deadly serious,' she said again. 'You *have* to tell me what happened. Was there an argument? Did it get out of control?'

Even as Melissa said it, it felt unfathomable to her. Sure, they had their disagreements, all families did. But an argument so serious it led to someone getting hurt?

No. No no no!

'This is stupid,' Lewis said, pushing away from the counter. 'We're not going to tell you, Mum, we're just not.'

Her mouth dropped open. This was unbelievable! She grabbed his arm and made him turn to her. 'How dare you? You *will* tell me. If you don't, I'm going to the police.'

Tears sprang to Lewis's brown eyes. 'Please don't, Mum,' he pleaded with her.

'Why?'

The doorbell rang, followed by knocking on the door. Melissa let out a frustrated moan. 'Okay, stay here, don't move. We're continuing this conversation in a minute.'

Melissa opened the door to see Jackie Shillingford holding a basket of something in her hands, her husband, Ross, beside her. They lived next door to Rosemary and Bill and were two of the original residents of Forest Grove too. Melissa had got to know them well after moving in with the Byatts, especially Jackie, who shared her passion for protecting the environment. They'd even attended a climate change march in London the week before.

'I hope you don't mind,' Ross said, taking off his signature flat cap, 'but we saw your car on the drive . . .'

Melissa forced a smile, aware of her three quiet children behind her. 'It's fine. I wanted to say thanks for looking after the kids last night anyway.' Her smile wavered and she felt the tears coming.

'Oh, darling!' Jackie said, pulling Melissa into her arms. 'We're all here for you,' she murmured in Melissa's ear. 'What a terrible thing to happen to you all. Here, sit down,' she went on, leading Melissa into the kitchen. The kids all paused, shocked to see their mum crying after how robust she'd been just a moment ago.

'Is it Dad?' Lilly asked, face white.

'No, Lilly,' Jackie said quickly. 'Sorry to make you think that. We just popped by with some sustenance,' she said, gesturing to the basket. 'Home-made brownies.'

'Oh, yummy,' Lilly said, taking the basket and pulling back the foil cover to peek inside.

'You take extra, darling,' Jackie said to Lilly. 'We're so pleased you got the lead in *The Sound of Music*. Your nan is so proud, honestly.' Lilly looked slightly overwhelmed, which was unlike her; she usually loved all the fuss she got from people, especially her grandparents. 'So good to have a small shimmer of light in the darkness with this happy news, isn't it, Melissa?'

'It is,' Melissa said, stroking Lilly's hair.

'How are you all this morning?' Ross asked, shooting the children sympathetic looks.

Lilly pouted as Grace shrugged.

'Not great,' Lewis said.

Jackie gave each of the children a hug. Grace looked uncomfortable, not being one for hugs with anyone but her parents. Lilly did too, though her discomfort was probably more to do with the fact she hadn't put on any make-up or brushed her hair. Lewis was happy to receive a hug, though, not getting embarrassed like other boys his age might. Patrick called him a 'proper hugger'. It was probably part of just how *physical* Lewis could be, whether it be on the football field as he smashed into opponents or with his family and friends as he pulled them into regular hugs. He'd been that way since a baby, rolling over earlier than Lilly and Grace, crawling and walking sooner than all his contemporaries.

Their first son, Joel, was the opposite. In fact, it was their first hint of the muscle-wasting disease he would eventually be diagnosed with. He was late walking, and when he *eventually* seemed to figure it out, he kept falling over. Patrick seemed oblivious to it at first, often declaring how *perfect* Joel was, how *advanced*. 'Look, he's only three months and he can hold himself up!' Bill and Rosemary had been the same, so proud of their first grandson, the latest addition to the 'perfect' Byatt bloodline. It made them blind to the signs Melissa saw so clearly. She'd finally booked in an appointment with their GP when Joel was two, and blood tests revealed that he had Duchenne muscular dystrophy, a serious condition that affects only boys and causes progressive muscle weakness. When the specialist consultant explained it was caused by a 'mistake' in one parent's genetic make-up, Patrick had walked from the room, unable to quite take it in.

So Melissa was alone as the doctor continued to explain that Joel's condition would deteriorate over the years, until he would eventually need to be in a wheelchair – maybe even as early as eight, which was exactly when Joel *did* end up going into his wheelchair. He'd need regular appointments with a specialist and a physiotherapist, the doctor continued. It would be a challenge, but many boys like Joel survived well into adulthood, thanks to advances in medicine, despite the average age of death from the condition being twenty-six.

Melissa had tried to remain calm up until then. Wheelchairs, she could cope with. Appointments and medicines, daily massages and around-the-clock care during bad times, she could cope with too. After all, they had so much support in the village. But the thought of her son dying before her, and so young too, made her feel like the whole world had dropped out from beneath her feet. Patrick had come back in then, drawing her into his arms.

'We'll get through this,' he'd said. And they had. Melissa threw herself into caring for her son, quitting her job as a receptionist at the forest centre to care for him.

She looked at the kids now. If she could get through all that, she could get through this. They *all* could, especially with people like Jackie and Ross to support them. But only if they told her what had happened!

Jackie let go of Lewis and rolled up her sleeves, turning the tap on. 'Don't you lift a finger, we're here for you. Why don't you get yourselves ready and we'll clear up?'

The kids all jumped up and headed upstairs, clearly desperate to excuse themselves from their mother's interrogation.

'So shocking,' Jackie said after they left, scrubbing at a pan as she looked over her shoulder at Melissa. 'In all my years living here, we've had nothing like this – *nothing*.'

Ross sat across from Melissa and shook his head. 'I can't help but wonder if the new factory in Ashbridge is related to all this.'

Jackie rolled her eyes.

'I'm just saying!' Ross said. 'I have nothing against foreigners, you know that, love. I'm just saying we've not had much trouble in these parts until that factory opened.'

Melissa kept quiet, forcing herself to nibble at a chocolate brownie, despite not being hungry. Was that what people were assuming? There *had* been rumbles of discontent since the factory opened and Melissa had certainly noticed more people with foreign accents shopping in Forest Grove's little boutique shops the past year. But in her mind, that didn't mean anything *negative*.

Melissa peered up at the ceiling, listening as the kids got themselves ready. They wouldn't cover for a random stranger, though, would they?

'I'm going to try to set up a proper search,' Ross said. 'I'm sure other Forest Grovians will be more than happy to help.'

'I don't know, Ross,' Melissa said. 'We need to leave the police to it.'

'Fat lot of good they're doing,' he said in disgust.

'There's not much else they *can* do, Ross,' Jackie said. 'We've all seen the police presence. Remember, it's been less than a day since it happened.'

'They don't know Forest Grove like we do, though!' Ross replied, picking his mobile phone up. 'If we want to get anything done around here, we need to do it ourselves. I'll give Tommy Mileham a call, get some of the crew together.'

'The Crew' was the name of the original residents of Forest Grove, a tight-knit group of five couples who'd ingrained themselves in each other's lives over the past twenty-six years, bringing their children up together, spending most weekends together, even holidaying together. It had been that *crew* who had all been there for Melissa and her mother all those years ago too.

'I think we need to let the police do their job, really,' Melissa said, panic fluttering in her chest. Usually, she'd be up for the rest of the community getting involved and sorting out any messes in the village, like when the local allotment was getting vandalised. Bill and Ross had set up a nightly watch and eventually found the culprit, a man from the next town who was trying to jeopardise their chances of winning the county allotment contest. His punishment? He was never allowed to enter the village again, even being marched off the premises of the Neck of the Woods pub when he was seen there a couple of years later with his grandchildren. That was what punishment meant in Forest Grove: ostracism, something that struck fear into the village's residents.

But this time, Melissa didn't want the full force of the village behind this, not until she knew what had happened herself.

'Melissa's right,' Jackie said. 'Don't go getting all gung-ho, Ross.'

'Fine. If you say so,' Ross said with a sigh as he put his phone away.

Melissa breathed a sigh of relief.

'You must be so worried about the kids,' Jackie said to Melissa, unplugging the sink and pushing her red glasses up her nose as she regarded Melissa. 'Any mother would be, to know her children saw their father like that, especially little Grace.'

'How did they seem when you came to look after them last night?' Melissa asked.

'In shock, sweetheart. What about you? It must be so awful for you, worrying about your husband, worrying about the kids too.'

Melissa nodded. Jackie always seemed to get to the crux of the matter. 'It is. I don't know how best to approach it. They're just bottling it all up.'

'Never any good,' Ross said.

'Only natural, though,' Jackie said. 'Same happened when our Riley saw the dog get run over when he was seven. Remember that, Melissa? You were living here then.'

'Oh yes, that was horrible.'

'Riley didn't speak for a week,' Jackie said. 'I even thought about taking him to see Kitty Fletcher.'

Kitty Fletcher was a local therapist whose book, *Raising Children the Kitty Fletcher Way*, was a bit of a bible for the mums of Forest Grove. Its premise revolved around not allowing children any screen time at all and focusing instead on outdoor activities.

Think of the glossy screen of a tablet, TV or phone like the open mouth of a dementor from the Harry Potter books, sucking the soul out of your children, Melissa remembered Kitty saying once when she launched her book in the village's courtyard. At that very moment, Lilly had been taking a selfie for her new Instagram account, which Melissa had let Lilly set up for her thirteenth birthday. Melissa was sure Kitty's eyes had been drilling into her as she'd said that and she couldn't help but feel an overwhelming sense of guilt. She and Patrick had promised themselves they'd reduce the kids' screen time, something Patrick was always banging on about anyway . . . but then he wasn't with the kids as much as she was.

Melissa had taken the kids to the Woodland Wonderland area that Kitty had helped create. It was behind the visitor centre and was a large outdoor sensory area that would supposedly keep children entertained for 'hours on end, whether they're one month old or sixteen years'. Alongside the usual bug hotels and wooden play equipment for little ones, there were also 'chillhouse' huts where teenagers could hide away and talk. There were 'reading trees' too, with comfy benches, a particular favourite of Grace's. It entertained the twins for a while, but the novelty soon wore off and Melissa found herself becoming more lenient again.

Maybe it was something to consider, the kids seeing Kitty? Maybe she could extract what happened out of them.

'Patrick isn't a dog, Jackie,' Ross scolded now. 'Melissa doesn't want to go seeing a therapist like Kitty who'll give anyone who pays her a diagnosis. All the kids need are their family and friends, not strangers poking their noses in.'

'Kitty's one of the good ones, Ross, honestly! All I'm saying is,' Jackie said with a sigh, 'it's no good bottling things up.'

'No, it bloody isn't,' Melissa agreed, peering up at the ceiling.

And yet wasn't that what she was doing too? Not telling the police . . . not telling anyone? Just keeping it all bottled up? But what would Jackie and Ross think if she came out with it right then, that one of the children might have stabbed their own father, because that was one of the possibilities, wasn't it? Forget immigrants, it was the children on your very doorstep you needed to worry about. And look what happened when a child *did* cause problems, like Jacob Simms! His promising career in football wiped away with one flick of a match.

She thought of his bruised face when she first saw him a year ago, fresh from St Fiacre's Children's Home. Then she imagined one of her kids looking the same.

She shivered, wrapping her arms around herself.

Chapter Ten

Friday 19th April, 2019
10.54 a.m.

'Morning, all,' a voice called from the hallway. Rosemary shut the front door behind her and walked into the kitchen.

Jackie strolled over and hugged her. 'Oh, my love, how awful this must be for you.'

'Any change?' Melissa asked.

'Nothing,' Rosemary replied as she yawned. 'They were cleaning him up, so I thought I'd come back, give my boy some privacy.'

Melissa took a deep breath, trying to wrap her head around the fact that her strong, handsome Patrick needed someone else to clean him.

Ross stood up. 'We'll leave you to it. Jackie did her famous brownies,' he said, gesturing to the basket. He went up to Rosemary and gave her a quick hug. 'We're here for you. Anything you need . . .'

'Absolutely anything,' Jackie added. 'Just shout. You too, Melissa.'

They both waved then walked out, shutting the door behind them.

'Kids upstairs?' Rosemary asked Melissa.

'Yes, getting ready. Bill's sleeping.'

'Good, I'll go and see them. I need some cuddles.'

Melissa paused. She wanted to go straight to the hospital but she really needed to continue her conversation with the kids. But how could she, with Rosemary here now too?

She'd do it on the way to the hospital. The prospect of seeing their dad laid up in that hospital bed with all those tubes coming out of him might help to drag the truth from them.

Sandy padded up to Melissa, nudging at her hand.

Melissa looked out into the forest, suddenly desperate to get out there. The trees always helped her to get her head straight, and God knows she needed some clarity now before she tackled the kids again.

'You okay with the kids for twenty minutes or so while I take Sandy out for a quick walk?' she asked Rosemary.

Rosemary's brow knitted. 'What if the person who hurt Patrick is out there?'

'I'll be fine, I have my guard dog,' Melissa said, gesturing to Sandy, who was now running around with his lead in his mouth.

'Okay. But you mustn't go too far. You know how easy it is to get lost in the woods when your mind's not on it.'

Rosemary was right. Many people got lost in the depths of the forest. Even residents tended to stick to the outer circle of the woods during walks, taking the designated paths.

'I know this forest like the back of my hand, remember?' Melissa said as she pulled on her wellies.

Rosemary wrinkled her nose, the way she always did when she was reminded of Melissa's origins, living in the woods.

'Can you make sure the kids are ready so I can take them to the hospital with me?' Melissa asked Rosemary.

'I don't know if that's a good idea, Melissa. It's rather harrowing to see.'

'He's their father.'

The two women held each other's gaze. Ever since Melissa and Patrick married, there had been this subtle underlying tug of war between them, especially when it came to bringing up Rosemary's precious *Byatt* grandchildren.

Melissa sighed. She shouldn't think like that about Rosemary, she was a good person, really . . . and her son *was* lying in hospital.

She put her hand on Rosemary's arm. 'You're right,' she said. 'I'll see how they are when I get back.'

Rosemary gave her a brief smile. Melissa grabbed Sandy's lead and headed out.

'Oh, there's been a problem with giant hogweed too!' Rosemary shouted after her. 'It's poisonous, so keep Sandy away from it, okay? Just stick to the designated paths!'

'Okay!' Melissa called back to her as the back door swung shut. When she stepped outside, she paused, taking in a deep breath. She instantly felt better, being out of the house. The late-morning sun was a bright yellow, casting light in fine gold diagonal slices through the wildlife meadow Rosemary had created in her garden. It was one of Jackie and Rosemary's little projects, encouraging residents to let their grass grow, including the prettier weeds, so their gardens became a haven for wildlife. Melissa had started growing one herself and she'd even helped Jackie write some leaflets to drop into people's letterboxes to encourage them to do the same too. The gardens of Forest Grove were starting to look rather wild but beautiful, with the soft white petals of mouse-ear chickweeds and the sprightly yellow of creeping buttercups beginning to thrive. Some people weren't a fan, though, like Andrea, who'd complained about it on the Facebook group last summer. But she was quickly shouted down by people who loved the scent of the petals and the draw the wild flowers provided for mini-beasts and for wild animals like hedgehogs and foxes seeking sheltered places to sleep during the day.

Melissa passed the meadow and headed into the forest, Sandy darting off ahead of her, leaping over roots and logs to sniff out deer and squirrels. At first, Melissa kept to the designated path, calling Sandy back each time he strayed too far. As a child, it was these paths that Melissa would keep away from, instead heading into the deepest, darkest heart of the forest with Ryan. She found herself stepping off the designated path now too, the soles of her wellies sinking into the quilted mulch.

In the distance, a fat red dog fox paused, regarding Melissa before disappearing from sight into a groove in the forest floor. She liked to think it was one of the four cubs she'd hand-reared five years earlier when she found their tiny forms gathered around their dead mother on the side of the road one cold spring morning. She'd spent day and night feeding and caring for them, using everything she'd learnt from her mother, who'd done the same when they'd lived in the forest. Then she'd released them back into the wild, the kids watching in awe as their little friends darted off into the undergrowth. Word had got out and now, whenever an injured or orphaned hedgehog or fox was found, Melissa would be the first port of call, the local wildlife centre being a good hour's drive away. She couldn't always help, especially now that she was working full-time, but she did what she could.

That was why Melissa liked going out in the morning: there was more chance of seeing wildlife, especially deer. Sometimes, if she was lucky, she'd catch sight of a herd of deer, the same herd that would sometimes venture out into Rosemary and Bill's back garden to lie in the afternoon sun.

Melissa finally reached the point where she needed to be – a small clearing right in the heart of the forest, where its ancient great oak stood. Several metal struts supported its structure, but it was clear it was nearing its end, grey and decaying. The wooden bench around it looked like new, though, designed and maintained by Ryan. Two initials were carved beautifully into the backrest: RQ.

Ruby Quail. Melissa's mother.

Melissa walked to the tree, ducking under the rods to reach its trunk. She placed her hand on the bark, feeling its rough texture beneath the soft skin of her fingers. She closed her eyes, breathing in and then out, finding a rhythm with the sway of the branches as her mother had taught her to. As a child, her mother told her stories of the Senoi people of Malaysia, who believe each person has a 'partner' tree, a specific tree that they 'bond' with. This could go on through the generations, her mother told her, with trunks growing from the roots of an original tree, providing new trees for generations to bond with. She would take Melissa's small hand and place it against this old oak.

'This is our tree,' she would say. 'We belong to it. It belongs to us.'

It was her mother's favourite topic, the healing properties of the forest, both physical and spiritual. She'd collect items from the forest, make herbal remedies out of them. She'd even started selling them to people she'd met in her old job working at a health supplies shop in Ashbridge. Melissa's dad didn't like that side of her, though, telling her she was talking 'mumbo jumbo' and that, if she wasn't careful, people would begin to think she was a witch. So she'd restrict that kind of talk and her potion-making to times when she was alone with Melissa.

But now the tree her mother so loved – the tree where she'd died – was dying itself. Maybe that was a good thing. Maybe it had been home to too much darkness. That was why she'd agreed to Patrick's proposal to fell the old oak tree to make way for a well-being centre. Ryan was against the idea, certain the tree had more time left in it. But anyone could see it didn't, and anyway, it was

Melissa's land. She'd been so shocked to discover, via a solicitor's letter, that her father had passed the land over to her, along with the small cottage that sat on it, after her mother died. He'd moved away from the forest not long after Melissa and her mother had walked out anyway, but had refused to let them return to it. Clearly, the news of his wife's death had softened him. She never heard from him after that and still had no idea where he was. Melissa had rarely visited the cottage, her childhood home – too many unhappy memories. By the time she was old enough to think of selling it, the cottage had fallen into such disrepair nobody wanted to buy it. In the end, it was knocked down after one of the walls collapsed during a bad storm. If the oak tree eventually went too, the solid patch of land would enable them to 'give something back to the community', as Patrick put it. And it would give Melissa some closure, too, after all that had happened at that tree.

Patrick had used the centre as part of his pitch to residents when he was campaigning to get the ten nomination signatures he needed to stand as a councillor for them.

In fact, Melissa now realised with a sinking heart, she was due to be in this very spot the next day with Patrick and the girls as they looked at plans for the new well-being centre. That would need to be cancelled. Patrick would be gutted.

There had been a lot of soul-searching about Patrick running to be a councillor: the extra hours he'd have to work on top of the time he already spent in his job as director for a marketing company, combined with his volunteer work for the forest centre. But when Melissa saw the sparkle in his eye when he'd learnt he'd got the ten signatures he needed to run – in fact, he got treble that – she knew he'd done the right thing. They'd all just need to adjust to the extra hours his campaigning had taken up lately and make the most of the free time Patrick had. Patrick would probably have to be withdrawn from the local elections now, considering his condition. After all that hard work too – he'd be devastated if he knew!

Tears flooded her eyes. Her poor darling.

Melissa sat on the bench, leaning her head against the bark of the tree and closing her eyes.

'What do I do now, Mum?' she whispered, imagining her mother standing before her with her waist-length golden hair. 'How do I get the truth out of those grandchildren of yours? It's *so* out of character for them. I'm sure they have their little secrets, all kids do. But this is huge. Do you think one of them did it, Mum?' she asked out loud. 'I know it's crazy, but . . .' She took in a deep breath. She couldn't believe she was really contemplating it. But what other explanation could there be? Wasn't there usually some kind of inkling, a hint of a deep-seated issue, for a child to *do* that to their parent?

Melissa sighed, raking her fingers through her blonde hair. Other than Lewis's occasional outbursts at school, the kids were pretty well adjusted. But then the twins *had* lived through their brother's death . . . What had that done to them, losing their brother at such an early age?

There was a crack of branches. She opened her eyes to see Ryan approaching in the distance, his terrier not far behind. She didn't see him much nowadays, only on the doorstep of one of her neighbours' houses when he was called out to check a tree overhanging their garden.

He played a crucial role in Forest Grove's fabric. Though living in a forest had many plusses, there were also many challenges. Trees had to be checked on a regular basis to ensure they didn't fall down and harm residents. Alerts needed to be put out via the emergency text service Ryan had set up to warn of weather events, such as high winds, that might create safety concerns. There was a problem with wildlife too, from mice to rats, foxes and deer, something Ryan oversaw. He may not have been as sociable as other residents, living in the forest as he did and never attending events, but he was an essential part of life in the forest.

Melissa took the opportunity to watch him before he caught sight of her. He was wearing his usual uniform of black cargo pants and his green forest ranger T-shirt, which revealed his scarred, muscled arms. His fair hair had grown since she'd last seen him, curling around his ears.

He paused when he noticed her. She sat up and wiped her tears away as he strode over, his one-eyed dog bounding after him.

'You okay?' he asked when he got to her, his vivid blue eyes full of concern.

'Not really,' she admitted.

He gestured over his shoulder. 'Need to be alone?'

She shook her head. 'Please stay. I could do with the company.'

Sandy appeared from a crop of trees then, jumping up at Ryan as Ryan's dog let out a low growl.

'As obedient as ever, I see, Sandy,' Ryan said as he crouched down to stroke the Labrador. He peered up at Melissa. 'How you holding up?'

'Not great.'

'The kids?'

Melissa looked down at her fingers, scraping bark from beneath her nails. 'Not great either.'

She looked up again to see that he'd kept his eyes on hers, and she wondered if he could see the secrets and lies within them. He did have a knack of knowing what she was thinking. Or at least he used to, anyway. They'd been so close as kids when they lived in the forest together. Ryan had arrived first, after his mother passed away giving birth to him. They'd lived in a miserable town a hundred miles away originally, but when his dad took a job as a forest ranger, they moved into the woods, Ryan's dad burying his grief in the trees . . . and in drink too. He'd let Ryan run feral among the trees, and though Ryan was fed and had a bed to sleep in, there was no proper sense of nurturing, especially when his dad took to drinking.

They were living alone in the forest until Melissa moved there with her parents three years later. Her dad had lost his job as a lorry driver and fell behind on the mortgage repayments on the house he owned in Ashbridge, the nearest town. He found the dilapidated cottage a few minutes' walk from Ryan and his dad's lodge and bought it at auction.

Melissa had loved it when she first saw it, all the graffiti on the walls and the big hole in the top floor exciting to her at the time. Her parents were excited too, her dad harbouring grand plans to turn it into the 'most beautiful cottage in the woods you've ever seen' and her mother finally able to live in the forest she felt so spiritually connected to. She'd grown up in the New Forest, brought up by her New Age parents there. When she'd met Melissa's father and moved to Ashbridge with him, town life had stifled her. But being back in the forest seemed to calm her. As the months wore on, though, and the strain of doing up the cottage intensified, that dream grew more distant, and Melissa's father's angry outbursts more frequent too.

So Melissa escaped into the woods one day as her parents argued, chasing deer and rabbits until she saw a muddy boy her age doing kung-fu moves on top of a tree trunk. His face was filthy, his fair hair long, his chest bare and muddy. Melissa thought he was the most fascinating thing she'd ever seen. That was it, they became firm friends then, their fathers striking up a form of camaraderie too when her parents finally came looking for her. As the years went on, and home got even tougher for the two of them, they found sanctuary in each other until the day Melissa had to leave the forest when she was fifteen, a year after she first saw Patrick.

Melissa thought back to that day. Her parents had been arguing as usual, but this argument was bad, *really* bad. Her father had this look in his eyes she hadn't seen before. Then he'd dragged Melissa down the stairs and slapped her right in front of her mother, saying, 'Look at this mess, look at it!' as he pointed to the remains of the baking session she and her mum had enjoyed earlier on.

Her mum had got this steely look in her eyes then and turned to Melissa. 'Run. Now.'

So that was what she'd done. Her mum had always told her the best hiding place was the hollow in the old oak. It was like she'd been training her over the years for this very moment. So Melissa had run to the oak and squeezed inside. It felt like she was there for hours, but she found out later it was only twenty minutes before Rosemary had found her and taken her to their home. Turned out Melissa's mother had managed to lock herself in the bathroom and call Bill, the only person she could trust, having got to know him over the past year while supplying him with herbal remedies.

Despite being worried for her mum, Melissa had welcomed the warmth of Rosemary and Bill's house, the sweet taste of the hot chocolate Rosemary made her. Then that glimpse of Patrick on the stairs in his pyjamas. Rosemary's friends had turned up then: Jackie Shillingford, Debbie and Tommy Mileham's wife, Megan, too. No men, though; even Bill wasn't there. The women gathered around the kitchen table, fussing over Melissa and giving each other worried glances as Rosemary anxiously watched the dark trees outside.

Eventually, there had been the sound of footsteps and the front door opened to reveal Bill . . . and Melissa's mother. Her face was swollen with bruises and blood, and she looked sunken, eyes hollow. Melissa caught a glimpse of blood on her pretty nightdress before she quickly covered it with the coat Bill had lent her.

It was decided Melissa and her mother would stay with the Byatts. Her father refused to allow them back into the cottage, his cottage by rights back then, considering it was in his name, even when he moved away.

Ryan and Melissa barely saw each other after that, as Melissa got wrapped up in Forest Grove life while living at the Byatts' with her mother. It was only when Daphne came on to the scene that Melissa saw him more around town. But it was different this time; they were wearing masks created by family life. The rawness had gone and, with it, the connection.

'Has Maddy talked to Lilly?' Melissa asked now. Though Maddy and Lewis didn't talk as much since splitting up, she was still close to Lilly.

Ryan nodded. 'They've all been messaging each other. Lewis too.'

That was good to hear. Melissa was worried the two may have drifted apart but now, more than ever, Lewis needed his friends.

'Did the twins say anything to Maddy about what happened?' she asked carefully, interested to know if they'd confided in her.

'Just that they found their dad like that. You know what kids are like, don't say much to us when it matters.'

Don't say anything at all, Melissa thought.

'Mads wanted to go over to Bill and Rosemary's this morning,' Ryan continued, 'but I told her you guys need space.'

'No, tell her it's fine to come over. It'll be good for the kids to see her.'

'Okay, I'll tell her.' Ryan's brow creased as he looked into the distance. 'Any news on who did it?'

Melissa shook her head. 'Nothing. Have the police come to see you? I heard they're doing door-to-door.'

'Yeah. They wanted to know if I'd seen anything.'

'Why would you have seen anything? You live at the other end of the forest to us.'

He shrugged. 'Whoever did it could have walked through the forest.' He pushed away from the tree, patting his thigh to beckon his dog over. 'Better head back. Andrea Cooper called earlier to say one of her trees looks like it's rotting. Got a feeling she's more interested in finding out what the police asked me.'

Melissa rolled her eyes. 'That wouldn't surprise me.'

'Take care out here, okay? You know I'm here if you need to talk?'

Melissa nodded. 'I know.'

She watched him walk off, his dog bounding after him. She missed how close they used to be, but Ryan didn't really let many people into his life any more.

Sandy jumped up at Melissa's legs, whining.

'Okay, I get the hint. But we'll have to head back soon,' she said, checking the time as she thought of Patrick alone in hospital. She stood up and followed Sandy into the undergrowth.

Then she paused.

On one of the trees behind the great oak was a poster fixed with bright blue tape. She approached it. It was probably about another missing cat or dog. She got her phone out, ready to take a photo, a habit she'd got into so she could refer to it if she saw any lost animals on her walks.

But then she froze.

There was no cat or dog on the poster. Instead, it was a family portrait of Melissa, Patrick and the three kids, two words in bold printed above the photo.

I know.

Chapter Eleven

Friday 19th April, 2019
11.37 a.m.

Melissa stared at the poster. It was a colour A4 sheet with a purple dotted border, even placed in a plastic sleeve to protect it from the elements. The photo that had been used was from Patrick's election website. He'd wanted to make sure people knew he was a family man so had included this family portrait, which they'd had done last year.

Melissa stared at the words printed above the photo.

I know.

What did that *mean*?

She realised with horror that it could be referring to Patrick's attack. It looked like it had been put up very recently, the paper within the sleeve still white and untouched by the weather.

Could someone have seen what had happened the evening before? Their kitchen could be viewed from the forest. But why not just go to the police? Why put this poster up?

Melissa peered around at the other trees, letting out a gasp as she saw more posters.

She yanked each of the posters off the trees, shoving them into her bag. Maybe she could show them to the police, even get them to extract fingerprints to find out who was behind them.

How many more were there? She hadn't seen any others on the way into the heart of the forest, not on the designated paths anyway. She started running through the forest, scouring the trees for more posters. But there didn't seem to be any beyond the ones she found around the old oak tree.

She turned to look at the ancient tree.

Maybe the location had been chosen on purpose? Whoever placed the posters might know Melissa had once lived here. They might know Melissa often came here to sit on the bench Ryan had made for her mother too.

I know.

The old branches of the oak tree creaked in the wind. Melissa shivered, drawing her cardigan around herself. She should get back to the children. She could spend all day searching the forest for these posters and still not cover every inch of the woodland's five hundred acres. Even Melissa, who'd lived there most of her childhood, probably hadn't visited every part of that forest. She just needed to hope her theory was right and only the area around the old oak had been targeted. People rarely ventured into that part of the woods.

She turned around and made her way back to Rosemary and Bill's.

These posters just proved it, she thought as she headed back; she needed to go to the police. She'd give the kids one more chance to tell her what happened, then she was taking this to the people she should have gone to in the first place.

She strode across Rosemary and Bill's garden then let herself in via the back door, kicking the leaves from her wellies. As she glanced up, she realised the police were already right there, standing in the kitchen with Lilly and Grace.

Chapter Twelve

Friday 19th April, 2019
12.01 p.m.

The detective who'd interviewed them the night before was standing with a female detective, a slim black woman, her dark hair up in a severe bun. Melissa looked between the two police officers, conscious of the scrunched-up posters in her bag.

Lilly hurried over to Melissa, barefoot, hair still wet from the shower. Melissa squeezed her hand, reassuring her daughter as much as she could with a touch, a quick smile, despite freaking out inside as well. Grace seemed unfazed, staring in fascination at the two detectives.

'They just got here,' Lilly said. 'Nan's sleeping and Grandad's in the loo.'

'How can I help?' Melissa asked the officers.

'We wanted to update you on the investigation,' Detective Crawford said. 'You might prefer the children to go into another room?'

Melissa thought about it. No, they needed to see how serious this was. Maybe it would prompt them to tell the truth. As for her telling the truth about the missing knife, and the posters too, she hadn't made her mind up yet. 'It's fine, they can be here,' she said.

'This is Detective Powell, by the way,' Detective Crawford said, gesturing to the other detective.

Melissa shook the stern-looking detective's hand.

'We've just been having an interesting conversation with your daughter,' Detective Powell said, raising an over-plucked eyebrow as she looked at Grace. 'She remembered *exactly* where the blood spatter was.'

Lilly's face flushed bright red in embarrassment. 'I *told* her not to go on about it.' She struggled with her little sister's obsession with the darker things in life. Lilly was all about the lightness and spark of life, silly social media photos with her friends plastered with neon-coloured statements. If Grace had an Instagram account – which she wasn't allowed to yet – it would be filled with photos of the dark forest, rotting animals and the dying roots of an oak tree.

'Don't worry, we don't mind,' Detective Crawford said, clearly bemused that such a young girl would talk of such a thing. But his colleague looked less impressed.

Melissa gave them a shaky smile. 'Grace devours any new information, don't you, darling?'

Grace nodded and Lilly clutched her mother's hand even tighter, Melissa's heart ricocheting against her chest. Maybe this really was the time to tell the police everything, just like she'd been so determined to earlier.

She would ask to speak to them alone, get Rosemary and Bill to be with the kids in another room. She'd explain it was all such a shock, so confusing, and she was *scared* for her kids because she had no idea what the hell had happened and now there were the posters to consider and then—

She took in a sharp breath.

And then *what*? The kids would be interrogated, maybe even taken to the station. They would feel betrayed. Maybe one of them would confess to an argument gone wrong, a moment of rage, and their whole lives would free-fall, just as Jacob Simms's life had. Not to mention the fact Melissa herself might be done for accessory to assault.

'Are you okay, Mrs Byatt?' Detective Crawford asked.

She blinked, focusing on the officer. 'Yes, sorry, just tired. Let's sit, shall we?' she suggested, gesturing to the large sofa at the back of the kitchen. 'Coffee? Tea?'

Lewis appeared on the stairs. He came to a sudden stop, eyes popping with fear as he took in the officers.

'The police have just come to update us on the investigation,' she called out to him, trying to give him a calm smile.

Bill jogged down the stairs then too, his newspaper in his hands. He paused a moment when he saw the police officers, then he patted Lewis on the back. 'Come on, son. Let's see where they are tracking down your dad's attacker.'

Lewis nodded and they walked downstairs together. Melissa saw the similarity in them then, just as she did when she saw Patrick and Lewis together. The same height, the same way of moving. Confident and assured, even in the midst of all this. Rosemary would call it the 'strong Byatt backbone', all part of a bloodline that went back centuries, as documented by the sprawling family tree that dominated the space above the fireplace in their living room. Soldiers, rugby players, field doctors and now world-leading dog breeders, each generation adding to a lineage to be proud of.

Bill put his hand out to the detective. 'Bill Byatt, Patrick's father,' he said. 'Detective Crawford, isn't it? We spoke on the phone this morning.'

Melissa looked at Bill in surprise. 'You did?'

'I called earlier for an update,' Bill explained. 'Right, let me get you some drinks,' he quickly said, switching the kettle on as he rubbed Melissa's arm reassuringly. 'I think I'll let Rosemary sleep a bit longer.'

Melissa went to the sofa, beckoning for the kids to sit with her. The girls sat either side of her as Lewis perched his tall frame on the sofa's arm. Bill remained standing, his arms crossed as he regarded the detectives.

Detective Crawford took a dining chair across from them, but the other detective walked around the room, peering at family photos. Melissa clutched Lilly's hand particularly tightly. She could sense her daughter was struggling with this. She was usually so good at putting a mask on things, unlike Lewis, whose emotions were always right at the surface. With Lilly, she trampled them down so well that when they came bursting out in an epic moment of drama the whole world seemed to take notice. Melissa didn't want that to happen now.

Detective Crawford smiled kindly. 'I appreciate this is a difficult time for you all. I hear Patrick has been placed in an induced coma?'

Melissa nodded, the kids remaining still and silent.

'This shouldn't take too long,' the detective continued. 'I wanted to give you a quick update on where we are with the investigation. We're treating this as attempted murder.'

Murder. Melissa had to squeeze her hands into fists to stop them trembling.

Lilly gasped, putting her hand to her mouth as Lewis bit hard on his lip, trying to stop himself from crying. Grace remained expressionless.

Detective Powell glanced over her shoulder at Grace, brow furrowed. Melissa pulled Grace close to her, feeling protective of her younger daughter and her quirky ways. Sure, Grace was a little stranger than other kids. In fact, Patrick had been sure at one point she was autistic. Melissa had disagreed. *She's unique*, she'd said to him, *our special little Grace*. When Grace was eventually assessed for autism at Patrick's insistence, she wasn't anywhere on the spectrum, proving Melissa right. She'd felt a sense of triumph then, proof of just how deeply she knew and understood their children, especially the often unfathomable Grace.

But recent events had blown that out of the water. She would never have dreamed her children would keep something so huge from her, but here they were, doing exactly that.

'Of course,' Detective Crawford continued now with a sigh, 'we have little to go on. As you said in your statements yesterday, you all found Patrick like this. First, the children,' he said, looking sympathetically at the kids, 'then you, Mrs Byatt, a few moments later?'

Melissa nodded.

'Forensics have been at the house,' the detective continued. 'There are no fingerprints of significance and the, erm, blood spatter,' he said, darting a look at Grace, 'suggests a small struggle of some sort may have taken place.'

Bill's nostrils flared and Melissa pursed her lips.

'There have been extensive searches of the area, both the village, where we've been doing door-to-door, and the forest,' the detective said. 'As you know yourselves, it's a large area to cover with plenty of opportunity for any assailants to make it away on foot.'

'Have you been searching the surrounding villages and towns too?' Bill asked.

Detective Powell nodded, finally walking over to join them. 'These are all things we're taking into consideration,' she replied in clipped tones. 'In fact, officers are in Ashbridge today doing door-to-door enquiries, and we'll be talking to Mr Byatt's colleagues at the council too.'

'We'll also be focusing on trying to find the knife,' Detective Crawford added. 'It's clear it's one of the knives from the knife block in the kitchen?' He looked at Melissa for confirmation.

She nodded, trying to stay calm as she thought of one of the kids hiding it. Even worse, one of the kids plunging it into their father's side.

'Then you know exactly what type of knife to search for?' Bill asked.

'Of course,' Detective Powell replied. 'It's all part of the investigation. Find the knife and we may even find fingerprints if it hasn't been cleaned thoroughly enough.'

Melissa examined the children's faces. Lewis started tapping his foot, a ball of pent-up energy, as Lilly went rigid beside him. Grace just continued staring into the distance, face unreadable.

Bill sighed loudly and went to the back door, staring out at the forest with his hands in his pockets. 'Surely there should be some kind of development,' he said, without turning. 'You really need to speak to those factory workers.'

'It's been less than twenty-four hours, Mr Byatt,' Detective Powell said in a defensive tone. 'Trust me, we're as committed to finding the culprit as you are.'

Melissa didn't doubt it as she looked at the detective's fierce expression.

'Has anything else occurred to you since we spoke last night?' Detective Crawford asked them all. 'Anything out of the ordinary the past few days – weeks, even? Any enemies you can think of?'

'I told you, my son had no enemies,' Bill said. 'The people here adore him. It'll be a stranger attack, mark my words. Remember what I told you about Patrick's watch being missing?' he said to the detective.

'Is it?' Melissa asked. 'Patrick hardly ever takes that watch off.'

Bill nodded. 'I noticed it at the hospital, so I asked the doctors. They said he hadn't been wearing it. Then I confirmed with Detective Crawford this morning that there was no trace of it at the house.'

'Yes, that's certainly an interesting lead,' Detective Crawford said. 'I was looking it up this morning – worth a few thousand if it went to auction?'

Bill nodded.

'Quite a motive,' Bill said.

Melissa looked at the kids. Did *they* know where the watch was?

Detective Powell followed Melissa's gaze, noticing how tense Lewis in particular was. 'Anything to add, Lewis?'

Lewis's brown eyes darted up, glassy with tears. 'No, nothing.'

Melissa put a steadying hand on her son's back, stroking it. 'Obviously, we're still in shock,' she explained.

'Understandably,' Detective Crawford said. 'There *are* things we can do to help.' He opened a folder and pulled out some leaflets. Among them was a booklet about child therapists. Melissa took it, staring down at it, not surprised to see Kitty Fletcher's name on it.

'I believe you haven't been to visit your father?' Detective Powell asked the children.

Melissa looked at her in surprise. 'He was only taken in yesterday afternoon.'

The detective glanced at the clock and Melissa followed her gaze. It was past midday. Melissa could see the implication in her eyes, how strange it was that the kids hadn't wanted to visit their seriously injured dad as soon as they could.

'We were all about to go before you turned up,' Melissa said, looking at the kids. 'Right?'

They all nodded but she could see the hesitancy in their eyes.

'Do you have any more questions?' Detective Crawford asked.

Melissa paused. This would be her chance to tell the police, right now. Before it was too late, before this really spiralled out of control.

But instead, she shook her head.

She just couldn't do it.

'When will our house be ready to return to?' Lewis asked.

Melissa looked at her son. He probably wanted to get back there, make sure the knife was hidden properly.

'Not for a few days, I'm afraid,' Detective Crawford replied, smiling kindly at Lewis. 'We have a scene guard on the house at the moment.'

'Scene guard?' asked Grace, curious.

'We need to protect the place where your father was hurt, Grace,' the detective said gently. 'Make sure nothing is tampered with.'

Lewis looked worried. *Was* he thinking of the knife? The other detective seemed to notice Lewis's concern too, her head tilting as she examined his face. Lewis caught the detective's eye and tried to adjust his expression, but it just made him look more suspicious. Melissa realised how important it was for her to hear the truth from the kids first, rather than going to the police. They wouldn't be able to handle being questioned by a detective like Powell!

Plus, Detective Crawford was right, it *had* been less than twenty-four hours. They needed time.

She thought of the posters she'd found too. Should she mention them? If she did, the police might begin to turn their attention to the family as they dug into the reason behind the *I know* scrawled across them. That in turn might lead to the kids. No, she wouldn't bring the posters up yet. She'd keep one just in case she decided to tell the police, but it would be best if she got rid of the others. Maybe burn them. For now, they'd just need to stay hidden away in the bottom of her bag.

'Anything else?' Detective Crawford asked. 'We really need to get on with the investigation now.'

'No,' Melissa said, smiling at him as she placed her hand over her bag, where the posters lay. 'We appreciate you coming over . . . and for all the work you've been doing too.'

She led the two detectives to the door but, before stepping out, Detective Powell peered back into the kitchen at Grace, narrowing her eyes.

Melissa bristled. What was her *problem* with Grace? She clearly had no kids of her own and didn't understand how *weird* they could be. 'Keep us posted,' Melissa said, keen for the detectives to leave.

As they walked down the path, Maddy appeared on the other side of the road, dressed in black dungarees and a bright yellow T-shirt. It still gave Melissa a bit of a shock when she saw her short pink hair. It used to be a lovely dark brown colour but then she'd suddenly dyed it earlier in the year. It was probably no coincidence it was around the same time Maddy and Lewis split up. Some kind of statement of independence, Melissa supposed.

Maddy froze when she saw the police, her brown eyes widening. The detectives nodded at her as they passed and she gave them a shaky smile.

'Hello, Maddy,' Melissa said when Maddy reached her.

'Dad called, said you were okay with me coming over?' she asked Melissa, wrapping her arms around herself, looking pale-faced as she peered behind her at the police again.

It must be so shocking to see all this happening in her village, Melissa thought. 'Of course,' she said. 'It's just that we're all going to the hospital soon.'

'Oh.'

'Do come in, though. The kids would love to see you, even if it's for a few minutes. How do the twins seem? Your dad mentioned you've all been messaging.'

Maddy looked slightly alarmed at Melissa's earnest expression. 'Upset, I guess? It's been pretty shocking for everyone.'

'Right,' Melissa said, exploring Maddy's heavily kohled eyes. Did she know something? It was hard to tell.

Before Melissa had a chance to ask her more questions, Grace ran outside and instantly pulled Maddy in. Maddy smiled, stroking Grace's silky blonde hair as she let Grace lead her into the kitchen.

'Hello, Maddy,' Bill said as Maddy walked into the kitchen. 'What are you doing here?'

Nice welcome, Melissa thought. Bill and Rosemary had never really warmed to Maddy, with her quirky dress sense and outspoken political views, which ran in direct contrast to the Byatts' more conservative political leanings. And then, when their beloved grandson started dating Maddy, they were *really* put out. It reminded Melissa of the way Bill and Rosemary had reacted when they learnt

Patrick was dating her and she felt quite protective of Maddy as a result, being even more exuberant in her praise for the girl. Not that Maddy couldn't handle herself.

Patrick seemed to sit on the fence about Maddy, though. Deep down, she sometimes wondered if he felt the same way about Maddy as his parents, but for Lewis's sake he kept his doubts to himself, apart from when Maddy contradicted his political talk at the dinner table. Melissa would notice a slight twitch of his jaw that showed his irritation.

Melissa took a deep breath as she thought of Patrick lying in that hospital bed. She peered at the clock. She really was desperate to see him.

'Shall we go to the snug?' Lilly said to Maddy, gesturing to the large summer house at the back of her grandparents' garden. During Rosemary and Bill's big barbecues, the kids would often disappear into the summer house to play games and listen to music.

'No time for that,' Melissa said. 'We're going to the hospital to see your dad.'

'I don't want to go,' Lilly said.

Bill looked at his granddaughter in surprise. 'This is your *father*. You must go, he needs to hear your voices.'

'Your grandad's right,' Melissa said.

'I just – I hate hospitals!' Lilly declared.

'Yeah, me too,' Lewis said, folding his arms.

'You think your father is enjoying his stint in hospital?' Melissa said, voice catching. 'You're coming, okay? *All* of you.'

Rosemary appeared on the stairs then in her dressing gown, face drawn. 'We mustn't force them,' she said, having overheard the conversation. 'Hospitals can be a difficult place for children. We need to be patient.'

Patience, Melissa, patience.

It was a phrase Melissa heard often from Rosemary in those days after she and her mother had left their cottage in the middle of the night. 'People like your mother are fragile, Melissa. Their hearts and minds can't heal in a day,' Rosemary would often say when Melissa asked when her mother was going to snap out of her malaise. 'It can take weeks, months – years, even. You need to be patient with her, Melissa, give her time.'

'Don't worry, Mum,' Grace said softly as she took her mother's hand. 'I'll come to the hospital with you.'

Melissa smiled down at her daughter. 'Good girl.'

'You should get changed first, Mum,' Lilly said, peering at a smear of blood on Melissa's sleeve. Melissa followed her gaze and the sight of Patrick's blood made it all come rushing back to her, the horror of it all.

She put her hand to her mouth, feeling a sob begin to build.

'I'll do that now,' she said quickly. Then she ran upstairs, waiting until she closed the door behind her before she began to cry. This was how it had been in the months and years after Joel died, still was. It came in waves. Sometimes, life seemed to go on as normal, which felt quite extraordinary, really, considering her son was no longer there. But she had had two other kids to look after, and then a newborn too. Other times, it would hit her like a sledgehammer.

But Patrick wasn't Joel, was he? He would live. He *had* to live. And she needed to bloody pull herself together. She wiped her tears away and grabbed one of Rosemary's old tops, replacing her dirty one with it.

Then she walked back downstairs.

Grace was waiting for her in the hallway, her jacket already on. 'Where are the twins?' Melissa asked her.

'In the summer house with Maddy.'

Melissa rolled her eyes. 'I'll go get them.'

She marched out into the garden, then paused. If the twins would tell anyone about what had happened the night before, it would be Maddy. Maybe they were talking about it right that minute? She checked Rosemary wasn't watching her, then quietly approached the summer house from the back, hoping to overhear them. She imagined what Patrick would say. He'd probably shake his head, joke that she was a hypocrite. She had, after all, told him off only a few weeks ago for suggesting they read Lewis's phone messages after Patrick mistakenly thought Lewis was doing drugs. Turned out the white powder he found in Lewis's school bag was some translucent face powder Maddy had asked him to give Lilly for an audition the next day.

Patrick did that a lot, getting hold of the wrong end of the stick, like the time several years ago when he told everyone Barack Obama was having a beer in the Neck of the Woods pub during his state visit to the UK. When people rushed down, it wasn't Obama at all.

Melissa smiled when she thought of that now, yearning to see her husband. First, though, she wanted to see if she could overhear anything.

Luckily, the summer house backed on to the forest, which meant it was easy to reach from beyond the trees without being noticed. It was also easy to hear whatever people were saying inside, as Melissa and Patrick had discovered to their horror after hearing his parents having a bit too much of a 'good time' in there once while walking Sandy in the forest. The look on Patrick's face when he realised what the grunting noise was! It still made Melissa smile to think of it.

The smile disappeared from her face. Would she ever be able to walk through the forest with Patrick again? Giggle with him, and watch his tanned cheeks turn red with embarrassment?

Melissa crept close to the back of the summer house. It was large, ten square metres, and painted a calming olive green. There was even a small veranda at the front, and inside it was adorned with two large wicker sofas, a fridge full of soft drinks and a large TV on the wall, with speakers on a shelf. Bill, Patrick and Lewis had put it up five years before. Melissa remembered sitting in the sun with Rosemary and the girls, watching with pride as a ten-year-old Lewis hammered nails into wood, Patrick patiently instructing him on how to get it perfect as Bill nodded in approval.

Melissa pressed her ear against the wall.

'You mean the New Year's Eve party?' she heard Maddy ask.

'Yeah,' Lilly said.

'What did Carter say about your mum?' Maddy asked.

'Don't worry,' Lewis replied. 'Lilly shouldn't have said anything.'

'But—'

'Just drop it, Mads,' Lewis said.

Melissa frowned. Carter was Andrea and Adrian Cooper's son. He was in the same year as the twins and Maddy. Lewis had never liked him, calling him an arrogant twat. As for New Year's Eve, there had been a party at the forest centre. Melissa recalled that Carter had got a bit drunk. Andrea had been mortified. Come to think of it, Patrick had seemed a bit subdued after the party. Melissa put it down to him being tired with all the hard work he'd put into the upcoming election.

'All I remember about that party is you guys playing happy families all night,' Maddy said.

Lewis gave a bitter laugh. 'Happy families. Yeah, right.'

'Mum?' Melissa jumped, turning to see Grace watching her from the side of the summer house. 'What are you doing?'

They all went quiet in the summer house, clearly having heard Grace.

Melissa's face flushed.

'Just getting the twins so we can go to the hospital,' she said loudly. Was it obvious she'd been eavesdropping? She decided to style it out, walking around to the front of the summer house and knocking on the door.

Melissa opened it to see the twins lounging together on the sofa, Maddy sitting on a beanbag.

'Come on, time to go and see Dad,' she said.

Lilly frowned, picking at the material of her ripped stonewash jeans. 'We're not ready, Mum.'

'He's your dad,' Melissa said. 'You can't *not* go.'

'We *will* visit him, Mum!' Lewis said. 'Just not now, okay?'

'Please, Mum,' Lilly said, eyes brimming with tears. 'I honestly can't face it right now.' Maddy put her arm around her friend's shoulders and Lilly leaned her head on her.

Melissa thought about pushing the issue, but Maddy was right there. Wouldn't it just look cold-hearted? Maybe Lilly was right, maybe it *was* too much for them. If they didn't want to go yet, she shouldn't force them. Plus, it would give her the chance to talk to Grace alone. She was probably going about it the wrong way, trying to get the truth from all of them at once. Maybe the best way was to ask them individually?

'Fine,' Melissa said with a sigh, making a note to herself to try to glean what they had meant about the New Year's Eve party later. 'Look after these two,' she instructed Maddy.

Maddy gave her a salute. 'Always.'

Melissa walked away, their words echoing in her mind.

What happened at the New Year's Eve party . . . and what did Carter Cooper say about her?

Chapter Thirteen

Forest Grove Facebook Chit Chat Group

Friday 19th April, 2019
1.05 p.m.

Tommy Mileham
Right, Forest Grovians, we need your help! I've just got off the phone with Ross Shillingford and, as much as I admire the wonderful job our boys in blue do (having been one myself), in light of the fact there has been no progress with the investigation into the attack on our much loved Patrick, including the location of the knife used to stab him, we're arranging a search of the forest to *supplement* the police searches that have been taking place. It will begin this evening at 5pm at the Forest Centre. Hope to see you there. Please share this post so other residents don't miss it in their timelines.

Rebecca Feine
How do you know the knife hasn't been found, Tommy?

Tommy Mileham
Still have some contacts in the police, Rebecca.

Andrew Blake
Here, here! Find that knife and we might find the DNA of whatever scumbag did this. No one messes with Forest Grove residents!

Kitty Fletcher
I don't think inflammatory posts like that are helpful, Andrew.

Ellie Mileham
I agree, Kitty! Anyway, Peter and I will be there! Was chatting to some of the other mums during swimming this morning and we're all in agreement we're very worried about the possibility of their being a violent burglar targeting the town. Trisha Price confirmed her house on Birch Road was burgled last month. I'll leave Trisha to share more if she wants but, put it this way, it wasn't pleasant. Will PC Adrian Cooper be there tonight so we can ask some questions?

Graham Cane
*There

Ellie Mileham
Grammar not exactly a priority at the moment, Graham Cane 🙄

Kitty Fletcher
Correct me if I'm wrong, Trisha Price, but there was no violence involved. Just don't want to create a sense of panic in the community, I know how these things can snowball.

Trisha Price
No violence but excrement smeared over the walls, sorry to be graphic. Was rather traumatising.

Andrea Cooper
I bet it was, Trisha. We wouldn't want to downplay what you went through. Tommy, I think your idea of a community search is wonderful. Carter is an excellent forest scavenger so will be a great asset tonight. I suggest we use the main events area for a community meeting before the walk too? Jennifer Range, can you help with this? Adrian is on the case with regards to a police update. Can I also add, I'm *so* shocked by this, with every hour that goes past. As a community, we have a duty to such a wonderful man as Patrick to catch whoever did this to him.

Charlie Cane
Well said, Andrea, well said.

Daphne Peterson
Shouldn't we check with the police first? Not sure how useful it will be having Forest Grovians trampling all over their evidence. What does Adrian think about this, Andrea Cooper?

Graham Cane
No point asking Andrea what her husband thinks, she thinks for him!

Jennifer Range
HAPPY TO HELP, WILL BE THERE WITH THE METAL DETECTOR.

Graham Cane
No need for caps *covers ears from the shouting*

Andrew Blake
Nice pussy picture, Jennifer Range.

Daphne Peterson
Andrew Blake, you're gross.

Jennifer Range
DON'T UNDERSTAND, ANDREW, I'M NOT WEARING A CAP IN MY PICTURE, AND THAT'S MY CAT, SHE'S NOT A PUSSY ANYMORE, SHE'S TEN!

Daphne Peterson
Jesus H Christ. Is there something infecting the water supply in Forest Grove at the moment?

Graham Cane
Daphne Peterson ☺

Daphne Peterson
I mean you too, Graham.

Jackie Shillingford
Daphne Peterson ☺☺

Pauline Sharpe
Any more details on what happened from Adrian, Andrea Cooper?

Belinda Bell
I saw the police at Bill and Rosemary Byatt's house earlier, bit odd?!

Jackie Shillingford
Why odd?! Melissa is staying there with the kids while forensics finish up at their house. The police will have probably been over to update Melissa.

Andrea Cooper

Okey dokey, to confirm, the hall is booked for 4.30pm with the search at 5pm. I'll advertise this properly to residents with some posters dotted around. I'm printing them off as we speak. But if people can spread the word, that would be super-duper.

Rebecca Feine

Blimey, that was quick.

Kitty Fletcher

Andrea is nothing if not efficient. Thank you, Andrea.

Tommy Mileham

See you all tonight. Even if we don't find anything, it'll show whoever did this to Patrick that Forest Grovians won't rest until we find out who did it!

Chapter Fourteen

Friday 19th April, 2019
2 p.m.

I knew Tommy Mileham would get involved at some point. Grandad says he's like a bear. He can be all warm and cuddly and protective, but he can show his sharp teeth too if he needs to. When Grandad said that to Tommy once, Tommy loved it, chasing us around the garden. I laughed, let him grab me and pretend to eat me, but that's because I always knew he'd never hurt me, that I'd never be his prey because he's Grandad's best friend.

Except it's different this time. He's super angry at the person who hurt Dad . . . and that person is me.

Thing is, people might go on about the police not having a clue, but they've actually got a lot of it right, how Dad tried to fight back, shoving me away then slipping. That horrible crack when he hit his head, that weird gurgling sound.

Oh God. Deep breaths, deep breaths. I keep thinking of that today. Not the blood, like I was obsessed with last night, but the sound *he made. Like when that mean-looking detective was staring at us with her beady eyes, all I could think of was Dad's gurgle and I just know she saw the thought in my head.*

I was watching her while the other detective, the nice one, was talking. She picked a photo up of us all, the one Mum has on her Facebook profile of us in the forest. I swear she looked right at my face in that photo, right at it, then turned to look at me.

Mum says Grandma Quail used to tell her you can sense things about people, sniff the darkness out in them. Is that mean detective sniffing out the darkness in me?

Maybe she's right, maybe there is a darkness in me. I stabbed my dad, didn't I? It takes something to actually drive a blade into someone's flesh, especially your dad's. It takes a darkness, right? Something a bit mental.

I overheard Grandad describing Grandma Quail as a bit mental once. I know everyone thought Grandma was odd, and maybe that's the problem, there's something inside me that's been passed over from her. Something wrong.

Now everyone's getting all excited about this stupid search they've arranged tonight. Tommy's even going to bring his big dogs with him.

'They'll sniff anything out,' he always says.

Will they be able to sniff me out?

Chapter Fifteen

Friday 19th April, 2019
2.30 p.m.

Grace peered out of the car window, her pretty blue eyes taking in the pattern of leaves in the trees above.

'How are you, Gracey?' Melissa asked as they drove to the hospital.

'Okay,' Grace replied.

Melissa's eyes slid over to her daughter, then away again. 'It must be very tough, keeping a secret as big as this?'

Grace continued staring out of the window, not saying anything.

'Grace?' Melissa pushed.

She shrugged. 'I suppose.'

'You're usually quite good at telling Mum stuff. You're not covering for someone else, are you?'

Grace shook her head.

Melissa went quiet for a few moments, then asked the question she'd been dreading. 'Has Dad ever hurt one of you?'

'No,' Grace whispered.

Melissa let out a sigh of relief. It had been in the back of her mind, a thought spun from her own childhood and her father's quick temper. She didn't see her father much when they moved to the forest. When he eventually found another job, he worked long hours, then when he was at home he'd either be drinking with Ryan's dad or working on the house. She never quite knew how he'd be with her. One minute, he could be utterly charming, showering her with gifts and making her smile with his handsome face and shock of Elvis Presley-style hair. But then other times, he'd be angry, picking at any little thing she did. Occasionally, he would slap her. She didn't have to endure it as much as her mother, but it still happened, always when her mother wasn't there. She'd explain her bruises away with a fall, like her father coached her to. He knew that if her mother ever found out, that would be the last straw . . . in the end, it was.

'Did he ever make you do something you didn't want to?' Melissa asked in a low whisper, another consideration that had haunted her in the night.

'No, Mum!' Grace shouted, turning to look at her mum in horror. 'Why would you say that?'

'I'm grasping at straws here, Grace! Look, I know the twins are older than you, but you've said yourself you feel like you act older. If they tell you to do something, that it's the best thing to do, that doesn't always mean they're right.'

Grace's eyes were expressionless. 'I know that. I know what's the right thing to do, Mum. We're *doing* the right thing.'

Melissa felt tears prick at her eyes. 'It makes me sad you don't think telling me the truth is the right thing to do. It makes me feel . . .' Melissa thought about it, choosing her words carefully. '*Lonely.* I want to be part of the secret. I want to be able to help you.'

Grace frowned. 'It won't help if you know, Mum, it really won't.'

'Why?'

Grace sighed, turning back to look out of the window. 'I can't say.'

'Well, Dad might wake up soon and he'll say.'

Grace's little face tensed slightly. 'That's up to him.'

Melissa looked at her daughter in surprise. 'That's a strange thing to say about someone you love, Grace.'

Grace shrugged, her reflection in the window showing a miserable expression. Melissa's grip tightened on the steering wheel. The truth was, she *did* feel lonely bearing this burden. She suddenly *yearned* to tell Rosemary and Bill. But this was their son, who had possibly been harmed by one of their grandchildren! How could she put that on them?

It was down to her.

She impulsively slammed the brakes on and turned into a small road, coming to a stop by the forest. Grace looked confused. 'What are you doing, Mum?'

Melissa twisted in her seat to face her younger daughter. 'You're going to tell me what happened last night, okay, Grace? I know one of you hid the knife, I know there's more to what happened to Dad than you're letting on. Tell me what happened.'

Grace's eyes widened. She almost looked scared. Melissa swallowed down her guilt. She had to find out, for the sake of their family. For the sake of *Patrick*!

'I can't, Mummy,' Grace said. She hadn't called Melissa Mummy for years.

Melissa felt her resolve weaken again but clenched her fists. 'You are telling me right now, Grace Byatt. Right this minute!' It felt so alien shouting at Grace. It was usually the twins she needed to shout at, not Grace, who was so well behaved.

Grace flinched at her mother's raised voice. For a moment, Melissa thought Grace might tell her everything, but instead she just put her hands over her ears, shaking her head over and over. Melissa tried to pull her hands away.

'Please, Grace,' she pleaded, 'what are you keeping from Mummy? Please?' Melissa was sobbing now, guilty and desperate. Grace started screaming, her high-pitched shrill filling the car.

'Oh God, I'm so sorry, darling,' Melissa said, pulling Grace into her arms, stroking her hair until she calmed down. She'd been too hard on her. Grace would tell her in her own time, Melissa realised. She couldn't force it.

After a while, Melissa wiped her daughter's tears away. 'I'll take you back to Nanny and Grandad's, okay?'

Grace shook her head. 'No, I want to see Dad.'

'Are you sure?'

Grace nodded, so Melissa started the car and headed towards the hospital, arriving in Ashbridge a few moments later. Ashbridge was a soulless concrete town filled to the brim with buildings, a complete contrast to Forest Grove. It always made Melissa's heart sink when she had to come to the town to do some clothes shopping for the kids. She'd even changed her food shop to be delivered to save going into Ashbridge once a week. She imagined her mother living there before she'd moved to the forest, away from nature. She must have hated it.

Melissa parked up in front of the characterless white building and walked inside, heading towards Patrick's ward through a labyrinth of corridors, her hand tight around Grace's. She was still reeling from that conversation they'd had . . . or that argument. She'd pushed Grace too much, taken it too far. Melissa felt a sense of anxiety as she approached the ward, looking down at her daughter to see if she felt the same. But Grace just peered into any open doorways to look at the wards, hungry to see any drama.

'There'll be a lot of tubes around Dad's bed,' Melissa said, slightly out of breath because of the long walk . . . and the nerves. 'They've shaved his head, too.'

'You said, Mum.'

Had she? She couldn't remember.

A familiar figure approached in the distance, dressed in a nurse's uniform. It was Debbie Lampard, Joel's old nurse and one of the original Forest Grove residents. She and her husband had been part of Bill and Rosemary's 'crew', but then something had happened and they'd grown apart. She'd never managed to get out of Rosemary exactly what.

'People change,' Rosemary would say.

Debbie was in her sixties now, still working hard in a job Melissa knew she loved. Like Melissa, she'd entered her profession later in life, having been a customer service manager before becoming a nurse. Her four children had left home now, and she'd had twins too, which had brought her and Melissa even closer. She'd been a godsend when Joel was alive, so loving and caring. Debbie saw Joel soon after he passed away in the night eleven years ago and had been devastated by his death too. Melissa often wondered if that was why she had moved away from paediatric care. Of course, none of them had expected Joel to live beyond his thirties, but for him to die so young had been shocking for them all. Yes, he'd been struggling leading up to his death. People forget there are muscles in the heart too, so Joel's circulatory health was always a concern, and sometimes he had problems with breathing. But none of them had expected to lose him so young. As a family friend *and* the nurse who was always there when Joel was admitted to the hospital with problems, Debbie took it really hard. Not only had she fought to give Joel the best possible care, she'd also been the one to really encourage Melissa to pursue a career in care. During those long days in the hospital, the two of them would discuss the different options open to Melissa when she expressed an interest in physiotherapy and had even got her on the path of taking up a part-time degree in paediatric physiotherapy after years of being a full-time mum and carer to Joel.

'Melissa!' Debbie said now, rushing up to her and pulling her into a hug. 'I'm *so* sorry about Patrick. It's such a shock to us all.'

'I know, I don't think I've quite wrapped my head around it yet.'

'You're strong,' the nurse said, grasping Melissa's shoulders as she looked into her eyes.

Melissa thought about the way she'd just been with Grace. 'I wish I had your confidence in me, but thank you.'

Debbie looked down at Grace and smiled. 'I swear you grow an inch every time I see you! Look at those eyes too. Such a vivid blue. You're a real beauty, like your mother and your sister.'

Grace smiled shyly at her.

'How *is* Patrick?' Debbie asked quietly, aware of Grace listening.

'No change as far as I know, which is probably a good thing. He needs rest.'

Debbie nodded, face serious. 'I was going to say that. No change is good. You know they'll take care of him here.'

'Just like they did with Joel,' Melissa said with a soft smile.

Debbie's face darkened. 'I still think about that boy every day . . .' She shook her head. 'Listen to me! Obviously everything with Patrick is bringing back memories of Joel. Anything you need, you just shout.' She looked at her watch. 'I'd better go. Take care, alright?' She squeezed Melissa's hand then dashed off.

'Did that lady know Joel, Mum?' Grace asked her.

'Yes, she was Joel's main nurse. Don't worry about all that, though. Come on, let's hurry up and get to Dad.' They continued walking along the corridors, the very same corridors Melissa would wheel Joel down all those years ago.

'Lilly says she senses Joel sometimes,' Grace said. 'Maybe he's here now, keeping an eye on us.'

Melissa's eyes filled with tears. It was the sort of thing her mother would say. 'That's a lovely thought. He can keep an eye on Dad too.'

Grace shook her head. 'I don't think so.'

Melissa paused, looking down at her daughter. 'Why not?'

Grace held her mother's gaze then shrugged. 'Don't believe in ghosts, that's all. I was just being silly. Oh look!' She pointed towards the gel dispenser outside the ward, her eyes lighting up. Grace was going through a phase of constantly washing her hands, over and over, so the sight of a gel dispenser was heaven to her. They both washed their hands before entering the ward then walked towards Patrick's bed, seeing Peter Mileham there with his wife, Ellie.

Patrick and Peter had hit it off right away when they'd met at school, both the same age and new residents in a new town. Bill also became good friends with Peter's father, Tommy, so the families spent a lot of time together. Back then, there was no Forest Grove High so they had to make the twenty-minute bus journey to Ashbridge Comprehensive. Melissa remembered watching Patrick and Peter that first term they arrived, two golden boys so confident and charming with their smart dark hair and handsome faces. The girls flocked around them, especially Patrick. He enjoyed the attention, Melissa overhearing all the chatter about the many girls he hooked up with. Patrick pretty much ignored Melissa at school. That was easy enough. She cut a lonely figure sitting at the back of the class, her scruffy blonde fringe in her eyes. She was often picked on for living in the ramshackle cottage in the woods and hanging around with 'Beast Boy', as everyone called Ryan back then. He didn't go to school, his father was homeschooling him . . . supposedly.

After that first day she and Ryan saw Patrick, they continued to spy on the new family from the forest. Sometimes, Melissa would watch them alone, without Ryan.

Bill had built Patrick a 'watch tower' in one of the trees, a square wooden platform with a ladder leading up to it. One day, Patrick was sitting up there in the sun, reading a comic book as his younger sister, Libby, twirled around the garden in a pretty pink dress. Melissa allowed herself to imagine what life would be like if she'd been born a Byatt instead of a Quail. A girl in a pretty pink dress with shiny hair and a pile of dolls. She noticed then that Patrick had disappeared from his watch tower. She'd scoured his large garden for him before feeling a tap on her shoulder and had been shocked to find him standing behind her.

'No Beast Boy today, then?' he asked her, with a charming smile.

Her first instinct was to run. So that's what she did, thrashing through the woods as he took chase until she finally stumbled over a root, smashing her knee against a rock. He'd come rushing to help her, pulling her up with his soft clean hands, apologising and insisting she come back to the house to get cleaned up.

For a moment, she considered it. But then Ryan had come charging through the forest, bare-chested and wielding the Indiana Jones whip he'd found in the woods, which he used to try to whip Patrick away. Patrick stood his ground, explaining in his calm, confident voice that he was only helping. That just wound Ryan up even more, so he punched Patrick and dragged Melissa away, the blood from her knee dripping on the fallen leaves.

She remembered turning to look at Patrick to see that he was watching with a small smile on his face, seemingly oblivious to the blood running from his nose. She realised in that moment he was just as intrigued by the two feral children living in the woods as she was by him.

'Here, sit down,' Peter said to Melissa now, standing so she could take his seat. 'The doctor's doing his rounds, he said he'd pop by within half an hour.'

'Good,' Melissa said, giving Patrick a soft kiss on the cheek. 'Hello, my darling, I'm back now. Grace is here too.' She watched his face for any reaction but there was nothing. He was usually so animated, so passionate. It was hard seeing him like this. She blinked away her tears as Ellie gave her a quick hug. She was a tall, elegant woman with short blonde hair and impeccable dress sense. Melissa had always known Peter would marry someone like her. Sometimes, she wondered if Bill and Rosemary wished Patrick had met a girl like Ellie too.

'Peter's been reading the newspaper to Patrick,' Ellie said. 'You know how he likes his news.'

'Yes, he does. Just don't mention the football results,' Melissa said, trying her best to be jovial, despite the fact that her husband was lying in front of her in a coma, tubes coming out of him.

'Or the elections,' Peter whispered. 'I spoke to the team. I think their only option might be to find another candidate.'

Melissa sighed as she looked at Patrick. He would be so disappointed.

'Hello, Grace,' Ellie said. 'Your dad's going to be okay, you know.'

Grace stared at her father, eyes blinking.

Melissa went to her, taking her hand.

'Twins not here?' Peter asked.

'Don't think they're quite ready yet,' Melissa said.

Peter frowned. 'Oh.'

'Any news on who did this?' Ellie asked.

'Nothing,' Melissa replied.

'Beggars belief in a town like Forest Grove. What's the world coming to?' Peter said, his anger betrayed by his clenched fists. 'Actually, I know exactly what the world's coming to.'

Melissa knew what he meant: the local factory workers; specifically, any of them who weren't English. Whenever Peter and Ellie came around for dinner and Peter had a few drinks, his 'dinner party racism' would rear its ugly head, the same as she remembered happening with his father, Tommy. Ellie always looked uncomfortable, Patrick too, but neither of them pulled Peter up on it. Once, Melissa couldn't take hearing it any more and, in as polite a way as she could, she asked him why he seemed to have such a problem with people who weren't English. He'd got defensive and, later that evening, Patrick had asked her why she'd made Peter feel uncomfortable.

'*He* made me feel uncomfortable with what he was saying,' she'd said.

'You know Peter, though, he's a good man. He'd just had a few too many drinks.'

'Yes,' Melissa had replied. 'A few too many drinks, which lowered his inhibitions, made him say what he *really* thought. Well, hopefully he'll know not to now.'

'No, what will happen *now* is he'll be too scared to say what he thinks around us.'

'That's totally fine with me!' And Patrick was right, Peter did tone it down.

But now it looked like the attack on his best friend had made him think his veiled racism was acceptable again in front of Melissa.

'I have to say it,' he said. 'This would never have happened before the factory opened. I'm all for multiculturalism, but if it means one of my friends being hurt, I refuse to hold back on my thoughts.'

'The man was British,' Grace said.

Melissa looked at her daughter in surprise. 'What do you mean, darling?'

'Yes, I thought nobody saw anything?' Ellie added.

Grace frowned and Melissa put her hand on her shoulder, squeezing it gently. 'Grace hasn't had much sleep. You know what her imagination is like.'

Peter and Ellie exchanged looks. Melissa knew they found Grace a bit strange. Their daughter Zoe was the same age, but she couldn't be any more different from Grace. In fact, Melissa was pretty sure Peter had been the one to encourage Patrick to get Grace checked out for autism after comparing the two girls.

'We really must go, Peter,' Ellie said, getting her coat. 'Will you be at the search tonight, Melissa?'

Melissa frowned. 'Search?'

'Dad arranged one for tonight,' Peter said proudly.

'It was just on the Facebook group,' Ellie said.

'What are they searching for?' Melissa asked.

'The knife,' Peter replied. 'Find the knife and you have a chance of finding the DNA of the scum that did this to Patrick,' he said, looking forlornly down at his friend.

Melissa noticed Grace's eyes widen and she struggled to control her own expression. He was right, of course. She really needed to find out what the hell had happened to that knife. She thought of the posters she'd found too. What if more appeared . . . what if people saw them when they walked through the forest to get to the meeting that night?

'I see,' she said. 'I had no idea.'

Ellie put her hand on Melissa's arm. 'I'm sure someone is planning to tell you, it was only just announced.'

'Right,' Melissa said, brow still knitted.

Peter squeezed her arm. 'Maybe see you there later, then? Stay strong, we're all here for you.'

'Thank you.' She gave them a brief smile and they left the room.

'Okay, sweetheart?' Melissa asked Grace when they left.

Grace nodded.

'Come on, let's sit with Dad.' Melissa pulled round the chair on the other side of Patrick so she and Grace could sit with each other. Melissa took Grace's hand as they sat, watching as her young eyes travelled over her father's shaved head, taking in the wires too and the blip of the monitor beside him.

'You can talk to him,' Melissa said. 'Take his hand too, if you want.'

But Grace said nothing, did nothing, just continued sitting still, a slight crease in her brow.

It broke Melissa's heart. How could she not talk to her dad, touch him? What had happened to create such a fracture between the two of them? Between Patrick and *all* his children, she wondered, as she thought of what she'd overheard Lewis say after talking about happy families.

Happy families. Yeah, right.

As far as Melissa knew, they *were* all happy. There had been a time when they hadn't been, after Joel died, but things had finally begun to feel good again.

Melissa placed her hand over Patrick's. She felt the strong blue veins beneath his skin, veins so familiar to her. But was he really so familiar? Did she really know him? She knew nothing of the true facts, of course, so it felt unfair to imprint the 'what if's on the man lying comatose in front of her. And yet if one of the kids felt they had a reason to *stab* their own father in the stomach, then nothing was familiar for Melissa any more and it made her feel sick to the core.

'Say hello, Grace,' Melissa said. 'Let him hear your voice.'

'Hello,' Grace whispered.

As Grace said that, the line in Patrick's monitor went up, a sign his heartbeat was accelerating.

'He can hear you, see!' Melissa said, pointing to the monitor. 'Speak to him, Grace. He's your dad.'

Grace shook her head.

'Go on, darling, please.'

'I said I don't want to!' Grace screamed, jumping up and running from the room. Melissa ran after her through the ward and out into the corridor. She found her sitting on a windowsill, gulping in deep breaths.

'Oh, darling,' she said, going to her. 'It's fine. You don't have to do anything, say anything.' She kissed her daughter's cheek, smoothing down her blonde hair. Grace buried her face in Melissa's neck, her whole body trembling.

'I'm so sorry you're having to go through this,' Melissa whispered to her, tears filling her eyes. 'I just wish you'd *tell* me what happened. I'm so scared for you all if you don't just tell me.'

Grace peered up at her with terrified eyes. 'I'm scared too, Mum. *Really* scared.'

Melissa's breath hitched. 'Oh, darling! Scared of what? Of *who*?'

High heels clicked across the corridor floors. Melissa looked up to see Andrea Cooper striding towards them with a plant in her hand, locks of her platinum bob lifting with each step. Melissa thought instantly of what she'd overheard about Carter saying something about Melissa at the New Year's Eve party.

What *had* he said? And was it related to what had happened to Patrick?

Andrea paused when she saw Melissa and Grace, her face hardening slightly. Then she put on a sympathetic smile and walked over to them.

'I was *so* sorry to hear what happened,' she said. 'We're all thinking about you – the whole community. How is Patrick?'

'No change,' Melissa said, annoyed that Andrea had intruded on what was clearly a sensitive moment between her and Grace. But then Andrea had never been the sensitive type.

'Is that a lemon plant?' Grace asked, pointing to the plant.

'That's right,' Andrea said. 'You know how your father loves his lemons.'

'Does he?' Melissa asked.

Andrea bristled. 'He does. I thought he could plant this when he wakes and, with each lemon it produces, remember how far he's come.'

Her voice quivered as she said that. Melissa ought to feel sorry for her, except it was well known that Andrea had a massive crush on Patrick, always had, since they were teenagers together at school. In fact, Melissa was pretty convinced Andrea had lost her virginity to Patrick.

Andrea peered around her. 'Twins not here?'

'Not today.'

'They've been to see their father, though, right?'

'Not yet.'

Andrea looked surprised. 'Really?'

'It's difficult for kids.'

Andrea forced a tight smile. 'Of course. Any more details about what happened? He has a stab wound, yes? Head injury too? Was he found in the kitchen? Or someone said the living room, so . . .'

'Not now, Andrea,' Melissa said firmly.

Andrea's eyes flickered down to Grace then away again. Melissa could tell she was desperate to hear all the gory details. Clearly Adrian hadn't told her much. That made Melissa respect him even more.

Melissa stood up and Grace stood with her, hiding her face in her mother's arm. 'We'd better go.' There was no point forcing Grace to sit with her dad if it was going to upset both her and Patrick.

She went to walk away but then Andrea shouted out, 'Oh, wait a moment!'

Melissa sighed and turned towards her. 'Yes, Andrea?'

'I presume you know about the community meeting and search later?'

'Yes, I just heard about it.'

'Oh, good. We'll all see you there, then.'

'Well, I'm not sure if I'm going yet.'

Andrea raised an eyebrow. 'Not going? But I naturally presumed you'd be there, Patrick *is* your husband. The whole village will certainly turn up, everyone *loves* Patrick.' Tears appeared in her eyes then and she quickly smiled to cover them. 'Isn't it a great idea, though, the search? You can always count of the Forest Grovians to get the job done!'

'It's a stupid idea, actually! And you're a stupid, nosy woman!' Grace shouted at her. Her little face was livid with anger, spittle coming from her mouth.

Andrea's heavily lipsticked mouth dropped open and Melissa looked at Grace in shock.

'Grace!' Melissa crouched down to look Grace in the face. 'Calm down!'

Andrea put her hand to her ample chest, face shocked. 'Well, I . . .'

'I'm so sorry,' Melissa said without looking at her, eyes still on Grace, whose face had now gone blank. 'We're all going through a lot.' She pulled Grace into a hug as Andrea backed away.

'Of course,' Andrea said, still flustered. 'You take care now.'

She darted off down the corridor as Grace pressed her face into Melissa's neck.

'What was that all about?' Melissa asked Grace.

'I don't know,' Grace said, face forlorn. 'I just got so mad at her.'

Melissa watched Andrea rush down the corridor, peering over her shoulder briefly to regard Melissa and Grace. She could imagine what she was thinking: *children not visiting their father, wife not attending the search, young daughter lashing out. Something's not right about all this.* It was a popular phrase in Forest Grove, like the community had this conjoined intuition about certain situations.

Melissa did *not* want to be the target of that but, more importantly, she didn't want *Grace* being the subject of it. Andrea was annoying as hell, but she was powerful too. Melissa realised she needed to keep control of this situation *and* keep Andrea on her side.

And if that meant going to the community meeting that evening, then so be it.

Chapter Sixteen

Friday 19th April, 2019
4.20 p.m.

Melissa sat at the front of the Forest Centre's large hall with Bill, her stomach full of knots as she thought about the search that was about to take place. She'd really rather not be there but it was clearly expected of her. Plus, it would be useful to get a sense of what people knew.

The centre was a large wooden building, much the same as the other houses in Forest Grove, with huge windows at the front looking out into the forest. It housed the small reception area where Melissa had once worked and a gift shop. Beyond that was a café, which was often busy during the day with mums walking their kids, and mountain bikers and joggers. Behind the café was an education 'walkway', which Patrick and Daphne had worked together to set up with funding from the council many years back. It featured interactive displays delving into the life of the forest and how the community was able to run on it. The walkway led to the big hall Melissa was in now, often hired out for weddings and parties. On the walls were beautiful drawings of trees. Being here reminded Melissa so keenly of Patrick's vibrancy, all the care and attention he'd put into this centre, the heart and soul of the village, as part of his voluntary work.

People were now blocking the paintings he'd commissioned, though, the hall so full there were no more spare seats left for what was clearly going to be a well-attended meeting and search. Melissa felt her cheeks flush, her breath come in small spurts.

Be calm, she told herself. *It'll all be okay. These people are here to help.*

She peered behind her, nodding at people who shot her sympathetic smiles. Lines of chairs had been laid out and there was even a podium on the stage, which Andrea was fussing over. It almost felt to Melissa like she was at a wedding . . . or a funeral. And as Melissa took in Andrea's expensive floral dress, she wondered if Andrea thought so too.

Melissa thought again of Grace's outburst. She was with Rosemary and the twins now. Melissa had dropped her off then returned to be with Patrick all afternoon before coming here. She didn't want the kids at the meeting, and Rosemary had agreed to stay behind to be with them. Grace had been almost clingy with Melissa when she'd returned from the hospital briefly to get changed, clutching on to her hand. It had clearly traumatised her, being interrogated like that by her mother. Melissa would need to rely on the twins for the truth.

But first, this bloody meeting.

'Looks like it's going to be a big turnout,' Bill said, looking over his shoulder as more people started filing into the room. Melissa followed his gaze, finding herself feeling conflicted. On one hand, it felt good to be in the warm embrace of this community. They were like a family, always had been, and she liked knowing they all had her back. But on the other, the truth was, these people were there to catch the person who had hurt Patrick . . . and that person could be one of her children. Not to mention those mysterious posters and the very real possibility that someone in this room was behind them.

She clutched her bag close to her, aware of the posters still lying at the bottom. She really must get rid of them soon.

'Are they from the local newspaper?' Bill said as a woman walked in with a man carrying a large camera.

Melissa looked at them in shock. 'Oh Christ. Why are the media here?'

'An upstanding member of the community has been stabbed,' Bill said. 'This is a big local news story.'

Melissa watched as the journalist went to the front of the stage, shaking hands with Andrea. Then Andrea gestured towards Melissa, and they both walked over to her.

'Great,' Melissa muttered under her breath.

'Melissa,' Andrea said when she got to her, 'this is my old friend Karin. She writes the crime-watch segment of the local newspaper.'

Melissa shook the woman's hand.

'I said you'd be willing to say a few words,' Andrea said. 'Drum up some attention.'

Melissa couldn't think of anything worse.

'Actually, no,' she said. 'The police have told me not to talk to the media until they decide to do something more official.' Sure, it was a white lie, but it was the only thing she could think of saying that the journalist couldn't push back on.

'But surely any attention is good attention in a case like this?' Andrea asked.

'I said no, Andrea,' Melissa said, flicking a quick smile to the journalist so she didn't come across as a complete dragon.

Andrea's face dropped and she narrowed her eyes at Melissa.

'It's fine,' the journalist said. 'Covering the meeting and search will be enough.' She gave Melissa her business card. 'Just call if you change your mind.' Then they both walked away, Andrea turning to regard Melissa with a sombre expression.

Tommy arrived on the podium, the room going quiet. He looked like his son, Peter, barrel-chested, with inquisitive blue eyes. Sometimes it seemed to Melissa that he still thought he was a police officer, the way he acted.

Tommy took a moment to contemplate the people in the room. People were standing at the edges now, including Daphne, her slim arms folded. She gave Melissa a curt nod when she saw her, unusually subdued.

'Thank you for being here tonight in what I appreciate are worrying times for everyone,' Tommy began in his gravelly voice. His eyes rested on Melissa and Bill as everyone shot them sympathetic smiles. 'The objective tonight is to find any evidence that might help the police track down the scum who did this to our friend Patrick.'

The scum who did this. Like one of her kids? Melissa thought, wrapping her arms around herself.

'As much as I admire the police,' Tommy continued, 'and I used to be a detective myself, after all,' he added, puffing his chest out in pride, 'the past twenty-four hours were crucial in the investigation and yet, from what I gather from my sources in the force, no progress has been made.'

That was good, wasn't it? Melissa thought. With it looking likely that one of the kids had stabbed their own father – the very idea made Melissa shudder as it crossed through her mind – she didn't want there to be progress if it led to them. She needed *time* to figure things out.

A hush fell over the room then as the two detectives in charge of Patrick's case walked in – and they did *not* seem happy.

Tommy looked slightly flustered for a moment but then gathered himself. 'Speaking of the police,' he said, gesturing towards the detectives. People turned to look at them, murmuring.

Detective Crawford marched up the centre of the room as the stern-looking detective stayed at the back, scrutinising everyone with narrowed eyes. Melissa shuffled about in her chair as the detective's eyes alighted on her, wishing desperately that she hadn't come.

'Sources?' Detective Crawford asked Tommy. 'What sources are these?'

'A man never divulges the identity of his sources,' Tommy said with a nervous laugh.

The detective turned to the room. 'Well, this is *quite* the gathering. We were walking by and were rather intrigued to see such a busy crowd in here. Now I know why . . . you're conducting a search?'

Tommy nodded. 'That's right, Detective,' he said in a loud voice, smiling at the crowds. 'We thought you could do with the help.'

Detective Crawford gave him a tight smile. 'May I?' he asked, gesturing to the microphone Tommy was holding.

Tommy hesitated a moment then reluctantly handed it over.

The detective turned to the room. 'For those of you who don't know, I'm Detective Crawford and I'm in charge of the investigation into the attack on Patrick Byatt. I want to start by reassuring you all we are doing *everything* we can to track down the perpetrator who injured him.'

There was some discontented chatter in the room.

'I also want to remind you all that this is an ongoing investigation,' the detective continued, looking into the crowd seriously. 'We have to be very mindful of not risking the investigation, or tampering with evidence, something an *unofficial* search like this could well do.'

Melissa could see how annoyed he was and, even worse, his eyes were on her now, a slight crease in his brow. She wished she could run up to him, tell him she hadn't agreed to this bloody search either!

'Found the knife yet?' someone shouted.

Melissa's stomach dropped. *The knife the kids had hidden.*

'Not yet,' Detective Crawford said with a pleasant smile. 'But regarding where we are with the investigation—'

'Nowhere!' Graham Cane shouted.

'Pipe down, Graham!' Rebecca Feine, the landlady of the Neck of the Woods pub, shouted out. 'It's only been twenty-four hours, give them a chance.'

'This lady is quite right,' Detective Crawford said. 'We're at the very early stages.'

'Then tell us what those early stages are,' Belinda Bell said. 'This is our community, we deserve to know. Did someone break into the house, for example?'

'There was *no* sign of a break-in,' the detective replied.

'So someone just walked in?' Peter Mileham asked.

'More than likely,' Detective Crawford replied. 'This seems like the kind of place where people are happy to leave their doors unlocked, am I right?'

Everyone nodded. Forest Grovians were proud of that fact.

'Not any more,' said a woman a few seats down from Melissa, crossing her arms and shaking her head in disgust. Melissa recognised her as being Charlie Cane, Graham Cane's daughter and the mum of one of the girls in the twins' year. Melissa had never quite warmed to her. She was one of those people who put photos of themselves on social media in revealing gym wear, pretending it was purely to 'inspire' people to lose weight when really it was a vanity exercise in getting social media likes, considering she'd had absolutely no weight to lose in the first place.

'What about all the immigrants who've moved to Ashbridge? Have you questioned them?' Charlie asked now.

'Oh Jesus,' Daphne said, sighing. 'Please don't turn this into a live version of the *Daily Mail*'s comments.'

Some people in the room laughed.

'Charlie's got a point, though!' Belinda Bell said. 'I bet crime's gone up since the factory opened.'

'The surrounding towns and villages are, naturally, being explored, and residents questioned,' the detective said. 'However, we need to consider the possibility that Patrick knew the person who attacked him,' he added, looking around the room.

Melissa kept her eyes down, her fists clenching and unclenching as she tried to keep her breath even.

'Unlikely,' Bill said, shaking his head. 'Nobody Patrick knew would do this to him.'

'How can you be so sure, Bill?' Rebecca said. 'The world isn't as black and white as you'd all like it to be.'

'Bill's right,' Andrea said. 'Nobody would hurt Patrick. He's well loved here.'

'Yeah, well loved by you, Andrea,' Melissa heard someone behind her whisper.

Melissa turned and shot the person a look. It made her feel uncomfortable, the way people talked so openly about Andrea's crush on Patrick.

'Let's hear what the detective has to say,' Tommy said. 'So, Detective, are you saying Patrick was specifically targeted? That this wasn't just a break-in gone wrong?'

'As I said, we're following a number of leads,' Detective Crawford replied, raising his voice to be heard above the whispers of discontent.

'What leads?' Bill asked.

'I can't go into that now.'

'It's probably a teenager, mind all warped with that Nightfort game,' said Pauline Sharpe, a woman Melissa had been at school with. 'There's been an increase in graffiti at the local park.'

Melissa noticed Kitty Fletcher nodding enthusiastically.

'*Fortnite*,' Daphne said under her breath with an eye roll.

'Yes,' Belinda said. 'Look what happened with Jacob Simms!'

Melissa's stomach turned at the mention of her client, Jacob.

Andrew Blake, a man in his forties with a pockmarked face dressed in army fatigues, crossed his arms. 'Well, if it is someone here in the village, they'll live to regret it. No one gets away with stuff like this in our village, old *or* young.'

Melissa looked at him in shock as others murmured in agreement.

'I will *not* put up with any vigilante action,' Detective Crawford shouted above the noise. The room went quiet. 'It will be severely punished. Am I understood?'

People mumbled, rolling their eyes.

'What about the argument that was reported between Ryan Day and Patrick?' Andrew asked.

There were gasps from the crowds, people turning to look at Daphne, Ryan's ex.

Melissa searched her mind for any memory of an argument between Patrick and Ryan. Yes, things had always been strained between them since that fight they had as kids, and more recently they'd been at odds over cutting down the oak tree. But it had never spilled out into anything more than a few tense words . . . from what she knew, anyway.

'Yes, weird he's not here,' Graham Cane said.

'It's all part of our investigation,' Detective Crawford said.

'Can we leave Ryan alone, please?' Daphne said. 'Just because he doesn't follow the Forest Grove conventions doesn't make him a suspect.'

'An overheard argument does, though,' Andrew said.

'Overheard by the man who's hated Ryan ever since Ryan caught him climbing the old oak when he was drunk,' Daphne said, shooting Andrew a look.

'You saying I'm lying?' Andrew asked her.

'Yes!' Daphne shouted back.

'Andrew may be many things,' Graham said, 'but he is *not* a liar.'

'Oh, please!' Rebecca Feine said, laughing.

'That's enough!' Detective Crawford shouted out. 'This is exactly why we wouldn't have agreed to an event like this.'

'We have every right to be concerned about what happened to Patrick Byatt,' Belinda Bell said. 'We have every right to meet as a community to discuss it.'

'Hell yeah, freedom of speech!' someone shouted out.

'Exactly,' Andrew said. 'Some little scumbag has got into one of *our* houses and stabbed one of *our* people. We will not stand for this.'

People started talking again, nodding their heads in agreement.

'Bring back the death penalty!' someone shouted out. 'Hang the little fucker.'

'Oh, for God's sake!' Daphne said, shaking her head. 'This is a farce.'

Melissa put her hands over her ears. Death penalty. Hanging. They all wanted blood, and it terrified her because it could be one of her children's blood they wanted, even if they didn't know it. No wonder Grace had seemed so scared earlier.

'Shut *up*!' Daphne suddenly shouted out. She pointed to the back of the hall. Melissa followed her gaze and let out a gasp. The twins were standing there with Rosemary, their eyes wide with fear, clearly having heard what everyone was saying.

Everyone in the room went quiet and Melissa jumped up, running to them.

'What are you doing here?' she asked.

Lilly shot her mother a fearful look. 'Grace is missing!'

Chapter Seventeen

Friday 19th April, 2019
4.49 p.m.

'What do you mean, Grace is missing?' Melissa asked.

'We thought she was still in the room,' Rosemary said, wringing her hands. 'But when I went up to check on her, she was gone.'

'We searched the whole *house*,' Lewis said, brown eyes filling with tears. 'The garden *and* the forest next to it too. Nothing.'

Melissa tried not to panic as she thought of what Grace had said earlier about being scared. A horrible thought occurred to her. What if Grace had been lying that morning when she said no one else had hurt their dad? What if someone else was involved and now they'd taken her?

Detective Powell strolled over to them from nearby. 'Grace is missing?' she asked.

They all nodded.

'Does she disappear like this often?' Detective Powell asked.

Melissa took a few deep breaths to calm herself. 'Grace does sometimes take herself off on little walks,' she admitted. 'She gets easily distracted, might see a fox and run off, that sort of thing. I'm sure she's fine.'

But as she looked out into the early-evening gloom of the forest, she wasn't so sure.

Tommy Mileham joined them. 'Everything okay here?'

'Little Grace has gone missing,' Rosemary explained.

'Oh Lord!' said Andrea, who was listening from nearby. 'Grace has gone missing!' she shouted out.

People gasped and Melissa closed her eyes, pinching her nose. This was the last thing they needed.

'I'm sure it'll be fine,' she said in a shaky voice. 'She's done this before.'

'Done this before?' Belinda Bell said. 'On her own in the forest in the *dark*?'

'But she's only little!' Andrea said.

'It won't be properly dark for ages yet. And she's ten, for God's sake, she'll be fine,' Daphne said. 'Ryan and I used to let Maddy wander the forest when she was that age.'

Some of the mums raised their eyebrows at Daphne.

'Bit irresponsible,' Belinda said, crossing her arms as Kitty Fletcher nodded. 'There can be some very dense parts of the woods. Adults easily get lost, let alone children.'

Thanks for making me feel even worse, Melissa wanted to say.

'What if the person who hurt Patrick is still out there?' Andrea asked, eyes wide with concern. 'We can't have a little girl wandering about on her own in the forest.'

'Come on, everyone, let's find little Grace!' Tommy Mileham shouted.

Everyone started heading into the forest, even the two detectives. Suddenly the search for the knife had turned into a search for the victim's daughter.

'We should get ahead of them,' Melissa said to the twins. 'It'll terrify Grace, seeing all those people marching up to her. Rosemary, Bill,' she said, 'can you go back home and wait for her in case she goes back there?' They both nodded and walked in the direction of their house.

'Grace will hate all this fuss,' Lilly said as they ran into the forest, her trembling voice betraying her fear.

'I know,' Lewis said with a shaky laugh. 'She'll probably be poking some dead animal with a stick somewhere.'

'How was Grace before she went?' Melissa asked, watching as torches flickered on in the distance, people shouting out Grace's name.

'Just reading in her room,' Lilly said. 'It's hard to tell with Grace.'

'I know Grace acts older sometimes,' Melissa said carefully as they stepped off the main path and trod over branches and leaves, searching for Grace's distinctive blonde hair, 'but she's still very young. This is difficult for you guys – imagine how hard it must be for her.'

The twins glanced at each other and Melissa could see they were doing that 'twin' thing where they somehow communicated without saying a word.

'We have to think about Grace,' Melissa continued, 'the impact this is having on her little mind. That's probably why she's run off! We have to think about what's right for her, for *all* of us.'

'No, Mum,' Lilly said. 'Grace probably ran off because you grilled her on the way to the hospital earlier.'

Melissa frowned. 'She told you about that?'

The twins nodded. Melissa came to a stop and grabbed both their hands. 'You understand why I'm trying to find out, though, don't you? Surely it's better I know so I can help you before *they* all find out,' she said, gesturing to the people searching in the distance. 'You heard what they said in there just now. This could easily spiral out of control. If we don't get a grasp on this, then people like Andrew Blake and Tommy Mileham will.'

Lewis's dark eyes sparked with fear. But then he straightened his shoulders. 'We've got it under control, Mum. We hid the knife, didn't we?'

Melissa felt her legs go weak. 'So you *did* definitely hide the knife, then?' It was the first time he'd properly confirmed it.

Lilly closed her eyes as Lewis sighed. 'Yeah,' he said in a resigned voice.

'Where did you hide it?' Melissa asked.

'Best you don't know,' Lewis said.

'Really? So a fifteen-year-old kid knows the best place to hide a knife that might incriminate him or his sisters in the stabbing of their father.'

The determined look on Lewis's face faltered.

She grasped his arm, pulling him close. 'When the police or any of these people find it, they'll have their evidence, and I get this feeling you'd rather they didn't have any evidence.'

'But they haven't found it yet,' Lilly said. 'Even after searching the whole house.'

'So it's in the house still?' Lilly's cheeks flushed and Melissa shook her head. 'Jesus, you two, are you mad? The police are there right now, probably searching this very minute in case they missed something.'

'Fine,' Lewis said. 'I'll go and get it and hide it somewhere else.'

'How are you going to do that, Lewis?' Melissa said. 'There's a police officer posted at the front door twenty-four hours a day.'

He shrugged. 'I'll figure it out.' He stalked off ahead of her. 'Come on, we have to find Grace.'

Melissa ran after him and grabbed his arm, making him turn to her. 'You do *nothing*, okay, Lewis? Do *not* mess this up more than it is already.'

Two people approached from the trees then: Eamon Piper with his son, Harvey. They were both short and stocky, with a shock of ash-blond hair and ruddy cheeks.

Melissa let go of Lewis's arm.

Harvey narrowed his eyes at Lewis as Lilly looked him up and down.

Lewis and Harvey had had an altercation the year before, which had resulted in Melissa and Patrick being called into school. Lewis had explained that Harvey had insulted Lilly on social media. Lewis's sisters were his soft spot. Say anything bad about them and you were in trouble. Everyone knew that. When Melissa got home, she found the comment Harvey had made on a Snapchat post of Lilly blowing a kiss to the camera, her full lips painted bright pink. *#Fakeasfuck* was what he'd written, and Melissa was secretly proud her son had stuck up for his sister like that. Ever since then, it had been awkward between the two families.

'We just searched the area by the courtyard,' Eamon said. 'No sign. I'm sure Grace'll be fine.'

'I hope so,' Melissa said. 'We really appreciate you helping us find her, don't we, guys?' she said, elbowing the twins.

'Yeah,' Lewis mumbled, not meeting Harvey's eyes. Lilly didn't say anything, just crossed her arms and scowled into the distance.

'You been that way?' Eamon asked, gesturing towards the patch of forest they'd just covered.

Melissa nodded. 'Yes.'

'Right,' Eamon said stiffly. 'We'll head to the east of the forest, then.'

They walked off, Harvey glaring at Lewis as he passed them.

'Come on,' Melissa said. 'Let's find your sister.'

As they walked through the forest, Melissa thought of the first evening walk she'd shared with Patrick, a few weeks after he'd moved to Forest Grove as a teenager and they'd had that first encounter where Ryan had fought him. This time, Patrick had sought Melissa out at her home. She was shocked to see him approach from the forest. After all, they'd already been sharing the same classroom at school for a number of weeks and he hadn't said a word to her. But he told her later he had already been quietly falling for her, mesmerised not just by her long blonde hair and naturally beautiful face but also by the fact that she wasn't like the other girls at school, who seemed to fall all over him. Instead of MTV and make-up, she was more into nature and art.

As he walked towards the cottage, she was outside, reading an old book as her mother hung out some washing on a line strung between two pines. Her mother had frowned when she saw him and told Melissa to get indoors. Melissa knew why. She didn't want anyone to see the bruise on Melissa's cheek. She'd already made Melissa take a day off school for it to calm down.

But Melissa didn't want to hide away – not from Patrick Byatt, anyway. So she'd ignored her mum and waited for him.

'Hello, Mrs Quail,' Patrick said to her mum, always so polite. She must have looked so strange to him. His mother, Rosemary, was a conventionally pretty woman back then, with dark hair and eyes. But Melissa's mum looked wild in comparison, with white hair to her waist, tattoos and a penchant for flicked-up eyeliner. She'd regarded Patrick through narrowed eyes that day, giving him the same look she would always give him: suspicion.

'Can I take Melissa for a walk?' Patrick had asked her.

Melissa's mother had hesitated a moment but then, to Melissa's surprise, she agreed, no doubt clocking the pleading look in Melissa's eyes.

As they set off, Patrick's dark eyes had alighted on Melissa's bruise, but he didn't say anything. Instead, they'd walked and walked, talking about the trees and school. Patrick seemed captivated by her, watching her talk, even brushing her blonde hair from her eyes. She thought for a moment they might kiss, but Patrick was the perfect gentleman, accompanying her home an hour later and watching as she let herself in.

He came every week then, on a Sunday, and their walks grew longer.

'Who's that boy?' Melissa's dad would say.

'Oh, he's from a very rich family,' her mother would exaggerate. 'It wouldn't harm to let Lissie be with him,' she'd added with a wink, playing up to her husband's greed. Looking back, Melissa thought her mother probably just wanted to see her daughter happy for once.

Nothing happened beyond talking during those walks with Patrick, which surprised Melissa. She'd heard all about his 'conquests' at school. Kisses stolen in storeroom cupboards. Notes passed from girl to girl. They became a regular thing, those long walks, until Melissa found herself in Patrick's kitchen in her nightdress in the middle of a dark night. Three months later, a week after Melissa's mother died, they shared their first kiss under the oak tree.

Melissa came to a stop now. 'Of course! I bet Grace has gone to the oak tree and Grandma Quail's bench.'

The twins nodded in agreement and they quickened their steps until they came to the great oak. Its huge branches creaked in the early-evening breeze.

Melissa saw a figure sitting there and for a moment she thought of her mother as she'd been found the day she died.

But it wasn't her mother, it was Grace. They ran over to her and Melissa folded her into her arms, pressing her palm to her eyes in relief.

Lewis and Lilly joined them and they all hugged each other.

Melissa looked down at her children's heads. Was Lilly right? Were her constant questions and demands to know the truth only making things worse? But that was all she could do, get the truth so she could protect the kids. There was nothing else to grasp at unless she decided to tell the police, and she just couldn't consider that possibility; it literally felt like throwing her children to the lions. But her husband was lying in hospital with a stab wound, and surely she had a duty to find out who the hell had done that to him?

The conflict between her different priorities was tearing her apart.

'Well, look who we have here,' a voice said. They all looked up to see the detectives watching them. Detective Crawford stepped forward, crouching down in front of Grace. 'You gave us quite a fright, young lady.'

Grace peered up at him with tearful eyes.

'She's been through a lot,' Melissa said, stroking Grace's hair.

People started appearing from the trees now.

'She's here!' someone shouted. 'Grace is here.'

'Can't fault their enthusiasm, can you?' Detective Crawford commented to his colleague as he looked at the gathering villagers. 'I doubt anything gets past this lot. I'm starting to think the best assets we have in your husband's case are the people of Forest Grove.'

Melissa regarded all the familiar faces as they began to gather in the clearing. Friends and family, wide smiles of relief on their faces as they saw Grace. These were people she'd counted on all her life, but the detective was right. They *were* his best assets . . . and therefore, her biggest threat.

She looked down at her children. If one of the kids *had* stabbed Patrick, these were the people she'd have to protect them from.

Chapter Eighteen

Forest Grove Facebook Chit Chat Group

Friday 19th April, 2019
9.05 p.m.

Graham Cane
Fat lot of good tonight's search did, then. Though someone did manage to find an original jar from an Ashbridge sweetshop from 1870 which might be worth a few bob.

Rebecca Feine
We found Grace, though, didn't we?

Belinda Bell
That was rather odd, you know, the way the girl disappeared like that. Anyway, the search was never going to be useful, let's face it. I actually found the community meeting before the search more insightful. I have an instinct for these things and something just doesn't smell quite right about it all.

Graham Cane

I know what Belinda means. It's clear the police think whoever did this to Patrick knew him. And wasn't it interesting that our local forest ranger didn't participate in the search?

Tommy Mileham

I noticed Ryan Day's absence too, Graham. What did you mean about the argument between Ryan and Patrick, Andrew Blake?

Andrew Blake

Renee from the chemist told me she heard the two of them arguing in the forest last month. She told the police when they came to chat to her the other day, but they didn't seem too bothered.

Debbie Lampard

I can't imagine Ryan hurting anyone.

Eamon Piper

Oh, come on! Rarely get a smile out of the man.

Rebecca Feine

Ah, that *must* mean he's violent, then. An unsmiling assassin.

Graham Cane

Sarcasm is the lowest form of wit, Rebecca. Ryan's always been an odd one, skulking about in the forest. You should have seen him when he was a youngster, like a wolf, snarling at anyone walking their dogs in the forest.

Belinda Bell
Melissa was the same for a bit before she moved in with the Byatts. A regular little girl Tarzan.

Andrew Blake
Yeah, and she was proper close to Ryan when they were kids. I reckon Melissa knows more than she's letting on, her body language was all off last night. I have a nose for these things. Probably my training.

Kitty Fletcher
Your 'training'? Do you mean the six-week orienteering course you did, Andrew? The woman's in shock, for God's sake! Leave her be.

Daphne Peterson
Leave Ryan be too. We all know why you're keen to point the finger at him. You're still stewing that he made you look like a dick when you were drunk and climbed the oak last year. Totally disrespectful, considering what happened to Melissa's mum there.

Andrew Blake
Stop bringing that up! I was trying to inspect it! And I had a bad knee, otherwise I'd have kicked his arse.

Jackie Shillingford
Come on, guys, the Byatts are going through a lot at the moment and last thing they need is everyone speculating and arguing. Andrea Cooper, I think this post needs to be removed.

Andrea Cooper
I won't delete it, I believe in freedom of speech. But consider comments CLOSED!

Chapter Nineteen

Saturday 20th April, 2019
7.45 a.m.

Melissa woke the next morning with a sense of determination. After getting ready and checking her messages from Bill, who'd spent the night with Patrick, she went straight to the attic room, gently knocking on the door. There was a sleepy answer of 'Yeah?' from Lewis. She walked in to find him half awake, playing some game on his phone as the girls remained asleep.

'Not sleeping well?' she asked him.

'When do I ever sleep well?' Lewis replied with a sigh. He'd always struggled with sleep, right from an early age. They'd even gone to see a sleep expert about it and tried all sorts of remedies, but nothing seemed to work. He told her he was used to it now, and Melissa had got used to hearing him padding around in the night too. Now, as she looked at him, *really* looked at him, she could see he looked more exhausted then she'd ever seen him, his brown eyes bloodshot, his handsome face drawn.

'It's probably good the girls are sleeping, actually.' She went to his bed and sat on it. 'The knife,' she asked quietly. 'Where did you hide it?'

He frowned. 'Why?'

'I'm going to hide it for you. *Properly*.'

He placed his phone down, sitting up straight. 'Really? Where?'

'You don't need to know. Just trust me when I say it's a good place.' She peered out at the trees. 'I lived in that forest all my childhood, remember? You get to know the best hiding places.'

Lewis looked unsure and she took his hand. 'You have to let me help you. One thing I know for sure, you can't leave it in the house.'

'But you said there's a police guard. How will you get in?'

'I'll deal with that.'

Lewis swallowed, peering towards his sisters' sleeping heads. 'Alright. It's under the sink, in that hidden bit beneath the built-in bins where we found that dead mouse last year after the place started to stink.'

Melissa nodded. It was actually a pretty good hiding place. Good enough for the police not to find it yet, anyway . . . but if they decided to pull the cupboards out, they'd easily come across it.

'So you're confirming you hid it, then, Lewis?' she asked her son.

'Yeah.'

'Finally, you tell me *something*,' she said. She took a deep breath, readying herself for the next question. 'Was it you who did it?'

Lewis scowled, turning away. 'Not saying.'

'Because maybe I'd understand, if you told me why.' She grasped his shoulder to make him turn back. 'We can figure it out, the two of us. We can—'

He shoved her hand away. 'Mum, I'm not saying, alright?' he hissed.

She suddenly felt the urge to slap him, then instantly felt awful. She wasn't her dad! She got up and went to walk out but Lewis grabbed her hand. She looked down at him. 'Sorry for shouting, Mum. I know you're trying to help, like, with the knife. Thanks.'

'It doesn't solve everything, though, you know. Your dad will still wake up and tell all.'

'Or he might never wake up.'

She looked at her son in shock. 'How can you say it like that? This is your dad. The man who held you in his arms after you were born, the man who taught you how to ride your bike and curve a football. The man who was there for you when you broke your leg that time, even taking time off work to look after you.' She grabbed his shoulders, shaking them. 'Your dad, Lewis. Your dad!'

'I know, Mum! You think I don't know that?'

'Then why don't you care if he lives or dies?'

'I do!'

She noticed he was breathing heavily. He'd been diagnosed with asthma a few years back. It was rare for him to have an attack like this, but when he did, it always worried her.

'Lewis, where's your inhaler?' she asked.

He gestured to his bag, which was lying on the floor. She grabbed it, searching the pockets until she eventually found the inhaler. He took some quick spurts from it then leaned back against his pillow.

Had she pushed him too far, just like she'd pushed Grace too far?

'Oh, my darling boy,' she said, drawing him into her arms.

He sank against her. 'Sorry, Mum,' he mumbled.

'I think you need to have a good sleep,' she said to him. 'It's still early.'

'You know I don't *do* sleep, Mum.' But as he said it, he yawned.

'Come on,' she said, pulling the duvet back so he could slide beneath it. She tucked the duvet around him like she used to when he was little and sat watching him for a few moments, stroking his tanned arm while he gradually began to fall asleep. She remembered doing the same when he was a toddler, marvelling at how different he was when he slept, all that pent-up energy at rest.

Then she left the room and walked downstairs to find Rosemary in the kitchen already. She looked exhausted, dark circles under her brown eyes.

'Any news from Bill?' Melissa asked.

Rosemary sighed. 'Nothing.' She got up and went to the kettle as her two dogs peered at her from the utility room. Sandy was lying on the other side, staring in at them. 'Coffee?'

'No, thanks,' Melissa said, grabbing her keys from the side. 'I'll head to the hospital and take over from Bill. I just need to pick a few things up from the shop first.'

'I was actually hoping to talk to you before the kids woke up,' Rosemary said. 'You can have some breakfast while we chat? Rebecca dropped some pastries off last night.'

Melissa paused. She really wanted to get over to the house and hide that knife.

Rosemary pulled out a chair. 'Sit, please,' she said firmly. Melissa looked at the table, laid out beautifully with pastries and fruit. It reminded her of another time, twenty years ago. Melissa had just told Patrick she was pregnant. They were not even twenty yet, and though they'd been dating for nearly five years by then, it wasn't how Patrick had mapped out his perfect little life plan: married at twenty-five, director level at twenty-seven, children at thirty. So Patrick had been completely bulldozed by the news and asked for some time to think. By then, they were already living together in the attic room. Rosemary and Bill hadn't been delighted when they discovered the two teenagers were dating. But when it became clear they were in love, Rosemary in particular preferred to be able to control the situation by letting them take over the attic room when they turned eighteen, and Melissa got a job on the forest centre's reception while Patrick tried to make his way up the ranks at a marketing company.

When Melissa came down for breakfast the day after she'd told Patrick she was pregnant, she was surprised to find Bill and Rosemary waiting for her with him, pastries piled on a plate in front of them. She knew in that moment that Patrick had told his parents and she was *furious*. They'd agreed he wouldn't until he and Melissa had had a chance to talk properly! It was bad enough when Bill and Rosemary discovered she and Patrick were secretly dating, something they'd managed to keep a secret since that first kiss beneath the oak tree. The feral little forest girl they'd taken in wasn't exactly who they had in mind as their son's future wife. Now she was pregnant!

But this *was* their grandchild growing inside Melissa, so they had it all planned out in true Byatt fashion . . . and that was what the breakfast was about. The chance to fill Melissa in on what they'd decided about *her* baby and *her* body. They informed her that Patrick and Melissa would marry before she showed too much, and Bill and Rosemary would lend them the money to get a small place of their own . . . in Forest Grove, of course. It wasn't exactly romantic, having their marriage decided by Patrick's parents. But it was hard to turn down a house and the chance to provide a decent life for the child growing within her. Looking back, Melissa could see the Byatts had steamrollered her into it, taken advantage of her naivety. But it wasn't about her. It was about the child growing inside her, her beautiful Joel. Two months later they were married in a hastily arranged ceremony in the forest. In the end, it really was beautiful, Melissa dressed in Rosemary's wedding dress, Patrick looking impossibly handsome in a new suit.

But still, Melissa never forgot that breakfast when she'd been forced into a decision she hadn't even had time to consider.

'It's just been so *hectic* the past couple of days,' Rosemary said now as she handed Melissa a coffee. 'I thought we could catch up.'

Melissa sighed and sat across from her. She might as well get it out of the way.

'I just wanted to make sure you knew we're always here for you,' Rosemary said. 'No matter what.'

Melissa looked at Rosemary's concerned face. *No matter what.* Did she know something wasn't adding up with Patrick's attack? It was probably the meeting last night, how the detective told them all the culprit might be closer to home than they thought. She had seen the way it had given the community pause, especially Bill.

'Melissa?' Rosemary pushed. 'You know that, right? That I'm here for you? Bill too?'

'Of course,' Melissa said, smiling. 'I know you're both here for me *and* the kids too. All of us know that.'

'Good.' Rosemary paused, taking a sip of her herbal tea. 'I just keep trying to wrack my brains about who might want to *hurt* Patrick.' She fixed Melissa with a look.

'We all have,' Melissa said, trying to keep her voice even as she picked up a pastry, taking a bite.

'I mean, you know my boy more than most.' Rosemary tilted her head, a small, strained smile on her face. 'How have things been at home lately?'

Melissa placed her pastry down, no longer hungry. 'Normal, completely normal,' she said firmly. 'I mean, Patrick's been stressed with the election coming up.'

'Yes, he has been a little more *pensive* than usual,' Rosemary said thoughtfully.

'Which is only natural, right?' Melissa asked, looking her mother-in-law in the eye.

Rosemary snagged her lip between her teeth. 'It's just . . . well, you know what a mother's instinct is like, Melissa, and I just noticed Patrick seemed to have a lot on his mind recently.'

'You know the way Patrick is,' Melissa said, trying to hide her frustration. 'He always wants everything to be perfect, so he's been working non-stop for the election. But it's nothing out of the ordinary – nothing that could explain why he was hurt on Thursday, anyway.' Melissa examined Rosemary's face. 'Why, did Patrick talk to you guys about anything?'

Rosemary quickly shook her head. 'Nothing. What about the kids?'

Melissa froze. 'What do you mean?'

'They must have sensed their father's stress. Have they been okay?'

Melissa swallowed nervously. Did Rosemary suspect the kids were involved? 'They've been absolutely fine,' she said. 'What's this about, Rosemary?'

'Oh, I'm just trying to place some context around things.' She peered at Melissa's plate. 'You've barely touched your pastry!'

'I'm not that hungry,' Melissa said, looking at the clock, suddenly desperate to get away.

'Poor love,' Rosemary said kindly, putting her hand over Melissa's. 'I haven't even asked how you've been.'

'You mean since Thursday?' Melissa asked. 'Or before?' she added, hoping she was making it known she wasn't exactly delighted with this line of questioning.

'Both,' Rosemary said. 'You said Patrick has been busy, so all the day-to-day stuff must have been falling to you?' She leaned forward, lowering her voice. 'I know how you've struggled before, Melissa. I just want to make sure we're not getting a repeat of the past.'

Melissa stood up, coffee spilling on her jeans. She quickly wiped it away as Rosemary watched her. 'I'm fine, absolutely fine,' she said. 'Look, I really need to go. I feel bad I haven't seen Patrick since yesterday evening.'

She grabbed her bag as Rosemary stood too. 'I hope you don't think I'm prying,' Rosemary said. 'I just wanted to make sure you're okay and to let you know that we're here for you – *all* of Forest Grove is.'

She walked around the table and pulled Melissa into an awkward hug. Melissa felt she couldn't breathe as she thought of what Detective Crawford had said the night before.

I doubt anything gets past this lot. I'm starting to think the best assets we have in your husband's case are the people of Forest Grove.

She pulled away from Rosemary and tried to smile. 'Thank you. Tell the kids I'll be back in time for lunch, okay?'

Then she grabbed her bag and walked out.

As Melissa drove down Old Pine Road towards her street, she mulled over what Rosemary had said. Did she know something? Or was she just worried Melissa couldn't cope?

She wasn't sure which was worse.

When she arrived at her street, the house coming into view, she took in a deep breath. Less than forty hours ago, she'd been cycling along this very road in the sunshine, looking forward to starting a lovely long weekend with Patrick and the kids. Now, her husband was lying in hospital with a stab wound almost certainly caused by one of their children and she had one hell of a mess to clear up if she wanted the kids safe.

She drove past the house, noticing a police officer sitting outside on a plastic chair. Then she parked down a side street which housed a collection of garages. She turned the ignition off then got out, walking past the garages and into the woods. She knew she couldn't just rock up to the front door and demand to be allowed in. It was a crime scene and they certainly wouldn't let her rifle about in the kitchen. Instead, she planned to get in the back way and quickly grab the knife. This all relied on there not being an officer out the back too, nor any within the house. But from a text she'd received from her neighbours, the police presence had been drastically reduced since the evening before, so she was hoping that was still the case now.

She walked around the edge of the forest until she came to her back garden. As she took it in, she felt tears flood her eyes. It looked lonely, no bike or scooter strewn across the lawn, none of Lilly's suntan bottles or Grace's books left on the table from an Easter Friday spent in the sun. She checked nobody was at the back door then walked slowly down the length of the garden, relieved to see there seemed to be no sign of movement inside the house. She passed Joel's tree, gazing at the orb that Lewis and Lilly had bought. Its turquoise green and bright blue swirled as it twisted in a light breeze. She felt tears prick at her eyelashes.

'Oh, Joel,' she whispered. 'What's happening to our poor family?'

She wished he was here. He'd be over twenty now. Despite his condition, she was pretty sure he'd be a pillar of strength for them right now. When you endure the kind of challenges he had, it surely gave you a strength to deal with adversities like this. He was always so brave when he had to undergo tests and when he watched his younger siblings do all the things he couldn't. Yes, he had his moments, the occasional epic meltdown. But on the whole, he coped so well, smiling and joking, jovially telling his brother and sister off. She imagined him sitting beside her now in his wheelchair, his dark hair and brown eyes so like his father's, the freckles smattering his small nose like his mother's. He was such a beautiful boy, had been from the moment she gave birth to him. She knew Patrick had struggled with her pregnancy, still unsure he even wanted the child and clearly not enjoying the way the growing baby changed the shape of his girlfriend's, then wife's, body. But as soon as he held his squirming, beautiful son in his arms, Patrick fell instantly in love. *Anyone* who came across Joel fell in love with him. It wasn't just about the way he looked, it was how he dealt with his condition too, with a laugh and a wink. His brother and sister in particular adored him, his death hitting them hard.

Melissa pulled out her set of house keys, finding the back-door key and quietly opening the door. Though she had a plan if there did happen to be someone inside – feigning pure naivety on her part: 'Oh, I thought it was okay to pop back to get some clothes. Nobody said otherwise.' – she still felt nervous. The silence struck her first as she walked into the kitchen, just like Thursday, when she'd come in to find Patrick on the floor. It was unusual then and it was unusual now. She sniffed the air. It smelt stale, a brief hint of chemicals and something off.

Old blood, Melissa realised. *Patrick's blood.*

She placed her palm on the door frame to steady herself before slowly walking into the kitchen. There was police tape tangled on the side, specks of dust everywhere, cupboard doors flung open. The police had tried to clean the blood away but there were faint swirls of pink on the floor, like whoever had done it had grown bored with replacing the bloody water for new. Smears of blood remained on some of the cupboards too.

Melissa imagined Patrick lying before her again, the kids standing in shock around him.

She pulled her eyes away from the stains and looked towards the front door, taking in the shape of the police officer sitting outside.

She needed to be quick . . . and very quiet.

She went to the cupboard under the sink where Lewis had told her the knife was and reached her hand under the bins, prising open the plasterboard protecting the 'secret place'. At first, she felt nothing and had to manoeuvre herself so her fingers could reach further, finally grasping the edges of a black bin bag. One of the kids must have had the foresight to wrap the knife up before hiding it. She took a deep breath then yanked it out, peeking inside.

Yes, it was the knife, their largest one, its silver blade stained with Patrick's blood.

She put her hand to her mouth in horror. It all seemed so horribly real now, the tragedy of it all rushing over her in waves. For a moment, she thought she might be sick. She bent over, taking in gulps of air. That was the last thing she needed. How would she explain vomit on the floor?

She sat down, putting her head in her hands. When her queasiness dissipated, she wrapped the knife up in another bin bag, then grabbed an empty cardboard tube that had at one time contained a champagne bottle, a leftover from their celebrations when Patrick was nominated to run as a councillor. Grace had been saving the tube to use in a science project. Melissa placed the knife inside it, then put the tube in a large shopping bag.

She'd leave it in the boot of the car while she was at the hospital then take it back to Rosemary and Bill's before burying it. She knew where to hide it: it was a place she used to go with Ryan when they were kids, sneaking out on summer nights, unnoticed by their sleeping parents. It was a place in the densest part of the forest, a place they considered *their* area, somewhere they would escape to and whisper in the darkness. Ryan would set up a campfire and they'd both bring snacks. They always knew exactly where to meet because the area glowed in the dark, thanks to the presence of foxfire, bioluminescent fungi that thrived on decaying wood. And for some reason, in this particular patch of the forest, there was a *lot* of decaying wood.

If more people knew about the place, she was sure they would descend upon it. But she and Ryan kept it a secret, protective of an area that had been their sanctuary all those years ago. She sometimes wondered if the reason they were holding off introducing it to their own kids as they grew older was that they *liked* the idea of it still being here, like a portal to another world where they would always be protected.

Now it felt like a portentous decision to Melissa. The fewer people who knew about their secret spot in the woods, the less chance there was that the knife would be found. Of course she'd considered the fact that the spot was alight at night, a beacon for anyone wandering by. But people simply didn't wander by the area at night. It helped that there was a ban on people going into the woods between the hours of 11 p.m. and 4 a.m., an attempt to deter teens from having drunken camping parties there. But they didn't really need it. There was something about this part of the woods that people stayed away from anyway – fearful they'd get lost, maybe?

Melissa's eyes went back to the bloodstained floor. She thought of Patrick, of his large bare feet on this very floor as he walked in to get her a glass of wine. Or chasing the dog as the children laughed. The parties they held here for Halloween and for the kids' birthdays. The big BBQs they held for all their friends. Christmases with Rosemary, Bill and Patrick's sister whenever she visited from Australia with her family. So much laughter, so much love.

How had it *come* to this?

The front door clicked open.

Melissa froze, the shopping bag containing the knife in her hand as she heard the distinctive sound of Detective's Powell's voice echoing down the hallway.

Chapter Twenty

Saturday 20th April, 2019
9.05 a.m.

As the detective walked down the hallway, Melissa looked at the back door. Would she have time to dart out or would it just look even more suspicious if they caught her doing that?

No. She had to stay.

She searched around her frantically, her eyes alighting on some dirty clothes that had been taken from the washing machine and placed in a basket during the police search. She grabbed a bunch of them and shoved them in the bag, covering the tube holding the knife. Then she took a deep breath and faced the kitchen door.

It opened and Detective Powell appeared, a uniformed officer behind her.

If the detective was surprised, she managed to hold it in, regarding Melissa coolly. 'You're not supposed to be here,' she said.

'I came to get some of the kids' clothes,' Melissa replied. 'I didn't realise I wasn't allowed to come.'

'It's a crime scene,' the detective said.

'How did you get in?' the other police officer behind her asked, a young man with red hair who she vaguely recognised. 'I've been outside all the time.'

'Through the back,' Melissa said, gesturing to the door. 'I honestly didn't realise I was doing anything wrong. I thought all the forensic work had been done. I'm *so* sorry.'

Detective Powell examined her face, then her eyes dropped to the bag and Melissa thought she might faint.

Thankfully, the detective's eyes lifted back to Melissa. 'Is Grace okay?'

'Yes, thanks. She does like her forest walks, bless her.' Melissa realised her words were coming out quickly, her voice a nervous pitter-patter. She started backing away. 'Right, I'd better go get these clothes in the wash before I visit Patrick. Again, I'm so sorry.'

'Surely you have clean clothes?' the detective asked.

Melissa held her breath a moment then gestured towards Lewis's football shirt. 'Yes, but Lewis needs this particular shirt.'

'Right. Well, just make sure you let us know next time you need anything from the house,' the detective said.

Melissa nodded then strode to the back door.

'Before you go . . .' the detective called out. Melissa paused, heartbeat throbbing in her temples. 'We'll need to search your bag.'

Melissa slowly turned around. 'It's just dirty clothes.'

'It's something we need to do, Mrs Byatt. I hope you understand?' the detective said, dark eyes cold.

'Of course,' Melissa said with a shaky smile as the detective jutted her chin at the uniformed officer, who reached into his pocket and pulled on some rubber gloves. 'Just warning you,' Melissa said to him, 'it's all a bit mucky. Teenagers can be pretty gross.'

The officer wrinkled his nose.

Detective Powell's phone rang. 'Excuse me,' she said, leaving the room to take the call.

Melissa handed the bag over to the officer with trembling hands.

It was game over now; she knew it. What had she been thinking, coming here? She had just made it a hundred times worse. How would it look, being caught with the knife that had been used to stab her husband . . . with *her* DNA all over it now, as well as the kids'?

'I don't know if you remember me,' the officer said as he rifled through the top layer of clothes. 'I brought a hedgehog to you with my kids last year?'

'Oh God, yes, I remember,' Melissa replied. 'Your little boy is gorgeous. You live in Ashbridge, right?'

'Yeah.' The officer paused, peering around him. Melissa tried not to stare at the bag. 'We'd love to live in Forest Grove, though,' he said, 'especially before my son goes to school. Even with what's happened with your husband, Forest Grove is still better than bloody Ashbridge.' His eyes widened. 'God, sorry, that was insensitive of me.'

'No, it's fine,' Melissa said, just happy he hadn't yet resumed searching the bag. 'I actually know someone who's about to put their house on the market on Birch Road. The garden is small, but the price will reflect that.'

The officer's eyes lit up. 'Really?'

'Yep. Give me your email address, I'll get her to contact you when it's going up for sale.'

He peered behind him to see the detective still talking on the phone, pacing the hallway. Then he placed the bag down, getting his notepad out and scribbling his address down. 'That'd be awesome, thanks.'

She took the piece of paper and tucked it in her pocket. 'No worries.'

'Sorry for what you're going through, by the way,' he said.

Melissa didn't need to fake the tears that flooded her eyes. 'It's very difficult. I'm just trying to keep things normal for the kids, you know? Sounds mad, but it's the little things, like them being able to wear their favourite tops,' she said, gesturing to the bag he'd been searching.

The officer looked at the bag then sighed, handing it over. 'Here, go home to your kids. I didn't feel right searching it anyway. Detective Powell can be a bit OTT, you know?'

She took the bag, holding it close to her like it was a newborn baby. 'Thank you. Take care, okay? Fingers crossed you'll get to move here.'

She turned on her heel and hurried out with the knife in her bag.

Tonight, she would bury it.

Chapter Twenty-One

Sunday 21st April, 2019
2 a.m.

It was a still night with very little breeze as Melissa set out to bury the knife. The forest felt like it was moving in the darkness as she entered it, a hive of hidden activity. The long trunks of the pines took on a different form, like the ash-riddled columns of a burnt-out mansion. The ground below felt hazardous and Melissa walked carefully, her torchlight not quite enough to illuminate every little root she might trip over. Beyond the path, in among the trees, she saw movement, flashes of eyes. She knew in her rational mind it would simply be nocturnal animals – deer, owls, maybe foxes and bats, wondering who this stranger was among them. It still made Melissa quicken her step, though, heart thumping loudly as she peered over her shoulder.

After a while, the place she was heading for came into view, a hint of luminescent green on the horizon: her and Ryan's old meeting place. She trod over tangled roots and brittle branches until she got to the clearing. It was filled with dying tree stumps, some decorated with the bulbous green glow of the fungi feeding off them.

Melissa walked to the stumps. She imagined Ryan approaching with his bag of goodies in the darkness like he once used to, eyes sparkling as he caught sight of her.

She sighed and placed her own goodies down: a bin bag holding the knife in one hand, Bill's spade in the other. She'd cleaned the knife in the darkness of Bill and Rosemary's kitchen before she came out, trying not to think that it was her husband's blood she was wiping off. It had worked to begin with, her mind too tired and foggy from waking at such an ungodly hour to think with much clarity. But as the blood disappeared and the blade began to shine, she saw her reflection in it and that was when she lost it, fat tears rolling down her cheeks, stifled sobs coming from the core of her as the full gravity of what she was doing hit her. The fact was, she was cleaning her husband's blood off a knife she was pretty sure one of their kids had plunged into him. Patrick had seemed paler to her when she'd spent the afternoon with him, a small rash appearing on his chest; Melissa couldn't help but panic that something was wrong.

As she cried, she'd heard a creak on the stairs and looked up to see Lilly watching her.

She put her finger to her lips. 'Shhhh,' she said. 'Go back to bed.'

Lilly did as she asked and Melissa felt an overwhelming tide of sadness rise within her. Had she looked to Lilly just as her mother had to her all those years ago, sobbing in the kitchen?

Melissa peered at her watch now. Nearly two-thirty already. How had time flown by so fast? She quickly dug the spade's blade into the soil and started digging, using the rhythm as a way to distract her mind from going elsewhere other than the task at hand.

In the distance, a branch cracked.

Melissa stopped, eyes searching the darkness. *Probably just a fox*, she reasoned.

But then there was another noise, like something – *someone* – taking a deep breath.

'Hello?' she whispered, slowly picking up her torch and searching the darkness with the light. She tried to tell herself again that it must be an animal, but all the hairs on the nape of her neck were up, just as they had been before she discovered Patrick on that kitchen floor.

That'll be your instincts, Lissie, she imagined her mother whispering.

She placed the spade down and walked around the area, shining the torchlight into the forest, illuminating the dark, hidden spots.

There was a loud thud, a sharp intake of breath, then another branch cracking.

Melissa swivelled the torch around, heart thumping. 'Hello?' she shouted out, trying to be brave.

There was a flurry of noise, then a large bird flapped out of the tree above. She wanted to feel relieved. That must have been where the noise had come from, surely? But something told her it wasn't.

She looked towards the hole she'd dug. If there *was* someone watching, they would have seen her. That meant they'd *know* the hiding place of the knife. Should she abandon her plans, find somewhere else to hide it? Or return to the house with the knife?

She closed her eyes, trying to calm her mind.

No, she was just being paranoid.

She took a deep breath and went back to the hole, picking up the spade. After ten more minutes, she'd created the hole she needed. She carefully took the knife out, still wrapped in the bin bag, then placed it in the hole, pushing it into the soil so it sunk even further down. She paused a moment, thinking of one of her children wrapping their hands around the now hidden handle and thrusting the blade into their father.

Then she imagined them doing it to her, their own mother.

She put her dirty hand to her mouth, shaking her head as tears flooded her eyes.

'Stop it,' she hissed to herself. 'Stop thinking about that!'

She forced herself to stand back up and started to scoop soil over the space until it was eventually full. Patting the top to make it flat, she grabbed some foliage and covered it, even digging up some plants and replanting them there just to make sure.

She surveyed her work, wiping the sweat from her brow. It looked good in a 'nothing to see here' way. As far as she could tell, even people searching the area specifically for disturbed ground wouldn't look twice. She was no expert, though. That was the thing with all this. She was fumbling in the dark! But she had to trust her instincts, just like her mum would say.

She felt exhaustion sweep over her. She'd been running on adrenaline since she'd woken but now the job was done, the 'three in the morning' fact of this moment hit her full force. Yawning, she started heading back through the forest, torch jumping over the trees and foliage as she quickened her step, looking forward to getting out of her dirty clothes and sinking into bed.

But then she heard another noise.

She turned, looking over her shoulder, and let out a gasp.

Someone was standing in the darkness, watching her.

Chapter Twenty-Two

Sunday 21st April, 2019
3 a.m.

The figure, clad in black, merged into their surroundings but Melissa could just about make out their tall frame and the white of their eyes. She turned her torch on whoever it was, but they darted out of the spotlight.

Suddenly feeling brave, Melissa ran after them. 'Who are you?' she shouted as they sprinted off into the foliage. But then her foot caught on a root and she came thundering down, the torch smashing to the ground and turning off, plunging her into darkness. She lay among the leaves and the roots, clutching at her shin, feeling it sticky with blood.

'Shit,' she whispered as the reality hit her: she was in the forest, *injured*, in the middle of the night with some stranger skulking about. And who really knew for sure if Patrick *had* been stabbed by one of the kids? What if it was someone else, someone they were so scared of they were covering for them?

Hadn't Grace said she was scared?

Melissa's heart thumped loudly in her ears as she grappled for the torch, trying to make it work, to no avail. She reached into her coat pocket for her phone, but it was gone. She slid her hands over the branches around her but couldn't find it. It must have fallen out as she was running.

She stood up and yelped as pain darted down her leg.

'Come on, you can do this,' she told herself, limping through the darkness. But it was useless; she was bleeding too much.

She peered to the right of her, a small yellow light marking Ryan's lodge out from the surrounding darkness. It was only a five-minute walk away.

She limped in the direction of the lodge, shoving branches and long grass out of her way. When she reached the lodge Ryan had once shared with his father, she rapped gently on the window where she knew his bedroom was. A light was on inside but, still, she didn't want to risk waking Maddy if she was staying there that night.

'Ryan,' she whispered, 'it's Melissa.'

The curtain twitched open, Ryan staring out at her. His eyes widened and he opened the window, leaning out.

'Melissa?' he asked in surprise. 'What the hell are you doing here?'

'Can I come in?'

'Yeah, of course.' He appeared at the front door a few moments later, and she noticed he was dressed already in cargo pants and a T-shirt.

'What's going on?' he asked her quietly, looking her up and down as she limped in. 'Jesus, are you okay?'

She followed his gaze to her shin. There was a hole in her jogging bottoms, blood seeping through it. 'I fell.'

He gestured to his sofa. 'Sit down. Let me look at it.'

She took a seat on his brown leather sofa and watched as he reached for a first-aid box in one of the kitchen cupboards. It was an open-plan area with two bedrooms leading off at the back, and a small kitchen overlooking a decent-sized living room with a massive fireplace. She'd been here many times before, first as a child when her father would come over to drink beer with Ryan's dad . . . and then there was a time when she was here many years later too.

It had changed over the years, once cluttered and neglected by Ryan's father, with tools and empty beer bottles all over the place, now tidy and smart. Ryan had built a workroom out the back for all his tools, giving the lodge more living space. He had replaced the old carpets too, with neat pine floors, and the walls were now painted a pale blue. The kitchen was small and the most familiar of all, with its original pine units and granite tops, but the units had been repainted as well.

Melissa could still see hints of Daphne's presence here from all those years ago in some paintings of the forest on the walls and a blue vase on the table, filled with wild flowers. Maddy's touches were here and there now as well, teen books and notepads strewn over the wooden coffee table in front of Melissa and a small black hoodie with *Free the press* scrawled on the back.

Ryan sat beside Melissa and lifted her leg on to his knee, rolling her jogging bottoms up to reveal a jagged cut in her skin. She flinched as he pressed a gauze hard against it, stemming the bleeding. Then he took out an antiseptic wipe, cleaning away the blood and dirt before placing a large plaster over the wound. He was quiet as he did it, every now and again examining Melissa's face with a frown.

'How'd this happen?' he asked eventually, 'and why are you in the forest at this time of the night?'

'I couldn't sleep so I took a walk . . . then I fell.'

He raised an eyebrow. 'I'll ask again. How did this happen?'

Melissa regarded her old friend's face, feeling the urgent need to tell him – to tell *someone* – what had been happening the past three days. But could she trust him, especially with that talk of him having had an argument with Patrick? But then that *was* just a rumour and there were always plenty of those in Forest Grove, many of them turning out to be untrue. She took in his earnest blue eyes, as familiar to her as the forest. She had *always* been able to trust him.

Still, she had to ask him: 'Can I trust you?'

'You know you can.'

She wiped her hand over her tired face. 'It's so hard keeping it all to myself.'

'Then tell me, like you used to when we were kids.'

She peered towards the other room. 'Is Maddy here?'

'Yeah, but she'd sleep through World War Three. What happened?'

Melissa told him everything, from the moment she walked into her house to see Patrick on the floor to just now, when she'd seen a strange, silent figure watching her.

Ryan stood up when she finished, going to the window and peering out, fists curled as he tried to find the stranger she'd mentioned. 'I wish you'd come to me sooner,' he said.

'I couldn't. Imagine if the same happened to you. Wouldn't you want to keep things as close to your chest as possible for Maddy?'

She saw him frown in the reflection of the window. 'Yeah, I would.' He walked back to the sofa and sat down, thinking about it all for a moment. 'So you're sure it's one of the kids? You *sure* they're not covering for someone?'

'I really don't know, Ryan. I can't imagine them hurting a *hair* on their father's head, but equally . . .' She shook her head, pursing her lips as tears flooded to her eyes. 'It's such a mess.'

'Have you thought about which of them could do that to Patrick, if it *is* one of them?'

She shook her head.

'I guess the obvious choice might be Lewis,' Ryan said.

She looked at him in surprise. 'Why would you say that?'

'He's been in trouble at school for beating some kids up, right?'

'Not quite *beating* them up, Ryan. Anyway, that's completely different!'

'Sorry,' Ryan said quickly. 'I didn't mean . . .'

'It's fine,' Melissa said with a sigh. 'They all have their quirks. Lilly can blow up at the smallest thing sometimes. Grace is fascinated by the weird and dark side of life, but they're all good kids!'

'They are,' Ryan agreed. 'If one of them did it, they'd have to have had a good reason.'

'That's what I keep thinking. But Patrick is a good man. Why would they want to hurt him? Why would anyone?'

Ryan looked down at his hands.

'I can't help but blame myself,' Melissa admitted. 'I've always been a bit lax about them watching films, you know? Letting them watch 12s when they were five. Especially Grace – she's always preferred the Disney villains to the Disney princesses. Maleficent is an icon to her!'

Ryan smiled. 'That's cool. She's different. I like that.'

'Then there's Lewis, with those video games. I let him buy that *God of War* game with his birthday vouchers last year, even though it's too old for him. What about Lilly, too, with her social media obsession, maybe I should have—'

'Oh, come on, Melissa!' Ryan said, interrupting her. 'You sound like Kitty Fletcher. It's all BS. I mean, look at Andrea Cooper's kid, Carter? She sticks to all Kitty Fletcher's stuff like Velcro, and Carter is a little shit – the number of times I've seen him wandering around the forest when he should be at school. No,' he said, shaking his head. 'Your kids are good kids. Something must've happened between them all, something so big it made one of them stab their dad . . . and then *not* tell you about it.'

'They won't say a word.'

Ryan nodded. '*One for all and all for one*. Wasn't that their and Maddy's motto when they were all little?'

'Yes.' She peered towards Maddy's room. 'Has Maddy said anything to you?'

'Nothing.'

She remembered the conversation she'd overheard between the kids in Bill and Rosemary's summer house. 'I overheard Maddy chatting to the twins about something,' she said, lowering her voice. 'They mentioned Carter Cooper saying something about me at the New Year's Eve party. I'm not sure it's related in any way, but the kids seemed cagey about it. Any idea what they might mean? You were at the party, maybe you overheard something?'

'Nope,' Ryan said, focusing on packing all the first-aid stuff away and turning the kettle on.

Melissa looked out at the trees, trying to find a familiar comfort in the dark, swaying branches. 'I do wonder if I should have just been honest with the police from the start. Do you think I should have?'

He shook his head. 'Nah. But then, you know me, not exactly a fan of the authorities.'

Melissa's eyes travelled over to the rifle that was leaning up against the wall. She knew he needed it in case he found a fatally injured animal in the forest that needed to be put out of its misery. But she still felt uncomfortable seeing it there.

'Did you hear about the community meeting?' she asked.

'Daphne told me a few bits.' His brow puckered with concern as he got some mugs out from a cupboard. 'I heard Grace went missing.'

'She was fine. We found her at the oak tree.'

Ryan smiled. 'She's always liked that tree, hasn't she? Just like your mum.' The smile disappeared off his face.

Melissa nodded. 'Andrew Blake mentioned a fight was reported between you and Patrick?'

Ryan's eyes flickered with something. 'Fight? Don't know anything about that.' He brought over her coffee then sat down. 'You need to stop beating yourself up, Melissa. I really think you've done the right thing not telling the police. You don't know all the facts yet, and the kids *have* to come first. I'd do the same thing in your position.'

'But the police might have a better chance of getting all the facts out of them!'

'And scaring the hell out of them in the process. Honestly, you did what any decent parent would in the split second you had to make the decision.'

Melissa surprised herself by letting out a sob, mainly out of relief from having someone validate her decisions over the past three days.

'Come here,' Ryan said, pulling her into his arms. She sobbed into his bare neck, comforted by the familiar forest smell of him. She'd done this before, in the days following Joel's death.

But then she thought of Patrick, lying wounded in hospital. How would he feel about her sobbing in Ryan's arms?

She pulled away from him, avoiding his gaze. He sighed and gave her some tissues. She wiped her face, blowing her nose. 'Sorry, I'm just tired and emotional,' she said. 'If I can just get a handle on things, I might feel better. Like figuring out what those bloody posters mean,' she said. 'And getting rid of them too, they're still in my bloody bag.'

'Let me,' Ryan said. 'I can burn them.'

'Thanks. I'll try to bring them tomorrow.'

Ryan sighed. 'What does the *I know* in the poster mean?'

'I can't help but wonder if they know what happened to Patrick,' Melissa admitted. 'It can't be a coincidence I found them the morning after, can it?'

'It's pretty easy to see through into your kitchen with that big window of yours, especially with binoculars.' Ryan's cheeks flushed. 'I imagine so,' he added quickly. 'But why not go to the police? Why make posters, for God's sake?'

'God knows.'

'Maybe they're waiting for the right time to blackmail you or something. Maybe that was them earlier and they were planning to ask you for money.'

'How'd they know I'd be out at this hour?'

He shrugged.

'As for the blackmail thing,' Melissa said, 'it's not like we have any money!'

'People aren't to know that, are they? Patrick swans around in that Mercedes of his, wears all those expensive suits. All this stuff with him wanting to be our local councillor now – he's always in the local paper, going on about how he's going to make this place better.'

'I sense a hint of disapproval.'

'Not exactly the man's biggest fan, am I?' Melissa gave him a look. 'I just mean, we're completely different, aren't we?' he said. 'My Land Rover is twenty years old and the only suit I own was from a charity shop in Ashbridge, which I bought for my dad's funeral all those years ago. I'm just not the flashy type.'

'Patrick isn't flashy! I wish you'd give him more of a chance, Ryan. He really cares for his community and wants to make a difference. There's nothing *flashy* about that, is there?'

'And fell your mum's oak tree in the process.' Ryan sighed. 'Let's agree to disagree, shall we? So, back to the posters. If we can find out who put them up, we *might* be able to find out what happened to Patrick. Plus, the last thing you want is more appearing around the forest.'

Melissa smiled. '*We*. So we're a team, are we? Captain Hawkeye and Major Wolf,' she said, referring to the characters they took on as kids when they played games in the woods.

Ryan laughed. 'Yes! I remember that now.'

'I was *such* an awesome Captain Hawkeye with my binoculars.'

'Not sure how awesome I was in my mum's old fur coat.'

They burst out laughing, then Melissa's laughter trailed off as she remembered the gravity of the situation she was in. Ryan put his hand on her arm. 'I got you, Hawkeye. You're not alone in this any more.'

Melissa took in a deep, shaky breath. 'You don't know how much that means to me.'

They held each other's gaze for a few moments, then Ryan got up, placing their mugs in the sink. 'I *might* just have an idea, actually. You know those wildlife cameras that have been set up for that school project?'

The kids at Forest Grove High had been doing a project on forest wildlife, which Ryan was helping them with by documenting nocturnal animals. Melissa nodded.

'Why don't I take a look at the footage and see if it shows who might have left the posters out?'

Melissa smiled. 'That is a genius idea!'

'I just need to get the SD cards out and check them. There are quite a few so it might take a while to get them down and go through them.'

'Are you sure? I know how busy you are.'

He raised an eyebrow. 'Funnily enough, things are pretty quiet next week – we've had quite a few cancellations.'

'Why would people cancel?'

He shrugged. 'You know what this place is like – outsiders are always grounds for suspicion.'

'You mean suspicion about Patrick?' He nodded. Melissa shook her head in anger. 'That's ridiculous! Anyway, you're not an outsider! You've lived here longer than anyone.'

'Living in the forest doesn't count, Melissa. To be a true Forest Grovian you have to live in the village.'

'That's silly, Ryan. Everyone made me feel like a Forest Grovian, despite coming from the forest.'

'Not your mum, though.'

'What's that supposed to mean?'

He looked out towards the oak tree. 'Forget I said it.'

They fell into silence.

'Anyway,' Ryan said after a while, 'it's given me more time to do some woodwork.' He gestured to some bird boxes in the corner. 'Sold ten of those last week on my website.'

'I'm not surprised,' Melissa said. He'd made one for Melissa's fortieth birthday the year before, leaving it outside the house with a note. Patrick hadn't liked it, said it looked too rustic, so he'd made his own. Patrick's was beautifully painted, all the sides perfectly sanded down. It was nice, but Melissa secretly preferred Ryan's and kept it in the garden, right at the back so she didn't have to endure Patrick clucking in disapproval whenever he saw it. The birds seemed to prefer it too, a gorgeous robin quickly making a home of it, while Patrick's birdhouse remained empty. One day, she found Patrick's birdhouse in the bin, its wood shattered. When she'd asked him about it, he'd said it had fallen off the wall. But she'd always suspected he'd smashed it apart in frustration.

Melissa yawned.

'You look knackered,' Ryan said. He stood up and got his coat. 'I'll walk you back.'

She took his hand as he passed her, looking up at him. 'Ryan, thank you so much for all this. I really *do* wish I'd come to you earlier now.'

'You're here now, aren't you?' He squeezed her hand, eyes scanning her face as his blue eyes flickered with emotion. Then he pulled his hand away from hers. 'Come on, let's get you back. It's nearly four in the morning now.'

A few minutes later, they were walking through the forest, Ryan's huge flashlight guiding them. After a while, he crouched down.

'What do we have here?' he said, shining his light on a mobile phone lying on the ground.

'My phone!' She picked it up, placing it in her pocket.

'This where you fell?' he asked.

She nodded, shivering as she looked around her.

'Come on, let's go,' Ryan said.

As the community centre came into view in the distance, Melissa sighed. 'Everyone was so *angry* at the community meeting. It surprised me.'

'Does it really surprise you?' Ryan asked as he angrily kicked at leaves with his boots. 'People don't let things go here. Not when one of their own has been hurt. Think of that kid you've been helping, Jacob Simms.'

'He *is* one of our own.'

'You wouldn't think it, the way they treated him, Andrea fucking Cooper writing that letter to the courts about them needing to give him a proper sentence.' He caught her eye. 'They'll turn against you as soon as they think you're not one of their own any more.'

'You're being paranoid,' Melissa said. But as they got to Bill and Rosemary's house, she couldn't help but wonder if he was right.

Chapter Twenty-Three

Sunday 21st April, 2019
4.15 a.m.

I had a nightmare. I was standing in the kitchen and we were all shouting, like Thursday afternoon, but this time, Dad's the one with the knife and he's sinking it right into me . . . and then I realise it's not him, it's Ryan! And he's stabbing me, over and over, and there's so much anger in his eyes.

I woke sobbing and so scared. All I could think was: I need Mum. So I went to her room, but she wasn't there. Bathroom, nothing. Kitchen, nothing. And that's when I saw her, just now, coming out from the forest with someone.

That someone was Ryan.

It's completely freaking me out after that dream. I'm not surprised to see them together, though. How can I be, after everything Dad said about Mum and Ryan? It makes me think how Dad must have felt, and now I'm feeling super-guilty. The guilt and the regret hit me right in my core, like it does when I let myself stop to think about it all.

I bend over now, clutching at my stomach, trying to stop the sobs.

What have I done?

The sound of the phone ringing makes me pause. The phone. At this time? I walk to the door and lean my ear against it.

'Oh God,' I hear Nan say. 'Bill! Bill!'

Chapter Twenty-Four

Sunday 21st April, 2019
4.20 a.m.

Melissa quietly let herself into Rosemary and Bill's house, frowning as she noticed the lights were on . . . and there was movement inside.

Rosemary appeared from the kitchen then, pulling her coat on, a panicked look on her face. 'Where have you been?' she asked Melissa.

'I – I went for a walk. I needed to clear my head. What's going on?'

Rosemary glanced at the dirt on Melissa's grey jogging bottoms and on her face. 'The hospital called. Patrick's taken a turn for the worse.'

Melissa's head span. 'Jesus, what happened?'

'Infection,' Bill said from the landing in a sombre voice. She looked up to see him standing with the kids, who were all in their pyjamas, bleary-eyed.

'Where *were* you, Mum?' Grace asked.

'Just a walk.' She caught Lewis's eye, and he nodded, knowing she had hidden the knife. Melissa turned to Rosemary. 'I knew something was wrong – that bloody rash! I mentioned it to the nurse.'

'I did too,' Rosemary said, tears filling her brown eyes. 'Come on, we need to get to him. They said it's very serious.'

The children exchanged worried glances as Melissa tried to stop herself from sobbing. Was this it? Was she going to lose Patrick?

No, no!

'Kids, get changed,' Melissa instructed. They needed to be there if he died. It didn't matter what had happened, he was their father! This might be their last chance to see him.

'No, let them stay here,' Bill said.

'On their own?' Melissa said.

Bill patted Lewis on the shoulder. 'The twins are fifteen, Melissa, you've left them all on their own before. They'll be fine.'

Will they be fine? Melissa couldn't help but think. The last time they were alone, one of them stabbed their father.

'No, you should come,' she said to the kids.

Rosemary shook her head. 'They're too young. Come on, let's go.'

Melissa blinked, trying to figure out whether to push the matter.

'Come *on*,' Bill said, grabbing the car keys. 'We need to get to Patrick, now!'

'Okay,' Melissa said, quickly running up the stairs to the kids and kissing them on their foreheads. 'I'll call with news. Stay safe, okay? Do *not* leave the house.'

'We're fine, Mum,' Lewis said, putting his arms around his sisters' shoulders.

Melissa gave him a look that she hoped conveyed her thoughts, then went back downstairs, looking at Bill and Rosemary. 'Let's go to the hospital.'

The journey was unbearable. Awful scenarios flashed through Melissa's mind: would they get there to find Patrick had passed away? Her husband, the love of her life, her *rock*: gone. Those thoughts mingled with guilt. Guilt that an hour ago she'd been hiding the very knife used to stab him. Guilt, too, that she'd allowed Ryan to hold her like he had earlier. Allowed those few extra seconds before pulling away.

When they got to the hospital, Bill pulled into a disabled parking bay. 'I don't care,' he said when Rosemary pointed it out to him. 'I'll pay the bloody fine.'

The three of them jumped out of the car, the sound of the doors slamming sending birds sleeping in the trees flying away. Then they ran inside, rushing down corridor after corridor until they eventually got to Patrick's ward, Melissa's head throbbing with the horror of what might await them.

Patrick, gone.

After giving their names at the intercom outside his ward, they were greeted by his young doctor. She looked dishevelled, tired.

'Is my husband okay?' Melissa asked, peering behind her into the semi-darkness of the ward as the doctor steered them towards the family room.

'The nurses are tending to him now. You can see him soon. Come to the family room, we can have a quick chat.'

The three of them followed her in.

'What's happened?' Melissa asked.

'I want to see my son now,' Bill said in a stern voice.

'Bill,' Rosemary said, placing her hand on his arm. 'Let the doctor explain what happened.'

Bill took a deep breath then nodded, taking a seat with Rosemary across from the doctor as Melissa leaned against the wall.

'Patrick has a hospital-acquired infection known as stenotrophomonas maltophilia,' the doctor explained.

'So he caught it from this place?' Bill said in disgust, looking around him.

'Yes, unfortunately,' the doctor said with a sigh. 'We do all we can to avoid such infections, but it does happen, especially to those in a critical condition like Patrick. His immune system is very compromised.'

'I noticed a rash on him yesterday,' Melissa said, looking out at the corridor, desperate to get to her husband. 'I told the nurse.'

'Yes, we were aware of that,' the doctor admitted. 'Infection was one of the many conditions that may have caused it.'

'Then why didn't you act on it?' Bill asked.

'We did, when we noticed his condition worsening,' the doctor said.

'How is he now?' Melissa asked, wanting to cut through to the facts.

'Better. There was a moment about an hour ago when we thought we might lose him.'

Rosemary gasped as Bill hung his head. Melissa hugged herself, trying her best to hold back the tears. She needed to stay strong for Patrick.

'But he's through the worst now?' she asked.

The doctor sighed again. 'Not necessarily. The next few hours will be crucial.'

'He could still die, then?' Bill snapped. Rosemary let out a moan and put her head in her hands.

The doctor looked up at them with sad eyes. 'As we've discussed, regardless of whether Patrick has an infection or not, it's always a possibility for your son, Mr Byatt. He sustained a very serious head injury.'

Melissa squeezed her eyes shut.

'One of us should have been here,' Rosemary said. 'He should never be left alone.' She gave Melissa a look and Melissa could see the message in her eyes: you were out, walking, when you should have been with your husband.

'I told you all yesterday that it's good for Patrick to be alone sometimes,' the doctor said quickly. 'Of course, it's a comfort to know one of you is there but there are also times when he needs to be completely alone. We've moved him into a private room now to give him more peace and quiet.'

'Not now, though,' Rosemary said. 'I'm not leaving his side.'

The doctor nodded. 'Of course. Let me check if you can go through. I'll be back in a moment.'

She stood up and left them alone in the room.

'Where exactly were you, Melissa?' Rosemary asked. 'It was four in the morning, for Christ's sake!'

'I don't get what this has to do with Patrick getting an infection,' Melissa snapped back, her face flushing.

'You should have been with him,' Rosemary said.

'So should you!' Melissa shot back.

'Going for a walk at four in the morning – really?' Rosemary said.

'I couldn't bloody sleep! You know walking in the forest helps clear my head.'

'Why not take the dog, then? You always take Sandy when you walk. Why—'

'Enough!' Bill said. The two women went quiet. 'The doctor's right, she *did* tell us he needed time alone, remember? And that it was best we got sleep so we could be strong for him. That's why we all stayed at home last night, to get a proper night's sleep. We need to stop bickering and focus on Patrick now.'

'Exactly,' Melissa said, crossing her arms and facing away from Rosemary.

Rosemary was right, though: she should have been there. Instead, she had been burying the knife one of their kids had used to put Patrick in this precarious situation. Had she made a mistake, deciding to protect them?

But as she thought that, she remembered them standing on the landing in their nightwear a few minutes ago, the vulnerable looks on their faces. Her poor darlings. All she knew was that something had gone badly wrong in their family and she needed to fix it.

The door opened, the doctor poking her head in. 'You can see him now.'

They all followed her through the quiet ward, past sleeping patients, until they got to the room Patrick had been moved to. When they walked in, Melissa tried to hide her surprise at the sight of her husband. He looked even worse than he had yesterday, a blue tinge to his lips, his skin horribly mottled. His breathing was ragged, a new machine next to him now pumping in oxygen.

Melissa went to him and kissed his face. 'I'm sorry I wasn't here, darling, I'm so sorry.'

As she looked at him, she realised she really could lose him . . . and if she did, one of their kids could be put away for his murder.

Chapter Twenty-Five

Sunday 21st April, 2019
10.45 a.m.

Dad nearly died. That would have made me a murderer.

A murderer!

That's all I can think when I look at him now. Mum made us come visit him. She said Dad still might not make it. That he has an infection. She didn't even sugar-coat it. I think she was just too tired. Too scared too. None of us tried to even push back. We knew we had to go, no excuses. So here we are, and I can't get a grip on how I feel. All I know is that Dad isn't Dad any more. I mean, we've kind of been saying that for the last few weeks anyway, how we don't see him the same way we used to. But to see him lying in that bed with all those tubes coming out of him and the way his head's all been shaved. Yeah, we all agreed it when Mum just went to the loo and left us alone with him. Dad totally isn't Dad any more.

It's like what Maddy said once about her parents splitting up. How they became different people in her eyes. Together, they were a unit, 'Mum and Dad', 'my parents'. But when they split up, they made different shapes in her mind. Even at just five, she could see it. Her dad got all withdrawn, quiet, and sort of turned his back on society again. But it was actually her mum who changed the most. The way she chopped off her hair and started going crazy for the gym. Maddy always says it's like she was thrown into a completely different life with different people.

I suppose that's the way it's been for us too with Dad, ever since we overheard that argument with Ryan last month. Our parents are different people than what we thought, more fragile and brittle, and it feels like we've been living a lie all this time. And now we're thrown into this new life Maddy talks about, except our new life is full of blood and lies and tubes, like the ones right there in front of us.

I put my head on the bed and the other two crowd around me, putting their arms around me and trying to shut me up before Mum gets in because I'm saying sorry, sorry, sorry *over and over.*

I took it too far. I know that now. But what choice did I have, in that moment? And now the whole village wants to kill me, see me hanged, according to that stupid community meeting. I wish we'd just said the truth from the start. But we're too far gone now, and we have to think about Mum, don't we?

Mum walks back in and comes straight to me, putting her arms around me. 'It'll be alright,' she whispers. 'It'll be alright.'

I think of that drawing of the oak tree with her hiding in it. I think of her arms like the bark, her scent like the smell of the forest.

Familiar. Safe. Protective.

But for how long?

Chapter Twenty-Six

Monday 22nd April, 2019
12.45 p.m.

Melissa dragged herself out of her car, putting her hand to her mouth and yawning. She'd spent most of the past thirty-two hours with Patrick in hospital, bar the time she went back to Rosemary and Bill's to collect the kids to see him the day before.

It had been strange seeing the kids at the hospital together, staring at their dad like he was a stranger. It made her heart break and all she wanted to do now was see them. They'd spent the night at Daphne's, Melissa not wishing to leave them alone, as Bill and Rosemary wanted to spend as much time as they could at the hospital.

Melissa had taken it in turns with them the night before, watching over Patrick. When it wasn't her turn, she'd tried to sleep on a battered leather chair in Patrick's hospital room. But every rasp of his breath, every tiny little movement from a patient or nurse outside, had her opening her eyes and rushing to his bedside, checking he was still breathing.

And he was, thank God. In fact, he was fighting off the infection and was past the worst now.

'Of course he is,' Bill had said that morning when the doctor told them. 'He has Byatt genes.'

Melissa had wanted to tell Bill to shut up when he'd said that. She wanted to tell him it had nothing to do with bloody Byatt genes and everything to do with how hard the hospital staff had worked to bring Patrick back from the edge. But she didn't because she knew this was his way of coping, telling himself nothing could possibly hurt his perfect son because he was a Byatt.

Melissa slammed the car door shut now and walked up Daphne's path. She lived in one of the smaller houses in the village, three roads away from the forest in the middle of a row of smart, identical semi-detached houses. In typical Daphne fashion, though, her house stood out with its bright blue door and pale green painted wood, much to the disdain of her neighbours. Melissa liked the look, though; it was subtle yet pretty.

She walked to the front door and rang the doorbell. There was the sound of chatter then Daphne appeared.

'Hello, my love,' she said with a sad smile. She drew Melissa into an instant embrace and Melissa found herself sinking into her friend's slim frame, welcoming her familiarity. 'How's Patrick?' Daphne asked.

'Through the worst,' Melissa replied. 'Rosemary and Bill are with him.'

'Good, you need the break. Come in, I've just started making lunch, actually. It'll be ready in an hour. Just home-made quiche, but it's yummy.'

'Thanks.'

Melissa slipped her trainers off then followed Daphne down the hallway, past beautiful, vibrant canvasses of art on the wall. 'How have the kids been?' she asked.

'Grace and Lewis seem their normal selves, a bit subdued, but that's only natural.'

'And Lilly?'

Daphne frowned. 'Not herself.' She peered up the stairs. 'She's up in Maddy's room now. Go and see her while the others are in the garden, if you want?'

'Good idea.'

Melissa found Lilly curled up in Maddy's room with her back to the door. She walked over to her, sitting on the bed and stroking her long, wavy hair.

'Lilly?' she said.

Lilly shuffled slightly but didn't turn around.

'Darling, look at me,' Melissa said, putting her hand on her daughter's head.

Lilly turned to her, tears falling down her cheeks, and Melissa's heart broke for her. It was rare to see Lilly like this; she was so good at keeping her emotions in check.

'Oh Lils,' she said, pulling Lilly into her arms and letting her sob into her shoulder. 'My darling girl. Let it all out.'

'It's just so shit, Mum,' Lilly mumbled into her mother's top. 'It's so fucking shit.'

'I know, darling, I know.'

'Dad looked really bad.'

'He's better now.'

'He's not, though, is he?' Lilly said, angrily wiping the tears from her face. 'He could still die.'

Though it broke her heart to see Lilly like this, it also gave her some solace. The kids had been so detached about Patrick's grave condition it had horrified her. But now here Lilly was, actually registering some fear for her father.

Regret too, maybe?

'I really think he'll pull through, darling, honestly,' Melissa said. 'In fact, I was chatting to the doctor this morning, and they might try to wake him later in the week.'

Lilly's eyes widened.

'That's a good thing, you know, Lilly,' Melissa said, hating her daughter's reaction to the news that her father might wake up. 'It means your dad will survive, that he'll be back to normal.'

Lilly avoided her gaze. 'Yeah, I know.'

'I haven't really talked to you,' Melissa said softly. 'Not just you and me. You know you can talk to me, don't you?'

Lilly nodded, suddenly finding her silver nail polish fascinating.

'I think we're pretty good at talking,' Melissa said. 'You always say that. Definitely compared to Maddy and Daphne, anyway,' she said, lowering her voice. 'I remember you telling me how Maddy was jealous about the fact us two could talk about *anything*. Heavy periods, boys, exam worries, anything.'

'We can,' Lilly said with a faint smile. 'You're the best.'

'Then why won't you tell me what happened on Thursday afternoon?'

The smile disappeared off Lilly's face. 'I can't.'

'Not even though you know I'd do anything to protect you guys?' She leaned in close. 'I hid the knife the other night,' she whispered in Lilly's ear. She clutched her shoulder and looked her in the eye. 'If that doesn't prove I'm on your side, then I don't know what does.'

'I know, Mum, Lewis said.'

Melissa sighed. They were all willing to tell each other everything, so why was she met with a wall of silence whenever she tried?

She decided to try another tack. 'I was looking at photos on my phone last night,' she said with a smile. 'I came across some of the New Year's Eve party at the forest centre. Look,' she went on, digging her phone out and scrolling through the photos to find the one she meant. It was of the five of them – her, Patrick and the kids – all dressed up in eighties gear and smiling at the camera. 'We were so happy, weren't we?'

Lilly's face clouded over as she looked at the photo. 'Yeah,' she whispered.

Melissa scrolled through some others, stopping at one that showed Carter in the background. 'I think Carter Cooper was pretty drunk that night.'

Lilly's lip curled. 'Yuck. I can't stand him.'

'I don't think he's a huge fan of mine.'

Lilly frowned. 'Why d'you say that?'

'Oh, apparently he was saying stuff about me that night?'

Lilly's face flickered slightly. 'Was he? Well, he's a dick, isn't he?' She put her hand to her tummy and winced. 'Actually, Mum, I have a *mega* heavy period. Can I just lie down for a bit longer? It really hurts.'

Melissa wasn't convinced Lilly was telling the truth. Lilly lay back down and pulled the duvet cover over her. As Melissa looked at her, a thought occurred to her: Lilly's period pains, Lewis's asthma attack, then Grace's outbursts. Were they all manufactured to make Melissa stop questioning them?

She peered over at the bedside table by Lilly to see some paracetamols there. Maybe she really *did* have period pains?

No, they weren't manipulative enough to fake it like that, surely? They were just kids. *Her* kids.

She stroked Lilly's head and gently kissed her cheek then walked out of the room, leaning against the wall outside and taking in an exhausted breath. She looked down at her phone again, finding the family photo from New Year's Eve. They really had seemed *so* happy then. Patrick was dressed in tennis gear with a mullet wig and neon headband while Melissa was in a silver dress with huge shoulder pads, her hair teased into perm-like curls by Lilly. Lilly was dressed as Madonna, with a pink net top, black flared skirt and leggings, and Lewis looked like his normal self but this time in an Argentine Maradona football T-shirt instead of a

Chelsea one. Grace was dressed as Matilda, her favourite character from the eighties book by Roald Dahl, her usually fair hair covered with a dark brown bobbed wig.

Melissa noticed Maddy was in the background, dressed in a power suit and with enormous earrings, her usually dark hair crimped. But it wasn't her costume Melissa noticed . . . it was the way she was glaring at Patrick's back.

She zoomed in. Yes, there was definitely hate in her dark eyes. What was *that* all about?

Melissa tucked her phone in her pocket and walked downstairs. She found Maddy and Grace sitting on a picnic blanket in the sun together, looking at a magazine while Lewis kicked a ball about on the lawn.

'Mum!' Grace said when she saw her mother. Maddy peered up from her magazine and smiled. Melissa examined her face. Sure, she knew she wasn't exactly a huge fan of Patrick's political views, but that was pure hate she'd seen in her eyes.

'Hello, darling,' Melissa said as Grace ran up to her. She pulled her into a hug and kissed her cheek. She gave Lewis a wave and he smiled.

'Dad's doing better,' she said, even though neither Grace nor Lewis had even bothered asking her.

'Hey, Maddy,' she said, strolling over to the young girl. 'What have you guys been reading?'

'Oh, just an article about plastics in the sea,' Maddy said, regarding Melissa over her John Lennon-style sunglasses. 'I mean, seriously, when are the powers that be going to do something about it?'

Grace nodded solemnly beside her, something she always tended to do when it came to Maddy, her real-life hero.

'Well, it's something Patrick might be able to take up when he wakes,' Melissa said. 'He knows a few politicians.'

She examined Maddy's face, but she didn't seem to react. Maybe Melissa was reading too much into that photo.

Maddy stood up and stretched, revealing the small piercing in her pale tummy. 'I'm gonna get a drink. Do you want one?'

'No, thanks,' Melissa said.

She watched Maddy pad inside and frowned. Just like the kids, she seemed so dismissive of Patrick, despite him lying in hospital in a coma. What had he done to make them all act like this? It was like the worst kind of puzzle to solve, and it was *exhausting* her!

She lay back on the picnic blanket as Grace continued reading Maddy's magazine beside her. She realised she hadn't really felt the sun on her face the past few days, and she had to admit it felt good. Before Melissa knew it, she was asleep, that same dream she always had shimmering into her mind: the sound of a branch cracking. A rope. A ballet shoe abandoned on the ground.

She woke with a start as she felt ice-cold pressure on her arms.

'Lilly!' she said as she noticed her older daughter sliding an ice cube down her arms.

'It was the only way I could wake you up!' Lilly declared. Behind her, Daphne smiled as she laid food out on the garden table with Lewis and Grace's help.

Melissa grabbed Lilly's arms, pulling her down as she giggled. It was good to see her smiling again.

'Is your tummy okay?' she asked, as their mock fight turned into a hug.

'Yeah, a little bit better.'

'Right, grub's up,' Daphne said. 'Alexa, play the Daphne Chill playlist,' she commanded the device sitting a few feet away in her kitchen.

The kids rolled their eyes as they sat at the table. They hated all their parents' 'cheesy playlists', as they called them. But as the music started, the kids ended up singing along to the tunes.

'This is lush,' Lilly said, leaning back in her chair as she ate, blinking up at the sun.

'I know,' Maddy said, doing the same. The two girls looked so different: Lilly with her long caramel hair and white and silver shorts, then Maddy with her bright pink hair and ripped black shorts. But somehow, they worked together.

'Ergh, I can't believe I'm back to school soon,' Maddy said. 'Why does *our* school have to make Easter half term so early? The kids in Ashbridge have another week.'

'Yes, but they only broke up last week,' Daphne said. 'You all still get the two weeks off.'

'I thought you liked school?' Melissa asked her.

'Only when Mr Quinn's doing Citizenship,' Lilly said, wiggling her eyebrows at Maddy. Lewis frowned, focusing on shovelling quiche into his mouth. He clearly still had feelings for Maddy. Actually, now Melissa thought about it, Maddy *had* split up with him early in the New Year. Was it a coincidence it was only a few days after that New Year's Eve party?

'Oh, shut up,' Maddy said, throwing a napkin at her friend as Grace laughed. 'It's the subject I like, not Quinny.'

Her eyes glanced over at Lewis then quickly away again. Lilly looked at them both then smiled.

'I've always had this theory that Mads will end up falling for a Tory boy,' she said. 'I mean, Mum was a bit of a leftie, weren't you, right, Mum? Then you met Dad?'

Melissa laughed. 'I didn't give a damn about politics back then, darling. And I don't think your dad did either, really. We were just kids.'

'Well, I'm totally up for marrying a politician,' Lilly said, twirling her long hair between her fingers. 'Even a Tory. Imagine all those magazine covers?'

'Oh my God, seriously?' Maddy said, shaking her head but smiling all the same.

'Yeah, I reckon Jeremy Leadsom would make an *awesome* husband,' Lilly replied, referring to the brightest boy in their year.

Lewis rolled his eyes as Grace quirked her lips into a small smile.

'Jeremy and Lilly, sitting in a tree,' Maddy started, before collapsing into a fit of giggles.

Melissa watched Lilly as she giggled with her friend. She was a compete contrast to the way she'd been an hour ago, full of light and fun. But Lilly was good at that, switching from darkness to light at the click of a finger, pretending everything was okay.

'Do you know what?' Lilly said. 'I think I'd like to go back to school tomorrow, actually.'

Melissa looked at her in surprise. 'Really?'

'Yeah,' Lilly said, popping an olive in her mouth. 'Beats moping around at Nan and Grandad's.'

'I hate it when you do that, Lil,' Lewis said.

Lilly stared at him. 'Do what?'

'Pretend like nothing's wrong.'

Maddy looked down at her plate as Grace sighed, used to the twins' arguments.

'Come on, you two,' Melissa said. 'No arguing at the dinner table.'

'Jeez, what's *wrong* with you, Lewis?' Lilly said, ignoring her mother as she flicked back her caramel locks.

'Oh, I don't know, our dad's dying in hospital?' Lewis hissed back at her.

Melissa took in a sharp breath. 'Lewis!'

'You are *such* an arsehole!' Lilly shouted at her brother.

'Lilly!' Melissa shouted back at her.

Lewis jumped up and strode inside.

‘That was out of order,’ Melissa said to Lilly.

Lilly frowned slightly but then shrugged. ‘He’s such a drama queen. Anyway, *he* was being out of order.’

‘You need to be a bit more sensitive round him, you know how he is.’

‘This is why I want to go back to school,’ Lilly said, pouting as she crossed her arms. ‘I can’t stand being cooped up inside. Lewis can’t either, that’s why he’s acting like this. We need to get back to normal.’

‘But things aren’t normal, Lilly,’ Melissa said, aware of Daphne and Maddy’s eyes on them. ‘Lewis is right, your dad nearly died yesterday, for Christ’s sake.’

Maddy grimaced as she looked down at the table and Lilly burst into tears. ‘Thanks for reminding me, Mum. Thanks a bloody lot.’

Then she ran into the house too.

‘I’d better go check on them,’ Maddy mumbled, scraping her chair back and walking inside.

‘Me too,’ Grace said, following Maddy.

‘Well, that went well,’ Melissa said as they all disappeared.

Daphne leaned over, putting her hand over Melissa’s. ‘They’re going through a lot. You are too.’

‘I shouldn’t have shouted like that at Lilly, though.’

‘I would’ve done the same. How are you doing, anyway? I don’t feel we’ve talked much.’

‘Better than I was yesterday. Honestly, Daphne, I really thought Patrick was going to die.’

Daphne pursed her lips, tears flooding her eyes. ‘That must have been awful for you.’

They fell into silence.

‘I keep thinking how much Patrick would hate all this,’ Daphne said eventually, chewing at her lip. ‘Lying there in hospital, not being able to control it all.’

Melissa tilted her head. 'Control?'

'Well, you know what I mean. Patrick always likes everything to be *just so*. Maddy loves watching him mow the lawn whenever she visits you guys at the weekend. She says Patrick has to get *every little* blade, even if it means getting down on his hands and knees to cut them with his scissors.'

Melissa smiled to herself. 'He *is* a bit of a perfectionist. That's why I need him.' Her voice broke. 'What will I do if he dies, Daphne? How will I cope?'

Daphne leaned forward, looking into Melissa's eyes, her own green eyes fierce. 'You would cope fine. If there's one thing I've learnt since Ryan and I split up, it's how *strong* you can be on your own.'

'But you've always been more independent than me. Stronger than me!'

'Rubbish. I'm not as strong as you think, Melissa, *trust* me. I'm weak.' Daphne took a deep breath then stood up, clearing the plates away as Melissa watched her. Weak was the *last* word she'd use to describe Daphne, but then everyone had their insecurities, didn't they? Even people like Daphne, who always seemed so confident and strong.

'So, will you let Lilly go back to school tomorrow?' Daphne asked as Melissa got up to help her.

Melissa looked in towards the kitchen, where the twins were now sitting with Maddy, watching something on the small TV in there.

'I don't know,' Melissa confessed. 'Maybe she's right, maybe she needs the distraction. It can't be doing them much good, moping around at Rosemary and Bill's.'

'I don't think that would do *any* of us any good,' Daphne said with an arched eyebrow. 'Seriously, though, I did wonder that. School can be a good distraction.'

'The school gate mums can be too,' Melissa said sarcastically.

'You don't need to endure that,' Daphne said. 'Lilly can walk in on her own.'

'I'd want to walk in with Lilly in case she changed her mind.'

'Fair enough. There are hardly any parents at the school gates now they're older anyway.'

'You'd be surprised. You know how mollycoddling the parents can be here, and the primary school is just a street away so you can't help but bump into mums.'

'Like Scandrea and Insta Charlie?' Daphne said.

They both laughed.

'What's for pud, Mum?' Maddy called through to Daphne.

'Who fancies devouring all my leftover Easter eggs?' Daphne replied.

'Yes!' the kids all chorused in delight.

Melissa smiled. For the first time since Patrick had been stabbed, she felt a small sense of normality sink in. Then she peered in the direction of Forest Grove High, imagining facing Andrea and Charlie at the school gates the next day.

How long would that normality last?

Chapter Twenty-Seven

Tuesday 23rd April, 2019
8.34 a.m.

Melissa walked with the twins to school the next day. Lewis had surprised Melissa by waking that morning and declaring that he wanted to return to school too. She wasn't sure that was such a great idea – he seemed a bit subdued – but he'd been quite insistent. Grace hadn't been so keen, though, so was being looked after by Bill while Rosemary stayed at the hospital with Patrick. Melissa was planning to go there too, straight after dropping the twins off. There had been no change in his condition, but she wanted to be there as much as she could in case there was.

Melissa took in a deep breath, trying to mentally prepare herself for the possibility of seeing other parents at the school gates. It had been a couple of years since she'd done the school run, with the twins now walking Grace to her primary school before heading into their own secondary school.

Melissa thought of the first time she'd ever done a school run with Joel, when he was five. He'd attended a specialist school ten miles away and a bus would pick him up and drop him off each day. But Patrick and she had insisted on taking him in for his first day. Melissa still remembered how confident Joel had pretended to be, using the special ramp to haul himself up into the car.

'My boy is all grown up,' Melissa had said to Patrick.

Her heart clenched at the memory of Joel, then at her husband's absence now. She bit her lip to stop herself from crying as the school came into view. It was a sprawling modern building made of wood and exposed brick. It sat right on the edge of the south side of the forest, a short five-minute walk through the woods for the kids, though that five minutes often turned out to be longer as they messed about in the forest with their friends. Among the trees around the school were wooden picnic benches forming 'forest classrooms', the kids encouraged to learn outside whenever it was dry.

They drew closer to the wooden school gates, pupils wandering around among the pine trees in their gold-and-green uniforms. Some glanced over at Lilly, the handful of parents there smiling sympathetically at Melissa.

Melissa noticed Andrea Cooper talking urgently to her son, Carter, nearby. Carter was a tall skinny boy with gelled-back hair, white like his mother's. Andrea grabbed her son's arm, pulling him close to say something, but he shoved her away and walked off, laughing.

Melissa frowned as she took in Andrea's wounded face. Carter was such an arse. Though Andrea irritated her, Melissa still felt sorry for her, having to deal with a son like that.

She thought back to what he might have said about her at the New Year's Eve party . . . the same party where Maddy had been pictured glaring at Patrick. She peered over at Lilly to see she was linking arms with Maddy now, her friends gathering around her and hugging her while Lewis high-fived his friends nearby.

Maddy turned to regard Melissa over her shoulder, brow creasing.

The school bell rang out and Melissa beckoned the twins over to say goodbye.

'If it gets too much,' she said to each of them, 'just tell Mrs Nightingale. She said she'd call me so I can come get you.'

'We'll be *fine*, Mum,' Lilly said, clearly desperate to return to her group of friends, who were waiting for her.

Melissa gave the twins quick hugs then watched as they walked back over to their friends. Before they got inside, Lewis turned to look at her, lifting his hand in a wave, reminding her of when Patrick had waved when he spotted a fourteen-year-old Melissa watching him from the trees. Lewis slipped into the school entrance with his sister, the two of them swallowed up by a sea of pupils.

Melissa sighed and went to walk away but noticed Andrea striding over. 'I was hoping to catch you!' Andrea called out. 'A few of us were chatting just now and we want to hold a charity raffle for you at the book fair tomorrow evening!'

Melissa frowned. 'For . . . me? I don't understand.'

'For the family! To raise money.'

'But we won't need money.' Andrea's expression faltered. 'I mean, it's lovely, but . . .'

'You can't work; obviously, Patrick can't either,' Andrea explained. 'And we thought we could raise funds to help with the search for Patrick's attacker, take out ads, get posters printed?'

Melissa felt a jolt at the mention of posters. She examined Andrea's face. Had she mentioned posters on purpose? Did she know something about them?

Or was she even *behind* them?

'Posters? No, I don't think we need any posters,' Melissa said quickly. 'Why would we want posters?'

Andrea shrugged. 'Oh, I don't know – a way to remind people to look out for evidence while walking the dog, that sort of thing.'

Melissa didn't say anything.

'You're lost for words,' Andrea said. 'I get it. So we're thinking if we send a message via the school's ParentMail today, that gives people time to bring in their items for the raffle tomorrow morning. I've already agreed it with the teachers.'

'Erm, wow,' Melissa said. 'It's *such* a . . . *lovely* thought, really, but we don't need any money. I'll be paid, it's counted as compassionate leave, and Patrick's boss has already told me they'll cover his wage. And we certainly don't need any posters,' she said meaningfully, watching Andrea's face for a reaction. 'We need to let the police do their job.'

But Andrea just raised an eyebrow 'Really? I think they're being rather useless. This was clearly the work of a druggie, the mess they made of it.'

'The mess they made of what?'

'The attack! Sloppy, apparently.'

Melissa frowned.

Andrea put her hand to her mouth. 'My God, I'm so sorry, how insensitive.'

'No, that's okay. I just didn't realise Adrian was allowed to share details like that.'

'Oh no!' Andrea said, looking aghast. 'It wasn't Adrian. It was Rosemary who told me.'

Melissa couldn't help but think it was a bit crass, Rosemary telling Andrea about the messy details of her son's attack. But then it was like Daphne had said: everyone's business was shared here in Forest Grove. That was what the raffle was all about, really, a way for people to get involved, frustrated that they were on the margins of the attack on one of 'their own'.

Melissa suddenly felt a flare of anger. 'I'm sorry, Andrea, but the truth is, I think the raffle would be a bit inappropriate.'

Andrea's face hardened.

'But do you know what would be even better?' Melissa added, aware the last person she needed as an enemy was Andrea Cooper.

Andrea tilted her head. 'What would that be?'

'If we could raise money for a Duchenne muscular dystrophy awareness charity. In honour of Joel. I honestly think if Patrick could hear me telling him we were doing that, it would mean so much to him.'

To Melissa's relief, Andrea smiled. 'What a wonderful idea. Are you happy for me to arrange it all?'

'Oh, absolutely.'

'Great! So we'll see you at the book fair tomorrow, then?'

Melissa faltered. They'd all been planning to go to the book fair before everything that had happened with Patrick, but it felt very strange to go now that there was going to be a charity raffle in their name. 'I'll have to see how the kids are.'

'Of course.'

Melissa's phone buzzed in her bag. She pulled it out to see Ryan calling. Andrea frowned as she recognised the forest ranger's name.

'He's helping me with something,' Melissa quickly explained. 'Excuse me a moment, will you?'

'Have to dash anyway.' Andrea looked again at Melissa's phone then tottered off on her high heels.

Melissa put her phone to her ear. 'Ryan?'

'Can you come by my lodge when you get the chance?' he asked her, voice strained.

'Why? What's wrong?'

'It's easier if I show you.'

Chapter Twenty-Eight

Tuesday 23rd April, 2019
9 a.m.

Ryan was outside his lodge, sitting on a tree stump as he drank coffee and stared at some items laid out on a plastic tarpaulin. He looked exhausted, like he hadn't slept a wink.

'What's going on?' she asked when she got to him.

'Some of my cameras have been vandalised.'

Melissa crouched down, taking in the smashed-up camera pieces. 'Jesus. When did this happen?'

He raked his fingers through his fair hair. 'Must have happened overnight. I didn't notice anything yesterday. I went out to get the SD cards and found a box hanging off the trees, the camera smashed up. I thought it might be a one-off. Squirrels, big birds, they can all do damage like this. But then I found the next one was the same.' He sighed. 'And the one after that. Twenty-three in all. Not all of them, but enough to *really* piss me off.'

'Who would *do* that?'

He picked up a stick and poked one of the broken pieces. 'All the damaged ones were around the old oak, same place you found the posters.' He looked up at her. 'Can't be a coincidence, can it?'

Her blood turned to ice. 'They didn't want us finding out who it was. How did they know you'd be looking at the footage, though?'

'I don't know. Maybe that person you saw was listening in on us?'

Melissa pulled the posters from her bag. 'Here, you said you'd burn them?'

He took them all and stared at them, pacing back and forth. 'I don't like this, I don't like this one bit.'

'Ryan, calm down,' Melissa said, going up to him.

He turned to her, blue eyes flashing with anger. 'Someone was following you the other night, and now this? Not to mention these bloody posters. It's aggressive behaviour, I don't like it.'

'No one's hurt me,' Melissa said, trying to hide her own fear as she took in the shards of plastic and glass on the ground. 'Whoever it is had a chance the other night, but they didn't.'

'Yeah, but they're trying to intimidate you.' He curled his hands into fists. 'I swear, if anyone tries to hurt you . . .'

Melissa looked at him in surprise. She wasn't used to seeing him so animated.

'I heard the sirens on Thursday night, you know,' he said. 'I ran to the end of the road, saw the ambulance heading to your place.' He peered at her, face taut with emotion. 'I seriously thought my world had just dropped out from under me.' He stepped closer to her. 'I thought you were hurt, Lis.'

Melissa remained silent, listening.

'I was out of my mind,' Ryan continued. 'I ran to your house, worried you were hurt. I kept thinking about all that time wasted . . .'

Melissa froze. 'Ryan, don't.'

'Don't what?' he said, shoving the posters into a bucket of wood nearby and grabbing her hand. 'I've made so many mistakes, messed *so* much up.'

'It's in the past.'

'Exactly! The past. If I hadn't ignored you after you moved in with the *Byatts*,' he said, spitting their name out, 'if I'd gone to you, told you how I . . .' He took in a sharp breath. 'Things might be different.'

'Ryan, please . . . you don't have to say all this.'

'But I do, can't you see that? That's what I'm trying to say, I do! Can I tell you something? Seeing Patrick like that, getting loaded up into the ambulance.' His jaw flexed. 'I thought about him being out of the picture.'

'Ryan . . .'

He circled her wrists with his hands. 'I know, I fucking *hated* myself for it. But I can't stop how I feel.'

The wind picked up around them, leaves lifting in the air, and for a moment Melissa felt as though she were a teenager again, about to share her first kiss with Ryan, the same way they had all those years ago. It was the night before she had finally left the forest. Things were bad between her mum and dad, the worst they'd ever been. Looking back, she shouldn't have been surprised matters would reach the state they did the next day. As her parents argued, she sneaked out at night and waited for Ryan. He was late and she started panicking that he wouldn't turn up, dreading the thought that she'd be alone out there. When he did eventually appear, she was so relieved she ran to him and wrapped her arms around him.

Somehow, their lips just found each other, even though they never had before. It felt exactly like it should, like everything in her world had been leading up to that point. She'd woken the next day smiling, desperate to see Ryan again. But then everything had kicked off and she ended up at the Byatts. She still sneaked out to find Ryan the night after, but he wasn't in their usual meeting place.

When she did eventually see him a week later in the woods, he told her to leave him alone. She'd never felt pain like it. She didn't understand at the time that he was just hurt, stubborn. He told her many years later that he'd seen her in town with Patrick a few days after she'd moved in with the Byatts. He could see she'd already been enveloped in the Forest Grove way: her hair was shorter, her feet clad in expensive wellies. A young Ryan saw no role in his old friend's life any more so he stepped away.

She looked up at his face now, eyes exploring the achingly familiar contours of his face. He was still a boy, really, barely changed by societal demands. He'd frozen in time here, and though in many ways he had grown – a father now, the town's forest ranger – he was still the Ryan she knew. She wondered what he saw when he looked at *her*? So many harsh waves had knocked at the rocks of her life, the death of a child and now all this. She knew she wasn't that pretty teenage girl any more. And yet that didn't stop him moving closer to her, his fingers trailing down her cheek, and for a moment she really *was* back in that clearing again, a whole lifetime of regret and love rushing to the surface too. She felt her body reacting to him, a feeling so bound up with the feel of his skin on hers it seemed as natural as the leaves on the trees above.

'I love you,' he whispered. 'You know I always have.'

Yes, she knew he'd always loved her. She had been too young to understand all those years ago that he was just pushing her away out of stubbornness and pride after he ignored her following that first kiss. But she grew to learn that Ryan had never stopped loving her, even when he met Daphne. He'd done the 'right thing', trying so hard to make a go of it with Daphne. But his love for Melissa was always there. She knew all this because he'd told her when he found her in the woods after Joel died. He found her at her most vulnerable and he became her sanctuary, her big, solid oak to hide away in.

And now she was desperate to hide away again, leave everything behind, just as she had in those days following Joel's death eleven years ago.

She leaned into Ryan now, like she would into a large oak.

He kissed her brow, her cheek, the imprints left behind like the warm shadow of leaves protecting her from the elements.

Protecting her, like she was protecting her children, her children who may have stabbed their father.

Their father. Patrick.

Oh God, Patrick.

She pushed Ryan away, shaking her head. 'No, no. I – I can't.'

'But you love me, I know you do.'

'Of course I do, but not the way you want me to, not like I love Patrick.'

His handsome face registered hurt, then anger. 'He's not the man you think he is.'

'Everything okay here?'

They looked up to see the two detectives working Patrick's case watching them with raised eyebrows.

'We're fine,' Melissa said, a flush travelling up her body.

'Surprised to see you here,' Detective Powell said, taking in Melissa's flustered face with a bemused expression.

'We're friends,' Melissa said, Ryan still staring at her, not saying anything. 'Are you looking for me?' she asked the detectives in as normal a voice as she could muster.

'Actually, it's Mr Day we're looking for,' Detective Crawford said.

Melissa frowned but Ryan didn't look too surprised. Instead, he just gave a resigned sigh.

'Why do you need to talk to Ryan?' Melissa asked.

Detective Powell tilted her head. 'Just following some leads. What's all that?' She gestured to the broken cameras.

'Just some old junk,' Ryan said, kicking it under a bush.

'You both used to live here in the forest, didn't you?' Detective Crawford asked. 'I was checking the old records – quite a few call-outs to your cottage, in fact, Melissa. It must have been difficult, enduring your father's treatment of your mother?'

Melissa gave the detective a quizzical look. Why had he been checking her family's records?

'You came to question me, not Melissa,' Ryan said, his voice hard as he stalked past the two detectives towards his lodge. 'I have an appointment at nine-thirty so best do it now.'

Detective Powell went to say something but the other detective put a hand on his colleague's arm, shaking his head slightly.

'Haven't you questioned him enough?' Melissa asked.

'It's fine, Melissa, really,' Ryan said, without looking at her. 'Just go home.'

She glanced at the broken camera pieces. 'Give me a shout later, okay?'

He didn't say anything, just opened his door for the detectives. She walked away, feeling the police officers' eyes on her back.

Melissa spent the next few hours with Patrick; Rosemary and Bill offered to take Grace to the cinema while the twins were at school. She got the impression they needed the reprieve as much as Grace. As Melissa approached Patrick's bed, she felt guilt dart through her. Yes, she'd pushed Ryan away, but she couldn't ignore how she'd felt as he'd looked at her like that. How must that have looked to the police too?

Melissa clutched Patrick's hand. 'I love you, darling.'

He moaned slightly. Maybe he could hear her? She leaned in close to him. 'Patrick? Can you hear me? Just squeeze my hand if you can, or blink.'

She waited, but there was nothing. So she reached into her bag, pulling out the book Patrick had been reading. It was a self-help book about becoming the 'best person you can be'. Patrick loved books like that and was halfway through this one, studiously reading it every night in bed with his black-rimmed reading glasses on.

'I brought the book you've been reading,' she said to him now. 'Who knows, maybe I'll learn a little something myself,' she added with a laugh. 'You always tell me I should try these books. Well, now you have your way.'

As she read to him, she examined his face. He was so handsome, even like this. It reminded her of the way he looked the night she was brought to his house. He must have heard all the commotion and came downstairs in his pyjamas, his brown eyes registering alarm when he saw Melissa standing in his kitchen in her nightdress.

'Go back to sleep, darling,' Rosemary had said to him, pulling Melissa's trembling body close to her. 'We'll explain in the morning.'

He'd taken one last look at Melissa, smiling slightly, then he'd walked back upstairs.

The next morning, they had all sat around the kitchen table – Melissa and her mum, Patrick with his parents and sister. It was a Sunday morning and Rosemary had laid out a feast of a breakfast with pancakes and bacon, muffins and eggs. Melissa's mum barely ate, instead just stared out into the forest. Melissa didn't eat at first either but as she watched the Byatts go about their breakfast, tucking in, laughing and arguing, acting like it was just a normal Sunday morning in the Byatt household, she started joining in, Patrick catching her eye and smiling. After they'd eaten, Bill had explained that Melissa and her mum would be staying with them for a bit, 'until they get back on their feet'.

It was the start of the summer holidays and the weather was perfect that first week, so Melissa was able to immerse herself in hanging out in the garden with Patrick and his sister, sunbathing and listening to music, pretending she was just a normal girl from a normal family. She tried to ignore the hushed talks between Patrick's parents and her mother. The glimpses of her mother crying at the kitchen table.

Melissa felt tears slide down her face now, imagining what that young teenage girl would think about the fact that the boy she loved would be lying in a coma over twenty-five years later . . . a coma caused by one of their children.

Melissa's phone buzzed in her pocket. Melissa wiped a tear away and pulled it out to see it was the school. She put the phone to her ear. 'Hello?'

'Hello, Mrs Byatt? It's Miss Milton, Lewis's football coach. I'm afraid Lewis had a little outburst on the pitch. I wonder if you could pop by and pick him up? It would be good to have a quick chat too.'

Melissa pinched the bridge of her nose. 'Of course, I'll be right there.' She peered at the clock on the wall. It was only half an hour until the end of the school day. She might as well hang around and wait for Lilly too.

Melissa leaned over Patrick. 'I love you,' she whispered, giving him a kiss. 'Your mum and dad will be here in an hour or so.'

Then she headed out, dreading what she was going to discover when she got to school.

Chapter Twenty-Nine

Tuesday 23rd April, 2019
2.30 p.m.

As Melissa drove to the school from the hospital, her mind ran over what Lewis could have done. He'd been so good lately. Should it really come as a surprise, though? She'd had a few calls like this over the years.

It infuriated Patrick. 'Why can't the boy control himself?' he'd say. What Patrick didn't seem to realise was that Lewis was *just* like him. Though Patrick gave off a calm exterior to the world, he was quick to lose his temper, swearing and throwing hammers in frustration when he got something wrong with his DIY efforts, or the times when Melissa would hear him late at night, yanking paper from the printer and kicking the door in anger.

In fact, father and son had locked horns more lately as Lewis grew more confident. Like the time a few weeks ago when Grace spilt some of her juice on the rug Patrick had spent ages cleaning the day before. Patrick had shouted at Grace in frustration, and Lewis had jumped to his little sister's defence, telling his dad it was just a mistake.

It was only natural as boys became teenagers for them to clash with their fathers, so it didn't concern Melissa. She just wished

Patrick didn't think Lewis was the one who needed to control himself when Patrick could be just as bad sometimes. But it was pointless telling Patrick that; he was blind to his own faults, like his parents were blind to the wonderful Byatt gene having *any* possible imperfections.

The fact was, Lewis was under particular strain now; no wonder he had returned to his old ways. But the first day back – *really*? She felt a burst of anger, punching at the steering wheel. Couldn't these kids just give her a *break*? But as quickly as the anger came, the guilt flooded in.

It wasn't their fault. They were just kids having to contend with way too much.

She drew up in the school car park and got out of the car, marching towards the football field. Lewis was sitting on the bench with his coach while the other players stood in a huddle, watching him. As Melissa drew closer, she noticed a boy being attended to by another teacher, a bloody tissue to his nose. She recognised that boy as being Andrea Cooper's son, Carter.

'Great,' she whispered under her breath. Of all the boys it could have been, it *had* to be the son of the queen of Forest Grove, Andrea bloody Cooper.

The coach stood when she saw Melissa approach. She only lived in the next street and had done wonders for Lewis, spotting his sporting talent and nurturing it. When Lewis *did* have his outbursts, they were restricted to the classroom: on the sports field, whichever sport he chose to play, he was calm and focused.

Not today, though.

'Hi, Melissa,' the coach said with a sigh as Lewis avoided his mother's gaze, looking down at the ground with an expression of anguish.

'What happened?' she asked.

'Lewis lost his temper and lashed out at Carter over there,' the coach said, gesturing to the boy with the bloody nose.

'Was he provoked?' Melissa flinched. 'Sorry, that sounds bad.'

'No, fair question,' the coach replied. 'I'm afraid not, though. It literally came out of nowhere. Carter made a very good tackle, a tackle that was perfectly above board, and Lewis punched him.'

Melissa looked at Lewis, taking in a deep breath.

'I understand you've been through a lot,' the coach said softly. 'That's why I'm being a little more lenient on this occasion. Maybe it was a bit too soon for Lewis to come back after everything, though?'

Andrea marched over to them then, drawing Carter along after her. Melissa watched the boy, wondering again what he'd said about her at the New Year's Eve party.

'You are going to apologise,' Melissa said to Lewis in a harsh whisper.

'But Mum . . .'

'There's no excuse for this, Lewis.' She shoved him towards Carter. Up close, Melissa could see the boy's nose wasn't as bad as she'd expected, just a bit of blood clogging one of the nostrils.

Still, it wasn't good.

Lewis sighed, forcing himself to look at Carter. 'Sorry,' he mumbled.

'I think you may have broken Carter's *nose*, Lewis,' Andrea said, her eyes sliding over to Melissa. 'I'm going to have to take him to A & E. I have to confess, I'm very disappointed. I thought you two were friends?'

Lewis gave a bitter laugh. 'Yeah, right. No chance.'

Andrea's mouth dropped open.

'Lewis!' Melissa said. 'I'm so sorry, Andrea. Lewis and I will be having stern words when we get back.'

'I should hope so. Look at this,' Andrea said, gesturing to the blood on Carter's bright blue puffa jacket. 'This coat cost me a fortune. I'll need to buy him a new one now.'

Melissa suddenly got a flashback to the blood all over Patrick's top. She forced the memory away. 'Lewis will pay for a new coat too, won't you, Lewis? You can use the money you've been saving for new football boots.'

Lewis's nostrils flared. She dug him in the ribs with her elbow. 'Al*right*,' he said through gritted teeth.

Melissa looked at him in surprise. She didn't like his attitude one bit. Yes, she wasn't exactly a fan of Carter, nor his mother. But there was no excuse for any of this. They needed all the support they could get in this town at the moment and having Andrea Cooper as an enemy was not going to do them any favours.

'Fine,' Andrea said curtly. 'Honestly, this was *not* how I imagined my day going.'

'Like I said, I'm *so* sorry, Andrea. It's just with everything going on . . .' Melissa let her voice trail off.

'I understand, of course I do,' Andrea said, 'but let's face it, Melissa, it's not like this is *unusual* for Lewis. The boy clearly has a propensity for violence – probably all those computer games Carter tells me he plays. It's *got* to stop.'

Melissa clenched and unclenched her fists. She was so tempted to tell Andrea to shut the *hell* up. But the fact was, she had a point.

'Right, come on,' Andrea said to her son. 'Let's get you to the hospital.' She stormed off, her son in tow.

Melissa watched them, blinking back tears.

'I'm sorry, Mum,' Lewis said. 'I didn't mean to upset you, but he—'

'I don't want to hear your excuse.' She thanked his coach then strode back towards the car as Lewis jogged to keep up with her.

'But Mum,' he called after her, 'seriously, he was being bang out of order!'

Melissa continued walking until they got to the car park, which was already beginning to fill up with parents, most of them driving from their jobs in Ashbridge to pick younger kids up on the way home, others no doubt noticing the dark clouds looming above and threatening rain. She jumped into her car, Lewis getting in next to her. She planned to wait in the car until the last possible moment to go and meet Lilly. The last thing she wanted was to be standing in the school playground.

'Mum, if you just hear me out . . .'

She grabbed the steering wheel, staring ahead of her. 'Miss Milton said it was a legitimate tackle,' she said, trying to keep her voice calm. 'I don't want to hear any excuses.'

'But it wasn't about the tackle,' Lewis whined. 'It's about what Carter said when he got up close to me.'

She turned to her son. 'What? What did he say that made you nearly break his nose, Lewis?'

Lewis frowned, dropping his eyes from his mum's face and looking at his hands. 'He said you and Ryan have been having an affair. He called you a slut.'

Melissa's mouth dropped open. 'You're kidding? Where the hell did he hear that?'

Lewis shrugged. 'Just some rumours going around.'

'Well, it's not true, *obviously*. Little shit,' she muttered.

Lewis raised an eyebrow at her bad language.

'Not that it justified you nearly breaking his nose,' she added quickly. 'Little finger, maybe,' she added as an afterthought.

Lewis smiled and Melissa sighed. 'Look, Lewis, I just wish you didn't lash out like that. It doesn't *look* good with everything going on, do you understand?' she said meaningfully.

'I know,' Lewis said with a sigh. 'I'm sorry, Mum, really. I don't want you getting upset. That's the last thing I want.'

'Oh, darling, come here and give me a Lewis hug.'

He leaned in, giving his mum a hug as she stroked his hair, not caring that it was all sweaty.

My boy, she thought to herself. *My poor, poor boy.*

She felt a surge of protection rush through her. She *was* angry at Lewis for lashing out, but Carter had been out of order. How dare he call her a slut?

A thought suddenly occurred to her. Had someone been watching Ryan and Melissa that morning? Is *that* how the rumour had started? Ryan was convinced someone was trying to intimidate her. The posters. That lone figure following her. The vandalised wildlife cameras.

And now these rumours.

There was a knock on the window. Melissa sighed and turned to see it was Andrea's friend, Charlie Cane. She made a gesture for Melissa to open her window, so Melissa reluctantly buzzed it down.

'Hello, sweetie,' Charlie said.

Sweetie. They rarely talked, so Melissa wasn't sure what the *sweetie* meant.

'How are you?' she gushed. 'How's Patrick? I *heard* the twins were back at school,' she added, eyes sliding to Lewis, who was now looking at his phone. 'Rather surprised me!'

'Why surprised?'

'Oh my gosh, sorry,' she said, touching Melissa's arm lightly. 'It has nothing to do with me.' She lowered her voice. 'Andrea told me what happened,' she said with a grimace, flicking back her long, highlighted hair.

'I see the Forest Grove rumour mill is working well,' Melissa said sarcastically. Lewis smiled but didn't look up from his phone.

Charlie's face hardened slightly. 'I can lend you Kitty Fletcher's book on managing childhood anger issues? Of course, I've never had to use it for my two, but I got it as part of a Kitty Fletcher bundle on Amazon. It might come in handy for you?'

Melissa thought about telling her where to shove her book, but she didn't need to give all the mums something new to talk about.

'Sure,' she said. She went to close the window but Charlie put her hand over the top, her long gel nails glistening in the sun. 'We're all here if you need us, Melissa. It's clear you're finding it *tough.* Just know we have your back. Us mums need to stick together, don't we?'

Melissa closed her eyes, taking a deep breath.

Calm down, Melissa, think of the kids.

She opened her eyes and smiled. 'Thanks, Charlie.' Then she closed the window.

'Why d'you let her talk to you like that, Mum?' Lewis asked her.

'We don't want any more drama, do we?'

'You should have told her to stick that number where the sun don't shine.'

Melissa smiled. 'I did think about it, trust me.'

'But you didn't do it, did you?'

Melissa turned to him. 'That's because I *think* before I do anything stupid, Lewis. We need these people on our side.'

'Do we, though?'

'You don't understand the way Forest Grove works.'

'Yeah I do. People like her and Andrea Cooper are twats, that's how it works.'

'Lewis!'

'They are. Why should we always try to keep them happy?'

'It's hard to explain, Lewis. One day when you're a parent, you'll get it.'

'Maddy does alright and her mum doesn't put up with all them lot,' he said, jutting his chin towards Charlie, who was now chatting to some other mums, showing them her nails.

Melissa opened her mouth then closed it, unsure of what to say. He was right. Why did she put up with it?

She took a deep breath, staring at the school. 'Right, I'd better go and get Lilly. You stay here, okay?'

She jumped out and walked towards the school gates. Some of the parents who were there looked up, watching as she passed, some nodding at her. Melissa noticed Samantha Perks, the receptionist at her physiotherapy centre, standing alone as she checked her phone. She made a beeline for her. Samantha was a safe bet. She *hated* gossip and had sent Melissa a series of lovely texts since hearing what had happened with Patrick. Even better, she didn't get on with Andrea and her cronies after her daughter Caitlin had a run-in with Carter.

'Hey, you,' Samantha said when Melissa got to her. She gave Melissa a quick hug. 'How are you? How's Patrick?'

'We're okay, and Patrick's hanging in there.'

'You're so brave.'

'Everyone keeps saying that, but I don't feel it.'

'Well, you look it to me! Are the kids back at school, then?'

'Just the twins. They insisted.'

'Good, they need the distraction.' She bit her lip. 'I hope Lilly wasn't too upset about the part?'

'Why would she be upset about it?'

Samantha's expression faltered. 'Oh, of course you're right, the Baroness role is just as good!'

'Baroness?'

'Yes, that's the role Lilly got, right?'

'No, she got the lead.'

Samantha swallowed, looking embarrassed. 'I don't think so. Caitlin got the part of Maria von Trapp.'

Melissa blinked rapidly, confused. Maybe she'd misheard Lilly when she told her she got the part. But she was so sure Lilly said she'd got the role of Maria von Trapp!

Why would Lilly lie?

'God, I feel awful now,' Samantha said.

'No, no, it's fine, really,' Melissa said, peering towards the doors to the school. 'Honestly. It's the last thing on our minds. What great news for Caitlin, though!'

Samantha couldn't help but smile. 'Isn't it? You know how shy she is. But she adores acting.'

'Good on her, really. I'm delighted for you.'

'Thank you. I was a bit worried she might not have a chance, what with all that stuff with Carter Cooper a few months back.'

'Why would that stop Caitlin getting the part?'

Samantha sighed, peering towards where Andrea usually stood with Charlie and a couple of other mums. 'You know what Andrea's like, finger in every pie. I was worried she'd do something to jeopardise Caitlin's chances. Oh, here they are!'

Melissa followed her gaze to see pupils spilling out of the school. She quickly spotted Lilly, with Maddy and a couple of other friends. Lilly's face lit up when she saw Melissa and she skipped towards her, her caramel locks lifting in the air behind her. She really was quite beautiful. Charlie whispered something behind her hand to another mum as she watched Lilly give Melissa a hug.

'You came to walk me home,' Lilly said. 'How sweet!'

'She was probably already here for Lewis, Lils,' Maddy said in a low voice.

Lilly rolled her eyes. 'That boy needs to control his temper.'

'Carter needs to stop being a dick, more like,' Maddy said.

'Is Lewis here, then?' Lilly asked, looking around her.

'In the car. Do you want a lift home, Maddy?'

Maddy peered towards the forest, a furrow in her brow. 'That's okay, I'm going to Dad's tonight. Thanks, though.'

Melissa looked down at the magazine in her hand. 'Latest edition of *The Grovian*?' she asked.

'Yep, hot off the presses,' Maddy replied with a proud smile. She lifted the magazine to her pierced nostrils and breathed in the scent. 'Still has that just-printed smell, lush. Here, have a copy,' Maddy said, handing Melissa one.

Melissa smiled. Maddy and Grace were so alike. 'Thanks.'

Then the smile disappeared from her face. There was an ad for the book fair on the back page – an ad that used the exact same font and border as the posters Melissa had found in the forest. She looked at Maddy. Could she be responsible for the posters? But why on earth would she do that?

She thought back to the look of hate in Maddy's eyes as she'd glared at Patrick in that New Year's Eve photo. If Maddy was behind the posters, could the *I know* refer to something she knew about Patrick? But why use a picture of the whole family, why not just one of Patrick?

'I'll WhatsApp you later,' Maddy said to Lilly. She turned to Melissa. 'See ya.'

Melissa forced herself to smile. 'Bye, Maddy.'

She watched as Maddy headed in the direction of Ryan's lodge. No, she just couldn't imagine Maddy doing something like that. There would have to be a serious reason for her to. There *must* be another explanation.

Lilly linked her arm through her mother's as they walked towards the car park. She seemed to be in such a jovial mood, considering what had happened to Patrick. Other people seemed to notice it too, parents frowning as they took in Lilly's smile.

'Darling,' Melissa said carefully as they got to a quiet part of the path. 'You didn't tell me Caitlin Perks got the lead role in the play.'

She felt Lilly tense. 'Oh, didn't I?'

'No. In fact, I'm pretty sure you said *you* got the part of Maria von Trapp.'

Lilly shrugged. 'I might have told a little white lie. I just didn't want to add to all the sadness.'

Melissa made Lilly stop, looking her daughter in the eye. She was still smiling, but her smile looked brittle. 'But darling, the role of Baroness is just as fantastic. You didn't need to *lie*.'

'Just a little white lie,' Lilly said, waving at a friend. 'Honestly, Mum, it's no big deal. I just didn't want to have to give you more shitty news after everything with . . . with Dad.' A brief hint of pain appeared beneath her mask. 'Especially Nan and Grandad, they really had their hopes pinned on me getting the part. I didn't want to let them down.'

'That's very kind, Lils.' She stroked her daughter's soft face. 'But I'd prefer you to tell the truth.'

Lilly laughed. 'Oh, Mum, who cares? It's just a school play. Come on, let's go see my *naughty* brother.'

She strode off towards the car as Melissa followed. Behind her, she heard Charlie raise her voice. 'So *weird* the way Lilly Byatt is acting like she doesn't have a care in the world.'

'Kids can be like that though, Charlie,' the other mum with her said. 'Pretending like everything's okay when it isn't.'

'Well, I've always found Lilly Byatt a bit fake.'

Melissa's eyes widened. Charlie was calling *Lilly* fake, when she was the one who posted those godawful semi-clad pictures on Instagram?

No, she'd had enough of this.

She turned and marched up to Charlie, crossing her arms as she stood in front of her. 'What was that you just said about my daughter, Charlie?'

A flush spread up Charlie's heavily powdered cheeks. 'Well, I – she – it—'

'Spit it out,' Melissa said.

'Mum, *stop* it,' Lilly said, pulling at Melissa's arm, trying to drag her away. But Melissa really had had enough. Lewis was right, she shouldn't put up with people talking about her family like this. So what if it rocked the boat? She wasn't this fragile thing people kept going on about. The way the kids walked on eggshells around her, Lewis not wanting to upset her, Lilly not wanting to tell her the truth about the role in case it made Melissa worse.

She thought of what Daphne had said to her the day before. Yes, she was stronger than they all thought. Stronger than *she* thought, *especially* when it came to her children.

'No, Lilly. I want to hear what Charlie said.'

Charlie looked around her at her friends, who all looked as embarrassed as Lilly. Then she took a deep breath, jutting her chin up. 'I just think it's a bit strange, that's all. The way you're all acting like your husband isn't lying in hospital. I mean, come on, the twins being at school already?' she said, gesturing to Lilly's uniform. Lilly stood stock-still, looking like she wanted the ground to swallow her up. Other parents walked around them to get to their cars, some stopping to watch.

'It was their decision,' Melissa said, trying to keep her voice strong. 'And frankly, it has *nothing* to do with you.'

'Really?' Charlie said, putting her hand on her hip as she looked Melissa up and down. 'This is our village, Melissa. We have every right to be concerned about what happened last Thursday.'

'That's no excuse to have a go at my kids!'

Charlie's mouth dropped open. 'I did not have a go at your kids.'

'You called Lilly fake!'

'Mum!' Lilly whined. She shook her head in embarrassment as some of her friends walked past, whispering.

'That's more about your parenting, to be honest, Melissa,' Charlie snapped.

Melissa narrowed her eyes at Charlie. 'Excuse me?'

'I mean, look at Lewis with his temper,' Charlie said. 'Then Grace just walking off into the woods like that. And now Lilly, acting like all is right with the world. You have to wonder what goes on behind closed doors.'

'Charlie!' the mum with her said. 'I'm *so* sorry, Melissa.'

'How dare you?' Melissa said to Charlie. 'You're essentially kicking us when we're down. Nice one, Charlie. I didn't think you could get any more shallow, but this has just proved it,' Melissa spat, buoyed by the clear support she was getting from other mums. She took Lilly's hand. 'Come on, let's head home.'

'I'm not the one kissing my ex in the woods while my husband lies in hospital fighting for his life!' Charlie called out after her.

Melissa froze. People's eyes widened, some whispering behind their hands to each other. Melissa felt a sudden ball of fury whip up inside. She turned around and went to run up to Charlie, but then she caught sight of Maddy standing on the path, Lilly's distinctive phone in her hand.

'I just saw Mr Quinn, he said you left it in class,' Maddy said to Lilly in a trembling voice. 'I – I came back to give it to you.' She marched up to Lilly and shoved it into her hands, her cheeks red. Her eyes then slipped to Melissa. She'd clearly heard what Charlie had said about Melissa and her father.

'Maddy, it's just—' Melissa started. But Maddy ignored her, rushing towards the woods.

'Nice one, Charlie,' Melissa hissed. She went to run after Maddy, but Lilly held her back.

'Please, Mum, let's just go home.'

Melissa closed her eyes, then she nodded. 'Let's get out of here.'

Chapter Thirty

Tuesday 23rd April, 2019
9 p.m.

So that's it confirmed, then. Mum and Ryan are having an affair or whatever it is they've been up to. Mum sat us down when she got back from school, telling us the rumours going around the village weren't true. But I've learnt not to trust what people say lately, even Mum. Now she's gone to the hospital to see Dad, probably feeling like crap, and I don't know how I feel. Kinda sick, to be honest. Shouldn't it make me feel better, though? It proves all the stuff leading up to last Thursday . . . all the stuff that made me do what I did to Dad. And that *means what I did was right because it confirms I stopped something even worse happening.*

Still feel like crap, though, because it proves, yet again, what a lie we've all been living. We're a fake family. This whole village is FAKE. The motto makes me laugh:

Welcome to Forest Grove, Utopia of the Woods
Home to Strong Branches and Deep Roots

I googled utopia*: 'an imagined community or society that possesses highly desirable or nearly perfect qualities for its citizens'. I like the way* *it says 'nearly perfect'. A little hint of something big and something bad that stops a utopia from being 100% perfect; that stops Forest Grove from being 100% perfect.*

That stops my family from being 100% perfect.

We did a good job pretending, though, that's why everyone's so shocked about what happened with Dad and all this stuff about Mum and Ryan. Like the morning before I stabbed Dad, the way my parents were with each other. All smiley in the sun. Pretending like we're just a normal family. A happy family. A family that doesn't have any secrets or any lies.

It's like Maddy says, when things are too good to be true, they usually are. When things are really *too good to be true, then you have to watch your back and the backs of those you love.*

I catch my sister's eye. She looks scared. I give her a reassuring smile. I hope she sees the message in it: we're going to be okay. I'm going to make sure we'll all be okay.

So why does it all feel so wrong? Why do I feel like I'm spiralling down a rabbit hole?

Chapter Thirty-One

Forest Grove Facebook Chit Chat Group

Tuesday 23rd April, 2019
9.05 p.m.

Pauline Sharpe
Absolutely disgusted with the vandalisation of the cameras in the forest! Those cameras hold precious footage for the kids' wildlife project. My husband and I found two of them smashed up on the ground early this morning. Does anyone else know who owns them? Is it the council? How can I report it?

Belinda Bell
What in God's name is going on with Forest Grove lately? First the incident at the Byatts' house, now this?

Jackie Shillingford
Pauline, contact Ryan Day, the forest ranger. He owns them. He's not on Facebook but google him, he has a website with a number you can call.

Graham Cane
Or ask Melissa to ask him . . .

Rebecca Feine
What's that supposed to mean?

Belinda Bell
Didn't you hear about the fight between Graham's daughter and Melissa earlier? Supposedly, Melissa was seen kissing Ryan Day in the forest.

Rebecca Feine
Pure speculation. Charlie shouldn't have mentioned it. I was there picking the grandkids up and heard about it after.

Graham Cane
Well, Melissa was rather aggressive with her when she asked a very innocent question about the twins being back at school.

Belinda Bell
It is rather soon for them to have gone back . . .

Pauline Sharpe
Clearly too soon for Lewis. I heard he got into some trouble on the football pitch. Andrea Cooper, wasn't it your son who was the brunt of an unprovoked attack?

Andrea Cooper
I don't really want to comment on Facebook. All I'm saying is I've just come back from a very eventful trip to A & E.

Rebecca Feine
What happened?

Andrea Cooper
Put it this way, I won't be letting Carter anywhere near the Byatt children any more. That's all I'm going to say.

Andrew Blake
Didn't Lewis Byatt beat the crap out of Harvey Piper too a year back, Eamon Piper?

Eamon Piper
He did indeed . . . not right in the head, that kid.

Kitty Fletcher
What an awful thing to say, Eamon. Mental illness must not be mocked.

Rebecca Feine
Oh, for God's sake, he's just a kid. Kids get in fights, doesn't make them mentally ill. Anyway, didn't you get suspended from Forest Grove rugby team for hacking down Sandra's boy a few years ago, Graham Cane? And I very much doubt Melissa was aggressive with your daughter, sounds completely unlike her.

Graham Cane
Oh, come on, that was rugby! And I didn't get suspended, you daft woman. The Byatt boy is a different matter altogether, full of rage, that one. Always getting himself in trouble. Mark my words, it'll be him behind the vandalism, and you need to wonder where he got it from. My bets are on Melissa, the way she was with my girl earlier.

Peter Mileham

Come on, guys, this is all a bit unfair. Lewis is a good kid and Melissa doesn't have a bad bone in her body.

Jackie Shillingford

Agreed. Can we calm down with the public lynching, please? Andrea Cooper, the comments on this post are getting out of hand.

Belinda Bell

Nothing wrong with airing one's views, we're a free country. You can't blame me for wondering.

Melissa Byatt

No need to wonder any more, Belinda Bell. Feel free to ask away!

Andrew Blake

Well, this just got awkward . . .

Jackie Shillingford

Don't feed the trolls, Melissa. I've reported this post to Facebook. Andrea Cooper, please get on the case.

Daphne Peterson

Good luck with that, Jackie. I guarantee Scandrea Cooper is sitting at home with her seaweed-flavoured popcorn, enjoying all this.

Melissa Byatt

No, it's fine, really. So Graham Cane, Belinda Bell, Eamon Piper. I'm here, ready to take your punches.

Daphne Peterson

Interesting. It's gone verrrrry quiet all of a sudden . . .

Debbie Lampard
Oh, Melissa, sweetheart, ignore them.

Andrew Blake
Grabs popcorn, takes a seat

Belinda Bell
I was just stating some facts, that's all.

Daphne Peterson
Belinda Bell, you criticise someone's kid, you criticise them. Right, Melissa?

Belinda Bell
What's this got to do with you, Daphne?

Daphne Peterson
Just sticking up for a good friend.

Graham Cane
Even though she's been seen kissing your ex?

Andrew Blake
What?!

Melissa Byatt
Here are my FACTS:
Lewis has always been violent: Not true
Unprovoked attack: Not true
Behind the vandalism of cameras: Not true
Me kissing Ryan: EMPHATICALLY NOT TRUE

Andrea Cooper

I promised myself I'd keep out of this, but sorry, Melissa, it was an unprovoked attack on Carter! It was a fair tackle, the coach said it herself, the other boys too. Lewis was out of order. I feel sorry for the boy, I really do, but Patrick being in hospital is no excuse to lash out.

Melissa Byatt

Really, Andrea Cooper? Ask Carter what he said to Lewis before he tackled him.

Peter Mileham

Ladies, come on, let's take this off Facebook.

Melissa Byatt

No, Peter. People can say what they want about me, but when it comes to the kids, I'm not going to turn the other cheek, especially when it's on a public forum like this.

Rebecca Feine

Hear hear, Melissa!

Debbie Lampard

Absolutely! Down with the trolls.

Andrea Cooper

Comments closed, and any more comments like the one you made about me, Daphne Peterson, and you're out of this group.

Chapter Thirty-Two

Tuesday 23rd April, 2019
9.10 p.m.

Melissa stared at the Facebook page on her phone as she sat in the hospital with Patrick, instantly regretting her outburst. She wished she hadn't got embroiled in it all, but she just couldn't help herself. Maybe it was a way of dealing with the stress of having to sit the kids down earlier and deny that she was sleeping with their friend's father. They hadn't seemed convinced.

'See, this is where I need you, darling,' she said to Patrick, stroking his prone hand, the lights of the monitor beside him blinking in the semi-darkness. He hated social media, said it was too easy to lose control on it and give the wrong impression. If *he* had been awake, he'd have stopped her.

But he wasn't, was he?

She took a deep breath and leaned back in her chair, rubbing at her eyes. She wasn't sure how much longer she'd be able to stay awake. That didn't matter, though; she'd already decided she was going to stay the night, give Rosemary and Bill a break. It was about more than that, though. She wanted to be close to Patrick, *especially* with all those rumours swirling around about her and Ryan.

Patrick would hate it. He'd always had a thing about her and Ryan, convinced that her old friend had a crush on her.

There had been occasions too, after a few too many beers on Patrick's part, when he even accused her of reciprocating those feelings, coming out with all sorts of wild suggestions. The next day, though, he'd wake with a hangover and not bring it up again, so she'd just put it down to too much red wine. She shuddered to think how he'd react if he was awake now, hearing all the rumours.

And poor Maddy! The look on her face after she overheard what Charlie had said about Melissa and Ryan. Melissa felt bad now, having suspected that Maddy might be the one behind the posters. She was just a kid. She should text Daphne and Ryan, check on Maddy *and* make it clear she was annoyed about the rumours. Who knows, maybe Daphne would begin to think the rumours were true, despite all her cynicism about the Forest Grove grapevine.

She reached into her bag, noticing a poster was still inside. She thought she'd given them all to Ryan. She checked nobody was watching through the small glass window in the door, then took the poster out, staring at it.

I know.

I know what?

There was a knock on the door and she looked up to see Detective Crawford peering in through the window. Melissa quickly shoved the poster in her back pocket and beckoned the detective in, heart thumping.

'We come bearing good news,' Detective Crawford said as he strolled in with Detective Powell.

'I could do with some good news,' Melissa said.

'There's been an arrest.'

'Really? Who?' she asked, hoping to God it wasn't one of the kids – but then why would he say it was *good* news?

'Turns out there have been a number of burglaries in the surrounding towns and villages,' Detective Powell said, 'and we've tracked down the person responsible.' She sounded almost disappointed.

'Even better,' Detective Crawford said, eyes dancing, 'the gentleman in question has previously been in prison for aggravated burglary and assault. He stabbed his last victim in the stomach with one of their kitchen knives.'

Relief made Melissa's legs weak. She leaned over and put her head in her hands.

The kids were off the hook!

'Are you okay?' Detective Crawford asked, sitting down beside her while Detective Powell stayed where she was.

'Just *so* relieved we've found the person who did this.' Melissa looked up at the detective, tears in her eyes. 'I presume he's not someone we know?' she asked, just to make sure.

'Unlikely,' Detective Powell said.

'Is he in custody?' Melissa asked.

The detectives nodded.

'And he's been charged with Patrick's attack?'

'Not yet,' Detective Crawford admitted as he looked at Patrick. 'But we have him for the next twenty-four hours, and can apply for another twelve if he remains tight-lipped. We're pretty sure he'll crack. We know this has been incredibly difficult for you, Melissa,' he added, putting his hand on her shoulder. 'But we have the fucker, excuse my language.'

She couldn't help but laugh. 'Thank you. Thank you *so* much.'

'We just need your husband to wake now so he can confirm what happened,' the other detective said as she regarded Patrick with hooded eyes.

Melissa followed her gaze. The detective was right, of course. In the end, Patrick would be the one to tell the truth about what had happened, a truth Melissa dreaded hearing. She'd just have to cross that bridge when she came to it. But there were still a lot of questions that needed answering . . . and wounds that needed healing.

But it was good news. Finally, things felt like they were working out.

Melissa walked through the forest the next day, heading towards the Forest Grove Shopping Courtyard with Lewis and Grace to meet Lilly at the village's annual book fair. Though she'd considered not going, especially in light of the raffle Andrea was holding and the awkward Facebook argument the evening before, Melissa decided the kids deserved some normal time, especially now an arrest had been made. Not to mention Grace was *desperate* to go and Lilly had volunteered a while back to work the tills.

It was busy as they entered the courtyard. Several rows of bookshelves had been wheeled out into the centre and residents wandered around among them, checking the blurbs of over-priced tomes while discussing how chilly it had got after the glorious Easter weekend. Hanging above them all was a banner announcing the *Annual Forest Grove Book Fair 24–28 April* in looping letters the same colour as the school's gold-and-green uniforms.

Around the shelves were the courtyard's shops, all open and enjoying the increased trade the book fair always brought. There were only eight shops, all adhering to the same colour scheme as the village's houses: muted greens and browns to mix in with the forest. Daphne had painted the exterior of her shop a bright emerald blue, though, and conveniently kept forgetting to book a decorator to paint it back after being told off.

The idea was that everything a resident should need was covered in the courtyard, from essentials such as a small library (Grace's favourite) and doctors' surgery, the tiny chemist's and quaint Forest Foods organic store. There was also the Into The Woods beauty salon (Lilly's favourite), the Neck of the Woods pub (Patrick's old favourite) and a gorgeous bakery (Lewis's favourite). There wasn't a newsagent ('We don't want to encourage use of paper' was how Jackie put it) or a sweet shop.

On a wooden table nearby, Lilly took payments from people, eliciting a rare smile from Belinda Bell. Melissa grimaced. Belinda was one of the people she'd had a go at on Facebook the night before. Next to her was Graham Cane, Charlie's dad.

A wind whipped through the late-afternoon air. Melissa wrapped her arms around herself, feeling the coldness seep into her bones as Lewis and Grace strolled over to see Lilly, leaving her alone. She noticed people watching her, some whispering. People she would usually expect to come and talk to her kept their distance.

Maybe she really *had* taken it too far this time by confronting Charlie then having a go on that Facebook post?

'Bloody freezing, isn't it?' a voice said. Melissa turned to see Daphne beside her.

'It sure is,' Melissa said. 'I texted you last night.'

'Oh yeah, sorry, I went to bed early.' Daphne put her hand on Melissa's arm. 'Don't worry about those stupid rumours, by the way, I don't believe all that shit about you and Ryan.'

Melissa sighed with relief. 'You shouldn't, it's all rubbish.'

'I believe you.' Daphne raised an eyebrow as she picked up Kitty Fletcher's book, *Raising Children the Kitty Fletcher Way*. On the front was a pair of hands formed from trees, 'nurturing' several children of different ages. Daphne most certainly *wasn't* a follower of Kitty's ways, the irony of which often made Melissa laugh, as Maddy wasn't as into her smartphone as other kids her age, even preferring to produce a physical copy of the school paper rather than an online version, like the village newsletter.

'Paper isn't killing the environment,' she'd say. 'Electronics are.'

Daphne picked up a book, looking at the price. 'You'll need to take a mortgage out for some of these books. I mean, seriously, have you seen how much they are? I thought we were raising money to extend the school library, not build a new one.'

Melissa laughed. 'Oh, come on, it's for a good cause.'

'Not the only cause either.' Daphne jutted her chin towards the raffle stall Andrea was setting up, face all flustered and stressed. Melissa followed her gaze to see Adrian hanging a photo of Patrick above the stall.

'Jesus,' Melissa whispered. 'I told them to make it about the Duchenne muscular dystrophy charity.'

'Oh, it just adds to the drama for them all. Look at all of them,' Daphne said, taking a sip from a bottle of water as she observed the residents wandering around and chatting, some of them peering over at Melissa. 'I bet all of them are whispering about you and the kids. Like leeches around a sick person.'

Melissa followed her gaze. *Were* they still whispering about them?

'I'm surprised she's here,' Daphne said, gesturing towards Charlie, who was talking to her father. 'I thought she couldn't read.'

Melissa shook her head, unable to stop herself smiling. 'You're terrible, Daphne.'

'And that's why you love me.'

Ellie Mileham walked by then, catching sight of Melissa and smiling. Melissa smiled back, pleased at least Daphne and Ellie were still talking to her. 'Hello, how are you?' Ellie asked her, kissing her on both cheeks as she gave Daphne a quick smile. 'I heard they made an arrest?'

'Did they?' Daphne asked.

'Yes,' Melissa said. 'It's such a relief.'

'For all of us,' Ellie said with a sigh. 'I wonder if that's why they're here, to reassure people.'

'Who are here?' Melissa asked.

'The detectives,' she replied, gesturing to Detective Campbell and Detective Powell, who were watching from a tree nearby. Melissa looked at them in surprise. What on earth were *they* doing there?

'That's strange,' Daphne murmured. 'Not exactly the sort of place for the police to come.'

'Probably trying to reassure us with their presence.' Ellie picked up a book, flicking through it. 'Gosh. A tenner for this. Really? I can get this on Amazon for half the price.'

'It's all for a good cause, Ellie,' Daphne said in a sarcastic voice.

Ellie laughed. 'Isn't everything around here? Did you hear about the tickets for *The Sound of Music*? They've added a fiver to the price just because some charity is attached to it.'

'Oh God, speaking of which,' Daphne said, 'did you hear about Caitlin Perks?'

'I did,' Ellie said with a sigh.

'What about her?' Melissa asked her friends.

'She's really ill,' Ellie replied. 'Samantha said she had an encounter with some giant hogweed this morning, even rubbed it in her eyes, which is horrible – it can cause blindness, poor thing.'

Melissa put her hand to her mouth. 'My God, poor Caitlin. Poor *Samantha*,' she added, thinking of her work colleague. 'They seemed fine yesterday.'

'How on earth did she do that?' Daphne asked. 'Everyone knows to steer clear of those plants.'

Ellie shrugged. 'No idea, I just got a rushed text from Samantha this morning. Looks like they'll be searching for a new lead for the play now, though,' she added. 'Right, better go and check the kids haven't pilfered any books.' She gave them a wink and strolled away.

'I can't believe that about poor Caitlin,' Melissa said, making a mental note to text Samantha later to check how her daughter was.

Daphne looked towards the entrance of the courtyard, raising an eyebrow. 'Well, well, well, that's not a sight you see often.'

Melissa followed her gaze to see Ryan standing with Maddy as she browsed through some books. He looked uncomfortable in his cargo pants and Forestry Commission T-shirt. His blue eyes scoured the crowds then stopped at Melissa and Daphne, a slight blush working up his cheeks.

Had he heard about the rumours too?

'Better go and say hello,' Daphne said. She gave Melissa a quick smile then walked towards her ex-husband as people watched her.

Grace approached Melissa then, with a huge pile of books balancing in her small arms. 'Can I have all these, Mum?' she asked.

'I think that's a tad above the ten pounds you saved, sweetheart,' Melissa replied.

'That's some bookworm you have there,' Detective Crawford said. He picked up the top book on Grace's pile. '*Britain's Taboo Crimes.* Interesting.'

'Grace, come on,' Melissa said, giving an embarrassed laugh. 'You know that's too old for you. Put it back.'

Grace's shoulders slumped and she walked off.

'Good reading taste, that one,' Detective Crawford quipped.

'She doesn't usually read stuff like that,' Melissa said quickly. 'I'm surprised to see you two here.'

'Police officers read too,' Detective Powell remarked.

'Speak for yourself,' Detective Crawford joked. 'No, we're here because we wanted to come and tell you ourselves.'

'Tell me what?'

'We released the suspect,' Detective Powell said, watching Melissa's face for a reaction. 'Turns out he has a watertight alibi for Thursday afternoon.'

Melissa tried to control her breathing. This was *not* good. 'Oh. That's a shame. I mean, we wouldn't want you to have the wrong man, but I thought that meant the case was all sewn up.'

'Sadly not,' Detective Crawford said with a sigh. 'We'll just have to—'

There was the sound of shouting from nearby.

Melissa turned to see Graham Cane staggering back against a tree, Lewis standing over him with his hand raised as Ryan tried to pull him back.

Melissa ran over.

'Take control of your child,' Graham shouted at Melissa when he saw her, eyes laced with fear. There was a red mark on his face and Melissa realised with horror it must have been Lewis who put that mark there.

The two detectives strode over, Detective Powell helping Graham up. 'He hit me!' Graham said to the detective. 'Did you see it? The boy actually *hit* me.'

'More a slap, from what I saw,' Ryan said, though his brow was knitted as he looked at Lewis.

'Dad?' Charlie said, running over as people turned to look. 'What on earth happened?'

'He hit me!' Graham repeated, pointing a shaking finger at Lewis.

Charlie's nostrils flared and she shook her head in disgust.

'Lewis!' Melissa said, grabbing her son by the shoulders and looking into his eyes. Lilly watched on, biting her lip, as Grace hugged her books to her chest, blue eyes wide. 'Lewis, what *happened*?' Melissa asked.

His eyes filled with tears. 'I had to, Mum. He was talking bullshit about our family.'

'Yeah, Mum, he was saying stuff about Joel too,' Lilly said.

'Shut *up*,' Lewis hissed at her.

'Joel?' Melissa turned to Graham. 'What did you say about Joel?'

'Does it matter what was said?' Charlie spat as she turned to her father, who suddenly looked his age, frail and scared. 'You can't just go around hitting a sixty-three-year-old man. Honestly, I think this just proves *everything* I said yesterday.'

'Oh, shut up, you silly bitch,' Lilly said.

Melissa's mouth dropped open as the two detectives looked on in surprise.

'Are you going to do something about this?' Belinda Bell said to the detectives.

Detective Powell sighed, getting out her notepad.

'What exactly happened, Mr Cane?' she asked.

'It all happened so quickly,' Graham said, putting his hand to his head. 'I was chatting to Belinda here and then the boy grabbed my shoulder and made me turn around. He started shouting in my face, I shouted back because I will *not* have a child tell me what to do, and then wham, he hit me.'

'Slapped,' Ryan said again under his breath.

Detective Powell gave him a sharp look.

Melissa closed her eyes, pinching the bridge of her nose as Grace grasped her hand. This was awful.

'I'm sorry, Mum,' Lewis said in a low, miserable voice. 'But seriously, what he said about you was out of order.'

'What did you say?' Ryan asked, crossing his arms as he looked down at Graham.

'I was only telling the truth, about you and Melissa having an affair,' Graham said to Ryan in a shaky voice. 'It isn't just Melissa either. The Byatts aren't as perfect as everyone thinks, you know,' he added, looking at the detectives. People around him murmured in disapproval. 'Oh, come on,' Graham said to them all. 'You all know what I mean, all those lock-ins at the Neck of the Woods when the Sharpes ran it, the tinkle of keys being thrown into a bowl. We all know Patrick has slept with half the women in this village.'

Melissa's stomach dropped. '*What?*'

Chapter Thirty-Three

Forest Grove Facebook Chit Chat Group

Wednesday 24th April, 2019
5.40 p.m.

Eamon Piper
Just wanted to post in support of Graham Cane. Hope you're holding up, old friend.

Rebecca Feine
Support? I can't believe the outrageous things Graham said about the Byatts. He deserved that slap!

Kitty Fletcher
What happened?

Pauline Sharpe
Weren't you at the book fair earlier?

Kitty Fletcher
I was at a lecture. Is Graham okay?

Eamon Piper

Lewis Byatt punched him. He's down the station now, being questioned by the police.

Rebecca Feine

Ryan said it was a slap. And can I just say, the Neck of the Woods is a very different kind of establishment now Bobby and I have taken over.

Belinda Bell

Slapped or punched, it was out of order. That child is feral.

Kitty Fletcher

What did Graham say to Lewis? And what has the pub got to do with it all?

Rebecca Feine

I don't want to repeat it here.

Belinda Bell

If you won't, I will: the Byatts have been swingers for years. Remember the old pub lock-ins back in the day? Well, now we all know what went on in there.

Ellie Mileham

What an utterly ridiculous thing to say!

Graham Cane

It most certainly isn't. It's been known by a few of us old crew for a while now.

Eamon Piper

He's back! Can't keep a Forest Grovian down. Tell more, please, Graham.

Kitty Fletcher

The Byatts are Forest Grovians too, you know. Can we be mindful of the fact that anyone can be reading these posts, please, including those poor vulnerable Byatt children? This is a police matter now so be careful what you say.

Graham Cane

Kitty is quite right, this is a police matter, which means I can't talk about what happened last night. However, what I will say is that this proves there's more to the Byatt family than the perfect picture they present to the world. And with the news that the police have released the man they arrested for the attack on Patrick, I think a lot of interesting developments will take place. Maybe this wasn't a break-in at all? Maybe the police will look at the family more.

Andrew Blake

And Ryan Day too. I've always wondered about him and Melissa.

Debbie Lampard

How exactly do you know all this, Graham? I can't imagine Melissa being unfaithful. And I certainly can't imagine Ryan Day being involved in any pub lock-ins and swinger parties, Andrew!

Graham Cane

Who said 'unfaithful'? Didn't I say they were swingers? All consensual.

Pauline Sharpe
My mum and dad used to run the pub back then. Debbie is right. Melissa was never involved in all that, nor Ryan.

Rebecca Feine
What about Patrick?

Pauline Sharpe
No comment. All I'll say is that those of us who went to school with Patrick will remember what he was like.

Ellie Mileham
What's that supposed to mean, Pauline? Peter used to stay on at those pub lock-ins with Patrick. It was just lads having a few drinks.

Graham Cane
You keep telling yourself that, love.

Rebecca Feine
Oh, come on, Ellie, surely you know what Patrick's like? I'm not saying Peter's the same but Patrick has always had a way with the ladies. The whole village knows it. I've always felt so sorry for Melissa.

Belinda Bell
Finally, it's out in the open! Been desperate to say something.

Kitty Fletcher
God, the poor man has only been in a coma a week and the rumours all start to come out.

Pauline Sharpe

I'm surprised it took that long for all the old skeletons to come out of the closet. Everyone knows what Patrick's like. He's a lovely guy but he really can't keep his pecker in his pants.

Andrew Blake

Yep, Andrea Cooper will tell you. She's been shagging Patrick for years.

Andrea Cooper

How dare you! Count this post deleted, and any more speculation like this will lead to an instant dismissal from the group.

Chapter Thirty-Four

Wednesday 24th April, 2019
5.45 p.m.

Melissa sat across from the two detectives with Lewis, trying to wrap her head around what Lewis had overheard Graham saying. Patrick *did* enjoy a few extra drinks with his friends when the Neck of the Woods used to have lock-ins many years back. Patrick would come in late at night, smelling of red wine and cigarette smoke. Melissa used to get annoyed with him, especially when she was pregnant with the twins and utterly exhausted. But that didn't mean Patrick was a womaniser!

The thing was, Patrick *had* had his indiscretions in the past. But that was years ago, when they were both eighteen. She'd caught him kissing Andrea Cooper behind the forest centre once after a Christmas party. When she confronted him, Patrick told her it was just a one-off. But a few weeks later she found a love letter from Andrea making it clear things *had* continued. When she confronted Patrick yet again, he told her he couldn't help himself. Melissa hadn't yet let him sleep with her, despite them being together for four years by then. They did everything else, but she was adamant she wanted to wait before losing her virginity, despite the pressure he put on her.

But Patrick made her wonder if she'd taken it too far. She'd deprived him of the satisfaction all young men needed . . . that was what he'd told her, anyway. So she eventually forgave him for his affair with Andrea and gave *in* to him too, finally losing her virginity to him on a cold autumnal night in the forest, sticks and dying leaves digging into her skin as he thrust into her.

Since then, there had been no more instances.

Or so she had believed, anyway.

Could he really have been cheating on her all this time? Oh God, this was all too much to take.

She pressed her hands between her legs, doing her best to suppress the tears.

'Tea? Coffee?' Detective Crawford asked. They were sitting in a small, cold interview room at Ashbridge Police Station. Lewis had been arrested and hauled in for slapping Graham Cane. But Melissa got the feeling it was more than that. The detectives needed an excuse to dig around in the family's secrets and lies, which had just been spilled out at the book fair.

'Nothing for me, thanks,' Melissa said, making her voice strong. She looked at Lewis. He'd gone into himself and was just staring down at his hands on the table.

'Right, Lewis,' Detective Crawford said, peering towards the whirring recording device, 'let's start with what you overheard Graham Cane saying.'

Melissa looked at Lewis, interested to know the details too, no matter how much it hurt.

Lewis peered at his mum, and the look of despair in his eyes made her feel terrible. 'Come on, darling,' she said softly. 'Answer the question.'

Lewis leaned back in his chair, putting his hands behind his head and taking a deep breath. 'I overheard him mentioning Mum's name so I stopped and listened.' His eyes flickered to his mother, then away again.

'What exactly was he saying, Lewis?'

Lewis put his head in his hands.

'Lewis?' the detective pushed.

'He said any family that's the product of Frank and Ruby Quail must be dodgy,' he mumbled, 'and that there's more to the Byatt family than the perfect picture we present to the world.'

A vein in Melissa's neck pulsed. *Bloody busybody.*

'What else did he say?' Detective Crawford pushed, his eyes on Lewis's.

'That Mum and Dad were involved in these, like, weird parties at the pub,' Lewis mumbled. 'That's it.'

'Do you know anything about these parties, Mrs Byatt?' the detective asked her.

'No!' Melissa replied. 'As far as I know, they were just pub lock-ins, a chance for people to have a few extra drinks, nothing more. And I never went to one, I promise.'

'But Patrick did?' Detective Powell asked.

Melissa sighed. 'He did, yes, but they were innocent, just a few extra drinks, like I said.'

Detective Powell tilted her head. 'How can you be so sure if you weren't there?'

Melissa didn't know how to answer that. She *wasn't* sure. She raked her shaky fingers through her hair.

Lewis watched her, his hands curling into fists.

'Mrs Byatt,' Detective Crawford started, 'has your—'

'You're here to question me, right?' Lewis suddenly shouted. 'Just leave my mum alone!'

'Lewis!' Melissa said, looking at him in surprise.

'Quite a temper you have on you there, Lewis,' Detective Crawford observed.

'Do you often lose your temper?' Detective Powell asked. 'I believe there have been a number of incidents where you've lashed out over the years?' She looked at her notepad, flicking through it before she got to a particular page. 'Sixteen separate occasions at school, I believe, resulting in two suspensions and a boy's broken nose.' She looked up at Lewis, raising an eyebrow.

'Yeah, there's been some stuff,' Lewis said.

'It's something we've been addressing,' Melissa added quickly. 'He's come on leaps and bounds. Not one incident the past year, right, Lewis?'

'Until football practice yesterday,' Detective Powell said.

Shit, Melissa thought. So they knew about that too. Who was telling them all this?

'Lewis has been through a lot the past few days,' Melissa said, knowing the excuse sounded weak.

'Yes,' Detective Crawford said. 'Of course we understand that traumatic events can trigger children with a condition like Lewis's.'

'Condition?' Melissa echoed.

Detective Crawford nodded his head. 'I believe you were diagnosed with an anxiety disorder when you were just six, Lewis?'

Melissa glanced between the two detectives, confused. 'What are you talking about?'

Detective Crawford looked at his notes. 'On the sixth of June 2010, your husband attended a meeting with Lewis's primary school teacher, Mrs Swan, about Lewis's violent outbursts during class time. During that meeting, your husband informed Mrs Swan that Lewis had been diagnosed with an anxiety condition during child therapy sessions the twins had with local therapist Kitty Fletcher.'

Melissa's mouth dropped open. She had had no idea about this.

She turned to Lewis. 'Is this true? *Did* Dad take you and Lilly to see Kitty Fletcher?'

Lewis's brow furrowed. 'I vaguely remember Dad took me and Lils there to play sometimes after pre-school. I didn't realise it was, like, *therapy*.'

Melissa looked down at the table, trying to gather her thoughts. There had been a year, after Joel died, when Patrick would leave work early to pick the twins up from pre-school two days a week. Sure, he'd sometimes come back late with the twins, taking them to the park or the café in the forest centre, sometimes to his parents' . . . or that was what he had told her, anyway.

Could he have been taking them to see a therapist once a week? Why not tell her, though? She wouldn't have minded. The kids *had* been through the trauma of losing their brother, after all.

Is that where it had all gone wrong? Lost in her grief for her first child, she hadn't even noticed the twins falling apart. Like when Lewis started wetting the bed and Lilly took to having full-on 'legs in the air' tantrums. And then little Grace, growing in her belly at the most awful time of Melissa's life. The twins were so young, their little minds still forming. Something that traumatic in their childhood could easily have repercussions later on in life. Even worse that their own mother wouldn't truly be there, mentally and emotionally, afterwards.

Could those repercussions be dark enough to make one of them one day lash out at their dad? How long before the police began to wonder the same – especially about Lewis, after that outburst?

She suddenly got a flash of Jacob Simms. She'd seen the photos of his injuries from his beating that last day in St Fiacre's, the sickening bruises and broken bones.

The thought of Lewis going through the same sent a knell of horror through her.

'You look shocked, Melissa,' Detective Crawford said.

'I – I wasn't aware Patrick had taken the kids to see a therapist.'

'Strange,' Detective Powell observed, 'for a husband not to tell his wife something like that.'

'Not really,' Lewis said. 'Mum was a mess after Joel died.'

Melissa felt her skin go clammy. She *had* been a mess . . . and Lewis, not quite four years old, had noticed it.

'So what happens now?' she said quickly, desperate to change the subject. 'Can you take into account what Lewis has been through the past week? What we've all been through?'

Detective Crawford took in a deep breath, watching Lewis. Then he nodded. 'On this occasion, you're released with no charge, Lewis.' Melissa looked up at the ceiling in relief as Lewis slumped back in his chair, closing his eyes. Detective Powell shook her head slightly, clearly disapproving. Detective Crawford leaned across the table towards Lewis, locking eyes with him. 'But any more incidents and I can tell you now, I will *not* be so lenient. Understood?'

Lewis nodded. 'Yes, sir.'

'Right,' Detective Crawford said, standing up with his colleague, 'we have work to do. Your father's attacker is still on the loose, after all,' he said, eyeing them both. 'I'm sure you're both keen for us to find that attacker . . . aren't you?'

'Of course,' Melissa said. She tried to sound calm, but the note of suspicion in his voice made her whole body quake with fear.

Chapter Thirty-Five

Wednesday 24th April, 2019
7.45 p.m.

Melissa stared at Patrick's face later, trying to uncover the secrets and lies there as she took in his familiar straight nose and high cheekbones. 'There was no one after Andrea, was there?'

She watched the monitor for a response.

Nothing.

'Knock, knock,' a voice said. Melissa quickly pulled away from Patrick to see Joel's old nurse, Debbie, peering in. 'I heard you were here. Mind if I join you?'

'Sure.'

Debbie walked in, face darkening for a moment as she looked at Patrick. 'How's he doing?'

'They said he's doing much better.' Melissa's voice caught in her throat, tears flooding her eyes as she thought of the shattered pieces of their family that he'd wake up to.

'Oh, love,' Debbie said, taking the seat next to Melissa and hugging her. 'He's strong, he'll pull through. And you're strong too,' she added, smiling sympathetically at Melissa.

'Really?' Melissa said. 'I honestly don't think so, Debbie.'

Another nurse rolled a trolley in then, stopping short when she saw Debbie. 'Oh, hello, you. I thought your shift had ended?'

'Just popping by to see one of my favourite people,' Debbie said. 'In fact, why don't you go get yourself a cuppa and I'll sort Patrick out. As long as Melissa doesn't mind?'

Melissa shook her head, looking at Patrick.

'You sure?' the nurse asked Debbie. 'Shouldn't you be going home now?'

'To what? Gary will be at work,' she said, referring to her husband. 'Go, before I change my mind.'

The nurse quickly left and Debbie pulled the trolley over, setting about washing Patrick: gently cleaning his legs and arms while Melissa used wipes to clean his hands. Melissa remembered sitting with Patrick as he had a bath a week before the incident. She remembered the way he had pulled her in with him, even though she had her pyjamas on. Had he been thinking of another woman when he did that?

She felt tears burn the back of her eyes.

'He has nice nails,' Debbie observed. Melissa wondered if she'd heard what Graham had said.

'Yes,' Melissa replied, 'he likes to keep them tip-top. He even lets Lilly and Grace give him manicures sometimes.'

Debbie laughed. 'I bet the girls love that.'

Melissa smiled at the memory. 'They adore it. They even set up a nail salon a few weeks ago. Grace made name badges and Lilly adopted the persona of "Sharon the Nail Technician". She even did the cockney accent. Lewis was *so* embarrassed.'

Melissa felt another sob building in her chest.

'Cry if you want to,' Debbie said. 'You've been through so much. I remember the way you were with Joel, so strong for him, so controlled. It's good to let go sometimes, though.'

'I *did* let go eventually, you know that.'

Debbie gently lifted Patrick's arm to wipe his armpit, the sight of his dark hairs and the outline of his ribs making Melissa's heart ache. 'It happens to all full-time carers of kids like Joel,' Debbie said. 'There comes a time when you simply hit a wall of exhaustion and frustration. Yours came a lot later than others'.'

'But if I'd held myself together and not given up being Joel's full-time carer,' Melissa said, 'I'd have been there when Joel died. And if I'd been there . . .'

'Now you listen to me,' Debbie said, grasping Melissa's hand and looking her in the eye. 'That was *completely* out of your control. Just so happens you were taking a well-deserved break, no connection.'

'But I was weak. I should have just sucked it up. I wasn't the only mum in the world having to deal with a child with special needs. I shouldn't have taken that break, it wasn't fair on Patrick.'

'It shouldn't all be on the mother,' Debbie said, face tense. 'You *needed* that time. You had the twins to deal with too, remember? It's not like Patrick took time off to help before he took the sabbatical.'

As Joel's condition had deteriorated, placing more demands on Melissa, it had got too much for her. So Patrick suggested he take a year's sabbatical from work so he could take over being Joel's carer and Melissa could retrain as a physio, something she'd wanted to do for a while after being inspired by the physios who helped Joel.

'I used to watch you and wonder how you did it,' Debbie continued. 'In fact, I remember when Rosemary told me you were having twins. Such a shock!'

Melissa thought back to that time. She hadn't even wanted another baby; her hands were full enough as it was with Joel. But Patrick had been desperate for another child – a *normal* child, as he'd put it once. In the end, she'd relented, then when she saw the ultrasound and heard those two heartbeats, her heart had sunk.

How would she cope looking after newborn twins while caring for Joel too?

Well, she didn't cope, did she? Patrick had to take over.

Debbie dipped her finger in some cream and rubbed it roughly over Patrick's elbows. 'It's not fair that you, of all people, are going through this now.'

'Tragedy seems to have a habit of following me, doesn't it? Not just Joel, but my mum too. Maybe it's the Quail genes.'

Debbie gave her a sharp look. 'Don't be ridiculous. Life is just a roller coaster of shit and we need to hold on tight as we ride it. Anyway, all that stuff about genes is rubbish. Honestly, the number of times I heard Rosemary and Bill bang on about the perfect Byatt bloodline, I could have slapped them. Irony is, it's the Byatts who are weak,' Debbie said. 'Patrick's always been a bit . . . fragile.'

'What do you mean?'

'Oh, you know, he struggled when Joel was born, didn't he? You had to do everything for the boy.'

'So did Patrick when he took his year off.'

Debbie raised an eyebrow. 'He left Joel with his parents most of the time while you were working.'

'He didn't!'

'He did, darling,' Debbie said. 'I used to see him drop Joel off before heading off to the pub.'

Melissa's face flushed with embarrassment.

'Look,' Debbie said with a sigh, 'I heard about what Graham Cane said.'

'Is it true?' Melissa asked, hardly wanting to know the truth.

Debbie looked at Patrick. 'Come and chat outside for a moment, will you?'

Melissa followed her gaze. She was right. What if Patrick could hear them? She followed Debbie outside and they sat on two seats in the corridor.

'I can't say for sure, but there have always been rumours,' Debbie said in a low voice. 'And I did always wonder what he was getting up to when he dropped Joel off at Rosemary and Bill's.'

Melissa put her head in her hands. It wasn't just humiliation in front of the whole village too: clearly, most of them knew but no one had said anything to her!

'He's just like his father,' Debbie said.

Melissa frowned. 'What do you mean?'

'Bill always had an eye for the ladies. Why do you think he was so keen to help your mother? Ruby was beautiful, just like you are.'

Melissa looked at her in surprise. 'Bill and – and my mum?'

'I'm not saying anything happened between them,' Debbie said quickly. 'Your mother wasn't like that. She was just supplying him with herbs for the dogs, that's how they got chatting. But for Bill, it was more than that. Everyone knows he has a wandering eye.'

'Jesus, I had no idea. I feel like a bloody fool.'

Debbie laughed. 'You're no fool, sweetheart. You've just had a bit more of a sheltered life than the rest of us, living in the forest all those years. And then the Byatts come along,' she said bitterly, 'with their shiny hair and shiny promises, taking you out of that horrible situation you were in out of the goodness of their hearts. Or so it seemed, anyway.'

'What do you mean?'

Debbie leaned towards her. 'I *mean*, Bill was about to run as councillor at the time, just like Patrick has been. Of course, helping the destitute wasn't going to do his popularity ratings any harm, was it? I think your mum clocked on to that pretty early on, that was why she didn't want to continue living there after a while.'

Melissa blinked. It made sense, really, how Bill and Rosemary had paraded Melissa around the village. And yet when it was clear their precious son was falling for the feral girl from the woods, they suddenly started to cool towards her, and it had been the same ever since.

'It did make me laugh when I heard Patrick had got you pregnant,' Debbie said. 'Quail genes sullying the wonderful Byatt bloodline.' She frowned. 'And the way they acted when Joel was diagnosed, like it proved their theory.'

Melissa clenched her fists. 'Or *disproved* it. Joel was the very best of the Quails and the Byatts.'

Debbie nodded, grabbing Melissa's hand. 'Absolutely, Melissa, absolutely. Oh, that boy, we all loved him so much.' Her eyes filled with tears. 'When I saw him lying there, so cold, *too* cold, I—' She shook her head. 'Anyway, that's in the past. I just wish I could have done more.'

'You did! You were his guardian angel.'

Debbie's face darkened. 'Hardly.'

Melissa leaned back in her chair, blinking back tears. 'I don't think I can deal with all this, Debbie.'

'You hold on tight, young lady. You'll get through this, just like you did when Joel died.'

'I didn't get through that,' Melissa said. 'You *know* I didn't.'

Debbie gave her a sympathetic look. 'You're still here, aren't you?'

'And look what a mess I'm in,' Melissa said, gesturing to Patrick's ward as she gave a bitter laugh.

'This isn't your fault!' Debbie said.

'Isn't it?'

Debbie's brow creased. 'I won't let you beat yourself up about all this. Whatever happened to Patrick, you can bet your bottom dollar he brought it on himself.'

'What's that supposed to mean?'

'Hello!' a voice called out. They both looked up to see Rosemary walking down the corridor. A frown crossed her face when she noticed Debbie with Melissa. 'Oh, you're here.'

Melissa looked between the two women. They used to be friends, once. But then something had pulled them apart.

'Right,' Debbie said, standing up. 'I'll get out of your hair now. The nurses will take the trolley away.' She gave Melissa a quick hug then walked down the corridor, giving her former friend a tight smile as she passed her.

Melissa and Rosemary walked back into the ward, taking a seat on either side of Patrick as Rosemary looked down at her son with loving eyes.

'Can I ask you something, Rosemary?' Melissa asked her mother-in-law.

'Of course.'

Melissa took a deep breath. 'Was Patrick cheating on me?'

Rosemary's eyes widened. 'For God's sake, how can you say that in here, in front of him! Honestly, Melissa.'

Melissa pursed her lips.

'Go and get a coffee,' Rosemary said sharply as she took her son's hand. 'Looks like you need it.'

Rosemary hadn't said no, had she? Melissa stood up and walked out.

Melissa leaned back in her chair that evening, staring out at the dark forest in the silence of Rosemary and Bill's living room. Outside, the trees whispered to her, leaves rustling. She took another slug of cider, enjoying the way it made her mind whir. She'd been sitting here like this for the past few hours, the kids asleep upstairs, Bill now at the hospital with Rosemary. She'd made the kids dinner, sat wordlessly as they all ate. She saw them exchanging worried glances, but she didn't have the energy to talk to them about everything that had unfolded. She needed to puzzle it out in her head.

Her husband had cheated on her. It was clear now. Their marriage was a sham.

She looked up at the ceiling, wondering if the kids knew too. That would explain their attitude to their father lately. Everything they held dear – the stability of their family – was starting to fall apart around their ears and their father was to blame.

But would that be enough to make one of them *stab* Patrick?

Maybe the seed had been sown before that, way before that, in the weeks and months after Joel died. Patrick had taken them to see Kitty: another deception on his part. But clearly, he had been concerned about something.

Melissa picked up her phone. There were some notifications on there but not as many as she'd been used to the past few days. People she'd usually expect to send a text of support or concern were notable by their silence. Daphne had messaged, though . . . and Ryan. Just a quick message. *Hope Lewis is ok. Here if you need me. R.*

She opened the phone's browser and did a search for Kitty Fletcher's website. She found it quickly, a light and airy design with a photo of Kitty on the home page holding her famous book. She clicked on the *Contact Me* page before she might regret it and typed a quick message into the form, along with her contact details.

Kitty, it's Melissa Byatt. I'd love to meet to get your advice at your earliest convenience. Do let me know how I can arrange this. Kind regards, Melissa

'There, sent,' she said to herself. Kitty would probably be bound by client–therapist privileges so wouldn't be able to say much. But at least she could try.

She placed her phone to the side and looked back down at Rosemary and Bill's photo albums, which she'd got out earlier. She'd reached for them in desperation, studying each photo of her, Patrick and the kids to try to decipher when it all went wrong.

'My darlings,' she whispered, tracing her finger over the last photo she'd been looking at. It was her last photo of Joel, from Christmastime, his freckled face all cheery and happy, his frail body wrapped up in a warm festive jumper. Patrick was next to him, wearing an elf hat, and the twins were in the background, ripping open one of their dozens of Christmas presents.

She peered at the clock. Nearly midnight: time for bed. She stood up, stretching, and padded to the kitchen, placing her empty glass by the sink.

Then she paused.

Was that someone out in the garden?

She leaned closer as she looked out of the window, heart thumping.

Yes, there was definitely someone out there, on the edge of the forest, just watching the house.

She opened the back door and stepped out, Sandy and the two other Labradors bounding out into the darkness. The motion-activated outdoor lamp switched on, flooding the back garden with light.

The figure had disappeared.

Melissa wrapped her arms around herself. She looked at the dregs of her cider. She'd had three glasses. Maybe she was just seeing things? The last batch of cider she'd made and given to Rosemary and Bill *was* pretty potent. She checked the back door was locked anyway after the three dogs came in, all the other doors too, then walked upstairs.

She got ready, slightly unsteady on her feet, and slipped into bed. But once again, she couldn't sleep. She was so used to Patrick being beside her as she slept she simply couldn't shrug off his absence. Now her mind was filled with his infidelities, his lies and his secrets.

She felt like she had all those years ago after Joel died. She'd overheard her mum once describing tough times as like trying to walk up a muddy hill, doing your best to make progress, but you just kept slipping down, grabbing clumps of mud as you did and making it even harder until, in the end, you just slid down, down, down.

Melissa eventually fell asleep with the image of her mother in her mind, her long white hair and kind blue eyes.

But then she was woken again by the sound of breaking glass.

'Mum?' Grace's scared voice called out. 'What was that?'

Melissa jumped out of bed and ran on to the landing to see Grace watching her from the open door of the attic room above, bleary-eyed. As always, Lilly was sleeping through it, able to switch her mind off just like that.

Lewis shoved past his sister. 'I'll go and check,' he said.

Melissa put her hand on his chest, stopping him. 'No, wait here.'

'But Mum . . .'

'I can handle it, Lewis. I'm not as fragile as you think.'

She turned on the landing light and walked tentatively downstairs towards Rosemary and Bill's moonlit kitchen, catching glimpses of jagged glass on the floor. She quickly turned the lights on, letting out a gasp when she saw that the back window had been smashed to smithereens. Lying on the floor among the glass was a brick. She stepped around the glass and picked it up, realising with horror that it was wrapped in one of the posters she'd found the week before. She turned it around in her shaking hands, noticing that Lewis's face in the family photograph was circled in red pen with the words DAD KILLER scrawled above it.

Chapter Thirty-Six

Thursday 25th April, 2019
1.24 a.m.

It feels like it's the night of what happened with Dad again in Nan and Grandad's attic room, cowering under the covers, terrified. Except I'm even more scared now. At least I knew the monster under the bed last week. It was me.

But now there's a new monster and Mum's scared, really scared.

Why would someone do *that, throw a brick through Nan and Grandad's window?*

There was something wrapped around it but Mum wouldn't let us see it. She shouted at us to go back in our room so we did, because seriously, when she raises her voice like that, we know she means business. It must have been bad, though, really bad, because why'd she not show us? Plus, she was all trembly and quiet.

I remember another time she was like this, after Joel died. Going into herself. Or down a tunnel. That was how Kitty Fletcher described it. Alice falling down that rabbit hole.

She didn't call the police. Instead, she called Grandad at the hospital, talking to him in this weird monotone voice. When he turned up with Tommy Mileham, Mum went with them into the living room and they all shut the door, whispering whispering whispering. That's when I saw the photo albums on the kitchen table, and all those old photos of Joel. Mum must have been looking at them before she went to bed. It's like she's trying to fit the pieces of the puzzle together, and she's close, so close.

Will she finally slot all the pieces into place? And what then?

The three of us talked into the night last night. We talked about finally telling Mum everything. It's crazy in a way: after putting soooo much energy and sleepless nights into not telling her, we were beginning to wonder whether we should.

But then we decided not to, for the same reasons we kept it from her in the first place: we might lose one parent; we don't want to lose another.

But maybe she'll figure it out before we get the chance?

Or, even worse, maybe Dad will wake up?

Chapter Thirty-Seven

Thursday 25th April, 2019
10.30 a.m.

Melissa nursed the tea Rosemary had made her and stared out at the forest, mesmerised by the rhythmic swaying of the branches outside. Upstairs, the faint sound of music trickled out of the attic room, the kids hiding away up there.

Melissa had phoned Bill as soon as she'd seen the brick. She'd thought about calling the police, but those two words had sent a dagger through her heart – DAD KILLER. She shuddered. No, it was bad enough with the police grilling Lewis after the incident with Graham. She didn't need their suspicions raised by this too. So she deduced it was time to get help. She simply couldn't deal with this alone any more. She could feel herself losing it, just as she had after Joel died. The brick through the window was the last straw.

Bill arrived twenty minutes later, with Tommy Mileham, who'd brought a board to place over the broken window. Melissa had ushered Bill into the living room and shown him what had been wrapped around the brick. When Bill saw the words scrawled above Lewis's photo, he hadn't said a word about it. Instead, he took the poster off and placed it in his pocket.

'We'll talk later,' he'd said to Melissa. '*Properly*.'

She'd agreed, wordlessly. They didn't even discuss calling the police. Melissa just let Bill and Tommy take over, like her mother had many years ago.

'You okay, sweetheart?' Rosemary said now, smiling sympathetically at Melissa as she sat beside her at the kitchen table. They'd agreed to give Patrick some rest from their constant vigils for an hour or two.

'Yep. Just tired.'

Bill took the seat across from Melissa and took a long slug of his coffee. 'So,' he said, placing his cup down, 'are you going to tell us what's going on?'

Melissa blinked.

'We know you're keeping stuff from us, Melissa,' Rosemary said. 'You shouldn't bottle things up. You did that after Joel died, and look what happened then.' She leaned forward, placing her hand over Melissa's. 'Let us help you this time, for the kids' sakes.'

They were right. It had gone too far. She took a deep breath. 'I've been keeping quite a few things from you,' she admitted.

'Not to worry,' Bill said. 'You're going to tell us now, aren't you?'

She nodded and, over the next twenty minutes, she told Bill and Rosemary everything. They listened intently and quietly, every now and again exchanging surprised or worried looks. This was their son Melissa was talking about, after all; their beloved grandchildren too.

When Melissa finished, Bill peered up at the ceiling towards the attic room where the children were, as Rosemary chewed at her lip, lost in thought.

'You're sure, absolutely sure, they're not covering for someone?' Bill asked for the second time.

'Yes, pretty sure,' Melissa said with a sigh. 'Call it mother's instinct.'

'I can't believe the kids would do this to their dad,' Rosemary said. 'How awful for that to be the last thing my poor Patrick knew before he collapsed.'

'There's nothing else you're keeping from us, is there, Melissa?' Bill asked, his brown eyes boring deep into hers. 'No reason you know of for one of the kids wanting to hurt their dad?'

Melissa shook her head. 'Nothing. I promise. Other than all those rumours about him cheating.'

Rosemary took in a sharp breath. 'There are rumours about you cheating too.'

'Which are *false*,' Melissa said.

'Even if the rumours are true, a child wouldn't attempt to murder their father over something like that,' Bill said firmly.

Rosemary looked out towards the swaying trees, tears falling down her cheeks. 'It must be a mix-up. Misinformation. Lewis would have got himself into a state – you know how he is.'

'Lewis?' Melissa asked. 'How can we be so sure it's Lewis?'

'Oh, come on, Melissa,' Rosemary said gently. 'We love our grandson with all our hearts. But he has a temper on him. And the police obviously have their suspicions. Other people too, judging by this,' she said, gesturing towards the crumpled poster Bill had pulled out, the words DAD KILLER scrawled above Lewis's face.

'Now, Rosemary, we mustn't jump to conclusions,' Bill warned.

'If I could go back, I'd just tell the police right from the start,' Melissa admitted.

'No!' Bill said. 'You did absolutely the right thing, not telling the police.'

Rosemary nodded. 'Yes, I think Bill's right. Keep it here in Forest Grove. That's always the best way.'

'What's the point of all this anyway?' Melissa said with a bitter laugh. 'Patrick will wake soon and tell all. Maybe if *you* guys talk to the kids, they might confess. If we know the whole picture, we can get ahead of the game before Patrick says something.'

As she said that, she realised how awful it sounded, the implication that they should try to convince Patrick to lie. There had been a voice deep inside her, building and building lately. A voice that said if one of the kids *had* hurt their own dad, then surely they needed to be punished. Or, more importantly, surely they needed to be looked after by professionals? But that voice was trampled down by her maternal instinct to protect . . . and also by her trust in her children. For them to do something like this, they must have had a reason, a bloody good one too.

'Patrick will protect those kids, no matter what,' Rosemary said.

'Just like you've been doing,' Bill added, taking Melissa's hands in his large ones as he smiled sadly at her. 'You've done the right thing, exactly what Patrick would do too, I'm sure of it. He'd want to deal with it within the family, get whoever did this the help they need. I'm proud of you, Melissa. Maybe you have some of that Byatt spirit in you, after all. Right, Rosemary?'

Rosemary nodded, reluctantly so it seemed to Melissa. 'It must have been such a burden for you the past week.'

Melissa felt tears prick at her eyes. 'It's been awful.'

'Well, you're not alone now, sweetheart,' Rosemary said, stroking her arm. 'You have us. You're right, I can talk to the kids, maybe get the truth out of them?'

'No,' Bill said, shaking his head. 'They've been through enough. No more grilling the kids, understand?'

The two women nodded.

'You can trust us to get this sorted,' Bill said to Melissa. 'Just like we did before.'

Melissa thought back to that time, how they'd found her hiding in the cavity of the big oak tree, shaking and terrified, waiting for her mum to come and find her. And then an hour later, when Bill and the other man returned from going back out to confront her father.

'Your father's not going to hurt you or your mother any more,' Bill said to Melissa, eyes deep in hers.

'Why? Is he okay?' Melissa had asked. Despite all Melissa had seen her father do to her mother, despite how he'd treated *her*, he was still her father.

'He'll be fine,' Tommy said, stroking the bruises on his knuckles. 'He just got a piece of his own medicine, that's all. Like Bill said, he won't be bothering you again.'

'You're not to mention any of this, you hear me?' Bill said to Melissa. 'We've sorted it.'

As he said that, she'd seen a face watching from outside.

Ryan.

'Melissa?' Bill had said firmly. She turned back towards him. 'Do you understand?'

She looked towards the window again, but Ryan was gone.

'Melissa?' Rosemary said. 'Are you listening?'

'Yes,' she'd said, nodding slowly. 'I understand.'

The next time she saw her father was two weeks later at the shopping courtyard. His face was heavily bruised and he was walking on crutches. He'd clearly taken a beating, and Melissa was conflicted. Half of her saw the justice of it. But she also felt a pinch of sadness. She'd seen glimpses of some good in her dad, like the way he'd orchestrate complicated games in the woods for her. Or at Christmas, when he'd come home dressed as Santa, bringing a mountain of presents. When she compared him to Ryan's dad, he really didn't seem so bad sometimes.

When she heard he'd left Forest Grove for good, she barely noticed. Life at Rosemary and Bill's seemed like a breeze compared to her old life. No more arguments in the night, no more enduring her mum's screams. No more rotting floorboards and freezing-cold bathroom; no more thin stews for dinner and holes in her shoes. Everything was better at Rosemary and Bill's. Even now Melissa knew they'd just been using her as a way to gain popularity in the village, it was still the best home Melissa had ever known and they were kind to her, if a little cold sometimes. Fact was, Melissa was a teenager with a new bedroom that had a TV and a wardrobe full of clothes, and there was Patrick too, gorgeous, charming Patrick, who seemed just as delighted with her presence in his house as she was.

Then her mum died and the honeymoon period came to an abrupt end.

'Melissa?' Bill said now, pulling her away from her memories. 'We sorted it before, we can sort it again, understand?'

Melissa nodded, just as she'd nodded at that very same kitchen table over twenty-five years ago. 'Yes, I understand.'

Melissa spent the next day with the kids while Rosemary and Bill stayed with Patrick. She'd pulled the twins back out of school. It *had* been too soon and, with all the rumours circulating, she felt it best to keep them away. While Patrick seemed reasonably stable, it was a good chance to spend some proper time with the kids a week after he was attacked . . . plus, with it becoming increasingly clear Patrick had cheated on her, she felt she needed to process it before she saw him again.

Bill came back from the hospital sometimes, but he seemed even more preoccupied than usual. Melissa tried not to think about why; all she knew was that he was 'handling' stuff. Part of her wondered if she was relinquishing too much control, but the truth was she was *exhausted* with the burden of it being solely on her shoulders. It felt good to spend a day with the kids, walking through the forest with the three dogs, wordless, quiet.

As they strolled in the forest, they bumped into Samantha Perks. Melissa felt awful. She hadn't even texted her to check in on her daughter, Caitlin, after her run-in with some giant hogweed. Samantha was walking her dog alone, lost in thought.

'Oh, hello,' she said, smoothing her fair hair back when she noticed Melissa and the kids. She frowned as she took in Lilly. Lilly raised her hand awkwardly and Samantha smiled tightly at her.

'I heard about what happened to Caitlin,' Melissa said. 'How is she?'

'Not great,' Samantha replied, her eyes still on Lilly. 'We think her sight will be okay, though.'

'Oh, thank God,' Melissa said, putting her hand to her chest.

'It'll take a while for her skin to recover.'

'Skin?'

'Yes, huge boils and burns to the skin. Horrible to see. Make sure you keep away from the stuff, Lilly,' Samantha said, eyes narrowing as she looked at Lilly.

Melissa looked between them both. What was that all about?

'Did Caitlin find the giant hogweed in the forest?' Grace asked, fascinated as she always was with anything like that.

'Oh no,' Samantha replied. 'Caitlin wouldn't go around picking flowers willy-nilly. They were left outside our house as part of a congratulations bouquet for getting the part, we presumed. It was an anonymous bouquet, just one word on the card: *Congratulations*.'

Lilly flicked at some invisible dust on her sleeve.

'What, someone put the weed in a *bouquet*?' Melissa asked Samantha, alarmed.

'That's my theory,' Samantha said, eyes still drilling into Lilly. 'But Caitlin's a lovely girl, as you know. She refuses to believe someone would be so *mean*.'

Melissa looked between Samantha and Lilly again. Did Samantha think *Lilly* had done it?

Why not? a little voice asked in Melissa's head. After all, she had thought she knew her children. She had thought they couldn't be capable of anything truly horrendous. But recent events had changed that.

'I'd better go,' Samantha said, turning away. But then she paused, turning back to Lilly. 'Congratulations on getting the lead, Lilly,' she said, her voice brittle. 'You be careful if you get any flowers delivered, won't you, now?' she added with a hard stare. Then she stalked off through the woods.

Melissa turned to Lilly. 'You got the lead role? Why didn't you say?'

Lilly shrugged. 'I only found out yesterday.'

'But you could have told us last night,' Melissa replied. 'Or this morning.'

Lilly let out a dramatic sigh. 'It's no big deal, Mum.'

'I presume you messaged Caitlin?' Melissa asked Lilly. 'Just to check she's okay.'

Lilly peered down at the ground. 'Why would I?'

'Well, it's just polite. You got the part after she got ill.'

'She's not my friend.'

'But imagine how you'd feel in her shoes?' Melissa said.

Lilly shrugged.

Melissa shook her head as she looked at Lilly. What had made her so cold?

And then a thought occurred to her: if Lilly *had* given Caitlin the giant hogweed to scupper her role, what else was she capable of?

When they got back from their walk, Melissa's phone buzzed. She picked it up, noticing it was an email from Kitty Fletcher.

Hello Melissa,

It's good to hear from you. I was very much hoping you'd get in contact. Probably too short notice but I have a cancellation this evening at 6pm? If you're free, please call me or email me back at your earliest convenience. Alternatively, I have a free spot next Tuesday at three.

Best wishes,
Kitty Fletcher
PhD, MBACP (Snr. Accred.) UKCP

Melissa looked at the clock. It was half five. She quickly typed back *I'll be there at six.*

As she finished typing, the front door opened and Bill walked in, looking exhausted.

'Bill, can you watch the kids for a bit?' she asked him. 'I just need to pop out for an hour or so.'

'Sure.'

After checking on the kids, she headed outside. Kitty lived on Birch Road, which curled around the inner circle, where Bill and Rosemary lived. As she approached the road, Melissa could see the therapist's house had been extended with the addition of a big area that jutted out from the second floor, a large window overlooking the treetops of the forest. Clearly Kitty's books were making her money.

There was a sign on the door announcing: *Kitty Fletcher, Therapist*. Usually you'd expect people would want some discretion when it came to visiting a therapist, but Kitty was seen as a Forest Grovian and thus *different* from other therapists. If you *had* to see a therapist, then Kitty was the one to go to, and that was absolutely fine by the village residents. It looked like Patrick had bought into that, considering he'd booked secret therapy sessions with Kitty for the children.

Melissa buzzed on the door, taking in the metal owl wall ornament that watched her from nearby. There was the sound of movement behind the door then Kitty answered it, the woody scent of her perfume drifting out of the door.

'Oh, Melissa, I'm so pleased you're here.'

It was strange being face to face with her. She was probably the village's most famous resident, with her occasional appearances on national TV to promote her books.

'Hi, Kitty,' Melissa said.

Kitty opened the door and Melissa stepped in, looking around her. It was a busy hallway, with a hanger full of different-coloured coats and a bench cluttered with books.

'Come up to my rooms,' Kitty said, steering Melissa towards the stairs. 'I'd usually charge but, due to the peculiarity of your situation, I'm willing to waive my fee.'

'Thanks,' Melissa said uncertainly. She hadn't really seen it as a *therapy* session. She just needed to get some answers about Patrick's visit here. Melissa followed Kitty into a side room upstairs. When Kitty opened the door, she realised it led into her extension, a vast room with great views of the forest from above. Colourful beanbags lay on the floor, a patchwork chaise longue at one end, two huge comfy sofas at the other, facing each other. There was a wooden desk too, with a chair on either side. Around the room were photos of Kitty at various events and a large bookcase was filled with her books.

'Choose where to sit,' Kitty said. 'Wherever you feel most comfortable.'

Melissa decided to sit in front of the desk. She wanted something solid between the two of them, as if it might protect her from Kitty's probing green eyes.

Kitty sat across from her, tilting her head, her face shimmering with some kind of light, translucent powder. Her lips were pearly pink and her scarf was the colour of the ocean, her dress too. Melissa suspected she was about sixty, but she looked younger.

'You look so like your mother,' Kitty commented.

'You knew my mum?'

Kitty's face darkened slightly, then she shrugged. 'Oh, just from around town back in the day. Now, how are you doing?'

Melissa shifted around in the chair, trying to make herself comfortable. 'It's been tough, I can't lie.'

'Of course, of course. Your mind feels rather busy, I expect. All jumbled up, like the back room of a charity shop.'

Melissa couldn't help but smile at the image. 'Something like that. Look, Kitty, I'm not actually here for a session. Just a chat.'

'That's a very healthy way of putting it, Melissa.'

Melissa sighed. No point contradicting her. 'I just wanted to ask about when we brought the twins here.'

Melissa had thought carefully on the walk over to Kitty's about how to approach this meeting. There was a chance Patrick hadn't told Kitty he'd kept the sessions from Melissa. He was astute enough to know a therapist would disapprove if they knew. So if Melissa could make out she was in on the sessions, she might get a bit more out of this conversation.

'That was a very long time ago,' Kitty said.

So that was it confirmed, then, Melissa thought. *The children were brought here by Patrick.*

'I know. About ten or eleven years ago, right?' Melissa said, trying to make sure her voice didn't betray her emotions. 'I was busy with my studies so Patrick was always the one to bring them.'

Kitty nodded. 'Yes, that's right.'

'Yes. So, how many sessions was it again?'

'Let me think. Maybe ten? Why are you asking about those sessions, Melissa?' She smiled, her eyes quizzical.

'Well, the kids are struggling.'

Kitty nodded. 'Understandable.'

'And I thought we might be able to glean something from the sessions you had with them back then to help with coping strategies now.'

'I see. As I always tell my clients, children are changeable creatures, evolving *all* the time, drawing on influences from all around them as they do and being moulded by those influences too.' She sighed. 'The children I saw back then may be very different from the ones they are now, Melissa. So the best way forward would be for us to book in some new sessions for the twins, for your youngest too.' She picked up the iPad in front of her, which struck Melissa as rather ironic, considering her teaching about the need for all people to reduce screen time. 'I have some availability next week?' she suggested.

'No, I don't want to book them in.'

Kitty placed her iPad down and leaned back in her chair, putting her fingers together as she examined Melissa's face. 'Looking back on past sessions will *not* help, Melissa. I want to make that very clear.'

'But your diagnoses will still stand? People don't suddenly change.'

'They can, especially with FPP.'

'FPP?'

'Fantasy-prone personality, the condition Lilly struggled with then?'

Melissa nodded but, inside, thoughts were raging through her mind as she recalled the encounter with Caitlin's mother earlier.

Kitty peered over at a pink beanbag. 'You know, I still distinctly remember Lilly sitting on that beanbag, talking away to her big brother like he was still there.'

'You mean Joel?'

Kitty nodded. 'I know you and Patrick were concerned for her but it's actually rather normal after a traumatic event, especially when the mother isn't present to support the child.' She turned back to Melissa, her smile sickly sweet.

Melissa gave her a look. 'I was having to contend with my own grief.'

'Of course! I'm not judging,' Kitty said quickly. 'In fact, when I heard, I was rather pleased. You know how I advocate getting away and immersing oneself in the forest.'

Melissa rubbed at her temples as she thought back to that time. It had been raining relentlessly and Joel's funeral had only been a week before. Patrick had had to attend an important meeting so Melissa was alone with the twins, who were themselves suffering from their brother's loss. They both had an epic tantrum, then the lid of Melissa's blender had flown off, splattering her with smoothie mixture. She'd slid down the kitchen wall, bits of strawberry and banana splashing over a top Patrick had helped Joel get her for her birthday, and she'd just cried and cried.

When Lewis then shoved Lilly and she started crying, Melissa couldn't face it. She just walked out of the back door and headed to the forest, walking and walking with no idea where she was heading until she got to her parents' old cottage, which she now owned. She'd let herself in and curled up on her mother's bed.

Melissa stood up, grabbing her bag. 'I really must get back to the kids.'

Kitty frowned slightly then stood with her. 'I'm here to talk if you need me, Melissa.'

At a hundred pounds a pop, Melissa thought. 'No, it's fine, really. Thank you.'

'Patrick would approve, if that's what you're worried about,' Kitty said. 'He knows himself how beneficial therapy can be, having been here as a boy. He was one of my first clients when I moved to Forest Grove, you know,' she said proudly. 'And look how well he turned out.'

Melissa frowned. 'Patrick came to you as a boy?'

Kitty's smile faltered. 'Oh. I thought you knew?'

'I didn't. What did he come for?'

'Client–therapist confidentiality!' Kitty said with a nervous laugh.

'Would it explain his infidelity? I presume you've heard,' Melissa said, unable to keep the bitterness from her voice.

Kitty's face closed up. 'I'm afraid I can't discuss other patients' issues. Let me see you out.'

Melissa sighed and followed her out. As she walked back to Bill and Rosemary's, she thought about what Kitty had told her. Why would Patrick have come to see her as a child? She tried to think of anything that would have made his parents take their son to Kitty, but nothing came to mind. Sure, he was a bit promiscuous for a boy his age but, beyond that, he seemed normal enough.

But then her kids seemed normal too, didn't they? And yet *still* one of them had stabbed their father.

As Melissa left Birch Road and approached Rosemary and Bill's house, she noticed a police car outside.

What now?

She took a deep breath and let herself in to find Detective Crawford in the kitchen with Bill and Rosemary. The kids were outside in the garden, darting worried glances towards the detective.

'Ah good, you're back,' Detective Crawford said when Melissa walked in.

'Is everything okay?' Melissa asked, her pulse throbbing in her throat as Bill put his hand on Rosemary's shoulder.

'We were just wondering if you'd come down to the station for a chat,' the detective said.

Melissa looked at him in shock. 'Me? Now?'

'Yes, you . . . and right now,' Detective Crawford said firmly.

Chapter Thirty-Eight

Forest Grove Facebook Chit Chat Group

Friday 26th April, 2019
6.45 p.m.

Andrew Blake
News just in: I just saw Melissa Byatt being led to a police car by one of the detectives in charge of the case.

Belinda Bell
Well, I can't say I'm surprised.

Rebecca Feine
Talk about jumping to conclusions! They might just be updating her on the case!

Belinda Bell
Can't they just do this at Bill and Rosemary's? No, something fishy is going on and, frankly, it doesn't surprise me.

Debbie Lampard
What a horrible thing to say, Belinda Bell!

Rebecca Feine

Yes, so much for innocence before being proven guilty.

Andrew Blake

How can we not when it comes to a Quail? My old ma always said the Quails were trouble.

Pauline Sharpe

Melissa's dad certainly was. Ruby wasn't trouble, though, she was just different, with all her herbal remedies. I used to think she was so cool when I saw her around town. It's such a shame what happened to her.

Belinda Bell

Oh yes, I remember Melissa's dad. He was a big handsome fella, very charming.

Rebecca Feine

Charming?! Are you forgetting all the bruises we'd see on Ruby's face when she popped into town to do the shopping?

Eamon Piper

It wasn't just Ruby either. Melissa would often turn up to school with bruises. It was well known around the village.

Daphne Peterson

And nobody intervened? God, this place!

Kitty Fletcher

It was different back then, Daphne. People tended to just leave it to the family to sort it out. And Ruby did eventually leave him when she went to live with the Byatts.

Belinda Bell

Fat lot of good that did her!

Jackie Shillingford

Don't say that, they were good for her! Sometimes people just don't want to be helped in the end.

Kitty Fletcher

Jackie is, sadly, quite right there.

Belinda Bell

Exactly! Why stay with Frank so long anyway? They say certain women are drawn to men like that. Maybe Ruby passed that penchant for violent men down to her daughter. Kitty, you'll know. Do women who are drawn to violent men tend to have daughters who are also attracted to violent men?

Kitty Fletcher

I won't comment on this out of professional courtesy. But there are some interesting studies into the genetic legacy of trauma.

Daphne Peterson

So you're saying it's the women's genes that draw them to violent men? Essentially, it's the women's fault? What utter garbage.

Rebecca Feine

Yes, garbage! And by saying that, you're implying that Patrick was a domestic abuser because Melissa must be attracted to violent men . . . and that's the reason she's just been seen with the police, because they think she stabbed him in – what? Self-defence? This is getting ridiculous!

Belinda Bell

It's just one theory . . .

Peter Mileham

How dare you imply that about Patrick, Belinda! I've known him for years, and there is no way he would hurt a hair on anyone's head. Am pretty disgusted by these posts, especially by you, Belinda. I thought better of you!

Rebecca Feine

What did I say to you all?! Be careful what you post.

Belinda Bell

Oh, Andrea will delete this thread soon anyway, mark my words.

Debbie Lampard

Where IS Andrea? I bloody hope she does delete it! This family does not deserve to be raked over the coals like this.

Rebecca Feine

Andrea Cooper, help, please! This post needs to be deleted.

Graham Cane

Looks like Andrea's done a runner!

Chapter Thirty-Nine

Friday 26th April, 2019
7.15 p.m.

'This feels rather formal,' Melissa said, looking around her at the small police room Detective Crawford had brought her to, a different one from the room she'd been in with Lewis just a couple of days before. Detective Powell walked in and Melissa's stomach sank even more.

'This *is* formal, Mrs Byatt,' Detective Powell said as she took a seat across from her. 'This is an investigation into the attempted murder of your husband.'

Murder.

The word whirred in Melissa's head, drilling painfully into the core of it. She tried to hold herself together. 'Have there been developments?'

'We just wanted to go over a few things,' Detective Crawford replied vaguely.

'Like this poster,' Detective Powell said, opening a folder to reveal one of the posters, all crumpled up.

Melissa gripped on to the edges of the table. *How* had they got it? She thought of the poster she'd kept. It had been at the bottom of her bag, hadn't it? Unless there were more around the forest. She took some swift deep breaths to calm herself.

'A nurse found this by your husband's bed,' Detective Powell said.

Shit, Melissa thought. It must have slipped from her back pocket when she'd tried to hide it a few days ago.

'You don't look surprised, Melissa,' Detective Powell said, tilting her head as she regarded Melissa. 'It's almost like you've seen one before?'

Melissa put her head in her hands. She just couldn't keep up the pretence any more.

She took a deep breath then told them all about the posters – *just* the posters. Not her suspicions about the kids or the knife.

'Any idea who put them up?' asked Detective Crawford.

She thought about it. Should she mention her suspicions about Maddy? She didn't want to get her in trouble and, anyway, it might not even be Maddy who put them up. 'Maybe someone with a political grudge against Patrick?' she suggested. It was halfway true, if indeed it had been Maddy who put up the posters.

'I thought you said nobody held any grudges against your husband?' Detective Powell asked, those suspicious eyes of hers right in Melissa's.

'It's just a suggestion,' Melissa said, shrugging.

'It seems to me you don't really know your husband very well, Mrs Byatt.'

'I'm beginning to wonder the same,' Melissa admitted.

'I presume you're referring to his infidelities?' Detective Powell asked.

Melissa didn't say anything.

'Did you have any suspicions before that Patrick was ever unfaithful?' the detective asked.

'No.' Melissa hesitated. 'Well, there was something before we married, years ago, but I know of nothing since.'

Detective Crawford looked down at his notepad, flicking back a few pages. 'With Andrea Cooper, I believe?'

Melissa nodded. 'Yes. Who told you that?'

'We can't divulge our sources,' Detective Powell said. 'It seems there's more to your marriage than meets the eye. And yet you gave the impression it was perfect.'

'No marriage is perfect!' Melissa said. She took a breath to calm down. 'But I never suspected any affairs. All these rumours are coming as just as much of a shock to me as well.'

'And what about the rumours about you, Mrs Byatt?' Detective Crawford asked. 'Have you ever been unfaithful to your husband?'

'Never,' Melissa said firmly.

'How would you describe your relationship with Ryan Day?' Detective Powell asked.

'I told you already, we're old friends.'

'Friends,' Detective Crawford said, drumming his fingers on the table as he mulled over something. 'I want you to think very carefully about this, Melissa. Are you *sure* it never went beyond a friendship between you and Ryan?'

'Yes, I'm sure,' Melissa said. 'There was a kiss once when we were teenagers, but nothing since. What's this all about?'

'We've had a new witness come forward,' Detective Crawford said. 'I'm afraid they tell a very different story.'

'What kind of story? What do you mean?' Melissa said, trying but failing to keep the panic from her voice.

'They tell us that you've been having an affair with Ryan Day for a number of years,' Detective Powell said, a satisfied smirk on her mouth.

Melissa leaned over the table towards them. 'No, no, that's not true!'

'And interestingly, Ryan Day has *quite* a rap sheet for a friendly little forest ranger,' she added, looking down at her notes.

'Rap sheet?' Melissa asked. She searched her mind. Ryan had got into trouble when they were kids. Vandalism. The odd fight with Forest Grove boys when they dared to venture into his neck of the woods. That was it, though . . . as far as she knew, anyway. 'Ryan wouldn't hurt Patrick, if that's what you're thinking.'

They both gave her sceptical looks.

Melissa pushed away from the table. 'This is ridiculous.'

'Is it really?' Detective Crawford said. 'You can't blame us for asking these questions.' He looked down at the poster. 'I mean, you're not *quite* the perfect family we first thought you were, are you? And it seems others feel the same,' he added, tapping the *I know* printed on the poster.

'No, we're bloody not, and it's tearing me apart, as I thought we were perfect once too!' Melissa stood up, clutching her bag to her stomach. 'Unless you're going to charge me with something, I'd like get back to my children, thanks.'

Detective Crawford stood up. 'I'll let you out.' They stepped from the room and walked down the corridor in silence until they got outside.

'You've got this all wrong, you know,' Melissa said.

'Time will tell, won't it?' the detective replied before stepping back into the station.

Melissa got back to Bill and Rosemary's to find Bill waiting for her in the living room.

'Rosemary's with Patrick,' he said.

'Is he okay?'

Bill nodded. 'No change. So what did the police want?'

'They found one of the posters,' Melissa said, placing her jacket on the side. 'And they wanted to ask me about all the rumours about me and Patrick.'

Bill frowned. 'I see.'

'You know I've never been unfaithful to Patrick, don't you?'

'To be honest, I don't know anything any more, Melissa.'

'What about Patrick? I think it's pretty clear he was unfaithful now, so don't deny it.'

Bill went to the window, looking out at the woods. 'Yes, he may have had a few indiscretions.'

Melissa slumped on to her chair. 'Jesus, am I the *only* person who didn't know?'

'There have always been rumours,' Bill replied. 'I asked him once. He said he'd change.'

Melissa put her head in her hands and Bill came over to her. 'Melissa, it doesn't mean he doesn't love you. God knows, I misbehaved a bit in my day. But that never stopped me loving Rosemary and the kids with *all* my heart.'

'Does *everyone* in the village know?'

Bill didn't answer. Melissa stood up. 'Look, Bill, I'm exhausted. I think I'll just go and check on the kids then head to bed.'

'Okay, Melissa. I'm always here if you need to talk. And you really should go and see Patrick. You didn't see him at all yesterday!'

She knew he was right. But with every new thing she learnt about Patrick, she felt herself getting further and further away from him. Like the man lying in that hospital bed wasn't her husband and, instead, her *real* husband would walk in the door any minute.

'I will,' she said. 'Tomorrow.'

She walked upstairs and went to the attic room, placing her ear to the door. She could hear a film being played. She opened it slightly to see the three kids squeezed up on one of the beds, watching something on Lewis's laptop.

'What are you watching?' she asked.

'*The Hunger Games*,' Lilly replied. She patted the space next to her. 'Come and join us.'

Melissa walked in and slumped down next to Lilly, placing her head on her daughter's shoulder. She breathed in her perfume, sweet tones with hints of honey. It made her feel safe, familiar.

'What did the police say?' Grace asked in a small voice.

'It's okay,' Melissa said. 'Nothing for you guys to worry about.'

Lilly placed her hand on Melissa's cheek, looking her in the eye, her forehead scrunched with worry. 'Are you okay, Mum?'

'Just tired, darling. I'd feel better if you guys told me what happened to your dad.'

'Can't we just watch a film together?' Lewis asked. 'Like we used to?'

'Yeah,' Lilly said as Grace nodded. 'I'd like to just pretend everything's back to normal for a bit.'

As Melissa looked at their sad faces, she wanted to break down and sob. But instead, she forced a smile. 'Of course.'

As they all watched the film, Melissa felt her eyes starting to droop and, before too long, she fell asleep. As she slept, she had her nightmare again. She was running through the forest in a nightdress, running from someone. Then she realised her hands felt wet. She looked down at them in the moonlight to see that they were caked in blood, so much that it dripped on to the leaves below. Then she saw the broken branch, the rope, that old silver ballet shoe. But this time, she heard a whimper from above her. She looked up and let out a cry: Ryan was hanging from a tree, a rope tight around his neck, his eyes desperate as he looked down at her.

'Mummy?' a voice said. She looked down to see Grace in her arms as a newborn. But she was talking. 'Why is he hanging there, Mummy?'

Melissa woke with a muffled scream, putting her hand to her mouth. She sat up on the bed, her head in her hands as she tried to control her breathing and push the remains of the dream away from her mind.

She quickly peered at the kids, who were all now sleeping soundly too, Lilly curled up against Grace while Lewis was sprawled on the single bed across from them all, his arm flung above her head. Melissa placed her hand on her younger daughter's warm cheek. Then she did the same with Lilly.

They were fine. They were all fine.

She walked back out of the room, then paused. On the landing below she saw Bill letting himself in through the front door, his coat on. Melissa stepped back into the shadows of the attic room, checking the time on the kids' alarm clock. One thirty in the morning.

He hadn't said anything about visiting Patrick, so what had he been doing out at that time of night?

Chapter Forty

Forest Grove Facebook Chit Chat Group

Saturday 27th April, 2019
7.30 a.m.

Andrew Blake
What's going on at Ryan Day's place? Loads of police there and forensics (I think that's what they are?) in white suits.

Pauline Sharpe
I saw that too while walking the dog just now, loads of police! Was wondering where they were heading.

Ellie Mileham
Oh God, not another attack!

Graham Cane
Not that, Ellie Mileham. I think it's pretty obvious what's going on . . . something I said right from the start.

Rebecca Feine
What's that, then?

Graham Cane
Well, Ryan Day and Melissa Byatt go back years, don't they? Can't be a coincidence that she was taken in last night and now the police being at Ryan's again. Why do things like what's happened to Patrick usually happen? Crimes of passion, aren't they?

Jackie Shillingford
Don't be ridiculous!

Belinda Bell
Is it so ridiculous, though, Jackie? I remember happening upon Melissa and Ryan in the woods once, just after little Joel died. Deep in conversation, they were . . .

Andrew Blake
Is 'conversation' code for something else?

Belinda Bell
You and your smutty mind!

Eamon Piper
Actually, just remembering something now. Do you remember when Patrick roped Ryan into doing that woodwork talk during the local Tory Party event last year? You could tell Ryan hated every minute and he was so dismissive of Patrick. I said to Andrew at the time, 'Ryan's not a fan of Patrick,' didn't I, Andrew?

Andrew Blake
You sure did, pal.

Belinda Bell Interesting. So let's get this clear:
1) Melissa and Ryan were, maybe still are, very close.
2) Ryan hates Patrick
3) Patrick gets stabbed
4) Police descend upon Ryan's lodge

Debbie Lampard
Pretty shocked by these posts. Is this really appropriate? Where's admin? This is an ongoing investigation, for God's sake.

Andrew Blake
Oh! They've definitely arrested Ryan Day! His daughter is hysterical.

Graham Cane
Andrew Blake, reporting direct from the scene of the incident. You hiding behind a tree, Andrew?

Kitty Fletcher
Poor girl. Witnessing something like that can be very upsetting for a child.

Pauline Sharpe
Oh no, this is awful!

Graham Cane
Why's it awful? Surely it's a good thing, the scum responsible for the attack on Patrick Byatt finally found.

Debbie Lampard

That's a bit of a leap, Graham Cane. Like Kitty says, think of his daughter too, witnessing that.

Andrew Blake

Something was just brought out in a plastic bag. It's a knife!

Graham Cane

That's it, then. Case closed.

Chapter Forty-One

Saturday 27th April, 2019
7.45 a.m.

No, no, no! This is all wrong! They can't have arrested Ryan, not him, of all people! Surely that Facebook post is wrong.

I never meant for this to happen.

I can't deal with this any more.

I feel like a fly in a web now, and this spider is about to come and eat me and all I want to do is untangle the web around my neck.

Chapter Forty-Two

Saturday 27th April, 2019
8 a.m.

Melissa woke to see Lewis looking down at her.

'Mum, have you heard?' Lewis said. 'Ryan's been arrested.'

Melissa struggled to sit up, noticing the girls across the room watching her with solemn looks on their faces.

'They found a knife,' Grace whispered.

Melissa peered out towards the forest, a pulse at the back of her head throbbing. 'Th— that's impossible! I buried it right in the forest. I don't understand!'

She got up and started pacing back and forth. Of course, she knew that was where the detectives were leading when they'd questioned her the day before, towards Ryan. She ought to be relieved, really, that their attention was off the kids.

But it was Ryan! Her old friend. He didn't deserve this. Plus, she'd now be dragged right into it, the detectives clearly thinking something was going on between her and Ryan.

A thought occurred to her then. Maybe the kids were covering for Ryan.

She looked at them all. '*Has* Ryan got anything to do with all this?'

They all exchanged looks.

'Has he?' she pushed.

'You tell us,' Lilly said, folding her arms over her nightdress.

'What do you mean?' Melissa asked her.

'We know about you and Ryan, Mum,' she said with a sigh.

'Oh, for God's sake, not this again. There's nothing between me and Ryan. He's my friend!'

'It doesn't matter, we're cool with it, Mum,' Lewis said.

'You really don't need to lie, Mum,' Lilly said. 'You weren't yourself back then, anyway, were you?'

Melissa looked at them in shock. 'Back when?'

'After Joel died,' Lilly said.

They were interrupted by the sound of footsteps on the landing.

Melissa looked up to see Rosemary standing at the door with Grace's distinctive Harry Potter rucksack opened to reveal a bloody broken watch inside.

Patrick's missing watch, caked in dry blood.

Suddenly, all thoughts of Ryan disappeared from Melissa's mind.

'I found the rucksack in one of the spare rooms,' Rosemary said as she regarded Grace with hooded eyes.

Lewis and Lilly craned their necks to look at what was inside, mouths dropping open. Grace just remained expressionless.

Melissa took the rucksack to her. 'Why would you keep Dad's watch, Grace? And why's it broken?'

Grace shrugged. 'Don't know. Just took it.'

'That's *gross*,' Lilly said. 'There's still blood on it.'

'Why on earth would you do that, Grace?' Rosemary snapped. 'It's like some kind of—' She paused. 'Some kind of *trophy*.'

Grace cringed, eyes brimming with tears. 'Sorry!'

Melissa gave Rosemary a look. 'For God's sake, it's just her way of dealing with things.'

'Can we talk?' Rosemary asked Melissa. 'Downstairs?'

Melissa nodded, following Rosemary down to the kitchen. 'It's not right for a little girl to do something like that, Melissa.'

Melissa sighed. 'It's just her way of coping, Rosemary.'

'Yes, *her* way,' Rosemary said as she gently took Patrick's watch from the rucksack and began carefully washing it at the sink. 'She's always been different, hasn't she?'

'Yes,' Melissa said, crossing her arms, 'and that's why we love her.'

'I know, but . . .' Rosemary's voice trailed off.

'Spit it out, Rosemary!'

'Her obsession with dead animals, with *crime*. It's not normal for a kid her age.'

'Actually, it's more normal than you think. Children are fascinated by blood and guts. You know that.'

'Not little girls,' Rosemary said sombrely.

Melissa laughed. 'Oh, come on, Rosemary! That's a bit of a generalisation.'

Rosemary sighed. 'I just wonder if I've been paying too much attention to Lewis. What if it's *Grace* who hurt Patrick?'

'A watch isn't evidence of that, Rosemary.'

'It's just a consideration,' Rosemary said sternly as she regarded Melissa over her shoulder. 'He loves this watch, we all know that! It was Bill's great-grandfather's watch, the war hero, remember?'

'How can I forget?' Melissa said sarcastically.

Rosemary narrowed her eyes. 'I suppose you've heard about Ryan being arrested?'

'Yes, the kids just told me. It's not him who hurt Patrick, Rosemary.'

'The whole of Forest Grove seems to think so.'

'You're talking about the bloody Facebook group? Don't tell me it's on there already. Honestly, that is not a barometer of how people feel here.'

'I think they get it pretty spot on sometimes,' Rosemary said. 'There's been some interesting stuff said about Ryan recently.'

Melissa put her hand on her hip, looking at her mother-in-law. 'Like what, Rosemary?'

Rosemary turned around, her eyes on Melissa's. 'Like about you and Ryan being *close*,' she said.

'Oh Jesus, not you too!' Melissa flung her hands in the air in frustration. '*Nothing* has happened between me and Ryan!'

'No smoke without fire.' Rosemary went to Melissa and grasped her arm. 'Is Grace Ryan's daughter, Melissa?'

'Jesus Christ, why would you say that? No!'

'What's going on here?' They turned to see Bill at the doorway.

'Look what I found in Grace's rucksack,' Rosemary said, gesturing to the broken watch.

Bill eyes widened. 'Is that . . . ?'

'Yes,' Rosemary said. 'It's weird, isn't it, Bill?'

'Stop it, Rosemary,' Melissa said. 'Just stop it.'

'What are you two arguing about now?' Bill asked.

'She just accused me of having an affair with Ryan,' Melissa said, '*and* asked whether Grace is Ryan's daughter because of *course* no child with Byatt blood running through them would keep mementoes like she has,' she said. 'The Byatts are perfect – *except*,' Melissa said, tapping her chin, 'Patrick *did* have to see a therapist when he moved here. Not so perfect, huh?'

Both Bill and Rosemary's mouths dropped open.

'How do you know that?' Bill asked, closing the kitchen door so the kids couldn't hear.

'I have my sources,' Melissa said, crossing her arms. 'In fact, I'm learning a lot about Patrick lately. Infidelities, therapy . . .'

'How dare you?' Rosemary hissed. 'Your husband is lying in hospital right this moment and you dare to say all this about him?'

'But it's all true!' Melissa countered. 'You're not denying it!'

'Calm down, Melissa,' Bill said, putting his hands on her shoulders and looking her in the eye. 'Are you okay? You don't seem yourself.'

'Oh, I don't know, my husband, who's been cheating on me most of our marriage, is in a coma possibly caused by one of our kids and my mother-in-law thinks one of those kids has been fathered by someone else!'

Rosemary shook her head and sat down, Patrick's watch in her hands.

'Maybe we should get you some help?' Bill said gently to Melissa. 'You were like this after Joel died.'

'I was *grieving*.'

'I don't just mean the grief. You seem a little . . . unbalanced.'

Melissa's shoulders slumped. How could she argue back? He was right.

'It'll all be alright, Melissa,' Bill said. 'We'll sort it, you know that. Ryan's been arrested, hasn't he?'

A sudden coldness hit at Melissa's very core.

We'll sort it.

'Did you plant the knife on Ryan?' Melissa asked him.

'Of course not.'

She examined his face. 'You're lying. I saw you come in the other night. My God,' she said as it hit her. 'Did you follow me when I buried the knife the other night?'

He sighed. 'I know this is hard, but it's the best way, really.'

'But Ryan is *innocent*,' Melissa hissed.

'Well, he did betray Patrick . . .' Rosemary said, shrugging. 'He took advantage of you at your most vulnerable when you had your little breakdown after Joel died, didn't he?'

Melissa let out a frustrated scream. 'How many times do I have to tell you, I did *not* have an affair with Ryan.'

Rosemary and Bill exchanged dubious looks.

Melissa's phone buzzed in her hand. She wanted to ignore it, to continue laying into Rosemary and Bill. She was *so* furious they would do this to Ryan and that they had such little faith in her.

But when she looked down at her phone, she recognised the number.

'It's the hospital,' she said.

Bill and Rosemary went quiet as Melissa put the phone to her ear.

'Mrs Byatt?' It was Patrick's doctor. 'I've just had your husband's new scan results and we've decided to try to wake him. Are you able to get here soon?'

Melissa's head span. It was finally happening!

Chapter Forty-Three

Saturday 27th April, 2019
8.30 a.m.

Melissa ran into the hospital with Rosemary and Bill, her bag swinging from her shoulder. Her phone fell out, smashing to the floor. She quickly picked it up, not caring that the glass was broken, and continued running until she got to Patrick's room. As they approached Patrick's bed, Melissa took in a sharp breath when she saw that Detective Powell was already there, standing at the foot of the bed. Patrick's doctor was on one side, a nurse on the other.

Rosemary went to Patrick's side, stroking his shaved head. 'Be strong, my darling son,' she whispered. 'Be strong.'

Melissa felt a strange kind of calm as she regarded her husband, his long, lean body and handsome face. Half of her wanted to slap him, to scream into his face: *Why? Why? Why?* The other half was desperate to hold him, to know he was okay.

One thing she was sure of, though: she was now ready for the truth to come out. The lies and secrets had been eating away at her, and she realised with a sharp clarity that she should have just been honest from the start. Ryan's arrest had made her realise that. Manipulating the truth, withholding it, was *wrong*. She had done that by not telling the police about the kids hiding the knife . . . and

Patrick had too, with all his indiscretions. And then the kids – their kids – their wall of silence, all adding up to rot their family to the very core.

The kids didn't want the truth coming out, though. She'd seen it in their eyes when she ran upstairs to tell them their father was awake and Jackie would be over to look after them.

'We'll deal with it, okay?' she'd said to them as they regarded her with wide, fearful eyes. 'Whatever Dad says, I have your backs, you understand?'

And that was true. She *would* deal with it, whatever Patrick said about his attacker.

She took a deep breath and approached Patrick's bed with trepidation. She looked down at him, wondering how she could pretend everything was normal when their marriage had been pulled apart at the seams. She had to try, though. He wouldn't be with it, would he? The anger and questions could come later.

Detective Powell gave her a curt smile, the first smile Melissa had seen from her since this all started, and Melissa realised then that she too was yearning for the truth.

'Come and stand by your husband, Mrs Byatt,' the doctor said, gesturing to the space beside her. 'It'll be good for you to be close to him when he wakes. He'll be very confused.'

Melissa slipped in past the detective and stood by Patrick, across from Rosemary and Bill, hands trembling and freezing cold as she held Patrick's hand. Rosemary and Bill looked nervous. They seemed so convinced their son wouldn't tell the truth if one of his children had hurt him, but Melissa wasn't so sure. She wasn't sure of *anything* any more.

'How's this going to work?' Bill asked the doctor, an obvious tremble in his deep voice.

'We'll gradually reduce the drugs that have been keeping your son in a coma,' the doctor explained. 'It may take some time for

Patrick to wake, so patience is key. He'll be very disoriented, weak, in a little pain. I'd take a seat, if I were you.'

Rosemary and Melissa sat down, but Bill and the detective remained standing.

'Is this really appropriate?' Bill said, gesturing to Detective Powell. 'Can't our son just be woken with his family around him, give him some time to adapt?'

'This is an investigation into a possible attempted murder, Mr Byatt,' Detective Powell said sternly.

The doctor turned her attention to the detective. 'Patrick's father is right, we don't want to distress Patrick when he wakes. It's unlikely he'll be able to talk much anyway.'

'We just need one name, that's all,' Detective Powell said simply, eyes sliding towards Melissa.

'Where's Detective Crawford?' Melissa asked, wishing it was him there instead of his stern colleague.

'On his way,' the detective replied.

'Are we all ready?' the doctor asked, looking around the room.

They all nodded and the nurse started pressing buttons on the machine by Patrick. Melissa took a deep, shaky breath as Rosemary and Bill leaned in closer to their son, scrutinising his pale face. There was no activity for a while, the nurse and doctor just monitoring Patrick's vital signs. But after a few minutes, Patrick's eyes started blinking rapidly beneath his soft blue-veined eyelids. There was a moan and Melissa put her hand to her mouth, suppressing a sob. She'd never in her life experienced such a confusing mixture of emotions, elation that her husband was waking, anger at what he'd done and yes, full-on fear of discovering the reason behind him being there.

'Patrick,' the doctor said softly, 'I'm Dr Hudson. You're at Ashbridge General Hospital. Your wife, Melissa, is here, and your parents are too. You have been placed in an induced coma for the past nine days to help you heal.'

Patrick coughed slightly, dark eyelashes beginning to flicker open.

Melissa held her breath, tears squeezing out between her eyes. Then Patrick's eyes suddenly fluttered open, out of focus, long eyelashes batting against each other. Melissa let out a sob. It felt like she hadn't seen those deep brown eyes for so long.

'Patrick, darling, it's Mum!' Rosemary said.

'I'm here too, son,' Bill added, voice choked.

Melissa found she couldn't say anything. Bill gave her a look. 'Me too,' she croaked.

Patrick let out an anguished moan, trying to grab at his feeding tube. The nurse gently restrained him.

'You have a head injury, but it will *all* be fine,' the doctor said, checking Patrick's eyes with a small flashlight and nodding, seemingly satisfied with what she saw. 'These tubes have been helping you eat and drink, Patrick,' she explained. 'The nurse will remove them now.'

'Is he okay?' Rosemary asked.

'He's fine, just adjusting,' the doctor said as the nurse began to remove the tubes, Patrick's eyes flitting about in confusion from one face to the next, finally settling on Detective Powell at the end of the bed. Then he pressed his cheek into the pillow, moaning. It took a while for him to properly come around, Melissa and his parents doing as the doctor said: watching silently, giving Patrick's hand reassuring squeezes every now and again. After an hour or so, the fog in his mind seemed to clear a little when he turned to Melissa and said, 'Twins?' in barely a whisper.

She stared at him, opening her mouth and closing it, so many words wanting to spill out.

'They're fine,' Bill said. 'Grace is too.'

'How are you feeling, Patrick?' the doctor asked.

Patrick gestured to his throat. 'Sore,' he said in a hoarse whisper.

The doctor nodded. 'Yes, that's to be expected.'

He tried to sit up but fell back against his pillow, exhausted.

'You'll be very weak,' the doctor explained. 'But we'll get you up and walking soon enough, you'll see.'

'When?' Patrick croaked.

'Being asleep for so long takes its toll on the human body,' the doctor explained. 'Muscles waste, ligaments tear.'

Patrick turned to his father. 'Election?' he asked.

Bill and Rosemary laughed. 'I think our son is going to be okay,' Rosemary said, eyes filling with happy tears.

'He's running to be our local councillor,' Bill explained to the doctor, a hint of pride in his voice. 'Don't worry, son,' he said to Patrick. 'I'll chat to your colleagues. Let's make sure your name is still on that ballot paper!'

Melissa looked at him in surprise. 'It's too soon.'

Patrick tried to grab at her arm. 'Do want.'

Melissa frowned.

'That's my boy!' Bill said, laughing. 'Never stops, this one,' he said to the doctor.

Patrick winced and looked down at his side, towards his stab wound. Rosemary and Melissa exchanged a look.

'Look,' he croaked. 'Want to look.'

Rosemary frowned. 'You don't need to look, Patrick.'

'Want to,' Patrick replied stubbornly.

The nurse gently lifted the sheet to show his bandaged side. 'It's healing well,' she said.

Patrick's jaw clenched and he shook his head, eyes filled with sadness.

The detective placed her hands on the rails on the bed and leaned towards him. 'I'm Detective Powell, Patrick. I've been working on your case. Do you remember who did this to you?'

Patrick turned to Melissa, his dark eyes on hers. The detective followed his gaze, frowning.

'Patrick, you were attacked,' the detective said bluntly. 'Someone did this to you. We'd all like to know who that is.'

'Okay, that's enough,' Bill said. 'I think—'

'Grace,' Patrick gasped. He turned away from Melissa, looking the detective in the eyes. 'It was Grace.'

Chapter Forty-Four

Saturday 27th April, 2019
10 a.m.

Melissa looked at Patrick in shock, but Bill and Rosemary didn't seem surprised.

'Our little Grace?' Melissa asked Patrick, unable to wrap her head around it.

Patrick nodded, tears brimming in his eyes.

Melissa shook her head and put her hand to her chest, feeling the erratic patter of her heart.

Not Grace, surely not Grace.

'Just to be clear, Patrick,' Detective Powell said, 'you're saying your daughter, Grace Byatt, stabbed you?'

'Yes,' Patrick said firmly.

'Could he be confused?' Melissa asked the doctor.

The doctor sighed. 'Well, there can be an element of confusion after waking . . .'

'He seems pretty sure,' Rosemary said.

Patrick pointed to his stab wound. 'Yes, Grace did this.'

Melissa started sobbing. How could it be her darling Grace?

'What happened?' Melissa asked him. 'Why would she *do* that, Patrick? You know Grace, you know she isn't capable of doing something like that. What did you say to her? What did you *do*?'

The words came out in a rush, and Patrick winced, shaking his head.

'Melissa!' Rosemary said, putting her arm around her son's shoulders and shooting her daughter-in-law a hard look. 'Calm down, for God's sake.'

Detective Powell stepped towards Patrick. 'Patrick, if I can—'

Patrick started spluttering, clutching at his throat. 'Hurts,' he said.

'Okay, you have your name,' the doctor said to the detective as she gestured to the nurse for some water. 'Time for us to do our work.'

'But we need to know *why*,' Melissa said.

'That's enough, Melissa!' Bill shouted.

'Maybe you should leave for a few moments,' Rosemary suggested, arm still protectively around her son. 'Just to calm down. It's a lot for you to take in. Detective Powell, you can accompany Melissa out, can't you?'

Detective Powell shoved her notepad in her pocket and curtly nodded. 'You'll let me know if he says anything else?'

'Yes,' the doctor replied.

Melissa let Detective Powell lead her away, thoughts running through her mind. She'd go home, get the kids, escape somewhere, just the four of them. She couldn't let her little Grace go through the system for this, *wouldn't*. Patrick must have done something to provoke her, something awful.

She twisted around as she left the room, looking at Patrick over her shoulder. He wouldn't meet her eye. Instead, he stared up at his parents and Melissa felt like she was in a bubble rolling down the hill, out of control and outside it all.

The door closed on them and the detective led Melissa to a quiet family room. Melissa sat down, her head in her hands, as the detective stared out of the window.

'Something must have gone horribly wrong for Grace to do that,' Melissa said. 'I know she seems different from other kids, but she's a good kid. Something must have gone really badly wrong.'

'Well, we'll find out soon,' the detective said.

Melissa let out a sob. How could it have got to this, her younger daughter stabbing her own father? She thought of the watch Rosemary had found in Grace's rucksack, Grace's fascination with blood splatter and dead animals.

On the surface, *yes*, it did all seem odd. But Melissa knew her girl.

Or at least she thought she did, anyway.

Detective Crawford appeared at the door then, out of breath. 'So?' he asked his colleague.

'Patrick's awake. He said it's Grace,' Detective Powell said.

'Interesting,' he said, not looking overly surprised. He turned to Melissa. 'We'll need to question Grace as soon as possible. The twins too, at some point. Probably best it's all done at the station.'

Melissa's stomach dropped. 'The station? But she's just a child!'

'We've had a lot younger do a lot worse,' Detective Powell stated.

'Grace isn't *like* those kinds of kids,' Melissa said firmly.

The detective raised an eyebrow.

'There will be a representative from the Youth Offending Team as an appropriate adult,' Detective Crawford said.

'A representative?' Melissa said. 'But surely I should be there when she's questioned?'

The detective shook his head. 'No. You're too close to the case. I'd recommend getting your daughter a solicitor too.'

'Solicitor? My God, this is madness,' Melissa said, her voice catching. 'She's just a child!'

'A child who has been accused by her father of serious assault,' Detective Powell said.

Detective Crawford sighed. 'Look, I know this seems harsh, but this is just the way it's done. I promise you we will make it as easy and as gentle as we can for your daughter. You can come with me to get her. You can even tell her yourself what's going to happen, if you want.'

Bill appeared from Patrick's room then, his phone in his hand.

'Are you going to talk to Grace?' he asked the detectives.

They nodded.

'Can you believe this, Bill?' Melissa said. 'Grace, of all people.'

He went to Melissa and embraced her in a hug. She sunk into him.

'I'll come with you, okay?' he insisted.

She looked up at him, wiping her tears away. 'But Patrick.'

'He has Rosemary. I'm coming with you, you hear me? You can't do this alone.'

She nodded, feeling so grateful for his presence, and they followed the detectives outside.

As they were driven back by the detectives to Bill and Rosemary's, Melissa tried to wrap her head around Grace being the culprit. Truth be told, she'd been last on Melissa's list. With Lewis's propensity for violent outbursts, he was the most likely. Maybe Lilly too, considering how she so easily blocked things out, and the possibility she'd sent Caitlin that bouquet.

But not Grace.

They pulled up outside Rosemary and Bill's house. She looked up at the familiar windows and the forest beyond. All the happy times they'd spent there, and it had come to this – having to go into the house to inform her youngest child she was going to be arrested for her father's assault. Not to mention the fact she'd be breaking the news to the twins too.

Detective Crawford twisted around in his seat to look at her and Bill. 'Ready?'

'Yes, ready,' Bill said. But Melissa didn't answer. How could she be ready for something like this?

Melissa got out of the car with Bill and the two detectives. In the distance, a couple walked their dog. They paused, eyebrows arching as they took in the sight of Melissa being escorted out of a police car. Melissa straightened her shoulders and followed Bill down the path, the detectives behind them. Her temples throbbed to the beat of her steps and her fingers trembled as she opened the front door.

As they entered, Jackie was crossing the hall, a tea towel in her hands. She paused, taking in the look on Melissa's face. 'Is Patrick okay?' she asked.

Melissa nodded. 'He's awake.'

'Doing well too, from what we gather,' Bill said, the relief clear on his face.

'Thank God,' Jackie said, putting her hand to her chest in relief.

'Are the kids in the living room?' Melissa asked.

'Grace is in there with Ross. The twins just went upstairs.'

Good, Melissa thought. *It would be too much for them to witness this.*

Jackie glanced at the detectives. 'What's going on?'

Melissa ignored her and walked through to the living room, the detectives and Bill behind her. Grace was in her usual spot at the window seat, reading, Ross nearby. When Melissa walked in, he glanced up, brow creasing when he saw the detectives.

Melissa paused a moment, watching Grace read. She thought their 'normal' had been shattered the afternoon Patrick was stabbed. But right now was when it was really going to happen, certainly for Grace anyway. Melissa walked towards Grace, her little Grace, trying to comprehend what she'd done to her father.

Grace darted her head up, paling when she took in the detectives.

Ross stood up. 'Patrick okay?' he asked Bill.

Stop asking about Patrick, Melissa wanted to say. *My younger daughter's about to be arrested!*

'He's fine,' Bill said.

'He's awake,' Melissa added, watching Grace for a response. But there was no response.

'Do you want to go and make us a cuppa with Jackie?' Bill asked Ross, the message clear in his eyes: *Leave us all alone.*

'Of course,' Ross said, placing his newspaper down and walking from the room, gently closing the door behind him.

Bill nodded at Melissa, a silent message that everything would be okay. Melissa went to Grace, crouching down on the floor and taking her hands. She explored her face. She looked so innocent, so young.

'Dad told us what happened,' she said, eyes still on Grace. 'The nice detectives are going to take you to the station and ask you a few questions, darling,' she said softly. 'And you *must* tell the truth, you hear me?'

'What did Dad say?' Grace asked.

Detective Crawford stepped forward. 'He said you stabbed him, Grace.'

'But I didn't!'

Melissa frowned. 'Then what happened, darling?'

Grace looked first at her mother, then her grandfather, then she sank her head. 'I can't say.'

'Come on, then,' Detective Powell said, giving Grace a rare smile. 'Let's head down to the station. My daughter will be *very* jealous you're getting to see where I work when she hasn't!'

Melissa looked at the detective in surprise. She'd presumed she didn't have children.

'Am I allowed to take my book?' Grace asked, hugging her battered book close to her chest.

'Of course,' the detective replied.

Detective Crawford peered up at the ceiling. 'We'll need to question the twins too. Best we chat to Grace first, though.'

'And me,' Melissa said. 'I want to tell the truth.'

'Melissa,' Bill said in a low, warning voice.

'It's time to tell the truth, Bill. The *whole* truth.'

Chapter Forty-Five

Forest Grove Facebook Chit Chat Group

Saturday 27th April, 2019
11 a.m.

Andrea Cooper
Just in case people haven't heard, I have some truly wonderful news: Patrick Byatt is awake and well! Wishing him a speedy recovery!

Charlie Cane
Oh, that *is* wonderful news . . . I wonder if they'll put him forward as a candidate now he's awake? I hope so!

Barbara Bell
Been reluctant to share this but it has to be said: I just saw Melissa and little Grace being led to the police station by the detectives in charge of Patrick's case. Looked very serious to me . . .

Graham Cane
Well well well.

Rebecca Feine
Why Grace? She's only little – what could she possibly have to do with it?

Eamon Piper
Melissa hasn't been by Patrick's bedside since he woke, according to my sister-in-law, who works at the hospital. Just his parents.

Belinda Bell
That speaks volumes.

Kitty Fletcher
Are you suggesting what I think you're suggesting?

Belinda Bell
That Melissa has been arrested for her husband's attack? Yes, that's precisely what I'm suggesting. These things are always closer to home than you think. What did I say about something not being right about this whole thing?

Pauline Sharpe
Her poor children.

Kitty Fletcher
Yes. People are very good at putting on these personas in public but, behind closed doors, it's a different matter. Imagine what those poor kids must have witnessed.

Rebecca Feine

Now come on. We don't know the whole story.

Belinda Bell

Exactly. We don't know the whole story. We never have with her. It'll all come out in the wash, it always does.

Chapter Forty-Six

Saturday 27th April, 2019
11.35 a.m.

'Must feel a bit like déjà vu?' Detective Powell asked as she sat across from Melissa in the small interview room, Grace next door with Detective Crawford. Melissa was pleased it was Detective Crawford interviewing Grace. He had kind eyes, not Detective Powell's hard, relentless, dark ones.

'Shall we start at the beginning?' the detective said. 'So, from the moment you arrived home from work the day Patrick was stabbed.'

Melissa nodded. 'It's exactly as I told you in my original statement. I walked in and found Patrick on the floor with what I thought was just a head wound but then turned out to be a stab wound too. The kids told me they'd found their dad like that too. What I *didn't* tell you,' Melissa added with a sigh, 'is that I saw a knife on the kitchen floor. The knife you discovered was missing from the knife block? When I left the kids alone to let the paramedics in and came back into the kitchen, that knife was gone.' She looked down at her lap. 'I knew then something wasn't right.'

'But you didn't tell us?' Detective Powell said.

'No. I don't know why. Looking back, I made a mistake, but you do stupid things to protect your children, don't you?' Melissa saw a hint of sympathy in the detective's eyes. 'Anyway, I didn't know *how* they were involved, but I knew deep down one of them must have hidden the knife. And the reason for that scared me. I guess I felt I needed to find out before you guys got involved. Does that make sense?'

Detective Powell didn't respond.

'I tried to get what happened out of the kids ever since it happened,' Melissa said. 'I just kept thinking, if I could only get it out of them first, *then* I could come to you.'

'What about the knife?' Detective Powell said. 'You mentioned the children hid it, but we found it on Ryan Day's property. We're currently getting forensics done on it for DNA but it looks very well cleaned so I'm not sure we'll have much luck.'

Melissa tried to keep her face neutral. She wasn't going to tell them Bill planted it there, that was a step too far. But she wasn't going to lie either. 'Lewis told me where they hid it, under the bin in the kitchen. I cleaned it then I buried it.'

'That's very serious, Melissa. That's aiding and abetting. You know that carries a prison sentence? Not just for you, but the twins too.'

Melissa swallowed. 'I know. But you need to remember, the twins were only protecting their little sister. She's just ten.' She leaned forward. 'They're all so close. How could they even comprehend telling you what she'd done? Their first instinct would be to protect her . . . As mine was to protect the kids. Wouldn't you do the same?'

'No, actually,' Detective Powell replied.

'I think you would, though, in the same situation. Think about it. *Really* think about it.'

The detective sighed. 'So how did the knife end up at Ryan Day's place? Why would someone unearth the knife you buried and plant it on him?'

Melissa paused. *Should* she tell the detective about Bill? She just couldn't bring herself to. He was family too, after all. 'I don't know,' she said.

'I'm not sure I'm convinced,' Detective Powell said. 'It all seems rather far-fetched to me, especially in light of how close you and Ryan are.'

'I already told you the truth about that,' Melissa said, wiping tears from her cheeks. 'Nothing happened between us. I swear I'm telling you the truth!'

'And yet you've not exactly been generous with the truth the past week, have you?' Detective Powell retorted. She leaned forward, her slim dark forearms on the table. 'I understand you found it particularly difficult after your first son, Joel, passed away?'

Melissa frowned. 'Of course I did. He was my son! What's this got to do with anything?'

'You disappeared for a week, I believe? Just walked out?' the detective asked, ignoring Melissa's question. 'In fact, you left your young children alone for a few hours, didn't you?'

'Who told you all this?' Melissa asked.

'We can't divulge our sources. Can you answer the question, please?'

'The twins weren't alone for more than two hours. Patrick's mum turned up. But yes, I'm ashamed of it, so thank you for reminding me,' Melissa said, her voice catching.

'Where did you go, Melissa?'

'My parents' old cottage. Well, my cottage officially after my dad passed it on to me.'

'Anywhere else?'

Melissa paused. 'I stayed with Ryan for a bit,' she admitted.

'I see. That was eleven years ago, right? Back in February 2008, a few days after your first son passed away in January, to be exact?'

Melissa nodded. 'Yes.'

'And Grace was born in October, eight months later?' the detective continued.

'Okay, I see where you're going with this,' Melissa said with a sigh. 'But Grace was not born prematurely so no, Grace is not Ryan's.'

'Is that another lie, Melissa?' Detective Powell said. 'She looks like Ryan Day, with those blue eyes of hers, and yet the twins have brown eyes.'

'Yes, Grace has *my* eyes and hair,' Melissa said, pointing at her own blue eyes and fair hair. 'Anyway, what has any of this got to do with it?'

'Everything,' Detective Powell remarked. 'Your husband said Grace stabbed him, but what we need to know is why? The possibility of Grace being Ryan Day's daughter certainly makes things interesting.'

'So *that's* your theory, then?' Melissa said with a bitter laugh. 'That Ryan is Grace's father and he somehow got her to stab Patrick? Do you realise how outlandish that is?'

'It makes sense, though, doesn't it?' Detective Powell continued. 'Ryan kills two birds with one stone, so to speak. Clears the way to get his child *and* his lover. You find out and decide to protect him by lying about burying the knife.'

'You're wrong.'

'Then tell me what happened in that forest in those days after your son died, Melissa,' Detective Powell said. 'Tell us why you disappeared for so long with a man who's *just* a friend? Tell me, why do we have a witness saying they saw you sleeping in Ryan's lodge for the duration of the week?'

Melissa swallowed. What witness was this?

'Melissa?' the detective pushed. 'What happened those few days in the forest with Ryan Day? Why did you stay with him when you could have stayed at your parents' cottage?'

She slumped back down on the chair. 'He was helping me,' she said in a quiet voice.

'Helping? Why?'

Melissa took a deep breath. 'I attempted suicide.'

Chapter Forty-Seven

Saturday 27th April, 2019
11.55 a.m.

Memories from those lost days after Joel died came back to Melissa. After walking out on the kids that day and falling asleep in her old cottage, she had woken in darkness, the familiar smell of the place confusing her, making her think her mum was still there, pottering around. But as she'd grappled through the darkness, seeing furniture covered in dust sheets, she'd remembered: her mum was gone . . . and Joel was gone too.

The pain overwhelmed her, making her double over. She just needed the grief to be *gone* too. Out of the corner of her eye, she saw one of her dad's old bottles of gin beckoning her, so she'd gone to it, doing what her father and Ryan's father did to chase their troubles away: she drank it. Drank it and drank it and drank it.

But the pain wouldn't go away. It was a toxic combination, grief, guilt and gin, like a million bugs all over her, itching at her.

As she'd stepped outside, ready to walk back, she'd hesitated before the ancient oak, looking up in the darkness at the moon-encrusted branches above. It felt as though her mother was calling for her to stay as they swayed in the breeze.

Stay, Melissa, stay.

She could imagine her mother doing that, telling her she needed time; that the forest heals. And God, she needed healing, because she felt broken, cracked open, ready to crumble.

So she *had* stayed. She'd sat on a log and she'd breathed in the night forest, stilling her mind. It was so quiet, the oak tree casting shadows across the forest floor before her. As she sat there, she thought of her poor mother. Her death had been a complete shock to them all. She'd disappeared in the night three months after they'd moved in with the Byatts. Bill had gone to look for her with Tommy and had discovered her beneath the old oak. It was a particularly freezing-cold night in late October and, unable to get into the cottage, which Bill had boarded up, she'd chosen to just sit by the oak tree rather than return to the Byatts'. She had passed away from hypothermia right there, by the tree she so loved. The guilt Melissa had felt had been unbearable. She had been so wrapped up in the excitement of being with the Byatts, and with Patrick too, that she hadn't noticed her mother was so desperate to leave that she'd sneaked out in the night.

The guilt had itched again. *Itch itch itch.* The grief swirled around, snapping its teeth. She threw the bottle away, watched as it smashed against the oak tree. A piece of glass rebounded, cutting her, but she didn't notice, just walked to the tree, her blood dripping on the leaves below. The rope from the makeshift swing her father had made her still draped from one of the oak's old branches, the seat rotten and black.

Melissa kicked it to pieces with her foot, her silver ballet slipper falling to the ground below. Then she took the rope that remained and twisted it around her neck, the only way she could think of getting rid of the pain. The last thing she saw before she passed out was her ballet shoe, the blood on the leaves, an image that had haunted her dreams since.

Looking back, it was awful to do that to the twins, who were themselves having to deal with the horror of losing their brother. But she simply wasn't thinking straight. She'd been drunk, out of her mind. It was something she'd never dreamed of doing. She was crazed in her mourning and, if Ryan hadn't found her, she wouldn't be here today.

She remembered Ryan's arms around her waist, his desperate pleas for her to open her eyes, to *breathe.*

'Melissa?' Detective Powell said now, dragging her from her past. 'Do you want to tell me what happened?' Her voice was unusually soft.

'I tried to hang myself, from the oak tree,' Melissa said. 'Ryan found me, he saved me. He took me to his lodge and he – he brought me back to life. He called a nurse we know, Debbie Lampard. She came over and they put me back together so my family would never find out. So *nobody* would.' She leaned forward, looking the detective in the eye. 'A week later, I discovered I was pregnant with Grace, *Patrick's* child. I swear to you. Take a DNA test if you want. There was no sordid affair.'

The detective was quiet for a few moments as she examined Melissa's face. Then she nodded. 'I believe you. I think it's time we talked to the twins, don't you?'

Melissa took in a breath of relief and stood up with the detective.

'What happens now?' she asked as they walked outside.

'I'm going to send someone to get the twins. In the meantime, you can wait here for Grace.'

'Will someone be with the twins when they're interviewed too?'

'Yes, but they'll be interviewed separately.'

They got to the waiting room. 'Look,' the detective said, 'I'm really sorry for all you've been through. I'm a mother. I can't even imagine the awfulness, back then and now. I just want to get to the bottom of it all. You understand that, don't you?'

'I do. You're just doing your job.'

The detective went to turn away, then paused. 'You said your husband's infidelities surprised you. That makes him a rather good liar, don't you think?'

Melissa frowned. Was the detective implying Patrick might have lied about Grace stabbing him too?

But why would he *do* that?

Melissa walked out of the police station with Grace later, blinking up at the bright yellow sky. In the distance, the sun gleamed down on the forest, making the trees appear ablaze with fire.

She looked down at Grace, squeezing her hand. They'd released her after her interview, pending further information. The twins were now being interviewed and, though Melissa wanted to wait for them, she'd been told it could be hours, so she and Bill had agreed on the phone that he would come and wait for them while Melissa took Grace home. He was on his way now.

Melissa didn't know much about Grace's interview, just that she kept denying she had stabbed her father. Other than that, she didn't divulge much information. With no proper statement from Patrick and the chance he might have been confused after waking, Detective Crawford had made the decision to wait until he could fully question Patrick and the twins.

In the meantime, it was agreed they'd release Grace to be with Melissa, which made Melissa so relieved. She decided not to push Grace about what happened. She'd already endured two hours of questioning, even if it *was* gentle questioning.

On the taxi ride back to Bill and Rosemary's house, Grace said nothing, just staring out of the window with a wrinkled brow. When they got to the house, it was quiet, Rosemary with Patrick, Bill now at the police station.

Melissa thought of Patrick. Rosemary had sent her a quick text, telling her he was sleeping, mainly . . . and that he was asking for her. Melissa had replied, asking Rosemary if Patrick had said anything else about what happened. *He can barely talk*, was Rosemary's curt reply. *He needs time. You should come and see him.*

But Melissa's priority right now was the kids, especially Grace. As long as she knew Patrick was awake and doing well, her time with him simply had to wait. Plus, what would she say to him after all she'd discovered?

'I'm tired,' Grace said. 'Can I go to sleep?'

Melissa nodded. 'Me too. Shall we go and have a nap until the twins get back?'

Grace nodded and they went upstairs, slipping between the covers of Melissa's bed. She folded Grace into her arms and stroked her hair as she fell asleep, savouring the feel of her.

Eventually Melissa fell asleep too, and it wasn't until she heard the front door clicking open that she woke. She sat up, checking Grace to see she was still asleep. Then she quietly went downstairs.

Bill was in the hallway, taking off his jacket as the twins went to head upstairs. Melissa was shocked when she saw Lilly. Her face was red and puffy from crying, her hair dishevelled. Lewis looked exhausted, his dark eyes haunted.

'How did it go?' Melissa asked.

'Conspiracy of silence,' Bill said with a sigh. 'They refused to say a single word.'

Melissa went to Lilly, stroking her cheek. But Lilly wouldn't look at her. 'Darling, what happened that afternoon?'

'I'm tired, Mum. I want to sleep.' She slipped past Melissa and went upstairs, pausing at the door to Melissa's room as she looked in on Grace. She let out a sob and ran up to the attic room, slamming the door.

'Lewis?' Melissa said. 'Look at me, Lewis.'

'What, Mum?' Lewis said in a weary voice.

'Why didn't you say anything?' she asked him. 'Dad said it was Grace. *Was* it Grace?'

'They've had enough questioning,' Bill said. 'Come on, son, get some rest and some grub, then we can take you to see your dad. He's looking good,' he added, putting his arm around his grandson's shoulders. Lewis looked over his shoulder at Melissa. Then he turned away, going into the living room with Bill.

Melissa stood on her own in the hallway for a moment, curling and uncurling her fists. Still this bloody wall of silence!

Only Grace had said something concrete: she didn't do it. Was she telling the truth or was she just a little girl scared of the consequences of stabbing her own father? That seemed more likely, didn't it? What reason would Patrick have to lie about it being Grace? And if it *were* Grace, that was one hell of a reason for the twins to keep quiet: to protect their little sister.

It was all pointing towards it being Grace, except for one thing: her motive.

Melissa sat at the dinner table later, playing with the omelette she'd made for Bill, Lewis and herself. She kept looking up at the ceiling, hoping the girls were okay. They were both sleeping when she'd gone up to see if they were hungry, so she'd decided to let them rest.

'Your nan said your dad's looking forward to seeing you, Lewis,' Bill said.

Lewis peered up, brow creased. He didn't exactly look thrilled at the idea.

Melissa placed her fork down with a clang. 'Why would Grace hurt your dad, Lewis?'

Bill sighed. 'Melissa, I told you—'

'This is my family, okay?' she snapped back at him. 'My children.'

'And my grandchildren!' Bill retorted.

Melissa ignored him and continued looking at Lewis. 'Lewis, why? What happened? You can't keep up this silence, not now Dad is awake and talking. He said it was Grace – done, over. The police know. All you need to do is fill in the missing pieces.'

Lewis remained quiet.

'Look, I know why you've been doing this,' Melissa said. 'It was to protect Grace, and I get it. I *admire* it. But there's no point any more. Once your dad is able to make a statement and confirms it was Grace, that's it. There's nothing more you can do.'

Lewis looked at Bill, then down at his food. 'I don't want to talk about it.'

'Leave it, Melissa,' Bill hissed. 'Can't you see you're upsetting him?'

Melissa put her head in her hands. 'I can't deal with this. I need to know.'

'You *need* to calm down,' Bill said in a low voice.

'How can I? My little girl has been accused of stabbing her father, and her brother and sister are refusing to say why.' Melissa shoved away from the table, grabbing her plate and taking it to the kitchen. She threw it in the sink then gripped on to the side, looking out at the forest as she took in deep breaths.

Then the doorbell went.

She closed her eyes. She really couldn't deal with Jackie or Ross right now.

She heard Bill walk down the hallway and open the door. Then she heard a familiar voice.

Detective Crawford.

She walked into the hallway to see him standing at the door with a uniformed police officer.

'We're here for Grace, Melissa,' the detective said. 'Patrick just gave us a statement. Grace definitely stabbed him.'

Chapter Forty-Eight

Saturday 27th April, 2019
12.42 p.m.

Melissa felt her legs lose their strength. Bill rushed to her, helping her to stay up.

'I . . . I thought he couldn't talk properly?' she said.

'It was a long process – we had to use flash cards in some cases,' he said. 'But he was very clear about it, I'm afraid. Grace stabbed her father, so we will be charging her with her father's assault.'

'How? Why?' Melissa asked.

'I'm afraid we can't go into that now. We're here to take her in, Melissa.'

'But where? Where will you take her?'

'We'll be taking Grace to a very nice place in Ashbridge for some further chats.' Melissa knew where he meant: St Fiacre's, the same home Jacob Simms was sent to as he awaited trial.

'No chance!' she said, trying to keep her voice low so the kids couldn't hear her. 'I know a kid who got a horrible beating there.'

'Things have changed since then,' the detective said. 'I promise you, it's the right place.'

'How can you be so sure?'

Detective Crawford sighed. 'Look, this is a very unusual case for us so there was a great deal of discussion about what will happen to Grace. In the end, we really felt St Fiacre's is the best place for her.'

'Surely home is!' Melissa said. 'She's ten!'

The detective shook his head. 'I'm afraid we can't risk that, in case she harms one of you.'

Melissa put her fingers to her temples, rubbing them. 'Harm one of us? She wouldn't do that.'

'Melissa,' the detective said in a low voice, 'don't make this more difficult than it needs to be for your daughter.'

'It's okay, Mum,' a voice said from the stairs. Melissa looked up to see Grace standing on the landing, wiping sleep from her eyes.

Detective Crawford gave a sad sigh. 'Hello, Grace.'

Melissa climbed the stairs and hugged Grace tight, every fibre of her body yearning to just run away with her daughter. But there could be no hiding any more. Patrick had confirmed it.

She crouched down, looking into Grace's eyes. 'Dad just confirmed what happened, darling, so the police want to take you somewhere to ask a few more questions.'

Grace placed her hand on her mother's cheek. 'Don't cry, Mummy.'

Melissa pursed her lips to stop herself from sobbing. 'I love you SO much, no matter what, do you understand? Mummy is always, *always* here for you.'

'What's going on?' Lewis said as he walked down the hallway.

'Your father confirmed it was Grace,' Bill said.

'No!' Lewis cried out.

He went to go to his little sister, but Bill stopped him. 'Come on, son, you don't need to see this.'

He took Lewis into the kitchen and shut the door behind them.

'The place we're taking you is great, Grace,' Detective Crawford said. '*Lots* of books, and the staff there are brilliant too,' he added, looking at Melissa.

'What about all her stuff, her clothes?' Melissa said, wrapping her arms around herself as she started to shake.

'Don't worry, Mum, I packed some stuff yesterday,' Grace said, gesturing to the Harry Potter rucksack Melissa had only just noticed on her back.

That made Melissa want to cry even more. Grace had known this was coming.

Oh, her little Grace. Her wise, clever, *knowing* little Grace.

'Aren't you clever?' Melissa said, wiping her tears away as she tried to smile. She gave Grace another quick hug. 'I will visit you as soon as I can. Is that possible?' Melissa asked the detective.

He nodded. 'Yes. I'll be in touch about the details.'

'I love you,' Melissa said to Grace.

'Love you too.'

She gave her mum a peck on the cheek then took Detective Crawford's hand and they walked off down the path.

As the front door shut, Melissa finally allowed herself to sob, leaning against the wall and letting it all out.

'What happened, Mum?' Lilly said, appearing on the landing. 'Where was Grace going?'

Melissa slid down to the floor. 'The police have taken her to St Fiacre's. Your dad gave a statement confirming what happened.'

Lilly blinked rapidly. Then she walked back into the attic room, gently closing the door behind her.

Bill peered out of the kitchen then and it occurred to Melissa: he hadn't even said goodbye to Grace. Was it as easy as that, cutting off his granddaughter because she had stabbed his son?

'Oh, Melissa,' he said, walking over to her and helping her back up.

'Where's Lewis?' she asked.

'Listening to his music. He didn't want to hear it all.'

Melissa grabbed her car keys. 'I want to see Patrick.'

'I don't think it's a good idea, Melissa. He needs to rest.'

'I'm going, Bill,' she said, grabbing her car keys.

Bill sighed. 'Fine. But be gentle with him, Melissa, he's still fragile.'

She left the house, her sights on the hospital.

Chapter Forty-Nine

Saturday 27th April, 2019
12.45 p.m.

I look at the picture Mum drew as a kid of eyes staring out of the old oak tree. There's a hollow inside that tree big enough for a child to cower in, hidden away from anyone who passes. The people of Forest Grove are like that old oak, dark places within where they hide stuff.

I'm the worst of them.

It's my fault Grace has been arrested. It's my fault Dad's lying in hospital. And it's my fault Mum's falling apart all over again. That was the whole reason we never told her. We didn't want her to try to kill herself again. We tried so hard, but I can see her breaking to pieces because I see it in myself too when I look in the mirror.

So that's it, game over. I ought *to go down to the police station now. But I'm such a bloody coward. I heard what happened to Jacob Simms at St Fiacre's! And yet how can I leave Grace in there for something she didn't do?*

Maybe there's another way. A way that means I don't have to go to that place. A way that means Grace doesn't have to stay there either.

Tell the truth in a letter, get Grace off the hook and then . . . nothing. A stop to the darkness inside, a stop to the itch of guilt and grief.

I hear the door slam and look outside.

Mum's going. Good. I don't want her to be the one to find me.

I look out of the window towards the woods where Mum tried to take her life after Joel died . . . and where Grandma Quail took her last breath.

I pick up a notepad and pen, then I walk downstairs, slipping out and going to the forest.

Chapter Fifty

Saturday 27th April, 2019
2 p.m.

Melissa walked towards Patrick's ward to find him sitting up in bed, Rosemary feeding him some porridge as Peter Mileham read the newspaper to him. Patrick was already looking brighter, with some colour in his olive cheeks. Rosemary had even given him a shave, brushing his hair to the side; it gleamed dark brown in the sunlight streaming through the window.

He really was so handsome.

Patrick looked up as Melissa entered, lips trying to form a smile as he saw her. 'Mel,' he croaked.

But she stayed where she was, wrapping her arms around herself. 'They've just taken Grace.'

Rosemary sighed. 'Yes, I thought they would.'

'What happened, Patrick?' Melissa said. 'Why did our daughter *do* that to you?'

'Argument,' Patrick said. 'Watch.'

'I'll leave you guys alone,' Peter said, placing the newspaper down and walking from the room.

'Watch?' Melissa asked. 'I don't understand.'

'He's struggling to speak, Melissa,' Rosemary said. 'The police had to use flash cards.'

'He managed to say enough to have our daughter arrested, though,' Melissa shot back.

Rosemary flinched. 'Melissa, honestly. *He* was the one who was stabbed, you know.'

'I *need* to know, Patrick,' Melissa said, ignoring Rosemary.

Patrick held her gaze, his dark eyes filling with tears. She felt her resolve weaken slightly. He *did* look upset.

'Shall I tell Melissa, darling?' Rosemary suggested to Patrick. 'Saves you struggling to speak again.'

Patrick nodded and tried to lift his hand out to Melissa.

'Go to him, Melissa,' Rosemary said. 'He's been asking for you.'

Melissa swallowed and went to him, taking his hand. His touch sent a bolt through her, so familiar and warm, her darling Patrick.

Her darling *cheating* Patrick.

'Grace accidentally broke Patrick's watch,' Rosemary said. 'The one we found in her rucksack.'

Melissa nodded. *That bloody Byatt heirloom*, she wanted to say.

'Not sure how it happened,' Rosemary said. 'Obviously Patrick can't go into detail, but he told her off, as you would if someone broke a family heirloom. I presume she wasn't paying attention or something – you know how Grace is sometimes.' Melissa felt like saying, *Actually, no, she pays attention to everything*. But she wanted to hear what had happened. 'Anyway,' Rosemary said with a sigh, 'Grace shouted back, the argument escalated, and – well, she stabbed her own father.' Her voice trembled as though she were still trying to comprehend it herself.

Patrick nodded, a tear falling down his cheek.

Melissa took the seat beside him, leaning close and exploring his face. 'It doesn't make sense, though. Grace doesn't *lose* her temper like that.'

'Sometimes children just snap, Melissa,' Rosemary said. 'You see it on the news all the time. Take all those kids from ordinary families who go into classrooms and start shooting people.'

Melissa looked at her in surprise. 'Grace didn't shoot anyone, Rosemary. And actually, there *is* usually something going on when you dig deeper.'

'Well, then, maybe there is with Grace?' Rosemary said.

'I *know* Grace. Look, can Patrick and I have some time alone, please?'

Rosemary frowned, clearly reluctant to leave her son.

Patrick nodded at his mother and she sighed. 'Fine, but call me if you need me. Be gentle with him, okay?' she said to Melissa as she left the room.

As the door closed, Patrick squeezed her hand. 'Love you,' he whispered.

She couldn't bring herself to say it back. His gaze faltered.

'I know everything, Patrick,' she said as tears gathered in her eyes. 'I know about all your affairs.'

He squeezed his eyes shut and started shaking his head. 'Sorry,' he rasped. 'Sorry.'

She gently put her fingers under his chin and made him look at her. 'You lied to me. What else have you lied about?'

He looked at her in surprise. 'No . . . lies.'

'But how can I ever trust you again?' She explored his dark eyes. 'Did Grace really stab you, Patrick?'

'Why would I lie?' he managed to get out.

Patrick was right. Why *would* he lie about Grace stabbing him?

'They've taken her to St Fiacre's, Patrick! If you're lying . . .'

She bent over, crying into her hands. She felt Patrick's hand on her back.

'Forgive me,' Patrick said. 'Please.'

She looked up at him, trying to find the man she'd married there. 'I don't know, Patrick, I just don't know.'

Her phone rang in her pocket. She sighed, taking it out. It was Bill.

She put it to her ear. 'Bill?'

'Lewis and Lilly have gone AWOL,' he said hurriedly. 'I went to check on them and they've both gone. Tried calling them, have been searching the village with some others too. Nothing.'

'When's the last time you saw them?' Melissa asked, giving Patrick a panicked look.

'After you left.'

'Shit.' She put her hand over the mouthpiece. 'The twins have disappeared.'

Patrick's eyes widened in alarm.

'You know the forest better than anyone, Melissa.' Bill said. 'I think they might have headed in there.'

'Right, I'm coming back.'

She put her phone down and Patrick reached out for her, his fingers grazing hers. 'Find them,' he said.

'I will.'

Ten minutes later, she arrived at Bill and Rosemary's to find Bill outside with Tommy Mileham and Ross Shillingford.

'We've searched the whole village,' Tommy said when she approached them. 'No sign.'

'Okay, let's go and look in the forest, Bill,' Melissa said. 'I'm sure they'll be fine. Tommy, Ross, you stay here in case they come back.'

The men nodded and Melissa and Bill headed to the forest, pushing branches out of the way to enter it. It felt dense and dark beneath the canopy of trees, the sun shrouded now by clouds, making it seem like night inside.

Melissa quickened her step, eyes scouring the trees. She had a sudden flashback to leaving her home all those years ago after Joel died, the distant sound of a three-year-old Lilly crying and calling out for her. Melissa had felt weightless, slightly unhinged, as if she could just lift her feet off the ground and fly.

She imagined feeling that way now.

She imagined Lewis or Lilly feeling that way now.

Her stomach dropped.

She started jogging, legs pumping, almost stumbling over roots and rocks as she flung branches out of the way. Bill ran beside her, panting, frantic too, until they finally got to the tree she was looking for.

The great ancient oak, right in the gnarly heart of the forest.

The place where she'd nearly died and her mother *had* died.

And there, hanging from it, a body.

Chapter Fifty-One

Saturday 27th April, 2019
2.45 p.m.

'Oh my God, it's Lilly!' Melissa screamed.

She ran to her daughter, holding her legs up as Bill jumped on to the bench to untie the rope, which was tangled around a branch.

'Hold on, darling, hold on,' Melissa said as she trembled beneath the weight of her daughter, stroking her leg as she looked up at her pale face.

'Lilly, oh God, not Lilly!' Bill shouted as he frantically tried to unknot the rope. 'It won't bloody budge.'

There was a sound from behind them and they turned to see Lewis sprinting over with Ryan.

'No!' Lewis screamed. He ran to his sister as Ryan jumped on the bench, helping Bill untie the knot and release Lilly.

They gently lowered her to the ground as Melissa started CPR, her tears spilling on to Lilly's skin.

'Is she gone?' Lewis asked as he sobbed. 'Is she dead?'

Lilly suddenly gasped a breath, her eyes opening and looking right into Melissa's. 'Sorry,' she wheezed.

Melissa sat watching Lilly in her hospital bed, Lewis curled up asleep on the chair nearby. Her caramel hair was spread out on the blue pillow and she was sleeping soundly. Bar a few torn ligaments in her neck, she was fine, thank God. They'd found her just in time. Lewis had noticed his sister missing and had headed into the forest to look for her, bumping into Ryan on the way.

The medical staff suspected that Lilly had had a psychotic breakdown, considering she was barely saying a word. So once they were sure the damage to her neck wasn't too serious and there were no other complications from having her airways suppressed, they told Melissa she'd be moved to the hospital's psych ward.

Melissa was horrified at the thought. Her confident, vivacious girl had been so horribly affected by recent events that her mind simply couldn't take it. And while she was officially conscious, Lilly chose to just sleep, moaning in sadness whenever she opened her eyes and promptly closing them again, as if she was too scared to be present in the world as it was.

Bill entered the room now, going to his granddaughter's bed and stroking her hair. He'd been there all afternoon with Melissa, allowing her to take breaks every now and again. Rosemary had arrived soon afterwards and the three of them had sobbed quietly in the corridor outside. They agreed not to tell Patrick yet.

'God, what a mess,' Bill said quietly, so as not to wake Lewis, slumping down on the chair opposite Melissa. 'Why would our Lilly *do* this?'

'I don't know. None of this seems real.'

'It's no coincidence she chose that tree, though, is it, Melissa?'

Melissa examined his face, heartbeat pulsing in her ears. 'What do you mean?'

He sighed, pressing his palm over his bald head. 'We know you attempted suicide there, Melissa. The twins told us.'

She reeled back, putting her hand to her mouth. 'No! How do they know?'

In her mind, she ran through who knew. Ryan. No, he wouldn't say anything. Debbie? Maybe, but why tell the twins?

Unless someone else saw her that day?

'They wouldn't say,' Bill said. 'Maybe that's why the kids didn't tell you what Grace did. They were scared you'd try to take your life again.'

Nausea worked its way up to Melissa's throat. She jumped up, running to the small bathroom and shutting the door, leaning over the toilet as she spat out bile. Then she stood up and wiped her mouth with trembling fingers, looking into the mirror at her haunted face.

'You did this,' she whispered to herself. 'You did *all* of this. It's *your* mess and you need to sort it out.'

'Melissa?' Bill knocked softly at the door. 'You okay in there?'

She took a deep breath and opened the door.

His face softened as he looked at her. 'Come here,' he said, opening his arms to her. She fell into them, just as she had as a child. 'It'll be okay,' he whispered in her ear. 'We'll make it all okay again, I promise.'

'How?' she asked as she looked at her sleeping daughter, the rope marks still present on her neck. 'How can we come back from all this?'

'You're their mother,' he said firmly. 'You're Patrick's wife. You need to pull yourself together, Melissa, for the sake of your kids. You can't fall apart like you did when Joel died. You need to do what's right.'

'But what's right, Bill?' she asked, honestly wanting to know the answer because she didn't have a clue how to fix things any more.

'Stick by Patrick,' Bill replied. 'Show the kids you're a family. Otherwise, you're right, the twins never will come back from this.'

'And Grace?'

'We can't control that now, but she *will* get the help she needs. What we can control is what happens to these two,' he said, peering towards the sleeping twins. 'You have a chance to make things right for them, and you won't be alone. Rosemary and I will help you do that, Melissa. We'll fix things like we have before.'

He pulled her into a hug and she felt like that little girl again, standing in his kitchen in a nightdress. Melissa pressed her face back against his shoulder. Yes, they would fix things. Rosemary and Bill always did.

Chapter Fifty-Two

Friday 3rd May, 2019
8.15 a.m.

Melissa tried to smile as she watched Patrick shuffle along with a Zimmer frame, his nurse behind him. It had been nearly a week since he'd woken from his coma, and it was a gradual process. But Patrick was his usual determined self, convinced he'd return home in time for his birthday at the end of June. Rosemary and Bill were delighted by his quick recovery, but Melissa was finding it hard to feel the same enthusiasm when her younger daughter was currently incarcerated in St Fiacre's a few miles away and her other daughter was spending her days in a ward for the mentally vulnerable. Not to mention Lewis, who'd sunk into a pit of silence and despair, just sitting in his grandparents' attic room whenever he wasn't with his twin sister in hospital.

He'd been there when Patrick had been strong enough to visit Lilly the day before, wheeled to her bed by Melissa. Patrick had just laid his head on her bed and sobbed as Lilly looked down at him, face expressionless. Seeing him like that, so vulnerable, made Melissa realise even more that Bill was right. She had a chance to make things right and sew her family back together if she could only forgive Patrick for his infidelities . . . what else could she do? Leave Patrick when he was in such a state, have the twins endure the separation of their parents when they'd already been through so much?

After talking with Bill on the day Lilly tried to take her life, she went to Patrick and told him she forgave him, that they needed to be strong for the kids. He didn't seem surprised. It seemed easy enough for him to fall back into his confident old ways, as though all the horror hadn't really happened. Melissa was too exhausted not to go along with it. Like today, watching him at yet another physio session, just as she used to watch him doing his speeches at local events as he tried to raise his profile for the election. She might as well; she was practically living in the hospital, dividing her time between Patrick and Lilly.

Today was different from the past week, though. Today she would be visiting Grace . . . plus, as their house was no longer under scene guard, she'd decided it was time to move back. Truth was, she'd been avoiding it – easily done as she was spending most of her time in hospital. She wasn't sure why she'd been avoiding it. Maybe because it would all feel so fake now, their seemingly perfect 'family home' that belied so many fractures. But it really was time to return, maybe even clean the place. Do something *normal.*

'Melissa, look!' Patrick said now. He'd reached the end of the bar, his handsome face alight with a bright smile.

'Isn't he doing well?' one of the nurses remarked as she passed. Melissa smiled.

Patrick really was doing so well. There was just one area of his recovery he was having particular problems with: his speech. His nurse said it was probably due to how sore his throat was after having pipes in for so long. It meant Melissa had to make do with brief sentences and laminated cards to communicate properly with him.

It was frustrating for him, but even more so for Melissa, as it was impossible to get a clear picture of what had happened that Thursday afternoon. She wanted to know all the nuances of it, what led up to it, how Grace had seemed to Patrick in the weeks and days before. They had always said they were a team when it came to the kids, but she still felt like she was a member down, even though Patrick was awake now.

Patrick threw Melissa another smile as the nurses helped him into his wheelchair. When he got to Melissa, he instantly looked at his phone. The local elections had been the day before, not that Melissa had really taken any notice. But it meant a lot to Patrick, and now he was desperate to see if the votes had been counted.

'Any news yet?' she asked him.

He shook his head, his forehead shiny with sweat and his dark hair glistening with it too.

'Well, you did great up there,' Melissa said.

He beamed at her. 'Did good, didn't I?'

'Wow, you are talking *so* much better too! That was really clear,' she said, clutching on to his hands. 'Did you hear yourself?'

He nodded, putting his hand to his throat and wincing. 'Hurt, though,' he whispered.

'But it's a good start. We should tell your nurse. Can you try to say something else?'

He frowned, shaking his head. 'Hurts.'

'Please try, Patrick,' she said, searching his face. 'It would be so good to talk. I still don't feel I've got to grips with what happened that afternoon, if—'

He shoved her hands away. 'Hurts!'

She looked at him in surprise.

The nurse strolled over. 'Everything okay here?'

Melissa sat back against the bench, watching Patrick. 'Patrick just said a few words. But it's clearly very painful for him.'

'Well done, Patrick,' the nurse said, crouching down in front of him. 'Want to try a few more for me?'

Patrick shook his head, gesturing to his throat. 'No worries,' the nurse said. 'We'll try later. Shall we get you some lunch?'

She wheeled Patrick away as Melissa stayed where she was for a few moments.

Patrick turned and looked over his shoulder, jutting his chin to beckon her to him. She got up and went to him.

St Fiacre's was a large three-storey house on the outskirts of Ashbridge with views of Forest Grove in the distance. Melissa had been desperate to visit Grace before, but this was the first time she had been allowed, two days before Grace was due in court to hear the charges against her. While Grace was there, the staff were focusing on getting her assessed.

'It will help her case,' Detective Crawford had told Melissa when she'd spoken to him on the phone. 'If we can get a full psychological assessment, and maybe her version of the story in the process, we can put together a fair trial.'

Trial.

Melissa couldn't believe her daughter would be dragged through the courts, even if they were the Youth Courts. At least the public and the media wouldn't be present. The thought of the media finding out it was Grace who had stabbed her dad, a man running to be the local parish councillor, struck fear into her heart. It hadn't got out yet, but it would. A ten-year-old from a village like Forest Grove stabbing her father was perfect tabloid fodder. Detective Crawford warned Melissa to brace herself; somebody was bound to leak it to the press.

Nothing yet, though, thank God. Even the Forest Grove Facebook group had gone quiet.

She walked towards St Fiacre's now with some trepidation. She couldn't help but play over Jacob Simms's experience there, despite Detective Crawford's reassurances that the home had had a complete overhaul since that incident. The house looked innocent enough from the outside, a fine white Edwardian property with large windows, the small silver sign and the buzzer at the front the only clue to it being anything other than a family home. Melissa pressed the buzzer and was allowed in when she gave her name. She was greeted by a woman with a name badge and taken through to the room where she would be seeing Grace. It had a range of comfy sofas and shelves laden with books and games. There was even a TV. Clearly the people running the place wanted to create as normal an environment as possible for the children there, and for their visiting families. But for Melissa, it was hard to see it as normal, especially when she took in the other visiting families and the children they were coming to see. Melissa wasn't the type to judge, or at least she tried her best not to. God knows she'd not exactly come from an auspicious background herself. But it was clear the people there had had hard lives. It was written across their faces, in their choice of clothing. Melissa stood out like a sore thumb with her Boden tunic and Salt-Water sandals.

Grace did too as she walked in, a book in her hand, a member of staff behind her. She looked particularly young, with her hair in plaits. She never usually wore her hair in plaits. Melissa jumped up and went to her, hugging her tight and trying her best not to cry. The woman behind her nodded, walking off to a nearby chair and taking out her iPad.

'How are you, darling?' Melissa said, leading Grace to a comfy chair. 'Have you been eating enough? Is the food nice?'

Grace shrugged and Melissa bit her lip. She looked exhausted up close, dark circles under her blue eyes. That shouldn't come as a surprise, really. But still, it worried Melissa.

'Are Lilly and Lewis okay?' Grace asked quietly.

'They're fine, darling.' She couldn't bring herself to tell Grace what had happened to Lilly. She had enough on her small shoulders as it was.

'When can I come home?'

Melissa forced herself not to start crying. 'There needs to be a trial first.'

'When will that be?'

'I don't know, darling, Detective Crawford said maybe six months. We have the court date first, of course. I'll be there.'

Grace tensed in her arms. 'I don't think I can do this, Mummy.'

Melissa grasped her shoulders. 'Nonsense. You need to be strong,' she said, realising this was the best approach now for Grace. No more mollycoddling. 'Think Maleficent kind of strong, when she gets her wings cut off in that Angelina Jolie film.'

Grace nodded, leaning her head on her mother's shoulder.

'Did Maleficent have a mum and dad?' she asked.

'You know what, I don't know.'

'Aurora was brought up in the woods with the fairies, right?'

Melissa nodded and Grace peered out of the window in the direction of Forest Grove. 'If I'd got to live with Ryan,' she said, 'maybe I would be living in the woods with him. Maybe I wouldn't be here.'

'Why would you live with Ryan?'

Grace turned back to look at her mother. 'He's my dad.'

Melissa shook her head, grabbing her daughter's hand. 'He isn't your dad, Grace. Where on earth did you hear that?'

'Dad told me.'

Chapter Fifty-Three

Friday 3rd May, 2019
11 a.m.

Melissa walked up the drive to her house, still trying to process what Grace had said to her earlier. She'd considered going to Patrick right away, asking him what the hell he'd been playing at, telling Grace she was Ryan's. But she needed time to think.

She put her key in the door, not quite believing it was just over two weeks since she'd done the same, expecting to be greeted by the usual chatter and calls for food. As she stepped inside, a bag with Lilly and Lewis's dirty clothes in her hands, she felt as though her legs were filled with lead.

She paused and looked around her. Things felt different now. It no longer felt like a home. She walked through into the kitchen and sat on a stool, staring at the place where Patrick had lain. Over two weeks ago, just two weeks, and yet so much had happened to change the course of their lives here. She yearned for the humdrum of the time before, the whir of the washing machine and the sound of music drifting from the twins' room upstairs. She yearned to see Grace reading in her favourite corner of the living room and Patrick throwing a toy for Sandy. But instead all she saw now was Patrick and Grace standing across from each other, shouting over a broken bloody watch!

She sighed and got the mop out, beginning to clean the floor. But the blood was so congealed into the grout that she had to get down on her hands and knees, scrubbing at it with a hard brush, tears rolling down her cheeks as she thought of Grace stabbing Patrick in this very spot . . . of Patrick telling Grace she was Ryan's!

There was a knock on the door. Melissa took a deep breath, wiping her tears away with her wrist, then she walked down the hallway, the scrub brush still in her hands.

She opened the door to find Daphne there.

'Oh, Melissa,' Daphne said, pulling Melissa into her arms. 'Maddy told me about Lilly. I'm so sorry you're going through this.'

'It's horrible.'

'I can't even imagine.

Daphne's eyes dropped to the brush in Melissa's hand, which was dripping bloody water on the floor.

'I've been trying to get the blood out,' Melissa said.

Without saying anything, Daphne took the brush and went to the kitchen. If she was shocked by the sight of the bloody swirls on the floor and the police tape on the side, she didn't show it. Instead, she knelt down and started scrubbing until every drop of the blood had disappeared. Then she turned her attention to the rest of the kitchen as Melissa sat at the kitchen table, watching her friend.

'Patrick recovering well, then?' Daphne asked, without looking up.

Melissa nodded. 'Yes, apart from his speech. It means we're not able to get much more out of him about what happened.'

'And what about you guys? How are you after, you know, all the rumours about Patrick?'

'We're hanging in there.'

Daphne's jaw clenched as she scrubbed harder at the kitchen worktops. 'So you're going to stay with him, are you?'

'I don't know yet.'

Daphne stopped scrubbing and looked up at Melissa, wiping her brow. 'You know people like him never change, Melissa. I just—' She sighed, shaking her head. 'Sorry, it's none of my business.'

'No, carry on. Maybe I need to hear it,' Melissa said, thinking of what Grace had just told her.

'I don't want you being influenced by Rosemary and Bill,' Daphne said. 'I hope you know you have your own strength without them . . . without Patrick too. You can do fine on your own. You need to learn to trust your instincts, something that can easily get lost when you're hugged too close.'

Melissa had heard a similar speech from her mother a week before she died. Her mother had broached the subject of them getting their own place a few villages away. Melissa hated the idea. She loved staying at Bill and Rosemary's, and she'd told her mother that.

'But I can't breathe properly here, Lissie,' her mother had said. 'I feel smothered by Bill and Rosemary, by the whole Forest Grove community.'

'They're not smothering us,' Melissa had whined. 'I love it here!'

Her mother had grown quiet and reflective. Then she'd looked at Melissa with her big blue eyes. 'There's this interesting story I once read about a forestry school in the Philippines.' Melissa had sighed. Her mother had a tendency to go off on tangents. 'The school decided to revive a forest nearby, which had fallen into disrepair. They planted a huge variety of trees in the woods, using various seeds, including mahogany seeds from India. And my, those mahogany hardwoods were wonderful, spreading like a good'un, nourishing those floundering forests and providing shelter to animals and students alike.'

Melissa had rolled her eyes. 'India. Philippines. Mahogany seeds? What's this got to do with anything, Mum?'

'Patience, child!' her mother had said. Melissa had gone quiet. Truth was, it was the first time her mother had properly talked since they'd left the cottage. It was almost like she was back to her old self. Her mother leaned forward, looking her daughter in the eye. 'Problem is, those trees began to take over. They became a nuisance, *stifling* the surrounding plants. Not to mention the fact those trees did *nothing* for the ecosystem, producing leaves that proved too bitter for animals to eat. In the end, the natural ways of those ancient woods were trampled on. They died.'

Melissa had sighed. 'So what am I, the ancient woods or the mahogany seeds?'

Her mother had taken Melissa's hand in hers. '*We* are the ancient woods, my darling. We were here before Forest Grove and its residents, and we would have survived without them, darling, *trust* me. Our roots are strong, you are strong. All I'm saying is, Lissie, save a part of yourself, keep it close, trust your *instincts.* You don't always have to look to the community, to Bill and Rosemary, to know what's right.'

Melissa had grown angry then. 'But they do know what's right, don't they, Mum? Because without them, we both might be dead right now.'

Her mother's eyes had narrowed. 'I had a plan, Melissa. I just never got a chance to follow it through, thanks to Rosemary and Bill. Be careful with those two, darling.'

Truth was, her mother had felt so stifled by them she walked out in the middle of a freezing-cold night.

Melissa shook her head now, the memories dissipating.

'Sorry. I'm going on, aren't I?' Daphne said.

'No, I was just thinking you sound like my mum, actually.'

'Now *there's* a compliment, from what I've heard of your mum.'

'Is it, though? My mum died of hypothermia in the middle of the woods.' Melissa fiddled with the sleeve of her cardigan. 'I think it's easy for people to look in from the outside and judge women who stay with their husbands. But sometimes, the decisions we make are based on bigger things, you know? Sometimes it's the best thing for the kids.'

'You think Patrick is the best thing for the kids?'

'He loves them.'

'There's something not right about him, Melissa. Always has been.'

Melissa frowned. 'What do you mean?'

'Did you know he was chucked out of his first school before coming to Forest Grove because he cut some girl's hair off? That's why Rosemary and Bill moved here. He told me when he was drunk once. *Really* drunk,' she added. 'The confessional, lay-it-all-out-on-a-plate kind of drunk.'

Melissa looked at her in surprise. When had they had a chance to get so drunk together?

'He told me he was thirteen,' Daphne continued. 'He had this thing for one of the girls in his class. But she dyed her hair for some charity event and he was so furious he cut it with a knife, accidentally cutting her in the process. Her parents went mental, the Byatts were driven out of town, so they ended up here,' she said, gesturing outside. 'Wasn't the first time he'd done something weird like that either, but Bill and Rosemary just kept covering for him, sending him to Kitty bloody Fletcher. He isn't right in the head.'

Melissa slumped back in her chair. 'Wow. I don't know what to say.'

'I'm sorry, Melissa,' Daphne said. 'I know he's hurt in hospital, but it's the truth, I *swear.* So maybe staying with Patrick *isn't* the right thing for the kids.'

Melissa bristled. 'He was just a kid then. And I know the right thing for my kids, okay?'

Tears flooded Daphne's green eyes.. 'You're not going to leave him, are you?'

Melissa examined Daphne's face. She looked really upset. Melissa suddenly felt bad for snapping at her. She got off the stool and put her hand on her friend's back. 'What's wrong, Daphne?'

Daphne shrugged Melissa's hand off. 'I don't deserve your sympathy. I really don't!'

That was when it dawned on Melissa.

Daphne had slept with Patrick too!

Chapter Fifty-Four

Friday 3rd May, 2019
11.30 a.m.

Melissa felt her legs weaken. She crouched down, putting her head in her hands. How could she not have known? Daphne went to put her hand on Melissa's shoulder, but Melissa batted her away. 'You slept with him too.'

'I'm so sorry, Melissa,' Daphne said. 'But maybe it's best you know anyway. Maybe it'll convince you to leave him.'

Melissa looked at her. 'You were supposed to be my *friend*.'

'I tried not to be. As soon as it happened, I regretted it. I tried to distance myself. But you were so kind to me . . .' Her voice trailed off.

'How could you?'

'It was a mistake. I was drunk, so drunk.'

'The lay-it-all-out-on-the-table kind of drunk?' Melissa asked sarcastically.

'Yeah. It was one of those lock-ins, not just one, but a few. There were other men too, it got out of hand. *I* got out of hand.' She hung her head in shame.

'Is that why you and Ryan split up?' Melissa spat.

Daphne nodded. Melissa stood up and went to the window, pressing her palm against the glass and looking out at the trees as she tried to catch her breath.

'Melissa . . .'

'Go away!' Melissa screamed at Daphne. 'Just fucking go away!'

Daphne stood up and let herself out. Melissa turned and threw the bloody brush she'd been using at the door, splintering the wood.

It was just betrayal after betrayal after betrayal. Ryan's betrayal too, as he hadn't told her. Why hadn't he told her? Only one way to find out.

She went to the back door and ran outside, gulping in fresh air. Then she headed for the forest, the soles of her wellies trampling leaves and mud. In the distance, several runners appeared from the woods. At the front was Andrea, clad head-to-toe in bright pink Lycra gym clothes.

Another one of Patrick's conquests, Melissa thought to herself.

Behind Andrea were Charlie and several other mums Melissa recognised from the school run, Rebecca Feine at the back, looking exhausted. Melissa had heard about the Forest Grove Runners' Club, had even considered joining it until she realised Andrea was leading it.

'Oh, hello, Melissa!' Andrea said.

Melissa looked at her in shock. How could she even *talk* to Melissa? Surely she knew the cat was out of the bag about her and Patrick? Melissa had seen the Facebook posts; it was clear that Patrick and Andrea's hook-ups hadn't stopped when they were young.

Melissa went to walk off but Andrea grabbed her arm. Melissa raised an eyebrow, looking at her hand.

'Shouldn't you be with Patrick?' Andrea said. 'If it were my husband, I wouldn't leave his side.'

'Oh, come on, Andrea,' Rebecca shouted from the back. 'He won't be alone, he has Bill and Rosemary, and Melissa's entitled to take a break. Come on, let's leave her with her thoughts.'

But Andrea didn't budge, instead looking Melissa up and down as she took a quick swig of water.

Anger burned inside Melissa and she slammed her palm into the bottom of Andrea's bottle, the top coming off and spurting her face with water. 'That's for fucking my husband.'

Then she strode off as Rebecca smiled.

Melissa continued walking until she got to Ryan's cabin and knocked at his door. He took a while to answer it. When he eventually did, she could see he looked like he'd been sleeping, hair all mussy, face creased.

His eyes widened as he took in Melissa's tear-streaked face. 'What's wrong?'

'I know Daphne slept with Patrick.'

Ryan raked his fingers through his hair. 'Do you want to come in?'

Melissa stayed where she was. 'No, no, I don't. I just need to know why you didn't bloody tell me. You must have known.'

He leaned against the door frame. 'I promised Daphne.'

'When did it happen?'

'Does it matter?'

'Yes, it matters! I want to know how long you've been keeping it from me.'

Ryan's eyes focused on something in the distance. Melissa turned to see Maddy walking through the forest towards them, her short pink hair distinctive against the green leaves. As Maddy drew closer, Melissa could see she'd been crying, her mascara running down her cheeks, her dark eyes glistening with more tears.

'Halloween, 2003,' Maddy said in a monotone voice. 'That's when it happened.'

Melissa frowned. 'I was pregnant with the twins then.'

As Melissa looked into Maddy's brown eyes, it all suddenly clicked into place. She put her hand to her mouth. 'Patrick's your dad.'

'Yes,' Maddy answered.

Chapter Fifty-Five

Friday 3rd May, 2019
11.50 a.m.

'Did you know Maddy is Patrick's?' Melissa asked Ryan.

'Yes,' Ryan admitted. 'That's why Daphne and I split up – I figured it out five years later. I could *see* Patrick in Maddy when I looked at her. I confronted Daphne when we were drunk, and she admitted it. I didn't know Maddy was aware too until a few days ago, did I, Mads?' Maddy shook her head.

'How long have you known?' Melissa asked Maddy.

'A few months,' Maddy said. 'Remember the New Year's Eve party when Grace wore that dark Matilda wig? Everyone kept saying how alike Grace and I looked with her dark hair like mine.'

Melissa nodded. 'I remember. Grace was delighted.'

'It just kept playing on my mind,' Maddy said, blowing her nose on a tissue Melissa gave her. 'Every time I saw Grace, I could *see* it. Same shape eyes, same mouth.'

Melissa examined Maddy's face. She was right. Now she knew, she could see Grace in her. The twins too.

Oh God, the twins. Poor Lewis.

'That's why you split up with Lewis?' Melissa asked.

Maddy's eyes welled up again. 'Yes. It was horrible. He's my half-brother!' she said mournfully.

'Oh, Maddy,' Melissa said, leaning over and squeezing her hand.

'Maybe that's how Patrick got the idea that Grace was yours,' Melissa said to Ryan. 'He heard the same comments about Grace and Maddy looking alike but came to a completely different conclusion?'

'Makes sense,' Ryan said. 'He came and asked me if Grace was mine a few weeks after the party.'

Melissa thought of the argument people had reported hearing between Ryan and Patrick. So *that* was what it was about. 'Why didn't you deny it?' she asked him.

'I did! He wouldn't bloody listen. I was tempted to tell him the truth, but I'd promised Daphne.'

'So Patrick really has no idea you're his?' Melissa asked Maddy.

'No, I don't think so.' She shook her head. 'That night with Mum must've been quite something if he didn't remember it.'

'That's what the lock-ins were like,' Ryan said with a sigh. 'Drunken messes.'

Melissa looked at Ryan, her heart going out to him. He'd held the secret for years and treated Maddy like his flesh and blood all the same.

'How did you finally figure it all out?' Melissa asked Maddy.

'I did some digging,' Maddy said. 'You know me, like a dog with a bone when I want to investigate something.'

Ryan looked up, smiling sadly. 'Yep, my little journalist.' The smile vanished from his face and Melissa realised what he was thinking: Maddy now knew she wasn't *his little journalist* – not biologically, anyway.

'Anyway,' Maddy said, leaning back against a tree and raking her ring-clad fingers through her pink hair, 'you know that dick,

Carter? Andrea's son?' Melissa nodded. 'He was totally off his head at the New Year's Eve party and he pretty much confirmed that his mum and Patrick had had sex. I don't know how he knew – maybe he overheard his mum saying something. He also told Lilly and Lewis that you and Dad were having an affair,' Maddy said to Melissa. 'I think he just liked winding us all up by repeating all the random rumours he heard . . . with a bit of truth mixed in too, it turns out. Anyway, it sort of cemented the idea in my mind that Patrick was a cheater.' She looked up at Melissa. 'Sorry.'

'It's fine,' Melissa said. 'I've got over the shock, sadly.'

'I put two and two together,' Maddy continued, 'and I was so *fucking* angry, and embarrassed too. Sorry, but Patrick is everything I despise. I know what Mum did was shitty to you both, but she doesn't try to make out she's some perfect person or anything. But Patrick . . .' Maddy wrinkled her nose. 'He's the opposite, gives off this "perfect family man" vibe, it makes me sick! So when I saw him parading you all around like you're the perfect bloody family, it made me furious.'

'That's why you made those posters?' Melissa asked her.

Maddy looked at her in alarm. 'You know?'

'I had a suspicion, but this confirms it.'

'*You* did those posters?' Ryan asked.

Maddy scratched at the remains of some blue nail polish on her thumbnail. 'Yeah. The plan initially was to confront him, face to face, but I chickened out.'

'So you put posters up instead,' Melissa said, 'in the place where you knew his event would be, by the plot for the well-being centre he had planned?'

Maddy nodded. 'I wanted Patrick to know *someone* knew he wasn't so perfect.'

'What about the brick?' Melissa asked. 'What was that all about?'

'The brick?' Maddy asked, frowning.

'We had a brick thrown through the window with one of your posters wrapped around it,' Melissa explained. 'Lewis's face was circled, with "DAD KILLER" written on it.'

'I swear, I didn't have anything to do with that!' Maddy said. She thought about it for a moment. 'Though it *does* sound like something Carter would do. He put a brick through a teacher's window once. He enjoys destroying things, the little psycho, and he was banging on at school about Lewis probably trying to kill his own dad.'

Melissa thought about it. 'It *did* happen just after some posts about Lewis on the Facebook group.'

'And Carter *probably* hated Lewis after their run-in on the football field,' Maddy added. 'Everyone was going on about what a wimp he was, crying when Lewis punched him. That would really piss off an arrogant twat like Carter.'

'But how did he get one of the posters?' Ryan asked.

'Shit,' Maddy said, rolling her eyes. 'I printed them off at school when I was working late on the newspaper. I might have left one behind. I did see Carter creeping around there once. He likes standing around in the dark like a complete weirdo.'

Melissa thought of the figure she'd seen watching from the forest the night of the brick incident. She'd thought it was the same person who'd followed her through the forest that time, but that had been Bill. No, this figure hadn't been quite as tall as Bill and had been skinnier too . . . and now she thought about it, in the moonlight, she could see they had been wearing a puffa jacket like the one Carter had spilt blood on after Lewis punched him, the same one Andrea had said she'd have to replace.

It *must* have been him.

'Do you think the little shit might have broken my cameras too?' Ryan said.

Maddy's shoulders slumped. 'Sorry. I did that. I overheard you guys talking that night in the lodge. I didn't want you seeing it was me who put the posters up.'

'Jesus, Maddy!' Ryan said.

'Sorry, Dad.'

Ryan sighed as he looked at Melissa. 'After all that, the posters had nothing to do with what happened the afternoon Patrick was stabbed.'

Maddy quickly shook her head. 'No way! You thought that?'

Melissa and Ryan nodded.

'Seriously, I have *no* idea what happened that afternoon,' Maddy said.

'The twins said nothing to you?' Melissa asked.

'Nada.'

'Anything else you noticed about the kids recently?'

Maddy frowned. 'When Lilly was drunk once, she kept saying something about Joel being too cold. I couldn't quite catch what she said, but Lewis basically told her to shut up so she did.'

Melissa suddenly felt giddy. Debbie had said something about Joel being cold too.

When I saw your little Joel lying there, so cold, too *cold.*

'What could she mean?' Melissa asked.

'Ask her?' Ryan suggested.

'She's not talking,' Melissa said.

'I thought she might have mentioned it in her suicide note.' Maddy flinched. 'God, that still sounds awful out loud. I can't believe she tried to kill herself.'

'She didn't leave a suicide note,' Melissa said.

Maddy's brow crinkled. 'That doesn't sound like Lilly – she loves writing in that journal of hers. I'd be surprised if she didn't write some sort of letter before she did what she did.'

Melissa looked towards the oak tree in the distance. 'You're right.' She gave Maddy a quick hug and squeezed Ryan's hand. 'Thank you for telling me all this. You did the right thing.'

Then she strode away, heading towards the great oak.

When she got there, she searched around it for any sign of a letter, but there was nothing. Then she caught sight of the hollow in the tree, the hollow where she'd once hidden.

She reached inside, fingers grasping the edge of a piece of paper, and pulled it out to see it was a folded letter addressed to her.

Lilly's suicide note.

Chapter Fifty-Six

Dear Mum,

If you're reading this, I'm gone. It's for the best, really. Truth is, I'm a bloody coward. And at least this way I won't hurt anyone else, like I hurt Dad . . . and poor Caitlin too with the hogweed.

But most of all, poor Grace.

It's just better I go now, even though I know how much pain it'll cause. The pain of losing me isn't as bad as the pain I know I can cause by sticking around, trust me. I'm just protecting you by doing this.

That's why I stabbed Dad, to protect Grace. I thought he was going to hurt her, just like he hurt Joel. I always think about how Joel must have felt in his last moments, and all I want to do is wrap him up in my arms to stop him feeling so cold.

Maybe he's here with me now, at Grandma Quail's bench.

Is this how you felt after Joel died? Like every route you considered taking was blocked, so there was only one sure way, the end of a rope?

I wish I had told you everything from the start, we all do. But when you leave it for so long, the words get stuck. Grace said that. She's so clever, isn't she? She said it's like when you leave a chimney for too long and it gets all stuck with soot.

The truth got stuck. And now I'm stuck. I want to help Grace. I want to march down to the police and say it was me who stabbed Dad, not her. But I'm so scared. I'm scared to see the disappointment on your face, on Nan and Grandad's faces too. I'm scared of what might happen to me in St Fiacre's.

It's easier if I just go.

So . . . that's it. I'm done. I know you'll be able to handle this, Mum, despite what Grandad keeps telling us. You have *to, for Lewis and Grace.*

I love you. Lils. x

Chapter Fifty-Seven

Friday 3rd May, 2019
1 p.m.

Melissa sunk on to the bench, putting her head in her hands, Lilly's letter by her side.

It was Lilly who stabbed Patrick . . . and she had done it to stop him from hurting Grace . . .

Just like he hurt Joel.

Melissa looked up at the sky, letting out a scream. Birds flocked away, wings flapping. She leaned her head back, tears streaming down her face.

What did Lilly *mean* about Joel?

And why had Patrick said it was Grace? Why had Lewis backed that up? Why didn't Grace *say* something?

What was it Ryan had said about them: *One for all and all for one.* A conspiracy of silence.

And as she thought of it, it made sense: if Patrick thought Grace wasn't his, then that meant she was nothing to him. He could use her to protect a *real* Byatt, his perfect daughter, Lilly.

Her phone buzzed and she looked down at it to see a message from Bill.

Patrick is asking after you. :-) See you soon? Bill

'Oh, I'll be there,' Melissa said to herself as she quickened her step. 'But first I have someone else to visit.'

When she got back to her street, instead of going to her car to drive to the hospital, she continued walking down her road and on to Old Pine Road, passing Bill and Rosemary's house until she was standing in front of Debbie Lampard's house. She took a deep breath and walked up the path, knocking on the front door.

Debbie answered in her dressing gown, yawning. Her blue eyes widened when she saw Melissa. 'Oh, Melissa! You must excuse me, I've just woken, had a late shift last night.' She examined her face. 'Everything okay? How's Patrick? And Lilly too? I heard she was taken ill?'

'They're fine. Can I come in?'

'Of course,' Debbie said, opening the door wide, worry registering on her face. 'Do you want a tea, I was just making myself one.'

'No, I'm fine, thanks.'

Melissa walked down the hallway. Debbie's house was one of the smaller ones on Old Pine Road but it had a lovely view right through the forest from the back.

Melissa sat across from Debbie on one of her comfy pink sofas.

'Can I just ask you something?' Melissa asked.

'Fire away.'

'You fell out with Bill and Rosemary after Joel's death, didn't you? Why was that?'

Debbie's face went very pale. She drew one of her cushions on to her lap and hugged it close. 'Oh, you know, over something trivial. I can't even remember.'

'It can't be trivial, Debbie,' Melissa said gently. 'You used to be so close. Trivial doesn't put a stop to friendships.'

'Why are you asking this, Melissa?'

'My family is falling apart at the seams and I need to know why.' She leaned towards Debbie. 'And I think it has something to do with Joel's death.'

Debbie looked out into the forest, eyes going glassy. 'I wondered if this day would come. I think I almost *wanted* it to.'

Melissa's heartbeat started racing. 'What are you trying to say, Debbie?'

Debbie took in a deep breath then stood up, taking the seat next to Melissa and clasping her two hands in between her own. 'The day Joel died, I received a panicked phone call from Rosemary.'

'Yes, she called you to come and check on him?'

'That's right. When I arrived, Bill and Patrick were locked away in Bill's study. I could hear Patrick crying and Bill talking to him in a low voice. I knew right away something had gone horribly wrong. The twins – they were three, nearly four at the time?' Melissa nodded, hands starting to tremble beneath Debbie's touch. 'They were sitting in the living room like meek little mice, all big, fearful eyes, and strangely quiet. Rosemary was in a bit of a state. I tried to ask her what was going on, but she wouldn't tell me, just led me upstairs.' Debbie closed her eyes as though seeing it happen all over again. 'Joel was lying in bed,' she said, eyes still closed, 'and I knew right away he was gone.'

Melissa let out a sob and Debbie grasped her hands tighter as she looked right into her eyes.

'Rosemary wanted me to check his pulse, just to be sure,' Debbie continued. 'So I did and, my God, he was *freezing* to the touch, even with a big duvet over him. It wasn't right.'

Cold, so cold.

'So . . . he'd been dead a while?' Melissa asked.

'No,' Debbie said, shaking her head. 'It wasn't that. It was freezing cold that day, so they had the heating on full blast, all of us did. No, it was like – like he'd been outside for hours.'

Melissa almost stopped breathing. 'Outside? But I thought Patrick found him in bed like that in the morning? How could he have been *outside*?'

'I know, it seemed like a ridiculous notion at the time, so I dismissed it. But deep down, I knew something was *off*.'

Melissa jumped up and started pacing the room, a million theories running through her mind.

'What, did you think they were covering something up?' Melissa asked. 'Something about Joel's death?'

Debbie started trembling, tears flooding her eyes. 'Yes. I should have said something at the time, I've lived with the regret ever since. I – I just hoped something would come up in the autopsy report, but they just ruled it was heart failure, which of course it would be if—'

'If what?' Melissa asked.

'If it was hypothermia.'

Melissa froze. 'But why would Joel have died of hypothermia?'

'I don't know, I really don't know, Melissa! I should have questioned them more at the time.'

She put her hand to her mouth and let out a sob, but Melissa didn't go to comfort her. Instead, she got up and walked out.

It was time to see Patrick and his parents.

Chapter Fifty-Eight

Friday 3rd May, 2019
1.45 p.m.

Melissa walked down the hospital corridor towards Patrick's room, her whole body trembling with anger. She could hear laughter, even music. When she got to the small room, it was crowded. Rosemary and Bill were there, Lewis too, sitting on a chair as he looked miserably out into the forest.

'You're here!' Rosemary said, giving Melissa a hug. Melissa stayed stiff in her arms and Rosemary frowned slightly.

'What's all this about?' Melissa asked, looking around her.

'The votes have been counted, and we've just had it confirmed that Patrick has been voted in as Forest Grove's next parish councillor!' Bill said, going to hand Melissa a glass of champagne. She shoved it away from him, the drink spilling over Bill's shirt.

He looked at her in surprise as she walked to Patrick's bed.

'Good news, isn't it?' Patrick asked her when she got to him, oblivious to how angry she was, his brown eyes alight as he took her hand in his. 'Finally, something to celebrate.'

Melissa noticed he'd conveniently forgotten he couldn't speak. It made her even more angry. 'Celebrate?' she said in a shaky voice. 'How can we celebrate when Grace is in that place?'

Patrick's face darkened as Bill and Rosemary exchanged looks.

'Seriously,' Melissa said, looking at the three of them, 'I can't be the only one who thinks all this is inappropriate?'

'Mum's right,' Lewis said. 'It's wrong. It's all so fucking wrong!'

'Lewis . . .' Bill said in a warning voice, squeezing his grandson's shoulder.

'Let him talk,' Melissa commanded.

'This is ridiculous, Melissa,' Rosemary said. 'Patrick has just received some wonderful news after all the tragedy of the past two weeks and—'

'Shut *up*, Rosemary!' Melissa said, her gaze not leaving Lewis's. 'Lilly left a suicide note, Lewis. She admitted to me it was her who stabbed Dad.'

Rosemary gasped, but Bill remained strangely quiet. Patrick just blinked, his face going pale.

'It's time to tell me, darling,' Melissa said. 'No more silence. It's time to tell the truth.'

Lewis's face crumpled. 'It was Lilly who did it.'

'He's lying,' Patrick said. 'Why are you lying, Lewis?'

'No,' Melissa said, walking over to her husband. '*You* are lying. You're always fucking lying.'

'Melissa!' Rosemary exclaimed.

'Don't deny it,' Melissa said to Patrick. 'You lied about Grace, you lied about *all* the women you slept with.' She got Lilly's letter out, waving it about. 'Why did Lilly feel the need to protect Grace from you? Tell me that, Patrick?'

Patrick swallowed as Bill stared at the letter in Melissa's hand. Rosemary looked confused.

'It was because of Joel,' a voice said from behind them all.

They all turned to see Lilly in the doorway. She looked fragile, pale, but she was standing, her hand on the door frame.

Melissa went to her, pulling her into her arms. 'Oh, darling.' She explored her face. 'What are you doing here?'

'I wanted to find Lewis so I slipped out when a nurse wasn't looking.' She turned to her father, her eyes darkening.

'Tell me what happened,' Melissa said.

'Don't, Lilly,' Bill warned his granddaughter. 'Remember what I said? This won't be good for your mum.'

'You're wrong, Grandad,' Lilly said. 'Mum can deal with the truth, can't you, Mum?'

Melissa nodded. 'I can.' And as she said that, she realised she *could* handle anything . . . even the truth. The final, horrible truth.

'Okay, then here's the truth,' Lilly said in a trembling voice. 'The truth about how Joel died.'

Melissa's breath became laboured. She held on to her daughter for support.

Patrick struggled to get up. 'Lilly, no!'

Lilly turned to him, eyes sparking with anger. 'Shut up, Dad.' He sank against his pillow and Lilly took a deep, calming breath before turning back to her mother. 'We went for a walk that morning, the day Joel died. I remember Dad said it might snow so I was proper excited.'

'For God's sake, you were only three at the time, how could you remember?' Bill said.

Melissa gave him a sharp look. 'You'd be surprised how much kids remember, Bill. And it was certainly a day that would stick in the mind, wasn't it?' she said, her voice catching.

Bill didn't reply.

'I remember, when we got there, Joel freaked out about something,' Lilly continued.

Lewis nodded, rising from his chair and going to his mother and sister. 'Yeah, Joel would do that sometimes. I think he just got so frustrated with being in that chair all day, especially when he saw me and Lils running around having fun.' He smiled sadly at Melissa. 'You always knew how to handle it, though, Mum, didn't you?'

'Yeah, you'd just hold him tight,' Lilly said as she squeezed Melissa's hand, 'telling Joel you loved him. He'd soon calm down.' Her face clouded over. 'But Dad, he couldn't handle it. He'd get all flustered, sometimes even tell Joel to "shut up, you're embarrassing me!" Remember that, Dad?'

Patrick put his head in his hands as Bill slumped on to a nearby chair, Rosemary beginning to sob quietly.

'Dad *really* couldn't handle it that day,' Lewis said, fists clenching and unclenching. 'I don't remember as much as Lils, but what I do remember is him shouting at Joel. It just made Joel worse, so Dad must've had enough. He left Joel there.'

Melissa glared at Patrick, her whole body trembling with rage. 'What the fuck is wrong with you?'

Lilly sighed. 'Dad told us Joel was going to be a big boy and stay out on his own, just like Grandma Quail did. I heard Joel crying out Dad's name,' she continued. 'He couldn't follow us, you see. He could try, but his poor legs . . .' She put her hand to her face as she started sobbing.

'I'm sorry, I wasn't thinking right,' Patrick whispered.

'Wasn't thinking right? Wasn't *thinking* right?' She ran up to him, but Bill held her back, wrapping his large arms around her chest. 'How could you?' she screamed at him, tears running down her face. 'He was our boy, our Joel. How could you?'

'I didn't mean it!' Patrick said.

Lewis shook his head. 'Don't lie, Dad. Do you remember what you said when we questioned where Joel was later that night?' Lewis asked. 'I do. It's always stuck in my mind 'cos I couldn't figure out what you meant. You said: "Joel's dead wood and he needed cutting out."'

'Jesus Christ,' Melissa sobbed, collapsing against Bill.

'You said the same thing to Grace two weeks ago, after she broke your watch,' Lilly said. 'Remember? You called Grace dead wood and I knew I had to protect her from you like I'd never been able to protect Joel. So that's when I got the knife,' she said, her whole body beginning to tremble as she hugged herself. 'I never really meant to hurt you. It was so you wouldn't hurt Grace, but then you ran at me and – and it just happened.'

'Look what you did,' Melissa said, managing to get away from Bill. She marched up to Patrick and started pummelling his chest. 'You killed Joel, you fucking killed him, and then knowing that scared Lilly so much she stabbed you in case you did the same to Grace!'

Rosemary tried to protect Patrick. 'You're just as guilty,' she hissed at her. 'Both of you are. You covered for your precious son and yet, all along, *he* was the dead wood! You at least owe me – *us* – the decency of telling us what happened to Joel.'

'We panicked,' Rosemary said. 'Wh— when Patrick got back without Joel, I knew something was wrong. Bill went out to find Joel, but he was already gone.'

'So you wheeled him back?' Melissa said to Bill. 'You wheeled his dead body back and pretended he was just sleeping? Made the twins *lie*?'

'I was protecting my son,' Bill said. 'Just like I've been trying to protect Lilly,' he added, going to take his granddaughter's hand. But she shoved him away, shaking her head.

Melissa frowned. 'You knew Lilly did it from the start?'

Rosemary looked just as shocked as Melissa. 'You *knew*, Bill?'

He didn't say anything, but Lilly nodded. 'We told Grandad that night when he got back from the hospital. He made us promise not to say anything. He said if we did, you would need to know why I stabbed Dad. Then all the stuff about Joel would come out and you might try to kill yourself again. That's when he told us you tried to commit suicide, Mum.'

Melissa shook her head in amazement. Bill had been *so* deceitful.

'But how did *you* know about that?' Melissa asked Bill and Rosemary.

'I saw you, that day in the forest,' Rosemary admitted. 'I came looking for you. I'd had enough of your little disappearing act, and I saw you,' she went on, voice trembling. 'I saw you tie that rope around your neck.'

'But you didn't help me,' Melissa said.

Rosemary put her hand to her mouth, sobbing as she shook her head.

'Like you didn't help Joel,' Lewis said. 'And I didn't help Grace. After Dad blamed Grace, Grandad convinced me it was the right thing to do. That I had to choose between Grace or Lilly, and as Grace is only my half-sister . . .' He let out a sob.

'Oh, my poor, poor boy,' Melissa said. 'You thought she was Ryan's too?'

He nodded. 'Why did I listen?' he wailed.

Melissa went to him, wrapping her arms around him. Then she reached for Lilly.

'Sorry,' she said to them, over and over. 'Sorry, sorry, sorry.'

Then she heard Patrick's voice. 'No, I'm sorry.' And Melissa could see it in his eyes.

It was over. It was all over.

Chapter Fifty-Nine

Forest Grove Facebook Chit Chat Group

Saturday 18th April, 2020
4.05 p.m.

Belinda Bell
A year to the day of the incident and I see the Byatts' house finally has a sold sign outside it.

Ellie Mileham
Hopefully Melissa and the kids can put the money from the sale to good use down in Sussex.

Andrew Blake
Won't Patrick get any money? Why's it always the bloody women who come out with the money in these situations?

Rebecca Feine
Jesus, Andrew, the man killed his son and accused the wrong daughter of stabbing him. Plus, I'm not sure what use he can make of any money at HMP Ashbridge.

Pauline Sharpe

I still think he should've got murder for what he did to poor Joel, not manslaughter. And twelve years? A disgrace. Should've been life for the life he took away from that boy. And the way he did it too: leaving him in the woods like that, making the poor boy die in the same way his grandmother had.

Rebecca Feine

I know, isn't it just awful? I still shudder when I think of what the prosecution said about Patrick being inspired by how his mother-in-law had died all those years back. And yet they still ruled manslaughter, when it's clear to anyone he knew exactly what he was doing, leaving that boy out in the cold like that.

Charlie Cane

Well, Patrick has always been a tricksy one, hasn't he? Managed to squirm his way out of that murder sentence by saying he didn't mean to kill his son!

Rebecca Feine

Haven't you changed your tune, Charlie Cane!

Charlie Cane

Of course I have, after everything that's come to light. I donated money to his campaign, you know, and then I find out he spent it on buying a Mercedes.

Belinda Bell

His party found out too. If all the stuff about Joel hadn't come out and got him suspended, then the misuse of election funds would have. He got his just desserts. At least we can rest easy, knowing it's all over now.

Kitty Fletcher
It's not all over, Belinda. It will have repercussions for those poor children.

Pauline Sharpe
Not to mention Rosemary and Bill. They might have got let off for their role in covering Joel's murder, but you've seen them around town. They'll never be the same again. And Debbie too, I don't think she'll ever get over the guilt of not saying something about her suspicions. I was so shocked when I read she was involved.

Rebecca Feine
Oh, I think Debbie will be just fine. I spoke to her last week. She's settling in really well at her new home in Richmond, though I could hear her grandchildren in the background making a racket.

Graham Cane
Speaking of deserters, did you hear Daphne's moving back to London too? Good riddance, I say.

Daphne Peterson
Why, thank you, Graham. You've always been such a charmer.

Rebecca Feine
I can see your red face from here, Graham!

Graham Cane

No red face here. Your loss, not ours, Daphne. You won't find another place like Forest Grove.

Belinda Bell

I agree. I bet poor Melissa is missing it here, it's a shame she had to move.

Daphne Peterson

Well, of course she bloody had to. As for missing Forest Grove, God help the next family who moves in.

Belinda Bell

Andrea, can we ban Daphne from the group now, seeing as she's leaving soon?

Andrew Blake

Sorry to hijack this thread, but has anyone seen the graffiti at the park near Birch Road? I guarantee it'll be kids from Ashbridge coming in and doing it.

Kitty Fletcher

Sad to say, I have to agree. I tried to drop off some leaflets about my books at the factory there but was told to leave with a few choice words! Clearly the factory workers let their children sit on iPads all day long.

Daphne Peterson

Jesus, Kitty, you do talk a lot of crap.

Graham Cane

Rebecca Feine

So do you, Graham. Actually, I know who did that graffiti. Carter Cooper. Isn't he one of your poster boys, Kitty?

Andrea Cooper

Right, that's it, this thread is DELETED!

Chapter Sixty

Saturday 18th April, 2020
4.05 p.m.

I'm getting used to the smell of the sea. Mum says Grandma Quail told her the sea heals because of the salt. I think it's more than that, though. I also think it's the fact it's so open and transparent and there aren't any trees to hide behind.

I miss Forest Grove. I miss my friends, I miss Maddy. I even miss Dad, despite all the bad things he did. I suppose he redeemed himself in the end, lying and telling the police he stabbed himself. I think he hoped that would make Mum not tell the police about what he did to Joel, but no chance. That was the first time I ever saw Detective Powell properly smile, when we all told her what had happened. All along, I thought she was hoping it would be one of us who hurt Dad, but the truth was, she just knew there was more to it than met the eye.

There's laughter in the distance. I look up, see Lewis chasing Grace down the beach as Sandy bounds after them. Mum is sitting on a picnic blanket and she catches my eye, waving at me. She's different now. Harder, like the wood of a helm oak. But that's good. She says she needed to harden up anyway. She seems happy here. I think she misses the trees, the feel of the bark beneath her palms. But as I watch her in the morning, kneeling down and waving her fingers in the sea, I think she'll get used to it here one day.

An engine roars and we all look up to see Ryan's Land Rover roll up, Maddy waving from the passenger seat.

I jump up and run to her, not caring that the scarf I'm wearing around my neck has escaped and drifted off with the sea breeze. Maddy jumps out of the truck and we rush into each other's arms.

Best friends. Sisters.

Ryan raises a hand in greeting. I smile and lead them down to the beach.

Mum's face lights up when she sees Ryan, and Lewis smiles shyly at Maddy as Grace wraps her arms around Maddy's waist. Maddy's hair is back to its old colour again and we all look so alike, like a family. A crooked one, like Joel's tree back home, scarred and hunched over, but our branches are still reaching for the sky, feeding off life, not blighted by poison any more.

'Your scarf!' Grace shouts, noticing as it floats away across the sea.

We all watch as it bounces over the waves. Lewis pulls his T-shirt off and runs to the edge of the sea, diving in.

'It doesn't matter!' I shout after him.

But he goes in anyway, swimming after it until he gets to it, grabbing it and holding it aloft in celebration, because that's what we do, don't we, risk our lives for those we love?

No more need to risk any lives here, though, just laughter and the smell of the sea.

Life is good. Life is sweet.

AUTHOR'S NOTE

Hello,

I hope you're reading this letter with a bit of a tear in your eye and a smile. That was how I felt when I wrote that ending, not just because I was saying goodbye to Melissa, Lilly, Lewis and Grace, four characters that have dominated my life the past few months, but also because this novel represents a first for me.

As those of you who have read my six previous books will know, this is the first time I've moved away from my usual beach location. Well, apart from the end . . . I had to get one beach in somehow, didn't I? Forests have always held a fascination for me – in fact, one wall of my writing study is even dominated by a woodland scene! I've always wanted to write something based in a forest, but it wasn't until the community of Forest Grove came to me that I felt able to finally fulfil that wish.

Did you enjoy the setting and the story? If so, I would be so grateful for a review on Amazon. It really means the world. I do actually read my reviews. In fact, I take into account what's said in them to help with subsequent books.

If you want to keep up to date with my news and my other books, including future novels, I'd recommend your first port of call be Facebook. Head on over to my author page www.facebook.com/

TracyBuchananAuthor, but if you really want the inside scoop from me and other authors, join The Reading Snug group. Just do a search for it in Facebook and request to join.

If social media isn't your thing, then come to my website at www.tracy-buchanan.com and contact me there. I love hearing from you guys!

Thanks,

Tracy

ACKNOWLEDGMENTS

Thanks, as ever, go to my awesome agent, Caroline Hardman. I am also deeply grateful to Sammia Hamer at my new publishers, Lake Union, for bringing me on board and helping me make this novel the best it can be. Speaking of which, heaps of thanks go to Ian Pindar, who helped me tame this novel, and the rest of the Lake Union team too, from the copyeditors and proofreaders to the publicity team.

I'd also like to thank Sam Matthewman for his help in understanding what it's like to be a coma patient.

Thanks to my family and friends, my ever-enthusiastic cheerleaders, as well. Too many to list here, but among them are, as always, my husband and my mum for their unwavering pride and support, my friends for their escape room and fun dinner distractions, and my fellow authors, especially members of the Savvy Writers' Snug, who never fail to be on hand for any questions I might ask. Thank you to my daughter, Scarlett, for inspiring me every day with her sass and creativity – many of her qualities shine through in Lewis, Lilly and Grace, especially Grace!

Finally, a big shout-out to my readers. Thanks for continuing to buy my books and leave such lovely reviews. You guys rock!

ABOUT THE AUTHOR

Photo © 2018 Nic Robertson-Smith

Tracy Buchanan is a bestselling author whose books have been published around the world, including chart toppers *My Sister's Secret* and *No Turning Back*. She lives in the UK with her husband, their daughter and a very spoilt Cavalier King Charles Spaniel called Bronte.

Before becoming a full-time author, Tracy worked as a travel journalist, visiting and writing about countries around the world. She has also produced content for the BBC and the Open University, and rubbed shoulders with celebrities while working for a London PR firm.

When she isn't spending time with her family and friends, Tracy now spends her days writing with her dog on her lap or taking walks in forests.

For more information about Tracy, please visit www.facebook.com/TracyBuchananAuthor and www.tracy-buchanan.com.